Memories Never Die

Memories Never Die

Alan D. Schmitz

ISBN 978-1468003321

Publishing history

Memories Never Die was first published in 2009 and printed through Create Space®. The first edition is reproduced herein with edits.

The author can be contacted at:

al@memoriesneverdie.com

Visit the Website:

Memoriesneverdie.com

Facebook:

Memories Never Die

Edited by:

Kara Brown
Shelly Rosenberg
Robert Schmitz

Interior Illustrations by:

Alan D. Schmitz

Cover by:

Blair Taylor Hardy
Osprey Designs

I want to thank all my family and friends who encouraged and helped me write this book in their own special ways. I want to give a special note of appreciation to my son Robert Alan Schmitz who became the force behind marketing "Memories Never Die".

Most notably I would like to acknowledge my wife Cindy for encouraging me from the first chapter on and for enduring my ceaseless discussions about "My Book."

****

While I did a great deal of research for the writing of this book, it is a book of fiction. All characters in the story are strictly fictional and are not intended to portray any particular person. Any political or religious references are used only to create the story and do not necessarily reflect my opinion nor can they be construed by anybody as an accurate representation of any particular religious or political group. All Geographic locations mentioned around the globe are accurate.

****

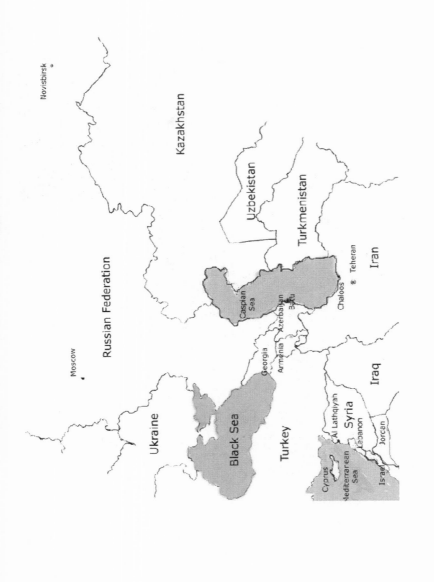

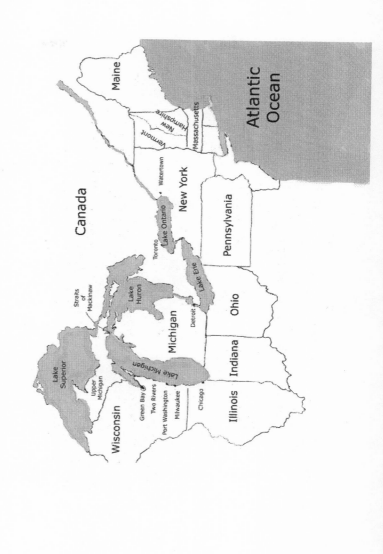

Chapter 1

Novosibirsk, Republic of Russia:

Professor Yuri Kromonov cursed the cold weather. He had walked these icy streets of the university most of his life. The University of Novosibirsk was world-renowned. The professor was proud of his work here and at the research institutes in Academgorodok. Academgorodok was about 20 km south of the city center of Novosibirsk and was a very special place with special perks for loyal Comrades. Yuri had the pleasure of living there as a nuclear research scientist for over 30 years.

During the middle of the so-called "cold war" it was a very good place to be, and it still was. This was where he met and married his wife. It was also where he and 65,000 other scientists and along with their families, lived a very privileged life. With the facilities located in the middle of Siberia, they were a captive crowd, but the cage was gilded, very gilded.

Academgorodok was a land of academia, with all the scientific lectures and discussions a scientist could want. It was a city within a city and in a town of academic elites, there was no end to the opportunities for scientific and philosophical debate. But if one wanted to stay in the gilded cage, it was wise not to question the motives or ways of the Union of Soviet Socialist Republics. All who lived at the research institute knew that the very existence of their community conflicted with the ideal of socialism. All comrades were not equal under the eyes of the politburo. Pay rates were perhaps the same, but what one could buy with that pay varied widely. Not one of the scientists would trade his apartment in Academgorodok for a miserable, small, dirty flat in Moscow. Nor would he trade his ample stores with the typically empty shelves throughout Russia and the lines a block long to buy stale bread. But then, the people in Moscow weren't contributing to the Mother Land as much as he and the other scientist did. The scientists did work hard for the good of the U.S.S.R., lest they were made an example of and kicked out of the gilded cage. Capitalism worked, but no one dared think of it in those terms. They were just being rewarded for their extra effort and given incentives to keep working hard. Of course, that was the definition of capitalism, but it was the one debate no one dared start; they were just being good Soviet citizens. And one thing a good Soviet citizen never did, especially if

1

Alan D Schmitz

he was being treated well, was to ask for more. Yuri never asked for more, until now.

The research institute was just a memory since he and his wife moved from their research cottage to an apartment near the University. And while the University was technically part of Academgorodok it was more aligned with the City of Novosibirsk, the third largest city in Russia. The center of Novosibirsk was 20km north, nestled against the river Ob. It boasted of having the largest library in Siberia and the biggest opera/ballet theater in all of Russia. It was even bigger than Moscow's Bolshoi Theater. Still it wasn't Academgorodok; he missed his old home. The professor pulled his wool hat tighter against his head with his gloved hands, as if that act would somehow keep him warmer. He watched his breath freeze as he exhaled. It was -23° C. Instantly his scientific mind calculated it in Fahrenheit to -10°. He took his arms and slapped them against his rotund body to bring some feeling back. Two more blocks to go, Yuri cursed. "Vsyo zayebis!" — "Everything's fucking great!" he said sarcastically as a gust of wind blew snow hard against his exposed face.

Yuri was officially retired. He and his wife lived in an apartment ten blocks from Yuri's university office. A nice walk in summer, ten blocks too far in winter. Yuri cursed some more, he should have taken the metro. It would have still been a cold ride but at least he would have been shielded from the wind. The professor hated the metro; it was filthy and full of human scum too lazy to walk. More than once he had found himself in an altercation with young hoodlums making sport of the way he dressed or trying to steal his umbrella. One good thing about the cold, the punks would be on the metro not on the street; they didn't know how to dress against the weather.

Yuri and his wife, Anzhela, had been asked to move out of their lifelong cottage in the research town a few years back. It seemed the institute needed the home for an up and coming scientist. And though they were asked in a polite, official manner to move to Novosibirsk, it wouldn't have stayed a request had they refused. He was told that as a "reward" for his retirement he would receive a private office at the university to continue his research and he would be given a professorship. So reluctantly they moved to the city, away from their friends and the life they knew.

The new apartment was much smaller than their private cottage. Their previous home had been grand, almost opulent by comparison. The new home was very nice by Russian standards, but to them it was bland. They were just one tenant in a building with twenty identical units. Each structure was just part of a cluster of twenty identical buildings. It was

2

over two years since they had moved; they both knew it wasn't home and it never would be. The couple had tried to dress up the apartment with some of the nicer things they had brought along, but most didn't seem to belong here. When they were forced to move it had been difficult to choose which items to keep and which to give away. Both realized that many of their precious and most personal belongings would have to be left behind; the new place was just too small.

Anzhela had been able to keep only a few of her cherished paintings. Her favorite, an impressionistic oil drawn by a then young university student, adorned one of the few small walls. To Anzhela it was an exquisitely beautiful painting, a quality that made it completely out of place on the drab wall in the dimly lit room. It wasn't a large painting but seemed to draw you into itself making it seem bigger. Staring at it long enough made you feel as if you were on the beach at the shore of the lake watching the sun go down next to the charming Swiss cottage. There was only the slightest hint of a person on the shoreline so as not to detract from the sunset and water, but Anzhela had imagined herself in the picture a million or more times.

Yuri pulled open the heavy door of the great hallway. The door pushed a mound of snow over his boots as he opened it and then his red-cheeked face was greeted by warmer air as he stepped in. The professor stomped his boots hard on the tile floor and brushed off his black wool coat, which was white with snow. He made his way down a narrow hallway toward his office. The long hallway was lit intermittently by flickering florescent lighting. The air smelled stale as if it was left over from 65 years ago when the large university building had been built. The walk to his private office was undisturbed, and it too was dimly lit. The office was small but warm and it was his.

Yuri hung up his wet coat, kicked off the over boots and surveyed his small domain. Any day now this small luxury of an office could be taken away from him too. Supervising classes wasn't one of his duties anymore. He realized that his professorship would only last until someone of more importance wanted this space. Every day that went by, Yuri realized that more and more people were becoming more important than he was. Retirement in Russia was very much like everything else; you hoped for the best and planned for the worst. Only, it was difficult to plan when you had no control over anything.

The monthly check would still come, and the couple had saved up some money. But it would be far short of what they would need to live comfortably anywhere in Russia, much less in a dacha in a warm climate. Anzhela earned some money giving piano lessons on their old but very

3

well cared for piano. Besides the piano money, his wife's monthly retirement check, which was much smaller than his, helped to make ends meet.

If they had any pride of ownership about anything, it was the piano. They couldn't bring themselves to leave it behind; that would have been too much to ask, even though it took up so much space in their small sitting room. Yuri Kromonov didn't play a note of music, but that didn't detract from his pride in owning the instrument. Having a piano in your residence for personal use was an oddity; it displayed class and a bit of economic superiority. Obtaining the piano would be impossible for him under his current situation, but back when he was important other important people had helped him with the ultimate surprise for his young wife.

Yuri thought about another disappointment in their lives. Early in their married life, he and his wife realized that they could not conceive. That need had been taken from them much too soon. But as the years went by they learned to replace the dream of having a family with one of living a life of leisure in a place with warm weather. It didn't matter where, but it had to be near a lake that never froze. Yuri could imagine sailing on that lake - a lake he envisioned, much like the lake in his wife's painting. The professor was sailing on that lake for a moment, then reality came back and he remembered his new mission. He patted his dark computer screen. "You will help me get to my lake, won't you my friend?" the warming old man said to his computer.

Another perk of professorship was having a computer. The Soviets knew the power of shared information and it often worried them. The old U.S.S.R. had been fairly successful in containing the Internet world, but the genie was out of the bottle now and Professor Kromonov could not imagine it would ever be put back in. He had grown up with computers, and in Russia that meant that you practically had to build your own. When the professor searched the Internet he knew how to cover his tracks, because if the wrong person discovered what he was looking for, he would not be considered a good comrade.

Yuri flicked the power switch on, his computer started to boot up. Then the Doctor of Physics turned around in the small room and started to boil some water in a teapot. He preferred coffee, good Columbian coffee, but in the last several years since leaving Academgorodok, he mostly drank tea. The scientist's mind wandered as he looked at a small glass jar of Nescafe instant coffee. It was a product he hated and was on the shelf for a colleague who insisted on coffee. The glass jar of coffee crystals made him recollect about his exposure to real Columbian coffee.

At the research center there was a coffee house. It was the most popular place for the young scientists and their wives to gather and chat. Yuri could almost smell the bold aroma as he reminisced about those days. He closed his eyes and mentally tried to inhale the wonderful fragrances of the *caffelatte* and *cappuccino* delights being served over and over again. Anzhela loved to sit with a good book at an outside table and enjoy her *caffelatte*. Yuri chuckled to himself as he pictured his young wife trying to read her book while squinting and putting up with the annoyance of the bright sunshine. It was an annoyance she gladly bore. For her, the sunshine was like being bathed in a warm regenerating elixir. Yuri tried to remember the name of the barista. The particular server Yuri thought about was a master at running the ancient shiny brass espresso machine. In his mind's eye he could hear the sound of steam traveling through the bright brass piping, hitting the milk and foaming it perfectly.

Yuri abruptly opened his eyes. The memories were becoming painful, though they had reminded him of why he had decided years ago that and if he couldn't have a good coffee, he would have none. The teapot looked out of place on the small hotplate that was borrowed from one of the labs. The hotplate was nestled not completely safely between stacks of paper and stacks of engineering books.

The computer took time to find all its connections. During the wait his mind drifted back again to that time 35 years ago when he was young and important. The scientist had done what everyone thought was impossible. Back then it was considered something of science fiction. And even to this day, though there were rumors of its existence, some being very credible rumors, nothing was ever proven. Today he was old and used up, though his designs were still being worked on and refined. In fact, the professor couldn't be sure, but he was almost certain that the United States had copied his design. A few years back, a respected source who still worked down in Academgorodok, said there was some compelling evidence that the great U.S. was improving on the supposedly secret design as was his own country.

The professor was well aware of the sad state of world affairs and quite frankly didn't give a damn. He had his own problems; the man who invented the most sinister bomb the world has ever known should at least be able to afford a small cottage on a warm lake for himself and his love of 35 years to retire on.

Yuri knew there were terrorists, or martyrs, depending on one's perspective, more than willing to blow themselves up. They would be willing to kill themselves in the name of God and jihad. And in the process, these men and women would strive to kill multitudes of innocents in the name of religion. Yes, he thought, these people would make his services in high demand. The world was a complicated place. Who was he to say who was right and who was wrong? His own country had placed a team of engineers and scientists at his disposal so that they could kill innocents too. Only his country didn't want to take the credit for the killings like the jihadist did. Mother Russia wanted it done covertly. But otherwise killing is killing; same difference in the end. The professor didn't have any false pretenses or moral justification to defend. When a young scientist was picked to design the special, small package, he knew that the only reason for such a bomb was to be used clandestinely. That meant any place, any time, with no warning. Innocents would be killed. But if the Mother Land decided that even the innocents were enemies, then who was to say differently?

To the professor it wasn't a question if one of the many terrorist groups or even a terrorist country would want his services. Undoubtedly, they would. The quandary was of letting them know a vendor was available without exposing himself. That was a problem worthy of a scientist to solve.

Yuri entered a few selected websites and Internet chat rooms looking for any sign that one of his alter egos was trying to be contacted. One of the websites he visited was al-Ekhlass. The professor didn't know what that meant, but did know it was a favorite site for militants to post messages. It was the un-official/official site of al-Qaida and it supported a forum where anyone can post comments. The trick was to keep invisible to the Russian authorities while visiting these dangerous sites.

There were services that promised to keep your identity anonymous, but those were the last Yuri would trust. After all, if you were the FSB, wouldn't you monitor those sites first? The scientist cringed at the thought of being caught by the FSB, which was short for the "Federal Security Service of the Russian Federation". The FSB was every bit as suspicious of its citizens as its previous self, the KGB. Yuri went to Yahoo! and checked the e-mail in a few of his accounts. These were accounts that he had routed through a server down in Academgorodok. And that server accessed through an Internet Protocol, or IP address, another that was routed through an acquaintance's computer. Sometimes it was convenient to be the resident "computer geek" as the Americans called them. When he fixed or set up a new computer, a trap door was always left open to give him a way into it. The professor scrolled through e-mails. His heart skipped a beat, and then it started to beat rapidly. *What had he done?* he thought to himself as a particular message caught his undivided attention.

Yuri had left small clues on how to be contacted in selected chat rooms such as al-Ekhlass. The scientist answered seemingly pointless questions with small inferences of having something they wanted. But someone had to put all the pieces of the puzzle together and responded with the right question for Yuri to take him seriously. Finally he was looking at a response. "Do you need a matchmaker? I specialize in matching people of unique skills with interested parties. Such work can be very lucrative for people with the right skills for my clients. Business is booming!"

The professor sunk back in his chair to catch his breath and then jumped in fear, nearly startled to death by the sound of his teapot's contents coming to a boil. He whispered quietly. "Ni khuya sebe!" – "No fucking way!"

In a daze, the professor turned off the hot plate and the teakettle slowly quieted. Without pouring the tea, he sat back down and pondered the situation. Why was he so surprised? Isn't this exactly what he had been waiting for? Maybe... the professor philosophized, maybe because for over a year, every day had been exactly the same until now. Every day the sly messages went out and every day the special "IN" box was empty. For the first time, Yuri admitted to himself that an answer was not really expected, not ever. No wonder he was surprised. The old man crinkled his wrinkled brow even more; he had never actually expected anyone to get his cryptic messages. And now that someone had, he didn't know what to do.

A strange thought crossed his mind. Though he had calculated every conceivable way to stay anonymous, the cunning scientist never contemplated the next move should there be a successful contact. Maybe he wasn't serious. Maybe this wasn't the right time. Yuri suddenly found that his stomach wasn't feeling that well. This was no longer a game; if the e-mail was answered, his life would never be the same. That was certain.

Yuri wrote down the sender's e-mail address on a small paper that was slipped in one of the many books on the neatly crowded bookcase. Then the professor did what was always done after going on line. He securely erased his session on the server at the research center. Then he securely erased his local hard drive to delete any references to the websites visited and lastly securely erased the e-mail files. The secure erase assured that

7

not only were references to these files erased, but each and every sector of his hard drive that was listed as available by the hard drive controller was overwritten with useless 0s and 1s to make sure even invisible files were completely erased. This had been taught to him very early in his career by the government. The concept of computer security had not been wasted on the security division of the huge government research complex, and it especially hadn't been wasted on him.

That evening, when safe and cozy in their small flat, Yuri felt rejuvenated, almost giddy. He looked across the beaten up laminated surface of the dining table. There his wife sat eating slowly and silently. The long winters were hard on her, harder even than they were on him.

"My little Angel, why so quiet?" The name Anzhela was from a Russian term that roughly translated to "The Angel." Yuri almost never called his sweet Anzhela anything else.

Anzhela had of course aged from the twenty something smooth skin beauty that he had fallen in love with, but she still looked every bit as desirable to him. And his love for her had only grown through the ages.

Anzhela smiled slightly and looked up from her plate. "Oh Yuri, you know how the winters make me feel. I don't even have the energy to read my books. You go to work and I miss you so when you are gone, but yet when you come home I don't feel any joy."

Yuri had just poured more gravy over a second helping of potatoes, but instead of eating the warm meal he set down his fork, got up and walked to his wife's side. "My sweet Angel, is there anything I can do?"

"Can you change the snow to a spring rain? Can you open the window and let in clean fresh summer air filled with the fragrances of blooming flowers. Can you give me summer sunshine on my back as I work in my garden?"

Yuri said nothing, but he leaned over in back of her and placed one of his massive arms around his suddenly fragile wife. That said more than he ever could have voiced.

Anzhela looked up at her husband with tired eyes. "My love, I'm not blaming you. It isn't your fault I miss the sunshine so much. I have had a good life, a very good life, and I owe it all to you. Without you, I couldn't have studied my precious literature and been given the opportunities to teach here at the university. But somehow I expected this part of our lives to be just as wonderful. It is wrong of me to be so selfish."

Yuri couldn't bring his big frame down to his wife, so he turned her chair around, practically lifted her out of it and into both of his arms. "To want more is not wrong. I used to be important, and important people would come to see me, to see us. Remember the parties we went to? OH

MY, the parties!!" Yuri's mind wondered back to those times. "Remember how we danced to live music all evening?"

Anzhela smiled and hugged her husband back. "Oh I remember, you were quite the dancer."

"I still am, Angel." Slowly, Yuri and Anzhela rocked back and forth, not dancing but transporting themselves back to earlier times with the gentle rocking motion.

Yuri whispered. "You talk like your life is over. It is not, I promise. Have I ever let you down before?"

"My Yuri," Anzhela scolded lightly, "you have never let me down, not ever! Perhaps I should get one of those lamps that help people feel better in winter. They are expensive but they are like sunshine."

"Yes, yes, my love. By all means we will find one of those lights. I know a scientist who works with full spectrum lights. I fixed his computer. He owes me a favor. I, Yuri Kromonov, will bring summer sunshine to my Angel, I promise. But first you must give me a smile."

Anzhela looked up at her lover and protector. She didn't have to force a smile, she was smiling already. "Just by being my Yuri, you have already brought some sunshine into my life."

****

The next morning the professor hated to leave his Angel alone again but he had some serious planning to do. His mind had been made up; it had been easy to come to a decision after seeing his Angel so sad. Anzhela was right about herself. Living her dreary existence day in and day out was killing her. What he didn't share with his wife was that it was slowly killing him also. Today, for the first time in a long time there was work to do. It was real work, important work, and his private office was the place in which to do it.

Yuri knew that he was about to play a very dangerous game. There could be no mistakes on his part. *If the mouse wants to tease the cat, it had better be a very, very cleaver little mouse!* he thought. This was going to take much more thought and planning than getting contacted had been.

9

Chapter 2

West Bend, Wisconsin; Two Years Later:

Scott Seaver didn't like the look of the sky; it was low overcast and no doubt filled with icy moisture. As a pilot, being aware of the sky conditions was second nature. There was a cold wind blowing in off the water from the east, a bit unusual as the prevailing winds were from the opposite direction toward the east. He also knew from sailing that with the winds from the east, the waters of Lake Michigan would be extremely rough and very cold.

Scott chuckled realizing that the song on the radio was the ballad of the "Wreck of the Edmund Fitzgerald" by Gordon Lightfoot. *How appropriate* he thought, the skies were certainly gloomy, though the month was October as Gordon sang, "When the skies of November turn gloomy." The helicopter pilot drove down the main highway toward the 832nd Medical Evacuation Company. The fiftyish pilot started singing along with Gordon, something that would be mildly tolerated by his wife, but totally unforgivable by their fourteen-year-old daughter. Alone in the car he belted out words somewhat in tune: "When the Gales of November came slashing." Well the winds weren't exactly gale force, he conceded; just the same, nobody would want to be out on the big lake on a day like today. Every wave that came up and slammed into the side of a ship's hull would send up a screen of icy cold water. During the colder months the icy water would freeze almost instantly on contact with the cold steel of a ship. Scott sang along some more, realizing that he didn't know the tune as well as he thought he did. Wasn't it always like that though? You could hear a song a thousand times, but that doesn't mean you actually know the words.

Scott respected the lake. He had grown up next to it and saw its fury and anger on many occasions. As a boy, he was drawn to it, and from the bluffs overlooking the endless expanse of water knew that it was as ferocious as any ocean. The young Seaver would marvel at how strong the outer breakwater must be to take the pounding of the waves over and over again. Maybe that was what drew him into engineering, a desire to understand such things.

As a helicopter pilot, Captain Seaver had flown over the lake many times, his lake, as he liked to call it. The Army Guard Captain often had thought that calling the Great Lakes, lakes at all, was a bit under rating, sort of disrespectful. They were, in fact, huge, more like inland oceans than lakes. If he had to fly over the lake it would be done over the shortest distance, which was from Manitowoc, Wisconsin, to Ludington, Michigan. The great lake was still over 60 miles wide at its narrowest and would take him thirty minutes or more in the "Huey," depending on winds. Seaver always thought of those minutes as the longest minutes in the world. Going down in the middle of a lake the size of West Virginia, even in the best of weather, would severely ruin a person's day.

When he turned off the main highway onto Chopper Drive, he stopped at the security gate. Sergent Lenny Sidowske was on duty at the guard post. Len saluted Captain Seaver and waved him through the security checkpoint of the Wisconsin Army National Guard. Lenny was the oldest son of one of Scott's high school buddies. The young man's father, Dan Sidowske and Scott had dated the same girl, Mary Ann Martin. Dan had eventually married her and the young Seaver had felt the pain of a love lost. Ten years later, Dan and Scott were on the same bowling team, became best of friends and still were to this day. Scott knew that Lenny wasn't married yet, but the young man certainly had his eye on a gal named Patti Mills, or Pat as he liked to call her. Captain Seaver laughed a bit at the thought that his high school buddy and former girlfriend might soon be grandparents. Life certainly passes quickly.

He kept his Huey at the 832nd unit of the Army National Guard. He liked to think of it as his Huey, though it actually wasn't, but then neither was Lake Michigan. He wouldn't be flying today, but was stopping by to check on his bird and make a nuisance of himself, even if today wasn't a scheduled on duty day.

"Hey Randy," Captain Seaver said as Lieutenant Schmidt saluted him. The captain saluted back casually. It was more like a handshake between friends than an official salute. Things were fairly informal around the small base.

"Have the bugs out of the new sim yet?" Scott asked teasingly.

"There aren't any bugs in it, sir," Randy answered, feigning being insulted.

Captain Seaver liked the flight simulator technician. In a way they were kindred brothers. They both were kind of techno geeks and proud of it.

"Don't blame the sim for your lack of flying skills, sir." Lieutenant Schmidt teased back. "If you fly boys would learn to fly properly, I'm sure you would find that the sim works just fine."

11

Alan D Schmitz

"Yea, Yea, Yea," Scott yawned out and patted the young technician on the back lightly as he walked toward the commander's office.

Lieutenant Schmidt called out and stopped the captain. "Did you get your new IT-Tech phone yet?"

"As a matter of fact, I did," the captain said proudly as he pulled it out of his pocket and held it up taunting the jealous simulator technician with it.

"Is it as cool as they say?"

"Nope!.... Way better!" Scott volunteered. "The video capture is amazing and it takes still pictures up to 10 megapixels. If I change my contacts or calendar on my phone it instantly changes on my home and work PCs and vice versa. It has GPS and security erase. Oh, and it also works as a great phone!" Scott added as an afterthought while the technician held it in his hand gingerly playing with the touch screen.

"And it has high speed Internet and e-mail functions," Randy Schmidt added reluctantly giving back the ultra high tech phone.

"And if I want it to do something else, I can just download any of about a zillion different applications. It is soooo way cool!" Scott added again as he smirked and slipped it carefully back into his pocket.

"What did you do with your old phone? I'll buy it from you," the lieutenant eagerly bargained. Scott was one of those guys who chased technology. His old phone was cutting edge, at least until the new phone hit the market.

"Sorry Lieutenant, I gave it to my daughter. But check this out."

Scott played with some buttons on the phone and pressed "SEARCH." Soon the map on the IT-Tech displayed a flashing yellow dot. "That is where my daughter is right now. I can find out where she is at any time."

"I can see from a parent's perspective that is awesome. Does your daughter know you can do that?"

"No, and neither does my wife; and what they don't know, won't hurt them!

Gotta go Lieutenant, see you later."

Scott walked past the simulator room and through the recently expanded and remodeled operations base. Its new walls were painted in the typical army drab green. The building may be brand new but once inside it looked like any other army base. Maybe that was the idea. You never knew how old or new a military base was because they all looked the same, at least on the inside.

The captain knocked on Major Robert Allen's door.

"Come in!"

12

Scott gave a much more formal salute to his commanding officer as he stepped through the steel doorway and stopped at attention.

Even though this was a reserve unit, army protocol was still respected and followed. And even though being in the National Guard meant that you were just part time, when on base or on duty you were always one hundred percent soldier. Scott understood the tradition and respected it, as did everyone else in the unit.

Without standing, Major Allen saluted back and welcomed Scott in with a smile.

"I thought you weren't scheduled in for another week?"

"Yes sir, I was hoping you wouldn't mind if I gave my old bird a once over, sir."

"Are you afraid that we won't take care of your UH-1 without your supervision?" The major tried to sound gruff.

"No sir!" Scott replied and then saw the hint of a smile on the major's face.

"Permission granted ... and Scott!" he added.

"Yes sir?"

"That vibration you noticed on your last flight was a dampener going on number two blade. Mark didn't find it at first. I told him to look again. I told him that if you said there was a vibration in that machine, then there was a vibration and he better find it. It took him a whole day, but he found it. You should have seen the smile on his face; you would have thought that he discovered the Holy Grail." Bob grinned at Scott.

"Thank you, sir." He recognized the compliment that the commander had just paid him and Mark, the head mechanic. After all, finding a slight vibration on a five thousand pound aircraft while it was sitting in the shop hangar was no small task.

"And in case you're interested," Major Allen paused for effect, "we checked out the H.S.I. you reported acting flaky. We replaced it also."

"Yes sir, good to know sir. I guess I wasted a perfectly good day off."

The commander laughed, "You couldn't have stayed away if you wanted to, which you don't."

Bob Allen and Scott Seaver had been friends for many years. Their sons had played on the same T-ball and later little league baseball teams together. Bob had been a good friend when Scott's son Brad died. He seemed to know what to say and when to say it and he also knew when to say nothing at all, but just be there for him.

"If you don't mind, sir, may I be dismissed so I can go and see my baby?" The Captain asked for the formal permission to be excused.

13

"Scott." Bob looked up and caught the pilot's eyes and gave him a serious look.

"I love those old birds as much as you do, and as long as they are here we will take care of them like our lives depended on them, because they do. But you know and I know that time marches on and those old birds are being replaced ASAP with or without our blessing."

"I know Bob." Scott dropped the sir and kept it personal; he knew when the formalities of rank were being pushed aside for a serious heart-to-heart. "I understand, out with the old, in with the new. Just like those young sky jocks that I am competing against. The old birds have been good friends and never let you or me down. I'm dreading the day when I come in and all the Huey's are gone."

"So will I Scott, so will I. But you know that the Black Hawk is one hell of a bird, and two engines are better than one. And the speeds, my god, are they fast. And with the modular components it should be easier to keep them ready to go at all times." Bob tried to sell the advantages of the new copters to his friend. "Captain Fredric has nothing but praise for the UH-60. I think that if I made him go on a mission with a UH-1 he would resign on the spot."

"I get it Bob, the UH-1 is yesterday's news, but I still like the old birds. I know where every switch, knob, light and lever is in my sleep. And you know that there isn't a sound that bird makes that I don't know by heart. I don't need a million dollars worth of computing power to tell me if it's a good sound or a bad one."

Bob changed the subject. *No sense beating a dead horse*, he thought. "Speaking of knobs and switches, how's the simulator training going?"

Scott knew what the major was getting at; he undoubtedly saw the sim reports and was just looking for Scott's perspective.

"Well..," Scott started hesitating. "I'll admit that it could be going better, but I'm getting it. Don't tell me about knobs and switches. The new Hawks have about a zillion more of them, and they're all in the wrong places. The controls are a bit tough to get used to for a ham handed pilot like me. Just a bit more time sir and I'm sure I'll have it down pat." Scott acknowledged that they were back to a professional discussion. Then he added. "And the sim, sir, I realize it is state of the art and costs millions of dollars, but it's still not the real thing. When I'm flying, I can feel the machine, I can sense it, and I can feel the air. To me sir, when I am flying the simulator, as realistic as it is, it is still just a simulator."

"You forget that I'm a pilot too Scott. I understand what you're saying. But just the same, satisfactory simulator performance is mandatory. And the reason the Army uses the sim is because we can have you practice emergency maneuvers without killing yourself or others and destroying a very expensive helicopter in the process. And by the way," Major Allen added in a deadly serious way, "according to the reports, you did die, several times as a matter of fact. I know you're a better pilot than that. What's up?"

"Like I say sir, just getting used to the simulator, it would never happen in the real machine," Scott said in the most convincing voice he could muster. "The multiple emergencies and unlikely situations that you guys cook up would never happen in real life anyways."

"Scott, you need to get your sim scores up. I know there is a lot of pressure on you because you are the most senior pilot here. Just relax a little; take deep breaths if you have to, maybe crack the books a bit harder before your next flight."

"Yes sir!" the captain replied respectfully and officially. Scott realized that it wasn't a request. It was an order, an order disguised in a friend's voice. The pilot also knew that his friend was right. Learning a new bird was a lot more difficult than he had imagined it would be. And, compared to the young aviators, being called the senior pilot was not necessarily a compliment. Those young jocks seemed to catch on to everything so much faster than he did. Sometimes the thought would cross his mind that it might be time to step aside and let the younger pilots be the heroes.

Bob caught the slight hesitation in his friend's expression and realized that the message was being considered seriously.

Major Allen's phone rang "Dismissed Captain and good luck."

Scott saluted and turned around as Bob picked up the phone.

"I thought Captain Fredric was scheduled. ...... I see. ....No, don't call Williams, Captain Seaver is still with me."

Scott was just about to close the door when he heard his name mentioned. He hesitated. Bob called out to him.

"Scott, hold on, come back in. It seems that Captain Fredric was hurt in a motorcycle accident on the way in. It doesn't sound like it was too bad, but he won't be able to go on duty. Would you care to take his spot until I find someone to fill out the rest of his shift? Ted's over his service hours and it could be a while before someone else could get here. And just in case there is some sort of an emergency, we need a pilot on duty."

Scott was caught off guard, but understood the question. "Yes sir, I can punch in anytime." Being given an extra opportunity to practice his skills was actually a lucky break. And being the boss at his own company had its perks, so taking the rest of the day off from the office wouldn't be a problem.

Bob was already on the phone telling Sergeant Lind that they had a pilot.

"I'll go to my locker and change into uniform, sir, and then I'll report back."

"Sounds like a plan Scott and thanks."

Bob was a good commander and being a good commander Scott knew that his good friend of so many years wasn't intending to let him sit around and play cards until his relief showed up. Captain Seaver wished that Major Allen would order him to practice with the Huey, but they both knew that more practice in the Huey wasn't needed. And burning up jet fuel just for the sake of a joy ride wasn't in the cards.

The captain quickly changed into a flight suit trying to prepare himself mentally for whatever challenge his commander cooked up for him. Scott admired that about Bob. He didn't let anyone rest on past training and often said, "I never saw a perfect training flight yet. And if I ever did, that would mean I didn't push the pilot's skills enough."

Bob was right, Scott had thousands of flights under his belt and never did he do EVERYTHING perfectly. Flying was a skill with a thousand tasks. Doing them all perfectly each and every time was impossible. There wasn't a pilot alive who could say he never forgot to switch frequencies at the right time, or dialed in the wrong navigation aid or calculated a decent profile incorrectly or didn't anticipate the ground wash.

Scott reported back to Major Allen's office with his flight helmet tucked under his right arm. The door was cracked open. He heard the commander on the phone. He knocked lightly and Bob waved him in as he hung up.

Bob looked up at Scott. "Looks like you'll be getting a chance to show the young jocks how it's done. Here's the scenario. There's a small sailboat capsized off Port Washington's breakwater, about 15 miles out. Lieutenant Schmidt will give you the coordinates. It's a family of five. They won't survive long in the cold water and it will be dark soon. Your team is on the way to Sierra Six, Six, Six. I'm giving you an authorized emergency takeoff. The flight line is only giving you enough fuel for about an hour and a half. You won't want any more weight on board than that. And you won't need any more time, because if you haven't brought them back by then, it will be too late anyhow. As of right now, the clock is running. Lieutenant Schmidt will be your ground support and give you further details when you're in the air."

16

"Yes sir! Has an emergency departure been filed with Milwaukee sir?"

"Being done now. From here on it's your mission, Good Luck!"

Scott quickly saluted and left. The clock was running as Scott rushed himself to the cockpit. *Old habits die hard,* Seaver thought as he tossed his "lucky" flight helmet behind the pilot's seat. It wouldn't be needed today. The Black Hawk had its own set of pilot and co-pilot helmets. This was high-tech time. The Hawk's helmets were actually much more than just protective devices. They were also part of the helicopter itself. The front shield housed a "heads up display" or HUD and infrared goggles were attached for night flying and rescue, not to mention the built-in microphone and ear sets and multi-channel mission radio. He adjusted the two quick adjust knobs and it conformed to his head perfectly. Well maybe not perfectly, but comfort wasn't a military prerequisite.

"Guard Base, this is Sierra Six, Six, Six. Team is aboard, departing with authorized emergency take off." The last call was a chance for the base to abort a potentially dangerous departure and at the same time verify over the radio frequency that he had authorization for the risky maneuver.

"Sierra Six, Six, Six authorized, frequency change approved."

Even as the pilot was being cleared to start the engines, his hand was on the switch and he started number one engine spinning up. The sound of a jet engine spooling up and the building up of internal air pressure began. Though typically the Black Hawk is flown with two pilots, today the luxury of a copilot wasn't available. So Scott was twice as busy going through the mental checklist. When the engine pressure was critical, the ignition switch was flipped and the powerful turbine produced its own power. He quickly started number two engine spooling while watching to make sure that the number one engine didn't go into a critical over speed. Turbines sometimes, though very rarely, did that on startup. If it did, an immediate shutdown would have to be initiated or the engine would blow itself up.

Scott glanced at the number two engine. The pressure was near critical and after another couple of seconds another switch was flipped and the second engine ignited. Temperatures immediately climbed and he had two powerful fifteen hundred horsepower engines spinning. *Shit!* he thought. He had taken his eyes off the RPM indicator for the number one engine for one second too long. It was in the red but he still had time to shut it down. It took him another second or two of staring at the cluttered instrument panel to find the shutdown switch. *Shit!* he thought again. But before shutting it down his eye caught the RPM gauge and saw it was back in the green. The captain didn't want to make the same

17

mistake twice and glimpsed at the number two engine. It settled in right away. It took five more long seconds to make sure both engines were secure. The time the engines needed to warm up was efficiently used to turn on the main electric power and set his radios.

"Milwaukee, this is Guard Sierra Six, Six, Six off of West Bend. I need an emergency departure, runway Zero Six, easterly, three thousand." In a few short words the pilot had given the Milwaukee radar departure group the critical information they would need to get him safely away from any other traffic. They now knew exactly what aircraft was calling them, where it was, where it was going and at what altitude.

The engine temperatures were still a bit cold. Under normal circumstances, the checklist would require a wait for them to warm before adding more power, but people's lives depended on every second he could save.

"Guard Sierra Six, Six, Six, cleared as filed, squawk guard frequency, departure 133.85. Hold for release for aircraft on final." Milwaukee, in equally efficient radio use authorized the clearance, but because of a landing aircraft it couldn't give the chopper permission to depart the field yet.

"Milwaukee, negative. This is an emergency and you get that pilot the hell out of here. I need air now!" Captain Seaver demanded.

"Guard, stand by."

Almost instantaneously he heard. "Guard copter cleared for departure."

Scott pushed both power levers forward and watched his radar altimeter begin to move. They were airborne. *Damn!* He thought. *This thing really does have power to spare, but now wasn't the time to spare it.*

The pilot put a bit more distance between the chopper and the ground and aggressively tipped the copter forward. The craft departed parallel to runway Zero Six. The aircraft would have to fly this heading a little northeast for just a few more moments, then he would turn it due east.

"Milwaukee departure, Guard Sierra Six, Six, Six, three thousand, Zero, Niner, Zero"

With just a small burst of radio time, he relayed the pertinent information to the radar controllers.

"Guard Six, Six," the controller shortened the call sign even more to save the precious radio time. "Go to emergency frequency for further assistance."

Scott retuned his radio and pressed the transfer switch to change the active frequency as he pushed the chopper into full forward motion one thousand feet over the surrounding rolling countryside. The captain realized that he was just below the cloud deck; he hoped that the ceilings wouldn't drop further before he got to the lake.

"Guard Six, Six to Guard Base, looking for last known coordinates of the water craft."

Lieutenant Schmidt responded immediately, "Last known position was 43 degrees and 23 minutes north and 87 degrees and 30 minutes west."

Captain Seaver responded by repeating the coordinates. Lt. Schmidt acknowledged that they had been repeated correctly. This time Seaver only keyed his microphone switch twice to reply an understood response, thus saving precious fractions of seconds on the radio. Scott reached his left hand toward the GPS in his radio stack. The GPS unit was state of the art, translation.... brand new to him. After pushing a few wrong buttons, it came back to him exactly how to set coordinates for a destination rather than just picking an airport or navigation aid from an alphanumeric listing. Soon the longitude and latitude were entered. With a push of the "DIRECT" button on the GPS, the course was verified. The pilot triple checked the numbers because even a small mistake here meant that he could be led miles away from where he wanted to be and that would mean certain death to the family.

Scott was starting to sweat. The pressure of doing everything just perfectly was getting to him. Not only did the GPS have to be reconfigured, a unit he wasn't as familiar with as he should be, but the course and altitude needed to be maintained. Also the engine gauges needed to be monitored and a visual watch for other aircraft was just as important, all while trying to remember exactly how to actually fly the high-tech device. The Black Hawk was still in visual conditions and that meant that other aircraft could also be flying visually, so all aircraft had the obligation to watch out for the other. *Right now going IMC could be a blessing,* the captain thought.

The heading indicator needle jumped into position. If it had been programmed correctly, it should now lead them directly to the last known position of the capsized boat. Seaver didn't actually expect to find the boat there. It certainly would have drifted, but he had to start somewhere and it might as well be there.

It was about fifteen miles to the lake on their current heading. Scott saw the blackness of the lakeshore approaching. The setting sun was casting a long, dark shadow over the water from the bluffs above it. He glanced at the flight timer and saw that a precious five minutes had gone by. The old Huey would have taken twice as long to get this far. At this speed, they would arrive at the scene ten to fifteen minutes sooner than in the Huey, which could easily mean life or death to the victims. Not hard to guess which aircraft any potential survivors would want.

Scott looked up from the moving map display on the GPS just in time to see a red flashing light coming quickly toward him. Instinctively pulling back on the joystick in his left hand the helicopter shot almost straight up. He didn't even know if the other pilot saw them as it took no evasive procedures. The small single engine plane shot past and under the Hawk. They probably wouldn't have collided but betting on "probably" wasn't good enough. Trying to be a hero and chancing a collision just to save a few seconds wasn't worth it. Flying and rescuing was all about risk management. Any potential survivors would no longer be survivors if the helicopter never got there at all because the pilot took a stupid risk.

The timer clicked six minutes just as the chopper crossed the bluffs overlooking the lake, which was quickly losing its shimmer. He wished that there were another set of eyes helping to look for the survivors. The rest of the team in the back of the helicopter including the "swimmers," would be getting ready at this time and wouldn't have time to help the pilot watch for survivors.

"Swimmers prepare, ETA five minutes!" the pilot announced over the onboard radio as he continued to scan the water's surface. Scott used a wide scan, assuming that the westerly wind would be pushing the capsized sailboat toward the shore. The time from the initial distress call and position report to their arrival could easily be fifteen to twenty minutes. A boat adrift could cover a lot of water in that time, and its passengers would be very cold and tired, probably near exhaustion.

The captain scanned the entire windscreen in front of him until he spotted something white in the distance. It could be a white cap, a nautical term for the crest of a wave breaking, or was it something else. The small movement was further north and would take him off course. Scott made the almost instant decision to investigate. The odds of the vessel being at its last reported position were slim to none anyway. Banking the copter instinctively to the left, the chopper turned too fast and he lost the line on the spot of white. With a smaller, careful correction to the right all they could do now was to fly with his best guess in the general direction of the last target. The sun was setting fast and the constant breaking waves made everything below look the same. Scott felt the tension in his right hand as it gripped the flight stick way too tightly. Usually adrenalin helped him in a situation like this, but right now it was causing him to over fly the aircraft. What was it that he had said to Major Allen, something about "a ham handed pilot like me?"

Scott took a deep breath and let it out slowly. He had taken a big gamble by going after a small glimpse of white. It could have been just another wave breaking, or nothing at all. Scott tried to keep up the scan of instruments in front of him and the water all around him. A copilot wouldn't be a luxury right now he reasoned. Another pair of eyes was desperately needed. Could he have missed something while he scanned the instruments? "Shit!" the pilot cursed. "I don't have time for this crap."

Their course was due north and they were getting closer to the shoreline. Captain Seaver banked right again a bit more aggressively and dropped the chopper a thousand feet. It was still a thousand feet above the water according to the radar altimeter. If he descended much farther his scan would be compromised, but the darkening skies were forcing him lower just the same.

It was time for another decision. If the pilot donned the infrared goggles, they might help him spot contrasting temperatures such as a warm hull or possibly even body heat against the cold water. But it would also severely limit his scan and the chance of glancing just past such an object would increase.

DAMN! Where are they? he thought.

"TEAM PREPARE TO JUMP." Scott practically screamed into the helmet mic. Was it just dumb luck or did his search pattern finally pay off? He didn't care right now; the rescue was on. An instant later the pilot switched to his military frequency and reported to Lieutenant Schmidt that they had located the capsized sailboat and were beginning the rescue operation.

The captain hadn't dared turn on the searchlights before now for fear of taking away his night vision and restricting the field of view. But right now, the search team would want all the light they could get. Scott, much more carefully this time, pulled back on the flight stick with his wrist and cut power slowly to settle the chopper over the water just above the capsized boat.

"Crew Chief, your chopper!" Captain Seaver instructed. From the pilot's position he couldn't see exactly where the rescue swimmers wanted to go or where they wanted the cable and winch to be centered. It was now the crew chief's job.

"Keep the chopper stabilized!" the crew chief cautioned.

Scott wanted to call back that he was doing his best against the gusting wind, but the crew chief didn't want someone doing his best. The

21

chief needed the chopper steady. If this was a land rescue, Captain Seaver would be able to engage the autopilot. The autopilot was a marvelous device that would use the current GPS coordinates down to the foot to keep the chopper in place. Over a land target, it worked great but their target was drifting with the wind and currents. It would take all the skill and luck the pilot had to keep the copter drifting with the survivors as he fought the gusting wind. Scott focused on the bow of the turned craft and decided that he would keep his Hawk in line with the boat below. It was at least some sort of reference. As the small boat drifted, the captain could assume so would the survivors below.

That seemed to work to the crew chief's satisfaction. "OK, let it drift left, but keep it steady. Now take her lower!"

Scott elected to keep the power up, but he changed the pitch of the rotating blades. They cut into the air less aggressively and the copter descended down to twenty-five feet above the water. He held it there. With the waves below swelling, he had better not settle down any lower.

Soon Seaver heard, "Swimmers away."

Scott tried to keep his heart from pacing too fast and did some slow deep breathing to calm himself.

Now there were two more persons he was responsible for in the frigid water. "Cable going down; we're going for the children first."

Scott could only picture what was happening directly beneath the beating thumping blades of the Black Hawk. He imagined the downwash whipping and pelting the people below with cold icy crystals of water. Captain Seaver struggled to stay both focused and as strange as it may seem, relaxed. A tight pilot wouldn't feel the buffeting and be able to correct for it. This was no time to be "ham handed" with the touchy controls. The experienced chopper pilot had the aircraft trimmed out as best as possible. That meant the aircraft was aerodynamically balanced and he could fly it all day without becoming physically tired. But the mental strain of keeping the aircraft essentially motionless, hanging in the air by the beating blades, took all the concentration he could muster.

"We have a new passenger on board, Captain!" the crew chief informed him in a matter-of-fact calm tone.

A third member of the rear rescue team would be administering medical help and getting each passenger safely positioned before the next rescued person would be brought on board.

"Cable going down!" He heard over the headset.

Well I wanted practice, Scott told himself. And, he was getting it!

The team was trained to work quickly and soon the team leader announced that the second survivor was onboard.

As one survivor was being hoisted onboard the big chopper, the divers would prepare another with the bright orange combination floatation ring and lifting sling. Not a second could be wasted.

Suddenly the chopper listed violently to the left. A big gust of wind had given the rotating blades, or more accurately the rotating wings, uneven lift. This caused the Black Hawk to tip left, which caused the chopper to make an aggressive sideways motion away from the bobbing hull and toward the churning waves below.

At this low height, the rotor blades could quickly catch the top of a swelling wave. The huge blades had over a fifty-three foot span which meant that a sideways tilt could put the tip of his blades within feet of the water. But the chopper didn't maintain altitude. It had lost lift with the uneven slant. In a blink of an eye the blades came dangerously close to the churning water. In another instant, they would catch on a wave with disastrous results.

Scott was glad he left the power up. The over sensitive controls were thankfully quick. Scott righted the copter while simultaneously pointing the copter into the gust. With a flick of his wrist the rotating wings took bigger slices of air and the copter shot up. It was a wild ride, but it worked.

"Nice catch!" were the calming words over the radio headset.

"Settle her down to twenty feet and let it drift left slowly," the crew chief said calmly into the onboard communication system as he repositioned the big chopper for the final rescue.

The pilot concentrated on not letting another gust catch him off guard and tried to keep the center of the copter directly over the rescue position. He then attempted another plan of letting the entire fuselage weather vane with the gust; it was something he should have been doing sooner. The new technique was helping. He thought that he must have been in some sort of trance when he heard from the crew chief, "All survivors aboard Captain; lowering cable for the dive team."

Scott didn't know where the time had gone. He was undoubtedly so focused on keeping the chopper steady that he had missed the other three calls, or had he, he wondered.

Just then the chopper shook; it was only twenty-five feet over the water. The chopper started losing precious altitude. With his right hand, which had been oddly idle for most of the time, the pilot pushed in full power on both engines. The chopper jerked and shot up forty feet in an instant. Scott repeated to himself an old flying adage. *Just fly the plane!* The saying was an automatically rehearsed response to an emergency situation in an aircraft. Many an airplane and crew were lost not to the emergency situation directly, but because the pilot became so transfixed on fixing the problem that he quite literally forgot to keep flying the airplane. A stall or bank would ensue and before he knew it, a perfectly flyable aircraft wasn't flying anymore.

The rescue swimmers were still in the water, but for now they were safe. The guard members had been trained in water survival and had on protective gear. The protective gear would help them last much longer in the icy water than if their bodies were unprotected.

Fly the plane! the pilot told himself once more as the chopper steadied at five hundred feet, giving just the least bit of safety. "Manage the risk," Scott repeated softly. A quick glance at the instruments told him that it was the number two engine. It had shut itself down for some reason. If he had been flying his Huey he and his passengers would be swimming right now.

Secure it or restart it, there were only two options. There was no time to waste. Losing an engine caused a cascade of events, all of which a pilot was suppose to be ready to deal with. But it happened so fast. Not only did the chopper lose the thrust of fifteen hundred horsepower but at the same time the aircraft picked up an extra eight hundred pounds of dead weight from that same non-working engine. The combination of negative lift factors could be and often was fatal.

The copter was stable at five hundred feet. Captain Scott Seaver was feeling more confident that he had the aircraft under control with each passing second. *Thank God it wasn't carrying a full load of fuel.* He realized that he needed to make another life or death decision and needed to make it quickly.

The whole point of two engines, besides giving more power, was the fact that if something happened to one of them, the Black Hawk could still fly home. Nobody ever promised it would fly well, but a competent pilot could or should get it out of harm's way and to safety as soon as possible. This pilot had five civilians onboard for whom he was responsible. They were possibly injured, but definitely suffering from hypothermia. There were also three other lives including his own. The decision was whether it was worth taking the risk of hovering over dangerous water with only one engine operative. Could he risk seven lives to save two more, even if they were his people in the water? If another gust came along, there wouldn't be the power this time to save it and the passengers on board.

The Black Hawk was still hovering five hundred feet above the floundering boat and the remaining team members in the frigid water. Every second of inaction over action was dangerous, wasted time. A glance at the timer showed that forty-five minutes had already gone by. Over half of the fuel was already used up, and no pilot wanted to make his landing with only minutes or seconds of fuel left. So that gave him one-half hour of flying time left at best.

"Sir!" A call came over the onboard radio. These people are in trouble; all of them are experiencing severe hypothermia and need to get to a hospital."

"DAMN!" Captain Seaver swore out loud to himself over his dilemma. The numbers weren't coming to him fast enough, if at all. *How much weight can the Black Hawk carry with one engine? Would lifting another four hundred pounds of swimmers below make them too heavy? Damn! I should know this.* The rescuers were in the water for approximately one-half hour already. *How much longer could they stay there?*

"Base, this is Sierra, Six, Six, Six! How far out is the coast guard cutter out of Milwaukee?"

"Sierra, Six, Six, Six. They left port at the same time you did, E.T.A. ten minutes."

"Base, we have an emergency; engine out, survivors all onboard, swimmers in the water." Scott was glad for government procedures and glad the government didn't mind burning up extra fuel. His rescue swimmers would be OK. Scott radioed his exact position; the Coast Guard Cutter's own GPS would guide them directly here.

Scott thought about his training. *Manage the risk! Can we wait ten more minutes?* Scott glanced at the fuel gauge; fuel reserves were OK. *SHIT!* Now he knew why the number two engine quit. *SHIT!*

OK, OK, Fly the plane! He calmed himself. *Don't do more harm.* That was more of a doctor's mantra, but it worked here too. The chopper was stable. Scott decided to secure the dead engine. That meant that he wouldn't attempt an air restart, which could be potentially dangerous.

"Medic, can the survivors hold on for another half hour until we are at the hospital?"

"Don't know Captain. They don't seem to be getting any worse. The young boy is in the worst shape and needs immediate care."

DAMN! Scott didn't want to leave the area until he was sure the coast guard could find his men. He didn't want to leave them in the frigid water alone. With his light on the small boat below, the coast guard would be able to spot the divers much faster, and time was everything.

"Coast Guard to Sierra, Six, Six, Six. We have you in sight."

"Roger that Coast Guard, they're all yours." With that, Scott peeled away carefully, realizing that he only had half the power with twice the

25

weight. Saint Joseph's was the closest hospital with a heliport and was thirty-five miles from their current location. Fuel was running low and they would be much slower going back in than going out.

It was just a matter of time now before the victims would be safely on the ground and under a doctor's care. Scott reminded himself not to get complacent; the Hawk was still overloaded for only one engine and it needed to be flown very cautiously. With Murphy's Law, anything that can and will go wrong still could. The pilot punched in the preset GPS coordinates for Saint Joseph's Hospital. At the speed they were flying the GPS calculated that it would be twenty-five more minutes to the hospital.

"Base, Sierra Six, Six, Six, please notify Saint Joseph's that we are twenty-five minutes out."

"Roger that, Sierra Six, Six, Six."

Scott could only imagine the ass chewing he would be getting. The only good news is he didn't crash the helicopter, at least, not yet.

Before long, the blue lights of the hospital helipad were in sight and Scott did a perfect one-engine landing. Captain Scott Seaver took a few very deep breaths as he shut down the simulator just as he would a real Black Hawk. The winding sound of a jet engine stopped as did the sound of the gyroscopic instruments.

It was uncanny how real the simulator was once the back door was closed and all you could see were the instruments in front of you and the high-resolution projection across the lifelike windscreen. Not only did the simulator look exactly like a real Black Hawk inside, the entire structure of the sim was mounted on huge hydraulic arms that mimicked every motion of the controls so the simulator handled identically to the real thing. But that was the point. Once a pilot saw the ground below him fade away and an exact replica of the West Bend Airport projected all around him on the windscreen as he departed the field it all became very, very real. And with the database in the computer it could simulate almost any airport in the world and quite a bit of the terrain surrounding it. To say that it wasn't a real experience would be a lie; everything about it was real.

Flying a real helicopter was mostly fun; the simulator was never, ever fun. That was why the pilots named it Sierra, Six, Six, Six. Sierra stood for S as in Simulator and the 666 signified it was the simulator from hell, and Lieutenant Schmidt was the devil in charge.

The lights flicked on and Lieutenant Schmidt opened the back door to the simulator. "Nice flying Captain!" The lieutenant complimented sincerely. "I tossed some pretty wicked winds at you for a while there."

It was also Lieutenant Schmidt who played the part of traffic control, crew chief, Coast Guard, medic and anybody else who interacted with the pilot during the session.

"Thanks, but why do I think I'm going to get my ass chewed out anyways?"

"It wouldn't be a sim session if you didn't, sir."

"RIGHT!" Captain Seaver drawled out, then remembering his helmet. It felt strange to not have it in his hand as he left the cockpit. He reached back, grabbed it and held it wearily in his right hand.

The cold air of the outer sim room felt good against his wet brow. Captain Seaver realized that his hair was matted from sweat. That wasn't unusual because the physical and mental workout was real. Scott had often thought that if he could convince himself that the entire sim experience was just a game, he would relax and do better. But once the programmed session got underway, it was all but impossible to not feel totally involved. It was just minutes ago that he had been focused on saving the young boy, even though the whole scenario was made up by Lieutenant Schmidt.

"Major Allen asked me to tell you that Lieutenant Mayor is on the way in to relieve you and he told me that he appreciates you sticking around, and that the sim session is on the house."

"Does that mean you will be burning the report Lieutenant?" Scott asked.

"Sorry sir, can't do that. But it won't go onto your official record and that might be a good thing sir. Your score wasn't real high."

"I know, I know," Scott walked away wearily to the showers as he said to himself sadly, "I know, I know!"

Captain Seaver went directly from the sim room to the washroom. First, he took a piss; it was something he seemed to need to do more often lately. Then the worn pilot splashed some cold water over his face. Scott looked in the mirror at himself as he wiped his face dry with a paper towel and saw every line of his considerably wrinkled face; the crows' feet around his baggy eyes were deep and furrowed.

"Where did you come from old man?" the reflection asked. Mostly, Scott didn't feel old. He kept himself in great shape, even for a man his age, he reminded the man in the mirror. Sometimes the captain even felt young. But more and more, he didn't have to remind himself of his age. His body did, in one way or another.

Scott knew that Lieutenant Mayor wouldn't be in for another hour or so. That meant there was just enough time to get his ass chewed out by Major Allen. Captain Seaver slowly straightened up and combed his still

27

full head of hair neatly to make himself presentable to his commanding officer. He took in a great gulp of air and exhaled it slowly. He lifted his six foot frame tall and braced himself for the coming simulator debriefing.

"Sit down Captain," Major Allen gestured with his hand warmly. "How about we go over the 'Good, the Bad and the Ugly,'" he joked.

It wasn't a particularly ominous suggestion. He had used the saying many, many times before to anyone who might be sitting in the hot seat after a sim session.

"How about we do the good first?" It was of course a rhetorical question by the major.

"I didn't know there was any?" Scott answered back with a bit of self-depreciating humor.

Bob just smiled slightly and started his review.

"Liked the way you handled the Milwaukee departure controller. A more inexperienced pilot might have let a controller get away with delaying an emergency flight."

Scott had forgotten about some of the good things he had done during the simulated rescue. "Yes sir, thank you sir." Scott knew that this was a very formal time between them. This was all business and his career in the guard was dependent on these types of reviews.

"Also your flying instincts are still well honed. Your evasive action prevented a probable mid-air collision. You missed the small plane that was coming right at you. Lieutenant Schmidt didn't give you much time to see it and respond. Good job."

"Yes sir," Scott responded quickly, not filling in the part that he had been looking away just before he luckily spotted the approaching light in time to dodge it.

"You could have been quicker with the GPS. As I said before a little more book time would help. I would also suggest that you take the portable GPS home and practice with it in simulator mode for a while. That will help a lot."

"Yes sir, I will do that sir," Scott replied respectfully.

"Your search and rescue instincts are still remarkable Scott."

Captain Seaver was getting a bit more comfortable in the chair as his commanding officer complimented him, but that didn't mean he was out of the woods yet. Scott knew better than that. The "Bad and the Ugly" were sure to come, but it was encouraging to hear that as a pilot, he wasn't a complete failure.

"Finding a capsized boat in that damned, rolling washing machine called Lake Michigan is more art than science, and more instinct than skill. I can honestly say that I don't know how to teach it to somebody. I truly wish I could. You have the instinct and always did. Even in Desert Storm you always knew where to fly and more importantly where not to."

"Almost always, sir!" Captain Seaver quipped back, correcting his commanding officer. Both of them clearly remembered the one time his instincts failed him, and nearly got the captain and his crew killed.

Scott reflected back to the failed reconnaissance mission. Scott thought he saw a missile battery and flew toward it. It had just been a decoy. Soon, a ground to air missile was headed toward them from behind. Scott realized his blunder and turned just in time to see the weapon coming right at them. On instinct he gyrated the Huey in time to save them, but the missile caught the edge of a runner, and when it exploded, shrapnel pierced the engine. The jets on patrol with them saw what had happened and immediately took out the missile site and its occupants. The Huey went down hard, and the team was captured.

They were locked in some sort of steel equipment container. The desert was hot that day, and the inside of the container was like an oven. Scott didn't remember much more than that. He had been injured quite severely during the crash. The report says that not only was the captain injured but he was tortured for a period of days along with the rest of his crew. It took another team from the Special Forces to rescue them. Even that, he didn't remember.

The last thing Scott did remember was waking up in the field hospital. His cracked flight helmet was sitting on the stand next to his bed to remind him of how hard his head had hit against something.

Bob Allen was the commanding officer for that mission; it was his face that Scott saw when his eyes finally opened. It had been Bob's job to do the debriefing of the crew for the official report. He immediately assured Scott that he had done a masterful job of landing the damaged aircraft and had acted heroically during the entire ordeal.

Scott was brought back to current debriefing when he heard Bob's voice say. "Sometimes even the best instincts aren't good enough," the Major found a way to break into the "Bad and the Ugly" part of his review.

Captain Seaver quickly lost his smile with that warning. The commander's voice changed to a quiet somber tone that sounded ominous to Scott.

Bob looked away for a second or two and said, "My god Scott, this isn't easy for me. You're a damned good pilot, one of the best." The major looked back at Scott. "Those heavy gusts of wind that Schmidt tossed at you have crashed many pilots doing the same simulation. Others couldn't

29

keep it over the target like you did and others would never even have found the target in the first place."

Scott couldn't contain his silence. "If all that is true, what are you trying to tell me Bob?" Out of place or not, Scott made it personal between them.

"Damn it Scott!.............., Damn it," Bob said more quietly the second time.

"If Lieutenant Schmidt wouldn't have reset the engines you never would have gotten off the ground in the first place." Bob looked down at his shinny black shoes for a moment and took a deep breath.

"What do you mean?" Scott demanded.

"The Ugly Scott, the Ugly." Calmly the commanding officer continued. "On start-up, the number one engine over spooled. It red lined. You took it out. Mission canceled before it began. All the instincts in the world won't help if you can't get the damned thing in the air."

"What are you talking about?" Scott asked calmly but confused.

"I watched the video of you in the cockpit. It's like you froze on startup; you looked right at the gauge as it climbed and did nothing, nothing. I don't understand it myself. Then you calmly started number two engine as if nothing had happened. You didn't even *try* to shut it down." Bob emphasized the word "try."

Scott tried to remember the start-up sequence, but for some reason it was a blank. The captain couldn't even argue with his commanding officer because for some reason he couldn't remember that particular string of events. Did the gauge red line? For some strange reason he couldn't remember starting either engine or remember watching the gages at all.

"Sir, I've been starting turbine engines for as long as I can remember. Waiting for the catch is something I don't even think about any more. It is automatic. I just can't believe that I could possibly miss something like that."

"It's not just that Scott. Do you know why your engine quit when you were out over the lake?"

Scott pressed his mind to remember the details of the simulation, gradually starting to remember parts of the flight. It was like the simulated rescue flight was playing in slow motion in his mind. He couldn't remember starting the engines, but did remember missing the small plane, so he tried to fast-forward his mind from that memory to the engine going out.

Major Allen waited for a response, noticing a blank look on his friend's face.

"Scott, Scott..., what's the matter?"

Seaver heard his name just as the simulator flight came back into focus. "Of course, I know sir; I lost fuel to that engine." Scott felt his palms sweat, but yet his body felt suddenly cold.

"Yes, you lost fuel to that engine, but the point was you had plenty of fuel on board. You never checked the fuel once, not even on start-up. You didn't know which tank your fuel was in or you would have switched tanks."

Scott suddenly felt disorientated and dizzy; his face felt flushed. He looked up at Bob and saw him talking but nothing was making sense.

Major Allen saw his friend's head bob and weave a bit. "Scott, Scott! Are you all right?" he asked, suddenly very concerned.

Scott looked up slowly and said. "May I please be dismissed? I am not feeling so well."

Bob picked up his phone and hollered into it. "Schmidt, Schmidt, get in here immediately. Something is wrong with Scott." Any sense of formality was gone. Something was wrong with his friend and the calm, cool commander was feeling a bit of panic for one of the few times in his life.

Chapter 3

The lieutenant rushed in without knocking; he was just in time to help his commander guide a limp Captain Seaver to the side couch. Lieutenant Schmidt was an emergency medical technician and took charge of the situation after helping his wobbly friend drop onto the couch.

"Let's get his legs elevated; he seems very light headed. What happened?"

Major Allen quickly explained how the captain's eyes had started rolling and how he seemed disoriented.

"He wouldn't be the first pilot who got sick from the simulator," the lieutenant explained.

The commander disagreed with the assessment. "Scott never got motion sickness in a sim or anywhere else. I've seen him do things with an aircraft that, well, shouldn't have been aerodynamically possible and he never got sick. I did, but Scott just laughed at me."

"Doesn't matter. Things change. People change. He isn't the young pilot you used to know anymore ... sir!" Schmidt thought he had better add a "sir" at the end of his statement when he saw his commander's annoyed expression at the reference that neither of them was as young as they once were.

As Lieutenant Schmidt checked the captain's pulse he added, "The simulator is high work load, high stress, and its motion, though simulating the movements of a real aircraft, are somewhat unnatural. Even the best can get sick from a tough simulator session."

"Not Scott," the commander said quietly, "not Scott."

"Look, he's coming around; his color is coming back," the medic observed.

"Captain, Captain, can you hear me?" he asked quietly as he knelt down next to the dazed pilot.

Scott realized he was lying down and his feet were propped up. Rather quickly he was gaining his senses. "What the hell happened," he asked somewhat woozily.

"Take it easy," Bob explained. "You fainted or something."

Scott tried to get up but the medic stopped him by using his flat palm to press gently on the captain's chest. "Just take it easy for a few more minutes, sir."

"Oww!" Scott grimaced and pulled his hand away from the EMT. "What are you doing that for?"

"I just had to prick your finger for a small blood test, sir. I need to do a blood sugar test."

"I don't remember what happened."

"That's not unusual," Randy reassured. "People seldom remember what happened immediately before a black out. The mind doesn't have time to file it away before things go blank."

"I think I'm OK. Let me sit up. I promise I'll be a good boy."

"OK slowly, and if you feel lightheaded I want you to tell me. Could you please get the captain a glass of water, sir?"

The lieutenant wasn't used to asking his commander's help, but in this case he knew that the ranking officer would be more than glad to do something to be of assistance.

When Major Allen returned with the water, Scott took it and joked, "Maybe I'm pregnant?" just to let the two concerned friends know that he was back to his old self.

"Let's hope not, Captain," Bob quipped back. "There are flight rules against that sort of thing."

"Yes sir!" Scott added smartly. "Besides, my wife would start wondering who I've been with."

"Doesn't seem to be anything wrong with your blood sugars," the EMT announced.

Scott stood up slowly as his nervous friends looked on. "I feel fine, honest. I don't know what happened but I feel much better now."

"Scott, I insist on giving you a ride home and I won't take no for an answer," the base commander said firmly. It wasn't an order and didn't need to be. Scott was more wise than macho at this point of his life. A ride would be welcomed, and he realized a doctor's appointment was inevitably in his future too.

Bob helped his friend pack up his civilian clothes. Normally Scott would have showered and changed out of his flight suit, back into his civilian clothes before leaving the base. But today things were anything but normal. He continually insisted that he was OK to anyone who asked, but the truth was he felt weak in the knees.

Still in his flight suit, he climbed into his commander's personal car. The ride home was uncomfortably quiet for both of them, though to Scott the car ride seemed to have passed rather quickly.

"I'll walk you to the house if you don't mind," Bob suggested.

"Really that's not necessary, I feel fine," Scott insisted.

Alan D Schmitz

"I'm sure you do. But I would feel a whole lot better if I knew that Elizabeth got an explanation from me about why you didn't drive yourself home. Remember you weren't even scheduled to be on the base today."

Scott realized that he would have a hard time explaining everything to Elizabeth by himself and actually welcomed the backup.

"Yea sure!" Scott agreed. "And driver, don't forget my bag," Scott wisecracked to his commanding officer.

"You're getting close to insubordination, Captain," Bob scolded with a smile as he grabbed the bag from the back seat of his car.

Scott walked through the front door of their brick two story home. "Honey I'm home," Scott announced as casually as usual.

"Hi hon!" came a voice from the other room. "You're home early."

"Well something came up at the office; Bob Allen is here with me."

Just then Elizabeth came around the corner from the kitchen where she had been preparing supper. As soon as she saw her husband in his flight suit she said, "Oh. That office! I didn't know that you were on duty today," Elizabeth said in a sweet voice.

A long time before they got married, Elizabeth had learned that flying was an important part of her new boyfriend's life. It was over twenty years ago when Elizabeth Marie London had first seen her sexy aviator in his green flight suit. She fell in love with him on the spot and was never afraid to admit it. It didn't take long for her to realize that if she truly loved him, she would have to accept his penchant for flying. Flying was his mistress and Liz knew that she would have to share Scott with her.

"To what do I owe this unexpected pleasure Bob? I hope you can stay for supper; we have plenty." Elizabeth shot a sincere smile at their mutual friend.

Major Allen could be as friendly as ice cream and apple pie if he wanted to, but right now it was business, serious business, and there was no point in putting it off.

"Sorry Elizabeth, not tonight," said the commander declining the dinner invitation.

Scott turned back to look at his friend and gave him a look that invited him to tell his wife what had happened. Bob caught his gaze. "Something happened at the base that I think you should be aware of," he started.

Elizabeth suddenly turned her smiling inviting face away from Bob and toward her husband, showing instant concern. This was highly unusual and that wasn't good.

"Scott passed out in my office this afternoon," Bob blurted out, as if saying it quickly would make it less painful to hear.

34

Immediately, Elizabeth Seaver took a position by her husband's side and held his hand.

"Smooth Bob, real smooth," Scott groaned. "I'm fine Liz. Something didn't agree with me and I passed out for just a second. No big deal." Scott for some reason was the only one who got by calling his wife Liz.

"No big deal?" Elizabeth protested. "Tell me exactly what happened." She wanted to know every last detail.

"I stopped in at the base to check on a few things; I was talking to Bob and passed out for just a minute."

Elizabeth became more concerned as the news started to settle in her mind. "Scott!" she ordered. "Sit down before you say another word."

Scott didn't have a choice, as he was immediately pulled toward the living room couch, almost falling onto it. Elizabeth sat down next to Scott holding his hand concerned. How such a petite, gorgeous woman could so easily overpower him, he still didn't understand. The fact that she could control him so easily whenever she wanted was spooky. It was as if his free will was instantly neutralized and he was subject to her will whenever the love of his life insisted. It wasn't that she was demanding, because she wasn't, not of him, but when she got serious like she was now, lookout! It was times like this that she took charge, and when Mrs. Seaver took charge, there was no negotiating.

Elizabeth reasoned that Scott would probably not be the best source of information in this case, so she held his hand tightly but asked her questions of their friend.

"Robert, tell me what really happened. And don't you dare leave out a thing."

"Scott stopped in to check on a few things, you know, some squaks on the Huey." Elizabeth was familiar with the flying term; it meant un-operational items that needed repair. "While he was talking to me about them, I got a call that Captain Fredric was in an accident and couldn't come in. I asked Scott if he could fill in until I could get a replacement."

"And that's when Scott fainted?" she asked.

"No, not exactly," Bob hesitated, suddenly feeling guilty for sending Scott into the simulator.

"You see, I thought that as long as Scott was hanging around he might as well get some sim time. You know, he needed, I mean wanted, the practice anyhow."

Elizabeth was quite familiar with the simulator training also. She had heard plenty of stories about tough simulator sessions, not only from Scott, but also from all of his pilot friends. Many of the stories were of course funny in hindsight, but often revolved around pilots who had actually for a second or two forgotten that they were safe inside of a simulator as they prepared to "land" for the last time of their life after having lost control of their aircraft due to some simulated failure.

Bob continued, "Scott flew the Black Hawk on a simulated mission. After he was finished we were reviewing things and that was when he passed out, right on the chair in front of me. Lieutenant Schmidt, who is a trained paramedic, looked after Scott until he felt better. When Randy thought it was OK for Scott to leave, I insisted on driving him home."

"That's all of it, Bob? Don't lie to me!" Elizabeth looked deep into Bob's eyes convinced that she would know if he were lying, but asking anyways.

"Elizabeth, I promise, that is exactly how it happened." Then Bob asked suspiciously. "Has this ever happened before?"

Without giving it a second thought Elizabeth said, "Never!"

Then she looked at her husband with a bit of doubt. She realized that pilots who loved flying weren't always the first to mention a physical ailment that might ground them.

"Scott..!" she warned with her most threatening voice. "Has this 'ever' happened to you before?" And Elizabeth emphasized the word "ever."

"Hey, don't look at me that way." Scott felt like a little child caught in a lie by his mother. "You know that I could never lie to you. This is the first time this has happened, honest. I skipped lunch today and I think I just got a bit light headed because I was hungry or something like that."

"You often get so wrapped up in your work that you skip lunch. Why would you faint today?" she quizzed back.

"I don't know, Lieutenant Schmidt said that I probably got sick from being in the motion simulator." Scott tried to make another excuse.

"Bull!" Elizabeth disagreed bluntly. "That's a lot of bull and you know it. I am calling the clinic right now and you are going to see the doctor immediately. We're going to the emergency room."

Bob felt compelled to reassure Elizabeth a bit. "Lieutenant Schmidt took his pulse and blood pressure, and did a few simple tests. He didn't feel that there is anything life threatening going on."

Scott was now really glad that his commanding officer had come home with him. Going to the emergency room wasn't something he thought he could argue against by himself.

"See Liz, I'm fine." So much for getting lucky tonight, he realized. There was no way that his wife would let him make love to her until she was satisfied such an effort wouldn't kill him.

"Bob..." she pleaded. "Are you sure?"

"I'm not a doctor, but I've watched plenty on TV, and I think he'll be fine until morning." Bob tried to lighten the situation.

"I agree with Bob, and I'd stake my life on it," Scott quipped back. Bob muffled his chuckle but Elizabeth didn't think it was very funny.

"I am calling the clinic, and you will do whatever 'they' say." This time she emphasized "they" and there was no question that she meant it.

Bob felt obliged to stick around until after Elizabeth was satisfied everything was OK. The hospital nurse agreed that since a medic had already examined him and that he was otherwise in good health, they could wait until the next day when his family doctor could see him.

Elizabeth had made the rules and now had to abide by them. "I am watching you like a hawk tonight, and if I get a hint of even the littlest complication, we are going straight to the emergency room."

As Bob excused himself, he gave Scott a firm handshake, a strong pat on the back and assured him that he would be in touch. But he didn't get to leave until Elizabeth had given him a very thankful hug.

As soon as Bob was out of the house, Scott asked his wife with an impish smile, "Do you want to make love tonight? I think you are so sexy when you act all worried about me."

"That's not funny Scott." Elizabeth wasn't amused. "This is no act, you have me very worried."

"I'm sorry, but think about it. People faint all the time. Heck, it happens so often they even made a television show out of showing people fainting at weddings and things."

"Maybe people do faint, but you don't, and that's what worries me. The emergency room nurse is leaving a message with Dr. Mooney's office and tomorrow we are going to be there at 9:30 sharp, and that's that."

Elizabeth went about her business in the kitchen while Scott showered and changed out of his flight suit. As Elizabeth was setting the table, the side door flew open as it usually did at this time of day. "Mom...! Mom...! I'm home.." Fourteen-year-old Avery Rose Seaver burst through the door.

"Hi honey."

Without acknowledging her mother's greeting, Avery continued into the room and slung her school backpack off her shoulders and into a corner on the kitchen floor. Elizabeth couldn't remember at what age Avery had claimed that small piece of real estate as hers, but it was, and her backpack lived there for nine months of the year. "You wouldn't believe what stupid Jeff Winfield did today. It was sooo...gross. And in gym, I was captain and I had to pick and I didn't want Julie Adams on my team in the worst way. I hate her. She is such a bitch."

37

"Avery!" Elizabeth scolded.

"Well, she is. But Debbie Ames was the other captain and she didn't want to pick her either, so on the last pick I had to take her, but then she got creamed on the first pass and I laughed. Then Miss Holden got mad at me." Without explaining more or skipping a beat, she continued.

"What's for supper? I'm famished. It smells like meatloaf. It better not be meatloaf. We have to work on a lab project tonight so Kelly is going to come over."

Scott came down the hallway. "Hi princess."

"Please Daddy, don't call me that." The youngest Seaver protested, though not too seriously.

Dad was quickly reminded that his little girl was turning into a woman. He had called her by that pet name since she was a little girl, always knowing that some day it would be out lived. Scott came up to her and gave her a big hug, which she still tolerated as long as no one else was around to see. "OK Rosie." Scott teased; his daughter hated being called by her middle name even more.

Scott knew that his little princess was growing up, and though there were days when the young teenager's hormones gave him a headache, for the most part he felt as close to his daughter as he ever had. He also accepted the fact that he had better relish every second of it, because one day soon, she would be a young lady, gone to college, married, and before he knew it, would be having a family of her own.

Then Avery Rose realized that her father's car wasn't in the drive. "Where's your car Dad? I didn't see it."

Scott wouldn't have expected the average teenager to have noticed such a detail. Mostly they were so wrapped up in their own small but ever so important lives that the details of life surrounding them were considered too unimportant to even notice, but not his princess. He was constantly impressed how she seemed to absorb the world around her and almost on a subconscious level know and understood things beyond her years.

Scott took a quick glance at his wife, looking for advice. He didn't want to worry his young daughter with the events of the day. But after a few uncomfortably silent moments, it was clear that Elizabeth wasn't going to be of help, at least not quickly enough. Liz she gave a slight shrug of her shoulders indicating that she didn't know what to answer either.

"It wouldn't start." Scott came up with a protective lie. "Bob gave me a ride home from the base." Scott thought he caught a slight knowing sign in his daughter's eye that Dad was lying, but if she did she let it go after giving her mother a quick glance just as Elizabeth turned away and busied herself at the sink.

"If you get right to it, you still have time to get some homework done before we eat," her mother coached.

That changed the subject, which was Elizabeth's hope. "Dad, Miss Salmon wants to know if you are going to help in Tae-Kwon-Do class. She says you are getting a bit rusty and should practice more. Mrs. Jocobson gave us two chapters to read, and she knows that we have to work on the lab project for tomorrow. She is such a bitch."

"Avery Rose!" her dad scolded her this time. "A young lady doesn't refer to her teacher as a bitch."

"Well, she is!"

Calmly Scott lectured, realizing he was talking to a teenager and his words were going in one ear and out the other. "She is doing her job, and I thought you liked Mrs. Jocobson?"

"Last year I had her for math and she was OK, but this year she's teaching English literature and she, like, became this book Nazi and thinks that we have to like all these books just because she likes them. She is such a bitch."

Both parents echoed at the same time. "Avery!"

Not wanting to hear another lecture, Avery grabbed her backpack off the floor and trounced to her room. As soon as she was out of sight the two parents looked at each other and laughed. Raising teenagers was a rough gig and even rougher if you took them too seriously.

Elizabeth took the opportunity to ask again for the fourth or fifth time since Bob had left, "How are you feeling?"

"I feel Miss Salmon should mind her own business. I don't think I'm getting rusty at my Tae-Kwon-Do skills," Scott defended himself sulking a bit. "And I can't help at practice this week; I have too much to do."

"You know what I mean, and don't change the subject," Elizabeth scolded.

"I'm fine Liz. I'm just fine and you will see tomorrow that the doctor will agree with me."

At the family doctor's office:

"All the initial tests came back fine, Scott. Blood pressure is normal, reflex, resting pulse are fine, and your blood sugar levels are normal."

"So Doc, you're telling me, I'm fine?"

"Nothing of the sort. I'm telling you I haven't found a quick reason for you to faint," Dr. Richard Mooney replied. "You fainted for a reason, and these quick tests aren't good for much more than confirming you are still alive."

Dr. Mooney had been Scott and Elizabeth's family's physician since they had moved to Port Washington fifteen years ago. He knew Scott more than well enough to let some of his professional facade slide.

"You and your family deserve to have a more definitive answer, and that's why I am prescribing more tests. First we will start with a stress test. I want to know what is happening when you aren't just sitting around doing nothing. I also want some blood work done. That should be enough to get me started. And Scott," Dr. Mooney added looking up over his bifocals, "no flying until we get this sorted out."

"Don't worry Doc, it's not like Bob is going to let me near a chopper until he gets the results himself. But you are going to find out that there is nothing wrong with me that eating a sandwich at lunch time won't cure."

"Go downstairs and they will take some blood. You will have to schedule a stress test at the main desk, and get it done ASAP. Got it?"

"Yes sir!" Scott saluted his long time doctor in jest, as he was already slipping on his shirt.

"And Scott," said the doctor, looking Captain Seaver square in the eyes over his glasses, "if you feel anything out of the ordinary at all, like a little light headed or dizzy, even for a moment, I want you to go to an emergency room and have them call me. Got it?"

This time Scott didn't joke. He looked his doctor in the eye and reluctantly agreed. "Yea sure, of course."

"I mean it Scott. We don't know what happened. Don't take any chances. It's just not worth it."

Scott just nodded in agreement this time. He knew what the doctor was trying to tell him and of course he was right. They both knew that one fainting spell could be medically excused as a fluke, another would indicate something more serious was afoot. However, if he returned to an emergency room, he knew that he would be grounded for a long time. The National Guard flight surgeon would have him go through any and every test imaginable before he would get his wings back. And at his age, they were bound to find something that could ground him forever.

The doctor left the small examining room while Scott finished dressing. He saw himself in the mirror and thought he looked like a small, broken man. But that wasn't who he was. He sucked in a large lungful of air and stood tall. He put his worries behind him and strutted out of the examining area and into the waiting room like a hero coming home.

Elizabeth looked up from her magazine the instant she saw Scott. Scott gave her a big wide grin and a thumbs up. "See, I told you I was fine."

Elizabeth didn't buy it already. "What did he say?"

"Quote un-quote!" Scott emphasized. "Everything is normal and everything looks fine."

"How can he be so sure, so quickly?" Elizabeth was suspicious.

"Well..," Scott tried to play things down a bit. "He wants me to have my blood checked just for the heck of it, so I have to go downstairs and give them some blood before we can leave."

"That's it, just a blood test?" she asked skeptically.

"Well, that and I'm supposed to schedule a stress test too."

"So everything isn't just fine and normal." Scott's wife of twenty-two years suddenly saw things adding up again.

"You know doctors. Once you walk in the door they got you. How do you think these places pay for themselves? Besides, for insurance reasons they have to throw the book at you if you just sneeze wrong." Scott tried to minimize the fact he had to have more tests done.

"Yea..., well, good for them." Elizabeth wasn't buying any of it as she walked down the stairs with her husband.

Scott tried to comfort his wife again, as well as himself. "Honey, I'm telling you, I'm fine."

On the ride back home Scott's phone alarm went off. Scott flicked it out of his belt clip and took a quick peak as they drove down the city side road. "Crap!" Scott swore.

"What's the matter?" Elizabeth knew the tone.

"With all of this medical stuff going on I forgot about a project meeting I'm supposed to be at in an hour." Scott looked at his watch out of habit, though the multi-function phone had just told him the time.

"I have just enough time to pick up my car at the base and get to the meeting. Sorry to ditch you so fast honey but I really need to be there."

"Can't you cancel?" Elizabeth's protective nature made her feel uncomfortable with Scott going to the office that quickly.

"I could, but it wouldn't look good, and besides, as I told you..." he said as he was quickly interrupted.

"I know, I know..., you feel fine!" Elizabeth finished his statement for him this time.

Scott chuckled and added. "See, we both agree!"

Elizabeth gave her husband a silly grin. "You can be such an ass," she said lovingly.

41

Chapter 4

Army Reserve base, West Bend, Wisconsin:

*T*hank god for my phone alarm, Scott thought. This was a meeting he couldn't miss. Jerry would have looked pretty foolish if he was left all alone with the owners who were clearly expecting both partners to attend. Granted, there had been a lot going on since yesterday when Scott fainted, but this project was critical to the company's future. He didn't know how he could have forgotten it.

Elizabeth pulled up next to the security gate. Private First Class Mueller, or Kev as everyone called him, immediately came out and asked how Scott was feeling. For at least the hundredth time since yesterday, Scott replied, "fine Kevin, I'm just fine." Scott smiled at the guard and then glanced at his wife as she choked back a small giggle at her husband's continued irritation at repeatedly being asked the question. Elizabeth drove her car into the open parking spot right next to Scott's. He leaned over and gave his wife a kiss goodbye.

"You take care of yourself today," Elizabeth Seaver warned.

"Yes dear," he replied dryly. One minute later he was speeding down the road and onto Highway 45 south to Milwaukee.

Jerry was his partner in their demolition and construction business. The two of them often kidded that one knocked the buildings down and the other re-built them. The truth was they worked great as a team in tearing down and rebuilding. It was amazing to Scott that what one of them didn't think of or anticipate, the other did. Of course, that was why they were so successful.

As soon as Scott was safely heading down the freeway he gave his partner a call.

"Hi Scott. Where are you? You had me worried. I wanted to go over a few things before the meeting."

"Sorry Jerry, you won't believe what happened to me yesterday. I'll tell you later. I only have time to go directly to the project site. I'll meet you there and we'll just have to wing it."

"Wouldn't be the first time," Jerry responded coolly. Scott was glad that Jerry didn't seem particularly upset.

"I shouldn't be late. Traffic is moving OK and…"

"Scott" Jerry interrupted. "I e-mailed you a new drawing and an updated spreadsheet. It's important that you please take a look at it before the meeting."

"Will do!" he acknowledged and then hung up. Scott prided himself on the fact that their company was one of the best implosion companies in the Midwest. Usually they used powerful plastic explosives to bring the larger buildings down. And when it came to engineering where to set the charges, he was the guy. In a way, there was nothing more beautiful than seeing a massive structure as it imploded perfectly on itself and settle down into a pile of rubble on its own footprint.

Once at the site, Scott looked at his watch and then out of habit glanced at his multi-use phone. He was a few minutes early and noticed that there were some messages waiting. He used the scroll wheel on his IT-Tech to scan the headings.

There were several e-mails, all of them important, including one from his partner Jerry. But Scott became lost in his own thoughts, dwelling on the previous day's events.

Jerry pulled up next to Scott and got out the car with an apology. "Sorry I'm a bit late. I thought we would be driving together so I was waiting for you."

Scott looked at his watch again and realized he couldn't recall what happened in the last ten minutes. "Jerry, I'm sorry I didn't call."

"No problem, we'll talk later. Did you look over the drawing and info I sent you?"

Scott hesitated a bit. "No.., not yet, ahh.., I just got here myself." Scott had forgotten about the e-mail Jerry said he should look at. That was so unlike him. And why had the last ten minutes gone buy so fast? Scott rationalized that there was a lot on his mind. He couldn't stop thinking about the day before and the simulator session. The businessman was more worried about his small fainting spell than he had let on to Liz and was anxious to go back to the office after this meeting to get his old routine back.

Scott got out of his SUV and gave his partner a firm handshake. "I'll just follow your lead Jerry. Then after this meeting let's get something to eat and I'll fill you in on why I was late this morning."

Both men grabbed their briefcases and walked into the doublewide job trailer.

****

After the meeting, the two men found a close restaurant.

43

"So you are telling me that you don't remember a thing." Jerry tried to understand as he listened to his friend while munching on some dinner rolls.

"Well, I remember things from before and after, but I don't remember how I got to the couch."

"That doesn't sound good."

"Anyhow..." Scott continued. "Bob gave me a ride home. Liz got all nuts about things and then made me go to the doctor this morning, which is why I was late. I'm just sorry that I forgot to call. In all the confusion and rushing around, I forgot completely about the meeting."

"Don't worry about it, I understand. And I'm glad that Elizabeth made you go to the doctor. So what's the verdict?"

"He said I'm fine. I think I know what happened. I skipped lunch yesterday and then I had that simulator session from hell. I think I just became dehydrated and that's why I passed out."

The partners saw their food coming and stopped talking as the waitress placed their meals in front of them. As soon as she was gone, Jerry asked as he picked up his fork, "So that's it? Doctor says you're OK and you are just going to pretend it didn't happen."

"No!..," Scott sounded insulted by the inference. "No, I'm not just going to pretend it didn't happen," Scott said sarcastically back to his long time partner and friend. "They're going to do some blood-work and I'm going to take a stress test. You know, I run my ass off on a treadmill while I'm connected to a bunch of wires."

"Yea smart ass, I know. I did one last year; piece of cake."

Scott took a big gulp of his Diet Coke, then added, "I keep telling everybody that I'm fine, but I know that nobody will believe me until I do the stupid stress test thing."

"Then just do the stress test thing and everybody will be happy," Jerry suggested with a smile.

"Enough of that!" Scott changed subjects. "I thought the meeting went well. Dennis said we have the job if our numbers are in line. I could tell by the way he looked at the drawing that he likes the new design; and so did I, by the way."

"Thanks.., yea, I think we're okay. I could have used some help in explaining why the demolition figures were higher than anticipated."

"Nonsense, you were doing fine," Scott complimented.

They both finished their meals. Scott paid the tab and they made more small talk walking out to their cars. "See you at the office, Captain." Jerry teased and saluted his partner as he slid into his car.

"See you in twenty minutes, smart ass." Scott gave his friend the one finger salute.

****

On the drive home from work Scott listened to the radio and, for the most part, had let the incident of the day before slip from his mind. Going to work and being in the office all afternoon with nothing but the usual crises to distract him made him feel normal again. He thought about the stress test a bit, not because he was worried, but because he was trying to remember what, if any, appointments he would have to change because of it. The clinic couldn't get him in any sooner than in a week and a half. That didn't concern him too much, but just the same he wanted to get it over with as soon as possible. He knew that things wouldn't get back to normal until everyone was satisfied that the stress test came out OK.

Scott heard the car "ding" at him. He looked around to see why and then on the radio LCD he saw a message that said, "Low on Fuel." A quick glance at the fuel gauge confirmed that he would have to stop for gas before heading home.

About two blocks from his home the fuel alarm dinged again. "Damn..!" Scott cursed. "You dummy!" he said to himself as he looked for a place to turn around. He had already passed the nearest gas station to his house. It wasn't far to backtrack, but he shouldn't have to backtrack at all if he had kept his wits about him. "Damn!" he repeated.

****

"Hi honey. I'm home."

Elizabeth came around the corner of the kitchen; she didn't have an apron on this time and it looked like she was still dressed from her interview. Scott was glad for the small hint from her clothing. It wouldn't do well for him to forget to ask about her important day.

Elizabeth beat Scott to it by asking him. "How did it go at work today?"

"I think it went pretty well. We'll know for sure if we get the signed contract back by the end of next week." Just as he finished Elizabeth pressed up against him and they gave each other a kiss and a hug.

"That sounds promising. Did you explain to Jerry why you weren't at the office this morning?"

"Of course."

Scott followed Elizabeth back into the kitchen, not wanting to discuss it further.

45

"When do we expect Avery home?" he changed the subject.

"Avery is still at school because of the Christmas play rehearsal so we might be eating a bit late."

"I had a late lunch, so I can wait," Scott replied.

It was coming up on the two-year anniversary of the death of their son Brad. Elizabeth had quit her teaching job at that time. The day-to-day pain of seeing young men and women the same age as Brad was too much for her to stand. The loss had taken a huge toll on both of them. It had driven them apart and pulled them together again. They learned how painful the loss of a son or daughter can be. But they also learned how much they both needed each other. Scott was still trying to work through the emotional trauma of blaming himself for his son's death. Rationally he knew the accident was a fluke and there was nothing he could have done to prevent it. But just accepting fate was much easier said than done. He needed to blame someone, but there was no one else to blame. Initially, Elizabeth not only let Scott blame himself, but she also needed to hold someone at fault, and used her husband as her whipping boy for a while. The last two years had been so emotionally draining that Scott often felt he couldn't go on living because of his guilt.

The tired businessman sat down in his recliner and opened the paper, but he couldn't stop thinking about the loss of his son and the guilt he had felt. It had taken counseling, a lot of tears, and angry words that had to be forgiven, but Elizabeth had eventually released him from his guilt. They both came to realize that even though there was a time she hated Scott and blamed him for killing their son, it was only because she needed somebody to blame as much as he did. In the end, Liz said that she didn't have to forgive him, because he had done nothing wrong. But no matter what she said, or what anybody said, to this day Scott often played the painful "what if" mind game with himself.

What if he would have seen the deer that jumped out of the woods a second or even split second sooner? Maybe he should have. Maybe he was driving too fast for conditions, even though no ticket was ever issued. *Too fast for conditions*; Scott thought about the phrase. *If you have an accident while driving, doesn't that mean automatically you were going too fast for conditions?*

Scott had been injured too, so he didn't remember much of what happened. In fact, the period of time from immediately following the accident to the time he woke up in the hospital was a complete blank to him. He did remember seeing a deer and swerving the truck. He also remembered the snowy road conditions of that December evening. He remembered that the pick-up didn't have a lot of traction on the slippery side-road. Scott even remembered the conversation he was having with his young fourteen-year-old son at the time.

They were returning home with the Christmas tree in the back of the old pick-up truck. Usually the whole family would have gone, but they decided that there just wasn't enough room for all four of them in the single front seat. Scott had brought the truck home from work just so they could get the tree that weekend. Brad was talking about the gun he wanted for Christmas. He was trying to talk his father into the merits of his having a .22 rifle. Of course what Brad didn't know was that the .22 was already bought and waiting for Christmas morning.

That's when things started getting blurry for Scott. He wasn't going that fast. The road was too slick. They came around a small bend in the country road. Scott could still see in his mind the big buck running out of the woods. The headlights must have blinded it, as it looked at them and stopped in its tracks.

But that was all he remembered until waking up in the hospital a day later. The police told him there had been another vehicle coming in the opposite direction and a head-on collision was barely avoided. But as he swerved to miss hitting the huge animal and the oncoming car, the truck skidded out of control. It went straight across the road and into the opposite ditch, hitting a large oak-tree dead-center. Both he and Brad had seatbelts on but it wasn't enough to stop them from flying forward as the truck stopped instantly.

The police told Scott that because of Brad's relatively small size, his body had actually slid through the seatbelt and shoulder restraint, which had done little to stop him. Brad's head hit the windshield hard and fast; the doctors said he had died immediately. It was a small comfort to know that Brad didn't feel a thing, and under the circumstances, even that small comfort was welcomed. Scott had hit his head on the steering wheel, receiving a severe concussion. He needed stitches on his forehead and some of his teeth replaced. Physically he had healed, but he knew the mental scars would never leave him.

Scott wiped a tear from his eye as he mournfully looked at one of the last pictures they had of Bradley Scott Seaver. It was from the summer just before his death, a much happier time. The picture showed Brad alone at the helm of the family sailboat; he was beaming a great big smile. A tear slid down and wet the smile on the father's face as he remembered that happy day and how much Brad enjoyed sailing.

Standing by the fireplace mantle with the picture still in his hand, Scott didn't recall getting out of his chair and picking up the photo. He still prayed that somehow God would let them relive that day but take him the next time instead of his son. Just because his wife had forgiven him didn't mean he had forgiven himself.

Elizabeth came into the living room to tell her husband about something or other, but when she saw him staring blankly at the picture of their young son with tears in his eyes, she decided to leave him alone with his thoughts. She knew what her husband was going through because she went through it every single day also. A certain type of mourning was best done alone.

Scott kissed the photo and set it down gently, as he said another prayer for his son. He again sat down in his favorite chair and tried to concentrate on his paper, realizing he had read the same article twice. He was starting to get hungry when he heard his teenage daughter bursting through the door like she always did.

"Mom...Dad... I'm home," she announced as if anyone could have possibly missed her entrance.

As Avery darted across the kitchen, in her typical fashion she rattled off a non-stop succession of assertions. "Peter Lance broke his leg playing soccer yesterday. But he is still going to be Charlie Brown in the play. He wasn't at school today. Are we having spaghetti? It smells good." Avery tossed her backpack in the corner of the kitchen and snitched a piece of garlic bread just as her mother was taking it out of the oven.

"I'm starving!" was all her excuse entailed as her mother gave her a look of patience.

Elizabeth set the hot pan down and gave her daughter a hug. "Your father is home."

Avery knew what that meant. She was supposed to go into the living room and give her dad a hug. That wasn't a problem. She was in a good mood and knew that with a hug and a kiss she could wrap her father around her little finger.

"Hi Daddy!" Scott set the paper down and relished the quick hug and peck on his forehead.

"How's my princess?" he asked like he always did.

"Fine," Avery replied as she ripped off a piece of the garlic bread and fed it to her dad.

"Mmmm! Delicious," Scott replied.

"I see you got your car started. What was wrong with it?"

"I must have left a light on and killed the battery."

"You can do that?" she asked. Avery was just starting to become interested in cars. She often reminded her parents that in two more years she would need a car of her own.

"Yes you can do that. And when you do, the battery doesn't have enough power to start the engine." Scott gave just a small lesson about driving and cars.

"Dinner is ready!" Elizabeth called around the corner.

Scott's princess dashed into the kitchen and the proud father felt another tear developing. She was at the same wonderful age as Brad was when he died. Scott excused himself to the bathroom so he could compose himself before sitting down with his daughter and wife.

The next morning:

Was it time to get up already? Scott wondered to himself though he knew the answer. He turned away from the sound of the alarm, trying to delay the inevitable. The soft bed sheet rolled with him. His lovely wife of twenty years couldn't ignore the annoying beeping of the alarm and lazily reached up to turn it off. As he turned, he wrapped his long strong arm around his wife's upper body and cupped her soft right breast in his hand as his forearm pressed against its mate.

They spooned together naturally, as they always had; he was still naked from the wonderful lovemaking the night before. Elizabeth was a bit more dressed just in case she had to get up for their daughter for some reason. Scott gave his sleepy wife a wet kiss on her neck.

"Stop that, you're tickling me," Elizabeth scolded playfully.

"You didn't complain last night about me 'tickling' you," Scott teased back. It had taken quite a bit of teasing and cajoling to get his wife in the mood. She was still suspicious of Scott's fainting spell, but after enough encouragement she couldn't say no any longer. And as they say, the rest is history.

"I thought you had a big day today at the office." Elizabeth swung her feet over the side of the bed.

"Every day is a big day," Scott said dodging the subject.

Liz wrapped her robe around herself and tied it off. "You get dressed while I get breakfast ready and make sure that 'Princess' is up." The last comment was a little tongue–in–cheek because their little princess was not a morning person and was known to be a little testy first thing in the morning. Often she was more like a little ogre than a little princess.

As Scott left the house for work he kissed the three middle fingers of his right hand and then touched them to the photograph of Brad hanging by the door. It was something he did every morning on his way out of the house. The picture was one of Scott's favorites. It showed his young son in a pose wearing his Scout uniform, standing in a wooded area. One foot

49

rested on an old log, with all his many merit badges neatly and properly displayed. Brad took his scouting very seriously and had pursued each merit badge with passion.

Two weeks later:

Elizabeth had insisted on going to the clinic with her husband. There was no getting around the fact that she wanted to be near "just in case" the test caused a serious complication. Her husband had walked back out to the small sitting area more than twenty minutes before and now they were waiting for the results. The stiff plastic chairs in the waiting area were becoming more and more uncomfortable by the minute as the Seavers sat in suspense, anxious for the doctor's report.

Scott knew everything went well; at least he was pretty sure. He kept himself in good physical condition by jogging and going to the "Y" whenever he could. Another routine that help him stay fit was practicing Tae-Kwon-Do. As a 2nd degree black belt in Tae-Kwon-Do, he often helped teach his daughter's class and did the routine calisthenics along with the much younger students.

Today, during the testing, it had actually taken a while for him to get his heart rate up to the optimum beats per minute and he thought that was a good sign. He watched the face of the doctor monitoring his tests and didn't notice any specific look of concern, so Scott assumed everything was OK. After the test, the administering doctor had secluded himself to a back office without saying a word.

"Scott!" He heard his name called by the duty nurse.

"Well, here I go," he whispered to Elizabeth with nervousness in his voice he couldn't conceal.

"I'm going with you, mister. You don't think that I am going to trust you to tell me the truth after he's done with you, do you?" Elizabeth insisted. Scott knew that was that.

"Hi Elizabeth." Dr. Richard Mooney greeted the couple as he walked into examining room three. Dr. Mooney hadn't done the testing, but as their primary physician it was his job to interpret the results for his patient.

"Scott, you were right. There is absolutely nothing wrong with your heart and lung capacity, and your blood work is also normal. A little high on the LDL cholesterol, but nothing we can't work with. I suspect a small change in diet might take care of it and in six months we'll do another blood test to see how it's going."

Scott let out a breath of air that he didn't realize he was holding. Elizabeth was the one who had the questions. "So why did he faint doctor?"

"The truth is, I don't know. If you want a diagnosis I would say that Scott had a Vasovagal attack."

"A what?" Scott managed to blurt out before Liz could.

"A Vasovagal attack. It basically means that you fainted from a loss of blood flow to the brain. It could come from anything and could very well be just as Scott said. Skipped meals, overtired, burning the candle on both ends, stress. It does happen. I suggest that Scott keep exercising as he has always done. For a man of seventy, he's not in half bad shape."

"Thanks Doc!" Scott grinned.

"I've got a small pamphlet on reducing cholesterol. You do want to follow its advice, or eventually you will be on statins and we would like to avoid that if possible. Otherwise, I don't have any advice except for you to take it easy. You know that as we age, we can't handle physical and emotional stress as well as the younger crowd."

"I hear you Doc, but I'm not stressed," Scott protested.

Unconvinced, the doctor perched on the edge of the examining table and draped a leg over it. He sat casually with his hands folded on his lap. He looked both Scott and Elizabeth in the eyes before speaking again. "I know that this is about the time of year that Brad died. I'm sure that it is on both of your minds constantly, especially now. It might just be coincidence, or it might have something to do with what is going on."

The doctor continued. "The body is a wonderful machine. Sometimes it senses a type of overload and shuts down rather than break. I see it all the time; the holidays are not always the happy, carefree times that the merchants and Christmas songs would like to have us believe. When there has been a tragedy in a family it often hits even harder during the holidays, when family becomes even more important.

Elizabeth and Scott looked at each other, realizing it was sound advice. Instinctively they reached out and held each other's hand.

Scott talked for the both of them. "Thanks Doc. Thanks for everything. We'll be fine. It is difficult, but..." Scott looked into his teary-eyed wife's eyes before finishing. "We'll be fine."

"If you need me, you know where I am." Doctor Mooney shook his patient's hand.

Elizabeth gave the doctor a hug. "Thank you." That was all she could manage to say as she held back the tears.

Chapter 5

Moscow:

Lev closed his Dell laptop. *America is an amazing country,* he thought as he looked around at the patrons of the very busy coffee shop. Nobody but the Americans would think that eager Russians would stand in line to buy overpriced coffee. He had to admit the coffee was better than coffee from anyplace else in all of Russia. Lev inhaled a deep breath through his nose. The aroma was even better. But what Lev liked even more than the coffee, was the free Internet connection. Of course he was no fool; nothing was free. The American based Starbucks was packed with other Russians getting the free Internet service. Each was drinking overpriced lattés and flavored coffees. Even free services had their costs. Lev stood up and walked past the row of coffee and cappuccino machines on his way out. *They didn't make coffee* he thought; the polished chrome and stainless steel coffee makers were actually money machines, and legal ones at that. If he got caught stealing as much money from his comrades as the American coffee company did, he would be facing many years in a very terrible prison. The forty-year-old Lev shook his head in amazement, walked out the store and whispered to himself, "Then don't get caught!"

"Lev Sidorov walked across the busy, six-lane city street with his laptop in its carrying case slung over his shoulder. In his right hand, he held his Starbucks cup, the very recognizable logo proudly announcing to the Russian world, *"I have enough money that I can blow it on American coffee."* The sun was warm today and many people were out and about enjoying it. He checked his watch as he crossed another busy boulevard in a dangerous manner, with cars honking and drivers yelling "Mudak." The American coffee in his hands made him think of the American translation, which would mean something between "asshole" and "dickhead."

He looked back and listened. Anyone trying to follow him would have to do the same thing he did, which would mean many more angry drivers yelling "Mudak" and honking their horns. Lev didn't hear or see anything. Apparently he was the only "Mudak" within shouting range, and that was a good thing. The city of Solntsevo was becoming a booming metropolis. The roads were busy, crowded with people doing whatever people did in and around Moscow. Solntsevo was a suburb of Moscow. It was a growing city with a questionable past.

The Solntsevskaya mob controlled Solntsevo. Everyone knew this, including the Russian police. They intruded on the mob's business only when it was absolutely necessary for political reasons.

Lev crossed several more streets in seemingly haphazard fashion, becoming quite used to being called "Mudak" or several other even less pleasant names. Eventually he came to a park. Convinced that he wasn't being followed, he glanced at his Rolex. It was a "gift" from a former colleague who had talked to the wrong people at the wrong time. Lev confirmed he was on time and then entered the park. He casually strolled to the back, where ivy filled a metal fence protecting the park from a busy thoroughfare. Along the fence he found a beat up, old, picnic table. There he took a seat and enjoyed his coffee.

He sat on the bench with his back toward the tabletop, watching the opening to the park for expected and unexpected guests. His position kept his back protected and his view of the park entrance unobstructed. He could see a man and a woman who were holding hands doing a subdued mating dance. They tried to hide their actions behind a large tree. There was a family playing on the park swings. As usual in Moscow, a drunk wasn't far away from either party. He posed no menace, half passed out on a park bench, clutching his paper bag tightly. Another young family was pushing a baby stroller and a mother was watching her two youngsters play in the sand. It wasn't long before squat looking Oleskandr Demidov walked in, also carrying a large coffee. Though, Lev immediately noticed, it wasn't from Starbucks. He sat down next to Lev and they both watched the front entrance as they talked.

"Are you sure this man can deliver?" Oleskandr asked as he took his left hand and rubbed it over his almost bald, fifty-year-old scalp.

Lev lit an American Marlboro cigarette and blew the smoke from it toward his companion. Oleskandr was familiar with the brand and liked them. "May I?" Oleskandr asked as he pointed to the pack still in Lev's hand.

"Of course," Lev flicked the pack toward his companion. It slid across the filthy top of the picnic table. Lev felt he was superior to most everyone he met, even his FSB companion. Lev was the opposite of his new comrade. Lev's hair was full, his forty-year-old body was lean and trim, and he oozed self-confidence to the point of being arrogant.

As Oleskandr lit the cigarette, Lev responded to his question. "First, I do not know if it is a man or a woman. You took the drawing to your experts. What do they say?"

Oleskandr puffed out a deeply inhaled breath like a man who had just tasted the finest cognac. At his government pay grade, American cigarettes would be too much of a luxury. For that he was sorry. *One more reason to work hard for the next pay grade*, he reasoned.

"They confirmed they are authentic enough. It is only one small part, but it is accurately drawn."

"If you know how to build this thing, why are you willing to pay me one million American dollars to get this information?" Lev asked as he enjoyed another inhale.

"Obviously, if the government was caught supplying the Russian mafia with the drawings or parts for such a device, it would be more than an embarrassment. Such an act would become an international political disaster. It would probably be considered an act of war. We cannot be involved in any way," the FSB agent stated flatly and unemotionally as he took another long drag on the Marlboro.

"Let me get this straight. You want this bomb to be built. Then you want me to sell it to the Iranians for whatever they will pay me?"

"Yes, the FSB will supply you with a contact name."

"You realize of course that the Iranians will probably use it against the Americans or the Israelis in some way."

"What the Iranians do with it is of no concern to either you or me."

"The Americans and the Israelis are both very good at putting the pieces of a puzzle together." Lev took a sip of his lukewarm coffee, letting the thought sink in. He liked his coffee hot, but this Starbucks was too good to waste. Lev's overconfidence made him assume he had told the agent something the FSB hadn't thought about. "And no doubt the British will be more than happy to help both of them, especially if they can lay the blame at Russia's doorstep."

"We cannot help it if a rogue scientist teamed up with an Iranian extremist to create such a disaster." Oleskandr replied.

"So you do not want me to kill this scientist after I have the plans?" Lev asked as he snuffed out the butt of his Marlboro on the side of the bench and threw it to the ground next to the hundreds of domestic butts already there.

"There is no need to rush into it. We can kill him anytime it is necessary." Oleskandr dropped his cigarette into his coffee; it gave a small hiss. Then he threw the coffee toward the already overfull garbage can. It missed and fell to the thin, brown grass. Neither man paid attention.

"What of me? Am I to be the scapegoat?" the leader of the Solntsevskaya Mob asked.

"That would depend on how well you do your job, wouldn't it? There are reasons the FSB likes to work with you. You know governments and bureaucrats. They can't keep anything secret and there is always way too much paperwork to trace. You should be happy that you do not work for the government."

"We all serve the government, comrade," Lev reminded. As a precaution, he was secretly taping their conversation just in case he needed a bit of insurance. He didn't trust the FSB any more than they trusted him.

"Yes, of course."

"I would imagine we never had this talk," Lev asked the agent seriously.

The agent responded with a small chuckle. "What talk?"

"Tell me this, comrade, as long as we are not having this discussion anyways. What benefit would it be to Russia if, per chance, the Iranians did set off a nuclear device inside the United States?"

Oleskandr didn't mind talking to the mafia boss candidly. In fact it was refreshing. *Strange* he thought; he could talk more honestly with a thief than he could with his own co-workers. Lev could never expose him because nobody would believe a mafia chieftain, and shortly after that, another overconfident petty thief would also be history. Oleskandr would see to that himself. But that made the agent wonder, who had killed more people, Lev or himself?

"I am only a lowly field agent, but if one wanted to guess, I would say that the prime minister wouldn't mind if the meddling Americans were kept busy by another attack on their soil. They take it so personally. And if they did discover that the Iranians were to blame, properly punishing the Islamic community some more would also take a great deal of time and resources for the Americans. It would pose a proper dilemma for the U.S. If they didn't do anything about the attack, they would become even greater targets in the future. If they attack another Islamic country it would only prove that the Americans wish to destroy Islam. Mother Russia, as a friend of the Middle East, could help save them from the Americans. Before the Americans would even know what happened, they would be out of oil and the Great Soviet Empire would become the new leader of the world."

Lev thought for a moment. Yes, he agreed as he nodded his head. As long as the Americans couldn't prove to the world that Russia was behind the attack, it would be a proper mess for the Americans to deal with.

"Comrade!" Lev announced with some pride. "We will help the Mother Land." Lev and his mafia comrades were many unflattering things, but that didn't mean they weren't patriotic; and for this help they would be paid very handsomely.

"Comrade Sidorov, your country is thankful for your services." Then he asked, "Do you enjoy Starbucks coffee?"

A bit unsure where that question was going, Lev answered with hesitation. "Yes, I find it to be a fine coffee."

"Then from now on you will get a cup of that fine coffee every Tuesday at 10:00 A.M. at the same shop you did this morning. If we need to communicate we will do it there. You will give a simple piece of paper with a question on it to an agent. The next week you will get an answer."

"How will I know the agent?"

"You will know."

Agent Demidov gave a signal to his fellow agents by standing up and brushing his hair back. At that sign, three men and a woman started walking toward them. One man was with a mother and two children; he had been busy gently pushing the swings on which the children sat. Another man and a woman, who were holding hands just moments before, doing the subdued mating dance around the tree, came up from the right. A drunk on a park bench stood tall and erect, and marched toward them with one hand under his coat.

Lev immediately noticed the four coming toward him. "What gives!" Lev asked surprised.

The mafia leader was so preoccupied with the agents coming toward him that he didn't see the gun come out of his comrade's coat pocket. But now he felt it being pushed firmly against his ribs.

"Don't be alarmed, just a precaution. There is a van parked just outside the park. I would suggest that you follow these people to it and get in without drawing any attention."

"What do you want? I said I would help you."

"They just want to search you to make sure that you weren't taping any of our conversation. You understand that we can't be too careful."

Lev carefully and slowly reached into his coat and handed Oleskandr the small recorder from his pocket. Then he unhooked the small microphone that was taped to his chest. "Hey, I was just trying to get a little insurance so I don't end up at the bottom of the Moskva River," he said as he handed it to Oleskandr. The cocky mafia leader was trying to play it cool though he was shaking in his boots over a possible loss of confidence, which could also mean his life.

Agent Demidov was now the one with the confident sounding voice. "I quite understand. That is why we take these precautions. Think of the body search as a free medical exam."

By this time the agents were upon them. Oleskandr dropped the recorder on the ground. He stomped on it roughly and ground it beneath his heel. Then he picked it up and broke the remaining pieces apart, dropping them in the over-full waste can carefully. He unwound the small micro tape inside the unit and crumpled it. Then he lit a match to it. It burned quickly, like a magician's act. When he dropped the flaming, tangled glob it was gone before it had a chance to hit the ground.

"Search him very carefully for any more surprises," he threatened Lev. "This will be a bit unpleasant but it is nothing compared to what will happen if you ever try to entrap me again in any way. Think of it as a very polite warning between friends."

Before the mafia leader was taken away, Demidov asked politely. "Would you mind terribly if I had another one of those fine cigarettes?"

Lev had quickly learned his place and tossed the slightly used pack at the agent. "Keep the change." He tried to be gracious but sounded more disrespectful; it came naturally.

Without saying a word, Oleskandr caught the package and slipped it into his coat pocket. Then he gave a nod. The other agents showed the butt of their guns to Lev to make sure he understood his options. Then the five walked toward the van.

Oleskandr sat back down on the park bench and guessed that he had time for two, maybe three, cigarettes before the search was done. The proud mafia boss would not be so proud by the time they finished with him. The senior agent believed that putting someone properly in their place before conducting business with them was an important part of control. If something else was found, he would be notified. Then he might have to make an example of Comrade Sidorov. The sunshine felt so good that he decided he could wait outside. *Besides*, he reasoned, *the inside of the van would be very crowded with agents and one naked mafia smartass.*

Alan D Schmitz

Novosibirsk, Republic of Russia:

Professor Yuri Kromonov stepped down off the stairs that led to his small apartment and smelled the fresh spring air. He looked at the sun and welcomed its warmth. The air was still cool and pockets of snow could be seen along the sidewalk. The godforsaken, long winter was over and today was a welcome confirmation of that.

Today the ten-block walk to his office would be a sunny treat; he had even left his hat and gloves behind on purpose. Coming home, the weather might not be as pleasant, but he was willing to take that chance.

Inside his small office, the day once again became as dreary as it was every other day. Maybe not quite as cold, but because it was an inner office with no windows, the outside weather was inconsequential.

Yuri turned on his computer and started to boil his tea. Carefully, the professor used his knowledge of computers and the Internet to connect to the World Wide Web, routing his own machine through a series of other unsuspecting computers. It was amazing how easy it was if you knew what you were doing. It would be impossible to trace anything back to his computer.

Yuri would have told himself, "Next to impossible to trace." But that wasn't correct. The truth was that it would be absolutely impossible; he was very confident of that. What he wasn't so confident about, was if his plan was actually going to work. It had been months of cat-and-mouse communications with his contact to get this far. And the more Yuri became involved, the more he accepted the fact that he was the mouse.

It had been six months since the initial contact with the man called "The Lion." During the previous six months, the professor had sent misleading information and deceptive directions to the mysterious contact. The misinformation was given with the intention of exposing his mysterious counterpart. Yuri had even "accidentally" left enough information on one of his blog sites to provide a trace back to him.

The information Yuri had planted was sufficiently buried to let anyone who found it think that he or she had got lucky. If the government was involved, it was information they certainly wouldn't have missed. The data trail he left led to a real computer at a real address. Only it wasn't in any way connected to him. Yuri had monitored the physical address and owner of the computer for weeks afterwards. It was only when nothing out of the ordinary happened that he trusted "The Lion," his contact, with more privileged information. They didn't communicate via e-mail or any other conventional manner. Through trial and error, mostly error, they had learned how to communicate through rotating blogs and electronic chat rooms. Even then, the communications were never direct but through a code. The professor hid the code in a blog that would have been almost impossible to find unless you knew to look for it.

"The Lion" had agreed to the professor's fee of one million dollars. Neither he nor "The Lion" were fools, nor did they trust each other. The professor had come up with an elaborate means to build the bomb and get paid. This was a very dangerous game. The professor hoped and prayed that he was a very smart mouse. The good news for the professor was that he didn't need any money to hold up his end of the bargain. What he needed was inside his head and in drawings that he had hidden away so many years ago.

The first engineering drawing the professor sent his contact had convinced "The Lion" that he was the real deal. It was understood that the professor wouldn't provide the fissionable material, just the design and construction.

Istanbul, Turkey:

The Russian mob boss, Lev Sidorov, had finally made contact with the Iranian agent that the FSB instructed him to meet. He arranged a meeting place where he and the Iranian would both be on neutral ground and able to talk freely.

As he walked through the crowded Turkish bazaar, people saw that he was of European ancestry and they tried to sell him everything from local candies, to tea, to hand woven rugs of various qualities. Lev brought his current girlfriend along though she wasn't with him at that moment. There was no reason he couldn't mix business with pleasure. She was still at the hotel, very impressed with her new boyfriend's obvious political connections. It had been relatively easy for him to get two travel passes out of Russia and two plane tickets to Istanbul. Lev himself was surprised at the ease of travel. It was almost as if he had a guardian angel watching over him, though he was pretty sure that his guardian angel was FSB.

Lev found the small café just around the corner from the bustling marketplace. He ordered a cup of dark, Turkish tea. What it was made from was anybody's guess, but it was good. More preferable would have been a Starbucks, but he hadn't seen any of those nearby.

The Iranian agent, Hamid Shukah, walked carefully through the busy bazaar looking for any suspicious signs. In his line of work, anyplace could be an ambush. The way this meeting came about seemed too good to be true. That made Hamid even more suspicious of the activity around him. As a major in Iran's IRGC or Iran's Revolutionary Guard Corps, he was used to danger, at least as much as anyone can get used to danger. Today, Major Shukah sensed deadly danger. What he was trying to accomplish at this meeting would have severe consequences in world affairs. If the wrong person knew of their plans, his life would be easily forfeited to stop it.

In disguise, Hamid walked past the small café. He carried a large woven basket on his shoulders like the many merchants working the busy street. The major spotted the Russian by the kerchief he was wearing, an agreed upon mark. The man appeared to be alone and seemed at ease sitting at the small table. Major Shukah turned down a very small alleyway and started to empty his basket. He watched the busy bazaar for European eyes, he could spot them a mile away. Convinced things were as safe as they were going to get, he carefully approached the café carrying the now empty basket. He walked past the Russian, carefully checking out his contact at close range. Satisfied, he put down his basket and approached the representative of the Russian mafia from behind.

"Are you the Russian Lion?" he asked in Russian before he sat down.

"I am!" The mafia boss answered in Farsi, the most spoken language in Iran. This established a sort of equality between them. Lev had no need to ask who the Iranian was, only one person knew he was there.

The Iranian sat down at the table, which had been carefully picked by the Russian. The chosen table was separated from the rest of the restaurant by a support pole and the busy pathway used by the servers. To most patrons it would have been the most undesirable table in the small café, but they weren't most patrons.

Both men should have been acting more nervous than they were. But they were both professionals and each knew that if it were a trap by the other, there was little they could do about it now.

"Cigarette?" Lev asked his company in Farsi, trying to ease the tension while at the same time making sure the supposed Iranian spoke his own language.

Hamid said back, in Farsi this time, "Russian cigarettes taste like rolled up camel crap."

The Lion spoke Farsi fairly well and understood the reply with crystal clarity. Convinced his new comrade was indeed Iranian, Lev said. "I agree!" Then he pulled the open pack out of his pocket and showed it to his guest. Hamid gave a small smile and quickly accepted the American brand smoke.

The mobster casually leaned forward and lit it for his new friend.

"I have a proposition for you." Lev spoke quietly through the noise of the café. "By what name may I call you?" he asked sounding very relaxed.

There was no point in giving this gangster his real name so he volunteered, "You may call me Kassim." He replied in Russian this time and then added some advice. "Most of these people speak Turkish but some may understand Farsi. As a precaution I would suggest we talk in your language."

Lev looked around at the patrons who were fairly distant from them anyway, shrugged his shoulders and agreed, "Da."

Hamid started the dialog. "My superiors tell me you have something very important for me."

"Well Kassim, I do, that is if you are interested in something that makes a really big bang."

"How do I know you have what you are selling?"

"Have you seen the latest morning news? I think you should look at it very closely." Lev pushed the morning newspaper across the small, round table.

The air was filled with the smell of spices, mostly cinnamon, which was being used for the morning specialty. The IRGC major didn't look at the paper; he knew the plans were inside of it. Looking at them would tell him nothing. Instead he studied the Russian's eyes, trying to guess what the real motive behind them was.

"And how do we know what you are giving us is real?"

"That, my friend, is a very good question. I am not a nuclear scientist, so I can't tell you. I would suggest you take this first drawing back with you, no charge. If your people like what they see, then we will continue to talk some more."

"Where did you get them?" the suspicious Iranian asked.

"If I told you that, you wouldn't need me."

A busy waiter, looking annoyed at the prospect of more work, asked the new patron what he would like to order. In perfect Turkish, Hamid asked for a cup of coffee and their version of the local morning specialty, a piping hot roll of soft dough with cinnamon and dates.

As the waiter walked away, Hamid raised his eyebrow at the Russian, indicating he was waiting for an answer. He didn't expect a direct answer, but he didn't think it would hurt to ask. What he did know was that his superiors seemed to have a lot of faith in these drawings even before they had seen them.

"If we like what we see, when will we get the rest? How do we know that you have the complete set? It is completely worthless otherwise."

"Four million American dollars," Lev whispered across the small table. "That is when you get the complete set."

"What if it doesn't work? What if we can't put it together from your plans?"

"Here's the deal. Take it or leave it." Lev's stomach was churning, he was bluffing for the biggest deal of his life. This deal was private and not even the other mafia bosses would know about it. The reward to him would be great. After paying one million to the "professor" as the bomb maker calls himself, there would be three million in cash for him, plus the one million more from the FSB for his efforts. "You don't put it together," Lev explained, "my associate will do that. But we need your resources to build the parts and to supply the fissionable materials. This is why we are offering it at such a low price. There are twenty sets of plans, not counting this one. I'll give you a bank account number and you put one-hundred thousand dollars in it each time I deliver a new set. Each time we meet, you will give me the parts from the drawings from the previous meeting."

Lev saw the waiter returning with the coffee and pastry. He warned Kassim with two raised eyebrows and a glance of his eyes in the waiter's direction.

Hamid took a small sip of his thick, syrupy Turkish coffee, waiting for the waiter to busy himself elsewhere.

"Do you take us for fools?" The Iranian cursed, barely managing to keep his voice civil. "We pay you. We make the parts. And then we are to give them back to you? You insult us."

Lev was prepared for this response; he would have said exactly the same thing.

"Wait a minute, before you pull out your sword, Kassim," Lev said with his typical sarcastic humor. "Remember, you will have the plans, the complete set. And if it is worth it to us to steal the parts from you, then it must be authentic. Only we won't steal the parts because once we deliver the completed unit, you transfer another two million to our account."

"I do not like that arrangement. We will put the device together ourselves."

"Unfortunately, my associate who has the plans, insists on putting the device together himself. He says that is the only way he can guarantee it will work. Once you have the plans you can make as many parts as you want. Besides...," Lev sat back in his chair pretending he had all the answers, "....what good is a nuclear bomb without the sizzle?" Lev responded with a sly smile.

"And how do I know that you don't already have the '*sizzle*' or that you will not sell it to someone else who does?" Hamid shot back, being equally sarcastic.

"Because Comrade Kassim, you have my personal guarantee."

"That is not worth any more than your weak tea, *comrade!*" He hissed out the word *comrade*.

"Then call it a risk of doing business. My associate will have it no other way; he is very firm on that. I remind you that until you get the bomb already assembled in your hands you will only have two million dollars at risk. And the plans alone are worth more than four million dollars all by themselves."

"The risk of doing business with us is very high if you do not deliver," Hamid threatened.

The Iranian pulled his pastry apart with his hands and casually slung a sizable piece into his mouth as he stared at his new collaborator.

Hamid thought about the arrangement some more. It wouldn't be his decision to make, but he felt that he could go to his superiors with a reasonable set of options. If they did not want to pay the extra two million, then his country would have to assemble the unit themselves. If the Russian was right and the assembly was much more difficult than they contemplate, they could have the bomb maker put the pieces together for another two million. The Russian was right about one thing: if the drawings were what they appeared to be, two million was a bargain. And to have a compact nuclear device in their hands needing only the fissionable material, which they had, could be invaluable.

The Iranian slung another piece of his bakery into his mouth, picked up the newspaper and left without saying another word. Killing the Russian very, very slowly would also have some value to him personally if Lev should fail or deceive them.

The Iranian quickly vanished into the crowd of morning shoppers. Lev looked at his watch. He had plenty of time to get in a morning slam with his girlfriend. She was probably still naked in bed. He realized that playing with danger sort of turned him on.

Alan D Schmitz

Novosibirsk, Republic of Russia:

The professor was busy working the keys of his computer. As he worked, he thought about Switzerland. He had seen many pictures of the lovely countryside with its mountains and lakes. It was some place he and his Anzhela would have to be sure to visit, but they would not live there. No, for them it would be someplace warmer like southern Italy or maybe Greece. But that didn't mean he didn't admire the Swiss. As the months would pass he would slowly become rich with the help of the clever Swiss bankers and the anonymous Internet.

Truckloads of supplies were constantly being delivered to the university from around the world - anything from unique lenses for laser experiments to computer paper, computers and printers. Cafeteria supplies went to the cold storage area and janitorial supplies seemed to end up everywhere. A month ago, one very special box was among the thousands delivered. It was a box of small, finely machined, magnesium parts. Yuri had been in the huge warehouse often, as were many of his co-professors and department heads. The real unfortunate thing was that the warehouse for the university was across town from the school. "Centralized planning," Yuri cursed. "Bullshit." Somebody owed somebody else a political favor and built a warehouse on otherwise useless property. It took an uncomfortable and time-consuming metro ride every time he needed to visit the huge building.

It seems that the warehouse was very good at collecting and storing everything that came into the college. What it wasn't so efficient at was getting the same items out to the proper departments. For anyone who was waiting for supplies and equipment, it was a mid-week ritual to wander the huge warehouse looking for whatever it was they were suppose to get. Personal knowledge of how the huge warehouse functioned was nowhere near as important as having paid off one's own personal spy within the huge walls.

As with many things in Russia, finding what you needed was usually a matter of bribing the right person at the right time. There seemed to be a strange fairness to the system. Even a low paid warehouse worker could influence his standard of living by being a bit more industrious. Not paying for their services could mean that the special package you were waiting for would get lost for a terminable-long amount of time.

Yuri had instructed The Lion to ship the machined bomb parts to the university's address, specifically to the food services division. But he had

64

cautioned. "Be sure to send the parts well protected and in an orange colored box marked with a wide green stripe around it."

The professor's inside man Georgy spied the orange box immediately. It was tucked neatly inside a pallet of various other products for the cafeteria. All the boxes were shrink-wrapped together into one neat blob of boxes that the forklift operator would quickly move to another location in the warehouse before moving it again and again, consistently demonstrating how important his job was. Eventually it would become lost in the sea of pallets and boxes until somebody important claimed it. If it was left unclaimed for long enough, he and his co-workers would assume that if no one else wanted it, then it must belong to them.

Georgy signaled his friend on the forklift to lower the pallet of boxes to the floor. Flicking open the knife from his back pocket, he cut a neat hole in the shrink-wrap.

"This is what the professor is waiting for!" Georgy yelled over the loud, gasoline engine that powered the forklift. The operator didn't really care. The small distraction would take a few minutes. Then he would take a break and very quickly a half hour of his day would be gone. He had learned long ago that one didn't need to accomplish anything all day; one just needed to look like he was accomplishing something.

Georgy carried the 30 cm square box away and stashed it under a metal staircase. This was where anything important was placed. Under the staircase it was practically impossible for the forklift operator to get at. That meant it wouldn't get moved over and over again, nor eventually lost to the world.

This was the third such package he had rescued for the professor. It wasn't a big deal to him and he didn't care what was in it, though he wondered why it was marked for the food services division.

Chapter 6

Milwaukee, Wisconsin:

Captain Seaver felt a small sweat building; he hadn't been on the treadmill for more than five minutes but the doctor had already increased the speed and the angle of the deck. Doctor Louise Strand was making his heart come up to a working speed.

Scott knew the drill pretty well by now. This was his second test in the month since he had passed out on his commander's couch. His first round of tests was with his family physician. He passed them all with flying colors. But that wasn't good enough for his commander. The regulations required that he be re-certified for flight by a licensed flight surgeon. So here he was, going through the same routine again. Only this time, the doctor promised him that the military version of the test would be much more demanding than the typical civilian procedure. The bright side was that his confidence was high and this was finally going to be the end of it. All of this work and effort was just because he had skipped lunch, he mused. From now on he was going to make sure that he carried some sort of energy bar in his car.

"Captain, please breathe into the tube until I say stop." The doctor pointed to the flexible tube mounted to the front of the treadmill, then made some notes.

Scott was past the point when he could talk relatively normal. His body was starting to demand more oxygen and his heart was beginning to pump faster to provide it. He placed the tube into his mouth and then used his teeth to hold it in place. That's when he learned that breathing through the tube required more effort than he thought. Wires and sensors were dangling from his chest as he ran. The treadmill inclined a little more, and it felt like it also sped up, though he couldn't be sure. The machines to his side were measuring his heart rate, oxygen level, blood pressure and who knows what else. This test was longer and harder than the previous. He was beginning to tire and his perspiration was increasing.

"OK Captain, you can stop breathing through the tube. Now I want you to begin the cool down process."

Scott didn't say anything but was relieved when the machine went from a steep incline, to level. Then after about a minute the speed began decreasing.

"How do you feel Captain?" the doctor asked.

"Just fine Doc, a little out of breath. So how did I do, Doctor?"

"You did fine Captain," the doctor reassured.

Scott felt his breath coming back and started to ask questions. "I guess everything checks out OK or you would have stopped the test, right?"

"I assure you Captain, that if I had the slightest hint of a complication I would have stopped the test. All in all, the initial indications are pretty much in line with the results I have from your family physician's report."

Scott continued at a slow jog, looking straight ahead for another minute. Then he looked at the doctor again and asked, "So how did I do, Doctor?"

The immediate repeat of the same question made the doctor look up at her patient a bit more closely. She took a small flashlight out of her white, medical coat pocket and shined it into the captain's eyes as the treadmill came to a stop.

Scott felt his breathing adjust to a more normal level. The flashlight test was something he couldn't remember his other doctor doing.

"Before my assistant unhooks all these wires, I would like you to fill out this small form. Please sit for just a moment."

Scott was used to being asked to fill out an ever-increasing number of papers, though he thought it strange that he was being asked to do it right then. "Sure," Scott responded slowly and sat down.

The doctor gave him a clipboard with a medical form on it and handed him a pencil. Scott placed the board on his lap and stared at the first question asking for his name. He almost immediately realized that he had written his first name first. Though it clearly asked for his last name first. Scott apologized, erased his first name and wrote his last name in the correct box. When it came to asking for his birthday, he labored over the question for a few seconds and chuckled when he realized the doctor was watching him closely. "It seems that I must have needed a bit more time to cool down. I feel a bit flushed."

Unemotionally the doctor said, "Please fill out the form so we can finish up."

"Sure Doc." Scott looked down at the form again and stared at the same question. He felt his heart begin to beat faster; his palms were cold and sweaty. This time Scott knew something was wrong; he started to panic. Why couldn't he remember his birthday? Then the words on the form began to blur.

The doctor took the clipboard out of his lap and started to examine the captain's eyes again. Then Scott inhaled a terrible odor and he snapped his head back.

"Captain Seaver, are you all right?" the doctor asked as she waved a small capsule of smelling salts under the captain's nose. Her assistant was by Scott's side, holding his shoulder to prevent him from falling off the chair.

Scott looked up a bit groggy. "Yea, sure Doc. I'm just fine."

"Captain, you passed out for a few seconds; are you sure you are feeling better?"

"I don't remember passing out," Scott assured.

"Trust me, you did. Captain, you need to be admitted to a hospital. There is something very wrong and we need to get to the bottom of it."

Scott looked up with the blood draining out of his face. All he could think about was that, with those words, his flying career was over. He immediately realized what failing this physical would mean and the thought of that caused his heart to skip a beat. Then he was feeling flushed again. That was all he remembered until he woke up in the ambulance looking at his beautiful wife and a couple of not so pretty male attendants.

Elizabeth was holding his hand and choking back tears. Scott felt a bit disorientated as they raced down the road. He lifted his left hand and touched the hand of his wife. She felt his hand touch hers before she realized he was awake.

"Oh Scott, you have me so worried."

Scott wanted to respond with one of his pithy comebacks, but he had some sort of mask over his face. Scott took his free hand and gave a small thumbs-up. He felt very tired, so he closed his eyes again and slept.

Novosibirsk, Republic of Russia:

The professor worked in his small basement. He had managed to create a fairly decent work area at the far back end. The remnants of old computers lay about. It was a collection of spare parts he amassed over the last two years. There was a pile of circuit boards, a bucket of hard drives and a snake's nest of computer cables. The basement wasn't part of their lease but he had never seen anybody go into it. He and his wife were leasing the area immediately above where he was working, so Yuri rationalized that the basement was his to use as well.

Fifteen orange and green packages had already been delivered. His Swiss bank account held 375,000 American dollars, 25,000 for each set of plans he supplied to "The Lion". Yuri was light on his feet. An ancient Russian tune flowed through his teeth as he whistled away like a teenager. His plan was working perfectly. Soon he could tell his Angel that a patent he filed away many years ago had been bought by a giant American company. They could soon retire anywhere in the world.

Anzhela so far had not discovered his secret work area. The professor limited his time working in the basement to days when his wife was away visiting friends. This severely limited his work time, but he couldn't take the chance that his wife would probe him about what exactly it was that he was working on.

Yuri didn't know how "The Lion" was getting the parts manufactured. But so far, each piece was perfectly made. The professor was also strict and precise about the composition of the metals being used. They needed to be of the highest quality and it appeared that "The Lion" had made good on his promise. What "The Lion" didn't know was that there were small imperfections purposely drawn into the design, each of which was perfectly machined into the parts.

The many imperfections were key to the Professor's plan. Whoever copied his drawings, or tried to manufacture a bomb from the parts, would be trying to put together a puzzle whose pieces didn't fit. The small keyways and protrusions were ambiguous to each part, and their placement made it impossible for many of the parts to fit together. The plans were nothing more than a collection of metal castings, machined parts and precisely bent tubes that wouldn't fit together even if it looked like one piece was designed to fit into another.

Yuri whistled away as he took a very small metal lathe and re-machined a small, precisely-measured angle of magnesium compound away from inside the cylinder until it was smooth. He had designed the mismatched parts so that with some relatively simple equipment he could repair the defects. Yuri whistled some more and thought that yes indeed, he was a very smart mouse. The professor smiled to himself and almost laughed out loud as he looked at the small collection of shiny metal parts under the workbench. Those parts were extra pieces and never intended to be part of the bomb. They were additional surprises meant to throw off any other potential bomb maker. The parts certainly looked like they were meant for the suitcase bomb, but in actuality they were extra parts that had nothing to do with its construction. They had another intendend use, but mostly the value they served was in misleading the cat.

This little mouse knew he would be safe only as long as the cat needed the mouse. The professor had gone to great lengths to make sure that the cat would always need the mouse if he wanted this bomb to work. And better still, if the mouse was the only one who could make more of these suitcase nuclear bombs, the mouse would be safe forever. Yuri made a decision. He would be sure that at their villa on the lake, he would have a beautiful workshop where he would make his beautiful bombs and be paid very, very well for his services.

Istanbul, Turkey:

Lev Sidorov stood outside the busy bazaar, leaning up against the outermost support post of a shopkeeper's tent. Today was his sixteenth trip to Istanbul in as many months. He knew with some certainty that he was the only Russian alive who could make so many trips to the same destination without FSB obstruction. He also realized that it was the FSB that had made this many trips so conveniently possible.

The mob boss raised his hand up to his mouth. The cigarette in it changed places and rested on his lips for a few seconds as his hands dropped to his pocket. He pulled out a small piece of paper. He double checked the time and address to confirm he was in the right place for his meeting. Comrade Sidorov, in a practiced, quick smooth-move, raised his right hand, took the cigarette out of his mouth and flicked some ashes on the ground as he slowly exhaled the smoke from the American brand cigarette.

He watched the busy, open marketplace searching for the crazy Iranian. This "Kassim" has been a very difficult man to get to know. Lev tried to come to friendly terms with the man, but that had proven to be very difficult. The Iranian seemed to despise him, though he could think of no reason why. Each of the previous meetings were short, with the exchange of plans for money and a small case of machined parts from the previous month's meeting.

Lev scanned the crowd for his unfriendly comrade. Suddenly Lev dropped his cigarette. The sudden, unmistakable feeling of a knife poking him in the side surprised him.

"We need to talk, Comrade!" the Iranian sneered.

The Major was in no mood for the Russian's cocky banter. He pressed his knife a bit harder into the mobster's waist. Lev knew the feeling of cold steel. It had easily penetrated his mocha colored cashmere sweater. *Damn*, Lev thought. He realized that he must be bleeding, and undoubtedly the sweater that he just bought and bargained hard for the day before was already ruined.

"If you try anything at all, I guarantee that you will die a very painful death. Once my knife cuts into your kidney, no doctor will be able to save you. Now walk toward the alley."

Lev thought about trying to talk his way out of whatever was bothering the Iranian, but the knife was already cutting into him as he walked. To provoke the Iranian even a little bit more would be unwise.

Hamid walked with his arm around the Russian's waist as if they were best friends. The knife was hidden by a scarf and the major's left hand was very firmly holding onto Lev's wrist.

The farther down the alley they went, the more obvious it became that very few people at the bizarre would dare to venture down the dangerous looking path to disturb them. Hamid suddenly turned the Russian's back against a filthy, ancient brick-wall; he pressed the Russian against it with the knife at his stomach and a strong forearm across his throat.

It didn't occur to Lev to worry about his life; he was too busy mentally cursing the Iranian for ruining his new sweater. Lev looked the angry Iranian in the eyes. "What the hell is the matter with you?" he demanded in Russian.

"I told you that you would pay dearly if you cheated me." Hamid could barely contain his anger as the knife dug into the Russian's flesh.

Lev knew that such a man would not respond to pity, nor would he respect him if he pleaded for his life. The mob boss figured he was probably dead anyhow so he might as well try to bluff his way out of this mess. Lev cursed at his attacker. "You dumb fucking Iranian. What the hell are you talking about?"

"Did you think we wouldn't find out?" The knife twisted a bit. It was just the beginning of the Russian's pain. "I can do that a thousand times before you will die," the Iranian warned as he watched his Russian comrade wince, "and I can make it a thousand times more painful."

It was too late to change track, so the Russian continued. "Listen cocksucker, I don't have a clue what you are talking about. Find out what?"

"Stop denying what you know," the Iranian insisted as he dug in the knife farther and twisted it more.

The pain was becoming very real now; Lev stopped worrying about his new sweater and cursed the pain and the Iranian. Lev caught his breath and gritted his teeth. "You're talking in circles you crazy Iranian. It obviously has something to do with the bomb, but I assure you, everything is going exactly as planned."

The Iranian quickly pulled his knife out in one swift move and pressed his left forearm against the Russian's throat even harder. The next thing Lev knew was that he was looking at the tip of a knife pressing against the bottom of his eye socket.

"Do you know why you have two eyes Comrade?" the Revolutionary Guard Corps major asked, not wanting or waiting for a response. "It is so that you can lose the first eye and be reminded of what will happen to your second if you keep lying to me." Hamid pressed the knife into the soft flesh below the eye socket. Small droplets of blood were forming.

"OK, OK I'll talk. What do you want to know?" Lev asked in a panic. He wasn't bluffing; he was truly frightened, unsure what the Iranian wanted from him. And if he couldn't give the crazy son of a bitch some answers, Kassim would probably kill him.

"The parts don't fit together, none of them," Hamid hissed.

"I've been assured that they do, I swear!"

Hamid brought his knee up between the Russian's legs.

Lev cringed from the pain and tried to double over, but Hamid held the knife and his arm tightly across the Russian's throat.

"Look Kassim, please listen, either I have been lied to also, or your guys don't know what they're doing. The professor assured me that he is making the bomb from the parts you supplied."

This was the first time the Russian had uttered his partner's name, even if it was just a moniker. The major pressed the knife a bit harder against the delicate skin of the eye socket. "Who is this professor?"

"I don't know, it's just the name he uses in his communications. He supplies the plans over the Internet."

"Then how does he get the parts we make?" The knife pressed a little harder still. Hamid was on the verge of removing one Russian eyeball just to make a point.

"I have important friends. If you hurt me they will not be pleased. How do you think that your government knew the plans were real?"

Hamid knew that the mobster wasn't lying about that. Higher-ups in his government had quickly rejected his skepticism with the bomb-making arrangement with the Russians. They knew something he didn't;

72

that part was true. Hamid re-thought indulging himself with the Russian's eyeball, though he still didn't remove any pressure.

"How does he get the parts we make?" He repeated his question, pushing slightly more on the knife.

"I mail them to a university," Lev replied choking on the arm pressed against his throat.

Hamid felt he was finally getting somewhere with his questioning. He released some of the pressure against the Russian's throat as a small reward.

"What is the address, you fool? Who do you mail it to?"

"Nobody," Lev responded accurately, but unfortunately for him, this was not satisfactory to the Iranian.

Major Hamid Shukah was tired of the Russian's bravado; he would have to fix that. The knife pushed into the eye socket farther, pinning Lev's head against the brick wall behind him. It only took the major an instant to carve around the eye socket and pluck it out with his knife.

The Russian tried to scream but the Iranian pushed even harder with his forearm against his captive's throat, muting any sound. Lev was weak in the knees and tried to drop to the ground, but the strong madman, who had just removed his eye, held him tight against the building. Lev's eye socket throbbed, though the real pain would come after the shock wore off.

"If you scream, I will cut your tongue out as well. Do not lie to me again. Now let's proceed before I become impatient and cut out your other eye.

"Who do you mail it to?"

Lev gasped for air, trying to choke back the urge to scream in pain.

The major released his throat-crushing pressure enough to let the Russian talk.

"Hurry, I am becoming impatient." The knife started to press against the other eye.

It was pure survival instinct that allowed Lev to continue. "I mail it to the university food services department. I don't address it to anyone; I swear I'm not lying," Lev sobbed.

Major Shukah for once started believing the Russian. "So how does he get the package?"

"I don't know, but he said to make sure that I sent it in an orange and green colored package. He must have someone watch for it."

"What about the money? Who do you pay?"

"It's just a number, a Swiss bank account number."

73

"Why do you trust this 'professor?' "

"I told you. I know people, important people, in my government. They told me he was for real."

"Then why don't the parts fit?"

"He told me that only he could put the bomb together. That is why I have to pay him a million dollars."

Hamid knew that his time was running out. Soon the adrenalin rush would wear off and the Russian would be screaming in pain despite any additional threats.

"I will deliver the package to your hotel. But the next time we meet, you had better have an answer for me on why the parts don't fit and have proof that the bomb is being built."

Major Shukah pulled the knife and his arm back quickly. Lev fell to the ground; he didn't realize that the only thing holding him up was the strong Iranian's arm under his chin. Lev spotted his bloody eye lying next to his hand.

By the time Lev looked up with his one good eye, the crazy Iranian was gone. He managed to crawl down the alleyway and out into the open bazaar. It wasn't until he saw the throngs of shoppers around him that he started screaming in pain, begging for help.

Chapter 7

Istanbul, Turkey:

Lev awoke but was still very groggy. Soon he felt a warm gentle hand in his. It was his girlfriend, Natasha. He looked around and realized that he was in a hospital. *Shit* he thought. His right hand reached up and gently touched his throbbing, left eye socket. He felt a mound of gauze and the bandage taped over it. He didn't remember how he got to the hospital.

"What happened?" he managed to croak out through his dry parched lips.

"Oh... sweetie, just rest. It doesn't matter. You're OK and safe here." Natasha didn't know how to explain to her boyfriend that his eye had somehow been ripped out of its socket.

Lev's strong left hand quickly turned and grabbed the small soft hand holding his. He squeezed the small wrist in his hand as hard as he could and twisted it.

"Stop Lev, you're hurting me!" Natasha tried to get her hand out of his strong grip.

Lev squeezed even harder and twisted it some more. "Tell me what happened!" he demanded angrily.

Natasha blurted out. "Nobody knows. Someone cut your eye out. No one knows why."

Lev let go of his girlfriend's wrist. His nightmares had been true.

"Where are we?"

"In a hospital, honey." Natasha cautiously picked up Lev's hand again. She forgave him instantly, as she guessed how confused he must be.

Lev was grateful for the forgiveness and gently squeezed her hand back to let her know.

"Where?" he wheezed. "What country?"

Natasha started to cry with the relief that something worse wasn't wrong with him. She took her free hand, wiped the sweat off Lev's forehead and brushed his full hair backward.

Her hand felt cool to the touch. Lev started to appreciate her for the first time in his life. "What country?" he repeated softly.

"We are still in Turkey. But you are safe now. They are taking very good care of you."

"We must go back to Russia immediately," Lev demanded in a weak voice.

"There was already someone here from the Russian consulate. They told me not to worry about a thing. The doctors said you can leave in a few days if there is no infection. Whoever did this to you was not very careful about it."

Natasha started sobbing again. "You poor baby, I can't imagine the pain you are in or what you have been through. Who would do this to you?"

"I was robbed," Lev stated calmly.

"The police were here and said that your wallet and Rolex were still on you." Natasha pulled the watch out of her purse as proof.

"The police were here?" Lev asked nervously.

"Yes, they wanted to ask you questions but the doctors wouldn't let them wake you."

"We must leave immediately," Lev insisted anxiously.

Natasha knew her boyfriend's line of work. She didn't ask questions and never wanted to know where he had been or whom he had been with. She understood his reluctance to meet with the local police even after having lost an eye. Natasha usually played dumb in this type of situation, but she knew that the police were right. This was a very suspicious attack.

Her mob boyfriend had his issues and sometimes treated her too roughly and cruelly. But she reasoned that she knew what she was doing and there was a price to pay to get the things she wanted in life. Her living standard was substantially higher than what most Russians could even dream for. She lived in a nice apartment with American designer clothes. She had been on several vacations with Lev to many exotic places; this was her third trip this year to Istanbul. Lev mostly treated her very well. She argued that the few bruises and demeaning acts against her were a small price to pay.

Though Lev realized that she knew what he did for a living, Natasha never asked about it, and the fact that they never talked about his particular profession spoke volumes about how much she understood. He didn't know what to call it; professional courtesy perhaps. Natasha wasn't a prostitute, at least he didn't think of her as one. He took care of her and she kept herself convenient for his needs. And his needs varied; sometimes he needed a beautiful, classy escort for a social event, or as in this case, a travel partner to make the days go quicker and the nights

76

more enjoyable. He, of course, could buy hookers at any time, and sometimes he liked to taste a different wine. But for the most part, he was comfortable with Natasha and he trusted her.

Natasha handed the parched Lev a Styrofoam cup of water with a straw in it. Lev took a long sip and let his head drop back onto the pillow. That simple act caused his eye socket to throb three-fold.

"You must have friends someplace, because after the consulate attaché spoke with the police, they never came back."

Natasha could sense Lev's agitation and who could blame him. Even for a mob boss he had been through a very traumatic incident.

"You should rest, my dear. We will fly back to Russia as soon as the doctors release you. Take your pain medication and try to get some sleep. There is nothing for you to do." It was none of her business what happened to cause her boyfriend to lose an eye so viciously. She assumed it was a price he had to pay for their lifestyle and she respected him for that. Natasha stepped beyond her bounds and cracked the façade of her dumb blond persona when she spoke a piece of wisdom to her nervous lover. "If he wanted to kill you, you would be dead already. Whoever did this wanted to send you or someone else a message. I don't want to know why this happened or who did it to you. Right now you can't do anything about it, so please rest. Your friends in Russia can help you take care of it when we get back."

Lev looked at Natasha with his one good eye and realized that he had underestimated her. That gave him pause; maybe he had underestimated the crazy Iranian and overestimated his own indestructibleness.

Natasha broke open a packet with two white pills in it. "Take these and go back to sleep. I will be right here when you wake up."

The mobster knew that the throbbing pain in his empty eye socket and the powerful pain medication could be affecting his judgment. Natasha's advice seemed sound, yes she was right, he was safe for now. The crazy Iranian would not hurt him again unless he couldn't find the professor and the proof he needed. But, how would he do that? Lev let his lover place the pills in his mouth; he took a big sip through the straw and swallowed them. He pondered his predicament some more while Natasha rubbed his face softly.

Milwaukee, Wisconsin:

"Scott, Mrs. Seaver, we have some good news and some bad news." The hospital had placed Dr. J. K. Guthrie as lead doctor. He was alone with the Seavers in the hospital room and started to tell them what the team of doctors thought they knew about Scott's condition.

Scott was sitting up on his bed, it was still morning but Scott was anxious to go home.

"Good news first, Doc," Scott said opening the discussion.

"Your physical health is excellent. Heart, lungs, blood, everything is normal."

Scott thought about making a joke, mostly to take the stress out of the situation for everyone. But he didn't feel like joking. This time he realized that something was wrong. If it wasn't his physical health then what was it?

"OK Doc, go ahead, what's the bad news?"

"The CT scan showed some abnormalities. That is why Dr. Louis spent most of the day with you yesterday." Dr. Guthrie paused expecting the normally quick-witted Scott to immediately press him for more information, but no one said anything. The room was deafeningly silent for a very long few seconds as the doctor tried to phrase his next sentence.

"We know from your health history that you have suffered multiple head injuries. You suffered a severe blow to the head when you crashed your helicopter during the war. Then several years ago, you had a very bad auto accident and experienced major head trauma. Before that, you could have injured yourself playing football or something else very early in life. Any one of these injuries, or all of them, could be contributing to your symptoms. In other cases, though it is rare, these abnormalities just develop on their own and quite frankly we don't know why."

Scott was trying to digest the information. He felt like someone had hit him with a brick in the face. This didn't sound like something a little exercise and a change in diet was going to cure. He heard Liz's voice and tried to pay attention.

"What does this mean? What exactly is wrong with Scott?" she demanded.

"It's called TBI, which stands for 'Traumatic Brain Injury'. It looks like parts of Scott's brain are shutting down. Slowing down would probably be more accurate." Scott thought back about the day before and remembered it clearly, or so he thought. "Is that why Dr. Louis asked me all of those questions and had me do that game on the computer?"

"Well.... Yes, but it was no game. It was a standardized test, called a mini-mental test, for testing memory skills. And I'm afraid that you didn't do very well, especially as Dr. Louis made it more stressful. As he

78

increased the stress on you, like when he pressed you to hurry, you did worse. In fact at times, the test itself became so stressful that you sort of blanked out, though you never fainted."

"I don't remember it being that difficult. I thought I did OK."

"That would be part of the diagnosis. You don't remember the times when your mind blanks out. These symptoms could be because of past traumas, or some other medical condition we don't understand yet. But, apparently Scott, you're suffering from a form of dementia."

"So you are telling me that I have Alzheimer's?" Scott asked incredulously.

"That is not what I am saying at all."

"Please doctor, what are you trying to tell us?" Elizabeth questioned painfully.

"Scott's brain activity is abnormal and appears to be getting worse. And for some reason we don't understand, stress seems to increase its severity. What actually caused the problem is not that important because unfortunately there is very little we can do about it at this time. There are some experimental treatments that have helped other war veterans, but these studies are highly selective. The truth is, we really don't understand the mind well enough to fully treat Scott's condition."

The doctor was quiet, as was everyone else. Scott looked confused.

Liz turned and looked at her husband; she gazed into his blue eyes and saw a tear. She squeezed his hand tighter. There was no doubt that he understood what was being told to him.

Scott started to feel anger build inside of him. During the war, he had been prepared to get shot at, captured and tortured, but nothing had ever prepared him for this.

Dr. Guthrie tried to expand on why exactly Scott would faint under stress. "It's impossible to know for sure, but Dr. Louis suspects that in Scott's case, fainting is his body's way of dealing with the stress. When the mind becomes confused, it stresses the body. Heart rate goes up, adrenalin starts pumping, blood pressure builds and breathing becomes rapid. It's all part of the fight or flight response. But when the mind doesn't give the body a command to do something, it just shuts down. These symptoms are consistent with PTSD or Post Traumatic Stress Disorder."

"Oh great, back to that again!" Scott moaned disgustedly. "I thought you said I had Alzheimer's?"

PTSD was not something that the captain cared to discuss with anyone.

Alan D Schmitz

"Scott, what I am trying to say is that there are several types of dementia, Alzheimer's is certainly one of them. You seem to have some form of dementia and could easily be suffering from PTSD on top of the symptoms we have been discussing. In fact they could very well be inter-related."

"I do not have PTSD, nor did I ever have PTSD."

"According to the doctor's report from Walter Reed National Military Medical Center, you exhibited all the classic signs of Post Traumatic Stress Disorder after your return from Iraq."

"I was never officially diagnosed with it," Scott argued.

"No you weren't, and you weren't treated for it either, because it says here that the patient was uncooperative and refused further diagnosis and treatment possibilities. But that doesn't mean you didn't have it or that you don't have it now. In fact, Mr. Seaver, the symptoms for PTSD, left untreated, often become more pronounced as time goes by. You need to consider the possibilities if we are to treat you properly."

"Wouldn't you think this discussion is a bit stressful, Doc? I'm still here. I still know that you are telling me I have dementia. Wouldn't that disprove your theory?"

The doctor moved closer to the couple, squeezed Scott's knee and looked him in the eye. "As far as the mind goes, there are no definitive rules. The test showed apparent abnormalities within certain areas of your brain. That is the only thing we know for sure. Like I said before, there is no way for us to test for or confirm exactly what kind of dementia you are suffering from at this time. All we can do is try to find out what it isn't and work from there. No one said you were becoming unintelligent. We are identifying the symptoms and have some ideas on what might be causing them. But that doesn't mean we understand why it is happening. I believe that if we can control the stress in your life, we can minimize the effects. Sometimes, though it is very rare, the disease stops progressing for a while." Trying to put a positive spin on things, the doctor added, "This is not a death sentence; you will live for quite a while yet."

"Yeah, as a vegetable," Scott added.

"We still have more tests that we can try in order to pinpoint what treatment will best serve you. You will both need to speak with the psychologist and she will run her own set of tests to determine the extent of the disease. I want you to stay one more night while we help you sort through this. Then you can go home tomorrow."

After Dr. Guthrie left, Liz and Scott were alone in the hospital room, neither of them said much to the other. What does one say after being told that you were literally losing your mind? Scott didn't agree with the tests that Dr. Guthrie scheduled for him the following day and angrily announced that he was checking himself out of the hospital.

Liz's first instinct was to calm Scott and insist that he stop putting on his street clothes, "One more night is all he's asking," she reminded gently.

"Why should I stay here another night, another day? PTSD? Is that the best they can come up with? That was what the shrinks told me I had when I couldn't remember the crash. They wanted me to remember the horror of being shot down and my men being hurt. You tell me. You tell me, Liz. Why would any normal person want to remember that kind of torture? If that is PTSD, you bet I have it; I wouldn't want it any other way. Those nutty doctors are the ones who need help, not me.

"Look honey, I'm the same man I was a month ago before fainting," Scott pressed. "Didn't think I would remember that did you?" he said crossly to his wife, though he was not angry at her.

"Scott, they just want to help you," she pleaded, not insulted in the least by her husband's anger.

"That's fine, but not now. Now I need to get out of here."

Liz understood and agreed with her husband. Today, right now, her husband needed time to accept and digest what was happening to him. She needed time also. Liz handed her husband his watch and rings.

"Don't forget these." She let him know the argument was finished. Liz went to the window and saw the children playing below, taking advantage of a beautiful November day.

"Let's go sailing," she suggested. "The boat is scheduled to be stored for the winter next week. This will be our last chance before Spring."

Scott stopped his angry rush to pack his things and went to the window alongside his wife. He looked outside. His sailor's eye gauged the breeze from the sway of the trees. The sky was deep blue with dotting clouds starting to form in the late morning.

He placed his right arm around his wife's shoulders and stared out the window for a while. They both said nothing until eventually Scott pressed her shoulders tighter against his and gently disclosed in a whisper, "I'm scared Liz. In my whole life I have never been this scared. I cheated death a few times, once I wish I hadn't, but this, this thing, how do you beat a failing mind?"

"I don't know, honey, I wish I did. We'll find a way to cope. We always do."

"I don't want to cope. I don't want to be a burden. I don't want Avery to see her dad forget who she is. We saw my mother disintegrate slowly with Alzheimer's; it hurt me so much to see that. I can't put you or Avery through that."

"Scott, there is so much we don't know, there might be a way to stop whatever's happening to you."

Scott changed the subject. "The breeze looks perfect. Let's get a quick wave-height report and forecast."

"Avery is going to my mother's after school, so we have the rest of the day," Liz concurred.

"I'm sure your mother is going to understand that after I have been in the hospital for four days, we decided to go sailing," Scott added sarcastically.

"Who is going to tell her?" Liz grinned impishly.

Later that afternoon - two miles east of Port Washington, Wisconsin:

Liz watched her husband standing tall and strong. He was guiding the fast sloop northeast, farther away from shore. The jib-headed mainsail was billowed out, filled with the wind pushing the cabin-sized cruiser along smartly. Scott was fully in his element. He looked back at Liz and gave her a giant, mischievous grin.

Their sailing cruiser was named "My Chopper." Scott called it that because of the powerful way it chopped through the water. And, of course, because he would never own a Huey, he settled on this cruiser as being his "chopper".

Like everything else Scott did, he did it big. "My Chopper" was elegant, sleek and long. She was a thirty-eight foot boat with beautifully done cabins and galley, including a head with a shower. Not only was it fast, it was comfortable enough to take the family on weeklong sailing adventures. It was a relatively short trip to the northern edges of Lake Michigan, where you could explore the many different islands. In the middle of summer, Scott would tell his family that they should imagine they were exploring the Caribbean.

Scott thought back to the wonderful trip the family took the summer before Bradley died. They had gone north on Lake Michigan and under the Mackinac Bridge into Lake Huron. It was an amazing adventure to sail under the five-mile long suspension bridge that connected the upper state of Michigan with the lower. If he remembered correctly, the Mackinac Bridge was the third longest suspension bridge in the world. It didn't take much imagination to see it as the "Golden Gate Bridge of the North."

From there they traveled south on Lake Huron to Detroit and then through the narrow channels into Lake Erie. The next day they crewed the craft northeast to Buffalo and into Lake Ontario. They went east as far as they could, all the way to the channel of the St. Lawrence Seaway.

Scott remembered pointing to it and telling the children, "Someday we will go through there and into the Atlantic, then down the coast to the real Caribbean Islands." Scott didn't look back at Liz as he remembered those days; he didn't want her to see him crying. Lord, he didn't want to lose those precious memories. They were all that he had of his son Brad now.

After returning to shore, Liz and Scott acted like newlyweds as they constantly hugged, kissed and touched each other intimately while unloading and winterizing the boat. During the short excursion they had both come to terms on their own. From now on, they would have to take life one day at a time and enjoy each and every moment to the fullest.

Novosibirsk; Russia:

It was difficult for the professor to put in the amount of time required to build the device. The problem wasn't that he didn't have the time. The problem was his Angel spent way too much time at home and not enough away with friends. Although he tried to work on it only when she was gone, eventually he had to admit to her that he was working on a special project in the basement workshop and she was not allowed to see it because it was a surprise.

However, one day when her husband was at his university office, Anzhela couldn't resist the temptation to see what her husband was working on for so long. She saw, unnoticed by the professor, where he hid the workshop key. It was silly of the professor to hide it in as convenient a place as under his favorite book, especially since he hadn't read or moved the book for years until very recently. Anzhela didn't consider herself a bad woman for snooping on her husband; she was just being a wife taking an interest in her husband's hobbies.

With key in hand, and the certainty that Yuri was gone for the day, she crept down to the basement through the outside entrance. Anzhela opened the door carefully. She felt like a thief. It was very exciting. The basement was dark, but not as cold as she had expected. Daylight streamed in through the open door, providing the only light. Besides the light, the open door let in a fair amount of snow that was blowing and swirling outside. She stumbled around the narrow aisles. Finally she found a light switch and twisted it. The lights flickered on.

Anzhela suddenly realized that snow was still blowing into the basement through the open door, so she rushed to close it quickly. Looking down she noticed her small footprints in the snow. Already signs of her entry were evident. She made a mental note to make sure she removed the evidence before she left. Her heart pounded as she realized that she should be more careful if she didn't want Yuri to find out about her nosiness.

Now that the lights were on, she set to the task of finding out whatever it was that her husband was building. There were wood shelves almost everywhere, with boxes of papers, old clothes, toys, and other trinkets. Most of the items were probably garbage; none of it belonged to them, she was sure. If she had time, she would examine the boxes more carefully for usable or valuable things, but for now she reminded herself to stay on task. Though she did wonder why she hadn't been down here before, or why Yuri never told her there were potential treasures below their apartment.

Anzhela glanced back at the doorway and her heart settled a bit when she noticed the snow on the floor was already melting. At the back of the basement there was an open area with a wood shelf that was unusually clean. Under it was a small stool. Undoubtedly this was the work area. An extra light was mounted just above the bench; she plugged the dangling cord into the nearby outlet. This was where Yuri worked on his special project, but where was it?

She thought back to her footprints in the snow. Certainly Yuri would have left tracks on the dirt floor also. Anzhela looked for obvious signs of foot traffic. She didn't find any, but she did see a fresh mark on the ground. Something had recently been slid out from under the shelves. Yuri's Angel felt her heart pound again. She was sure she had found the secret project. Making careful note of exactly how the box was placed under the shelf, she slid it out toward her.

It was at least ninety centimeters high and about forty centimeters wide, about the size of a small refrigerator. It wasn't as heavy as she expected. Her heart was thumping hard from excitement. What if Yuri found out she had snooped on him? Would he be angry? Would he leave her? For the first time Anzhela's conscience was expressing some doubt about what she was doing.

The box was out in front of her now; all she had to do was unfold the top covers and Yuri's secret would not be a secret any more. Anzhela stared at the top of the cardboard box for some time. It wasn't a decision if she was going to open it or not. That decision had been made when she opened the basement door. What she was staring at, was the top of the box. She was trying to memorize it so that she could close it exactly as it was. The price for snooping on her husband could be several weeks of terrible, deafening silence. To not be spoken to by Yuri until he forgave her would be a terrible price to pay. In his stubbornness, he might punish her with silence for a week or more.

Carefully she opened one flap and then another. Once it was open, she instantly knew what it was. The clean polished metal and small copper piping made it obvious. She fell back against the shelves behind her, causing them to tip; Anzhela quickly turned and caught them. She had almost caused them to fall. No wonder Yuri was keeping this a secret from her. Her heart pounded more. This was something she was not supposed to see, of that she was certain.

Ever so carefully, she closed the top of the device exactly like it had been, then she pushed it back exactly into place again. Retracing her steps, she unplugged the workbench light and then the main lights. She quickly slid out the door and locked it, promising to herself that she would never go into the basement again or snoop on her husband. It would be difficult to pretend she hadn't seen what she had.

Chapter 8

Novosibirsk, Republic of Russia:

L ev stepped off the train, cursing as he mis-stepped and tripped over a landing. With one eye gone, his depth perception was non-existent. He was told that in time he would adjust, but that didn't help him now he thought, as he cursed some more.

It was cold in Novosibirsk, and the long, slow train ride had been anything but pleasant. He would have flown, but he needed to follow the package. Finding the right material to create an orange-colored box marked with a wide green stripe around it had been a real pain. But right now, it was very convenient. There was pallet upon pallet of shrink-wrapped boxes being unloaded, but keeping an eye on his particular box was made easier thanks to the unique coloring.

The mob boss knew that his carefully wrapped package was going to the university. What he didn't know was exactly where. The orange and green package was loaded onto a delivery truck, one of many parked at the train station. Lev walked up to the truck parked next to his target and leaned against it. He glanced at the driver carrying his package. To make sure the truck driver watched him, Lev took a pack of American Marlboro Lights out of his jacket pocket, adding a touch of theatrics. He shook one out slowly and lit it, making a bit more out of the ordeal than necessary. On his first exhale, he acted as if he just had the first sex of his life and had found it very satisfying.

The burly truck driver watched with envy. Through his open window he could smell the quality in the exhaled smoke wafting around him. It was obvious to Lev that the driver had noticed the American brand marking the hard pack of twenty smokes. There was no doubt that the man in the torn, standard issue, drab Russian coat knew a good smoke when he saw one. Some of his thick fingers stuck through the worn gloves at the fingertips. They made a clicking sound as he nervously rapped them on the large driving wheel.

Lev played with his gold lighter, pretending he didn't notice the driver in the truck. The mafia boss flicked the hinged lid open and lit the flame. He then twirled it in his finger and with a practiced move, closed the lid with a click. Then, just as quickly, he had the flame lit again. It was a move that he perfected to create a distraction whenever he needed someone to notice him. This was one of his earliest lessons in thievery: create a diversion and you can get away with almost anything.

The pack of cigarettes was out in the open, tempting the driver further. Finally the exasperated driver could take no more and asked, "Comrade, it has been such a long time since I had a quality smoke. Would you mind sharing one?"

Lev looked up as if he hadn't even noticed the driver was there. In his friendliest voice he replied, "Of course Comrade, how American of me not to share. Shame on me."

Lev opened the pack and tapped it against his hand gently until one of the smoky treats fell to his fingers. He placed the cigarette gently between his lips and lit it for his new comrade. It was a simple and accepted sign of courtesy in his homeland to light a cigarette for a friend.

The driver took a long puff, clearly enjoying it, and then commented during his exhale, "The Americans are assholes, but they sure can make a fine cigarette."

"That they can Comrade. And where are you off to on such a miserable day?"

"You must be new to Novosibirsk. This is a garden day compared to the weather we usually get here."

Lev laughed. "Indeed you are correct sir; I am visiting my son at the university. He has told me about the miserable weather, but he exaggerates about almost everything, so I assumed he was just looking for sympathy from his papa."

"A son at the university; you must be very proud!"

"Very proud and very broke. Sending a son to the university is costing me a small fortune."

"Can't be that bad Comrade," the driver corrected as he exhaled again very slowly and nodded towards the half smoked Marlboro he held with fingers poking out of his tattered glove.

Lev laughed again, trying to cover up his lies. "This was a going away gift from my wife. She was so happy that I agreed to make the trip to see our son, she somehow found two packs of this American brand."

Lev continued softly, "We couldn't afford for both of us to visit. Besides, her health wouldn't have allowed her make the long train trip. I assure you Comrade, it was quite uncomfortable."

"Where are you from, my friend?"

"Moscow. It was a very cold, bumpy ride."

"I think I would like to go to Moscow someday."

Alan D Schmitz

"You are missing nothing but a truly nasty, uncomfortable, bumpy ride to nowhere."

From behind the truck, a horn on the lift beeped four times and a voice hollered for the truck to move out of the way. The driver ground the gears of the truck and started to pull away as he tossed out the butt of his cigarette.

"Did you say you had more of these American Marlboros?"

Without asking a question, Lev pounded one more out the pack and handed it to the driver.

"If you want a ride to the university, jump in. I'll show you cold and bumpy."

Lev grinned widely and offered deep thanks as he got into the passenger side. Finding a taxi at the train station wouldn't have been a big problem, but just the same, Lev wanted to stay as close to the package as possible. After all, he had followed it over 6,000 Km and to lose it now would be a disaster. His life depended on finding the man who called himself the "Professor."

Milwaukee, Wisconsin:

The nurse came to get Scott and lead him into the doctor's office. He drove himself to the clinic and was alone today. The current prognosis was that the disease was under control and it was safe for Scott to continue with a fairly normal schedule. This was just another one of his weekly sessions with the psychologist to see how he was doing. He was also being taught mental exercises to increase his memory and to help him cope with the shortfalls.

Scott struggled to come to terms with the fact that he would eventually be alive only as a shell of himself. He would surely become a burden to his family, both physically and, even worse, emotionally. For now he would do what he always did; he would persevere. He would look for and create an escape. Scott Lowell Seaver didn't give up so easily, he would find a way to stop it. Scott felt that if he could keep his mind active, he could stop the disease from stealing it. The doctor told him that sometimes a different area of the mind can be trained to make up for the deficiencies of another. Scott intended to become one of the success stories. "Hi Doc!" Scott greeted cheerfully. The nurse closed the door with a click as she left the doctor and patient alone. Scott wasn't all that happy to be there, but he knew that if he acted depressed it would mean more pills, more therapy and probably less freedom.

"Hello Mr. Seaver. How has the week been going?" As usual, Doctor Maslow decided to get right down to business. Dr. Howard Maslow was dressed in casual street clothes. He felt that the casual look was a good practice to help relax patients.

"Pretty good I think, but then again I can't remember." Scott wisecracked.

The doctor smiled at Scott's humor, then asked, "Please sit down and tell me about your week. How did it go at work since we last talked?"

"Fine Doc., I don't feel any differently. In fact I feel normal. I know your tests tell you I'm losing it, but I am still the one everybody, including my partner, comes to for information. I feel just as productive as always, if not more."

"Even more productive...that is encouraging. And why do you say that?"

"I hate to admit it, but you know all that memory stuff you are teaching me?"

"Yes, of course."

"It actually works."

"Well, thank you Mr. Seaver for reaffirming my life's work," the doctor quipped.

"You know what I mean. I use it all the time. It's the little stuff like not forgetting where I put my keys, or not forgetting what I was talking about. I also write lots of notes and record memos to myself on my phone. These types of things have actually made me less forgetful than before. I'm developing those important habits you keep preaching about."

"That is very encouraging. Now is the time to reinforce those habits. Keep doing the same thing, the same way, over and over again so that you don't have to think about it. Then what will happen in a pinch, is you will only have to remember what you are doing, and not what you did the moment or hour before."

"I know Doc, you keep telling me."

"Have you felt any panic attacks coming on?"

"No Doc, I haven't. Why would I? Things are going great."

"Don't fool yourself, Scott. If you haven't, you will. And by definition, it will be when you least expect it. Let's say you do. What would you do?"

Scott sighed heavily. The doctor made him do this exercise several times during each session. There were times when Scott felt that the whole diagnosis was wrong. He felt so normal lately, it made him upset to think he was wasting his time doing mind and body control exercises when he didn't need to.

Scott stood and started the drill in a mundane tone. "If I feel a panic attack coming on, and I don't, but if I did, I would stop trying to remember whatever it was that caused the panic. Then I would slowly inhale and exhale through my mouth. Nice even breaths." Scott then demonstrated the breathing technique.

"If I can, I should walk away from the stressful environment and find a private area where I can relax. I should remind myself that forgetting something is okay. In time I will remember it and life will go on. NO BIG DEAL!" Scott added the last words with emphasis, just as the doctor did when teaching him the relaxation technique.

Dr. Maslow offered hope that keeping Scott's stress under control would help his short-term memory. He also reminded Scott that when his mind becomes confused, it creates a type of panic attack. The more panic that sets in, the more disorientation the mind feels, which in turn causes more panic. This causes a cascading effect until the mind decides it has had enough and shuts itself and the body down.

"Scott, you need to be aware of the feeling coming on before it overtakes you. You can control it in the early stages, but if you don't stop it right away, it will be like a monster that keeps growing until you can't control it. And when it starts, the response needs to be automatic and immediate. Things that can set off a panic attack might be forgetting something that you know you should remember, such as your wife's or other familiar people's names, birthdays, where you are, or other types of everyday information. Any and all of these types of things create a panic situation. We need to teach you to control these attacks from the start so that they don't build."

Scott volunteered more information, "I think I am wound a little tightly sometimes, despite your pills. I'm afraid that I take it out on Liz from time to time."

Another part of the therapy was an anxiety-reducing drug. If it could help keep Scott's anxiety threshold low, he could better deal with uncomfortable situations.

"Scott, some anger is expected. You have been dealt some very bad cards through no fault of your own."

"Yeah, I sure have. But it's my problem, and Liz has been wonderful about it all."

"Just keep remembering that. I'm sure Liz can understand if at times you don't seem quite like yourself."

"Another thing I would like to talk about is your experience during the war. You have never brought it up, not once."

"I assume you are referring to when I crashed and we were captured."

"Yes, I am. Do you care to talk about it?"

"Look Doc, I'm sure you already know that I don't remember any of it."

"That is what concerns me. You don't remember the many days of misery and torture."

"I hit my head; I was sort of unconscious."

"According to the reports, your crew said you were quite coherent. In fact, you were an inspiration to them."

"Inspiration? I got them captured and caused their torture. Trust me, I was no inspiration."

"They thought you were, Scott. I could be completely misguided, but part of your memory problems could be a condition from that terrible experience. Post Traumatic Stress Disorder is very real Scott. Whatever happened during that time was not your fault. You were completely exonerated. In fact, you were given a medal for bravery."

"Look Doc!" Scott was becoming more agitated and angry. "I don't remember, and I don't want to remember. Why does everyone insist that I have PTSD?"

"Scott, let's not call it PTSD. Just call it what it was, a very nasty and frightening experience that you choose to forget."

"OK Doc. I'm sure it was, maybe that is why I don't WANT to remember it? Did you ever think of that?"

"Maybe you need to remember. Maybe you need to forgive yourself. Did YOU ever think of that? You don't remember the crash that killed your son either, even though you were found at the scene of the accident conscious, holding your son in your arms, trying to revive him. Just because it wasn't war, doesn't mean it wasn't just as traumatic."

"Now you want me to remember how I killed my son. I don't want to. I won't."

The doctor realized that, at least for now, Scott wasn't ready to talk about his feelings. But for Scott's sake, Dr. Maslow new that his feelings were something that needed to be addressed in the near future whether Scott wanted to or not.

Scott took a deep breath then asked, "Will all my memories eventually die? I mean, even the good ones?"

"I hope that in your case the memories never die. My guess is that at times you have problems accessing them. ·

"The short answer is that we really don't know, it depends on if your mind continues to degrade and how far and fast. I'm encouraged that maybe there is more behind all this than strictly a physical disorder. Dementia is usually a slow deterioration of the mind as it becomes more and more impaired. On the other hand, Traumatic Brain Injury, or TBA, often takes time for its effects to be felt and can stop progressing, or even reverse at any point, even reversed. Likewise, the more traumatic symptoms of PTSD often don't become problematic until well after the disturbing event, so it is another very real prospect for the cause of all this.

"You need to accept the possibilities Scott. I feel that you have a great deal of denial and self-blame bottled up inside of you. This guilt has become a tremendous burden, but you are so used to carrying it that you don't realize the toll it is taking. Intentional memory suppression can be very detrimental to your mind's overall health."

The doctor let that sink in a bit before continuing.

"What we know is that your mind has been physically damaged. It may be getting worse or maybe it's not. We can't be sure. But what if that isn't the only problem or even the main problem? I would like to explore this possibility with you in our next sessions.

"Unfortunately, another avenue I think we have to consider is the possibility that you do have early age dementia. There are many experimental drugs that can slow the disease down. However, medical science is at its infancy here. We don't understand why these drugs sometimes work and sometimes don't. That is why they are potentially dangerous."

"How do I get these experimental drugs? I have nothing to lose."

"There are some that I am currently evaluating. You are relatively young and in good physical health. You would be a perfect candidate to participate in a drug trial, but we need special permission to put you on the list."

"I haven't had anyone call me young in a long time Doc."

"In the world of dementia, you are unfortunately on the young side of things. But you are wrong about not having anything to lose. Some of these drugs have very nasty side effects, and some could even make things worse."

"If you were me, wouldn't you want to try something, even if it is risky?"

"Scott, truthfully, if I were you, and if I could, I would. I already submitted your file for review. I didn't want to tell you until I had some sort of answer, so please don't get your hopes up."

"Well Doc, I do have my hopes up. And I am going to keep them up as long as I can. I still feel like I can beat this thing."

"I applaud you; a positive attitude is very healthy. Miracles can happen. Medical science has had its share. But I don't want to give you false hope. If you do have dementia, it is a long shot in anybody's book."

Scott stood up. "Thanks Doc., I'll see you next week. Keep working on those special drugs. I know that we'll find something. Like you said, I am not your typical patient. I've won a few long shots in my time, and I think I have at least one more in me."

Scott got into his SUV and turned his car onto the busy street outside the doctor's office, as he strategized about his near future. It might be only a matter of time before he could no longer fulfill his duties at the office. If he didn't get the experimental drugs or if they didn't work, the charade would come to an end sooner or later. How long that took would be anybody's guess. So far no one suspected he was literally losing his mind, at least he didn't think anyone did. Scott lifted the center console between the light-tan leather seats where the bottle of anti-anxiety pills was safely tucked away. He looked at them begrudgingly; for now they were his only lifeline to sanity. It was impossible to know if they actually worked for him or not. Scott laughed to himself as he thought about the ridiculousness of it all. If they didn't work, he wouldn't know, and if they did, he wouldn't know either.

He parked his car at his office and opened the SUV's door into the cold. It was as windy as it was cold. The combination made for terrible winter conditions, especially when combined with the pelting snow. The wind had already blown a small drift around his partner's car, though the blue Jeep Patriot's four-wheel drive would see to it that Jerry wouldn't have any problem getting home tonight.

"How did it go at the site? Did Sam's wife have the baby yet?" Jerry asked as Scott fumbled with the keys to his office door.

"Just fine...," Scott answered and started to panic when he couldn't remember who Sam was, much less about a baby. Then he realized that he couldn't remember which key on the key ring was for his door. He recognized the panic starting to overtake him. The training by Dr. Maslow had thankfully made Scott aware of an onset of a worsening situation. He quickly placed the keys back into his pants pocket, draped his coat over a chair and explained that the morning's coffee had taken a toll and he needed immediate relief. He embarrassingly excused himself to the restroom. Jerry and the receptionist, Kim, laughed at his predicament and made sure neither of them hindered him in his race to the bathroom.

Inside the restroom, Scott did the breathing exercise that the doctor had showed him. When he felt under control, he took the keys out of his pocket and looked at the set. Immediately he knew which was the right key. It had a worn face. There were three keys that were shaped exactly the same; the other two were shiny and new looking. One was for Jerry's office and the other was for the accountant's office. They had been seldom used compared to his own office key.

Scott lifted his IT-Tech phone from his pocket and made a verbal note. "Get covers for my keys so I know which key works what door." The voice recorder on his phone came in very handy lately. He had learned to make memos to himself during the day. He actually felt that he was becoming more efficient in some ways. He saw that there was another memo that was time stamped from that morning and he played it back. *That's right*, he remembered as the message played back, "Sam had a boy and couldn't be prouder. Five and one half pounds. They named him James."

Scott came out of the bathroom and made some fun at his own expense while he poured himself a cup of coffee. "Sam had a boy!" Scott announced loudly for all to hear. "Five and one half pounds. They're naming him James."

"Good for them!" Jerry said before he changed the subject to the winter storm. "Radio said the roads are getting icy. What do you say we close the office down early? Mary never even came in, she was the smart one."

"You guys go ahead; I have a few things I need to get done here before I can leave." Scott turned the key and opened his office door as he had done thousands of times before.

"Don't stay too long, buddy. They're expecting the wind and the snow to keep building. Good thing tomorrow is Saturday, because it looks like it's going to be a snow day," Jerry cautioned.

"You two get going; I'll slave away here all by myself." Scott played for some false sympathy.

Inside his office, Scott sighed and felt a wave of release. It was strange, but alone in his office he felt safe. It was his haven. Home was nice. He loved being with his family, but his office was different. Maybe because he had spent so many years in this room, each and every memory of it was so ingrained he didn't have to pretend to remember. Scott knew every nick in his desk and where every folder was in the file cabinet.

Or maybe he felt secure in the knowledge that he was alone and didn't have to fear saying the wrong thing or accidentally repeating himself. But for whatever reason, Scott felt relaxed and content for now.

He sat down by his old desk and turned on his computer. He opend his computer's calendar and scanned it for memos that he left to himself for the next week. Scott also scanned it for any notes that his partner or secretary might have left for him. Things looked pretty slow, but that wasn't unusual for January. Looking at his desktop display he saw the memo that he made at the construction site this morning. Even though he made the memo on his IT-Tech phone, it automatically downloaded onto his computer in the office. His laptop computer, which was also his home computer, was also updated as soon as the computer found an Internet connection. This was a tremendous time saver, one that he tried to get his partner to adopt. Jerry wasn't as tech savvy as he was and was content to keep just one calendar on his office machine.

Not only did the IT-Tech update his computers, but if Scott made a change to his contacts or calendar on either of his computers, his IT-Tech was also immediately updated. To Scott, that was a comfort regardless of his memory problems. He liked knowing that wherever he looked for information, all his computers were up to date.

Scott's friend, Lieutenant Randy Schmidt from the base, helped him set up the system. It wasn't really that hard to do; the lieutenant had finally bought his own IT-Tech and wanted to show Scott what he had learned to do with it. Even though Randy was quite a bit younger than he was, they had become close friends. Ever since Scott had to take a medical leave of absence from his duties at the base, the lieutenant and Scott had made sure that they stayed in contact. They often used their mutual love of technological toys as a common thread. Every time either of them purchased a new application for their IT-Techs, they would tell the other of the virtues.

Jerry and Kim peeked into Scott's office and said their goodbyes for the weekend. Scott started to go through his e-mails and his snail mail. Then he caught himself up on the current news and sports scores. Liz called and asked if Scott had taken his noon medication and if he was coming home soon since the roads were getting really bad. Scott assured her he had, though he really couldn't remember. Scott looked out the window at the blowing snow and, before hanging up his office line, agreed that he would be leaving soon.

To Scott, it seemed like only minutes had passed before the phone rang again. As soon as Scott answered, he got an immediate earful. "Scott, I thought you said you were coming home soon. I'm so worried. Avery got home an hour ago and said the roads were terrible. I want you to leave right now!"

Scott looked at the clock on the wall; over two hours had passed since their last conversation. His desk was clear of all his paperwork and he wondered how the time went by so fast. What did he do during that time? He couldn't remember. With a couple of clicks, he shut down his computer, closed his leather-bound, hard-cover briefcase and was out the door. Grumbling, he scraped the accumulated ice and snow off his windshield and windows. He felt the stinging of sleeting rain and snow. The wind was blowing much harder now.

Captain Seaver jumped into the car shivering. He programmed his car's GPS for home while the engine warmed. Scott wasn't afraid of forgetting his way home, but the blowing snow would no doubt be worse on the country roads and create a visibility problem. Knowing exactly what road he passed and what was next could be very helpful to anybody in these conditions. Soon his GPS had drawn a blue line for his route home and his "lady friend" inside the computer began talking him home.

Evening darkness came quickly; the blowing, drifting snow was becoming much worse than he thought. Taking the extra time to program the GPS was paying off because the slow ride and extremely reduced visibility made him feel disoriented. Scott followed the tracks in the snow from the car in front of him and hoped he didn't follow it blindly into a ditch. He could barely make out the taillights through the swirling icy crystals. He wouldn't be the first driver who crashed his vehicle into a line of cars that had all made the same mistake; it was known to happen under these conditions. Scott watched the side of the road. His headlights were barely illuminating the roadside. Undoubtedly his headlights were also covered with snow and becoming less and less effective.

Scott lost track of time, he couldn't remember exactly at what time he left the office, but that wouldn't have been much help anyway. Because of the slow ride, he may have only gone five or ten miles. Scott dared to take a quick glance at the GPS; he was still on the blue line, which was good.

Suddenly the red taillights in front of him became much brighter, before they disappeared completely. The next thing he saw was the side of the vehicle in front of him as it spun around on the slick pavement. Scott instinctively pressed his breaks gently, trying not to skid out on the slippery road himself, while at the same time avoiding the out of control pick-up. It only took another second before the truck had spun one hundred and eighty degrees around so that its headlights were pointing at him. In that instant, Scott remembered the last time he saw headlights coming directly at him. He heard the sound of the truck hitting the tree; he heard the sound of his son's head hitting the windshield. Then everything was quite, very quiet.

"Turn right at the next exit. You are five miles from your destination on the left."

Scott stared out the windshield. Where was he? How did he get here? He remembered the snowstorm but that was all. Scott panicked. He hit the brakes, but he pressed them way too hard. The anti-lock breaking system kicked in and saved him from an out of control skid, before he came to a stop in the roadway. Midway through his sigh of relief, a glance at the rear view mirror showed a set of headlights coming at him. Any vehicle behind him would have no chance of stopping in time when they saw him, if they saw him. Scott pressed on the accelerator and the SUV started down the road again. The still shaken driver was thankful for the automatic four-wheel drive. He picked up enough speed to stay in front of the approaching headlights, narrowly avoiding being rear-ended.

Scott didn't know what to do, so he kept driving straight ahead. When he dared take his eyes off the road, he glanced at the GPS. He was still on the blue line, but to where?

"In one-quarter mile, turn right," the voice in the GPS reminded.

Scott turned right but the signs were covered in snow and impossible to read. He stopped at the end of the exit, looking for a familiar building, but the snow reflected the light from his headlights, disorienting him more. A horn honked loudly behind him; again Scott felt panic set in. He didn't know where he was or where he was going.

"Proceed to the right; your destination is four miles on your left."

The calm voice of his "lady friend" in the GPS settled him down. *No need to panic, she will take me wherever it is I'm going, and I'm almost there,* Scott reassured himself. Slowly he pulled away from the stop sign and cautiously went down the road.

"Turn left in one-half mile," the friendly voice coached him.

"Left turn in one-eighth mile."

Scott saw a green road sign and turned left. Somebody still had their Christmas lights on; they looked pretty all covered with fresh snow. Then absentmindedly, Scott said out loud to himself. "The Michelson's should really take down those lights soon. Christmas is long over Ralph."

Then it dawned on him. He was home. It was their subdivision.

"You are at your destination. Trip guidance is being canceled."

"I love you!" Scott said to his GPS unit. "Thank You!"

He pressed the button for the garage door and when it was open, he drove his SUV through a two-foot snow bank into the garage. Scott turned off the SUV and trembled, resting in his car.

All of ten seconds later, Liz was out in the garage and at the door of the car, which still hadn't opened. She opened the ice-encrusted door and cried. "Scott, Scott, are you OK?"

"Yeah, sure honey. That was a hell of a ride home. I'm just a little shaken up yet."

"Come in the house. I'll warm up some dinner for you. You look like you've seen a ghost."

Scott's hand was trembling a bit, enough that Liz picked up on it. She didn't say anything. It must have been a horrendous drive home, but still, she had never seen anything shake up Captain Scott Seaver before.

Scott too realized that his hand was shaking but knew it wasn't from the cold. It was because he realized that he couldn't remember the ride home. That was a very freighting thing for him.

Liz thought immediately about the anti-anxiety pills. Under the circumstances, she toyed with the thought that she could use one herself. "Where are your pills?"

"I keep them in the center console."

Liz reached into the SUV and brought them into the house with her. It would be time for her husband's evening dose in about an hour. Liz counted the pills and realized that there were two more than there should be.

"Did you take your pills today?" she asked casually, already knowing the correct answer.

"Yes dear!" Scott answered sarcastically but as truthfully as he knew it.

"Just checking honey," Liz smiled back, hiding her true feelings. She believed her husband was telling her what he remembered, but now she knew that she had another problem: how to make sure her husband took his pills when he was supposed to.

Chapter 9

University of Novosibirsk, Republic of Russia:

"**L**et me help you," Lev offered to his truck driver friend. "It is the least I can do for the ride."

"I only drive. The dockworker unloads. Here he comes now." The driver pointed to a forklift truck coming their way.

"Then my friend, we have time for one more American cigarette," Lev suggested.

They both stood out of the wind and snow inside the partially heated warehouse, watching the truck being unloaded. They had enough time for last cigarette in his pack, which he crushed and tossed into a corner. The orange-colored box marked with a wide green stripe hadn't been unloaded yet. Half way through the cigarette, Lev watched curiously as a worker opened a shrink-wrapped pallet and removed the one box the crime boss was interested in and placed it under a stairway.

The truck was soon emptied and the driver announced he was leaving. Lev said he too must be going. "I am sure my son will be surprised; perhaps I will find him in bed with a beautiful young lady to warm him on such a cold day."

"You should be so lucky, Comrade."

Lev grabbed his small suitcase and disappeared outside for a moment, then made his way back inside the warehouse by another door. There was no way he was letting the special package out of his sight. He hid behind a work curtain and patiently waited. The dockworker who had removed the orange box, made a phone call.

The Russian gangster was becoming more and more impatient. It had been hours since the truck was unloaded and still the package stayed unclaimed under the staircase. Lev had another pack of Marlboro Lights but he dared not smoke one and be found out. The lack of a nicotine fix was making him fidgety and nervous. Besides that, he was hungry and thirsty. *The professor would pay for his discomfort*, Lev thought to himself repeatedly.

Not long after, the mobster noticed the workers were starting to do even less than they were before as they began to turn off the lights. *Good*, he thought, *at least there wouldn't be a night shift*. He was certain he

Alan D Schmitz

would be able to find some food once the warehouse was empty. After
that, he would find a place to sleep somewhere in the big warehouse; he
couldn't leave the package and risk losing it.

Then Lev noticed a squat-looking, elderly man walk toward the
stairway; he certainly was not a worker. With a firm handshake the
dockworker who had placed the package under the stairs and the elderly
man exchanged something. Lev had seen enough pay-offs in his time to
recognize one. The worker turned off most of the lights and walked away,
while the man took the special package, tied it to a wheeled carryall and
walked toward a far exit pulling his package behind him.

Lev grabbed his small suitcase and followed the man he assumed to be
the professor. Unfortunately, the mobster's expensive hard-soled shoes
made every step a challenge to keep quiet. The professor on the other
hand was whistling some tune, oblivious to being stalked. Lev hoped the
melody would help conceal his steps.

The professor reached the far end of the warehouse and was just
about to turn the handle of the exit door when he stopped to listen. He
couldn't be sure, but he thought he heard a sound come from behind
him. Something was different. The hair on his back and arms stood on
end. The scientist had an eerie feeling that he was being watched. Lev
had taken two more steps before noticing his prey stop to listen for him.
The crime boss tried to be silent, but his last step had crackled on floor
debris. The professor spun in his direction just as Lev ducked between
two pallets. This time his movements were not only quick but they were
soundless. It was fairly dark in the warehouse with only some
background lights on. This wasn't the first time the mobster hid in the
shadows spying, though two eyes would have made the job easier.

The professor looked for the source of the small noise, seeing nothing
but darkness; *probably a rat or two had become emboldened now that
the lights were off.* He turned up the collar of his coat, turned down the
muffs of his hat and slipped on his gloves. The cold was becoming less
and less tolerable to him as he aged, so he had learned to protect himself
from it when possible. His dress wasn't very fashionable, but he was
warm, and at his age being warm was immensely more important.

The professor opened the door, braced himself against the cold and
slid out into the night, dragging his package over fresh snow. Lev raced
for the door, afraid that after all of this time he would lose the package to
the darkness. He was only moments behind the professor when he set his
suitcase down and cracked open the door. "Govno!" (Shit!) The professor
was getting into a taxi that had been waiting.

100

With no other choice, Lev grabbed his bag and sped out the door. "Wait!" He screamed and waved his hands. "I need a ride. My car broke down." The taxi was already moving away from him. For all of his efforts, the Mafioso envisioned the taxi and his orange package disappearing forever down the snowy road. In desperation, Lev whistled as loud as he could. It was a sound every good taxi driver recognized immediately.

"Why are you stopping?" the professor asked, annoyed.

Before the taxi driver could answer, there was a pounding on his window.

"My car broke down and my friends have all left." Lying came naturally to Lev. He sounded very convincing.

"I do not have time. Sorry!" The professor patted the driver on the shoulder to proceed.

"I will pay you well; I need to get home to my family." Lev talked to the driver through his partially open window. At least he gained the driver's attention. If this didn't work, Lev was prepared to use the handgun in his overcoat. The bomb making components would not leave his sight.

"I do not have time Comrade," the professor explained. "I cannot miss my metro."

"We will go first to the metro station; I don't live far from there. Then the driver can take me home. I will even pay some of your fare," Lev pleaded as he reached under his coat with his right hand, palming the gun while leaning against the open window with his left.

The professor didn't want to ride with a passenger, especially one from the warehouse. He was afraid that the rider might ask questions about what appeared to be some sort of present he took from the huge building. He started to protest again. The taxi driver made the decision for him and motioned with his head for the new rider to get in. This wasn't a well paying route; an extra paying passenger would not be turned away.

"Thank you, Comrade. And you Comrade." Lev nodded sincerely to his co-passenger as he sat next to him. The professor was glad the colorful package was tucked in the trunk; he didn't want any questions asked about it.

It was an oddly quiet ride to the metro station, which was in the same station as the train that had brought Lev to the university town. Lev didn't want to be asked any questions, nor did the professor, so neither encouraged conversation. The driver was also tired of passengers and their stupid questions, so he didn't initiate conversation either.

101

At the metro station, the professor got out and paid the agreed upon fare. He didn't want to force the issue of a shared fare or give this man any reason to remember him.

The professor walked away from the taxi with his box dragging though the deep snow, the wheels of the carryall useless. Lev instructed the taxi to drive to the parking lot. "I remembered that I have a friend who works here. He will give me a ride; I see his car now. Here is a nice tip for you Comrade; you were very kind to give me a ride."

Pulling his cart over the packed snow in the station the professor glanced at the people standing in the cold, forming a line to buy a metro pass. He was happy that he had purchased his ticket home earlier. It would be a long ride, and avoiding the line for ticketing meant he would probably get a seat. The side door was open, so he walked onto the waiting metro. Lev didn't have any choice but to wait for his turn like everyone else in the long line to buy metro tickets. He stomped his cold feet on the wood platform and watched the old man he was following disappear into the third car. Lev boarded the train in the car behind the one into which the orange box disappeared. He would have to watch each and every stop the metro made to ensure that he didn't miss the special package depart the train. Just because he saw one man take it onto the train didn't mean the same person would depart with it. He reminded himself that the target was the package, not the man, at least not yet. The metro rumbled on in the darkness. The seats were hard and the cushions tattered. The swaying back and forth made the mafia boss feel nauseous. Some of the overhead lights worked, but not all, so he made sure that his seat was in darkness.

Lev watched intently at each station, hoping that his prey wasn't smart enough to change cars. Even as the metro would pull away, he watched out the window just in case he could spot a glimpse of his target. After several stops, the metro sped up. There was only one stop left. If Lev missed the professor getting off the metro, his trip would be wasted. He would not be able to meet up with the crazy Iranian again because he would surely kill him this time. Besides that, he would have to disappear to another country because the FSB would also be looking for him.

Soon the train screeched to a stop. This was the end of the line, but Lev held back, his heart pounding. He knew his life depended on what happened in the next few seconds. There was always the chance that he missed the old man getting off the train, and that he also missed the brightly colored package. If that was the case, he could possibly go back to the warehouse and hope that the worker knew the name of the man who paid for the special package.

Lev was about to curse his luck, but then he spotted the elderly man, and he still had the orange package. It was time for introductions. Lev stepped off the metro and casually walked toward the man who was already walking away from the station, his package in tow.

"Professor, do you have a light?" Lev asked, testing his theory that this was indeed his prey.

Yuri turned around to see who had recognized him. The man's face was shadowed by the street light in back of him.

"I'm sorry, I do not smoke. Are you a past student of mine?" It wasn't unusual for a past student to remember him even after many years.

"No professor, I am a business associate of yours."

"I do not know what you are talking about. I have no business."

"But you do, professor. You make things, and I supply you with the materials."

The rotund old man was immediately frightened and started running down the road, towing the small luggage carrier with the box tied to it. Lev was amused at the man's attempt to outrun him. He would be no match even without pulling the heavy package.

"Get away from me; I don't know what you are talking about," Yuri repeated.

Lev walked quickly but didn't need to run. He would catch up with the old man soon enough and by then his prey would be too tired to resist him further. Professor Kromonov looked around for someplace to run, to hide. The narrow road he was on didn't offer many options: there was a river to his left and to his right were small, dark buildings, abandoned factories and warehouses. The packed snow alongside the roadway was slippery and made it all the more difficult to pull the handcart, which he dared not leave behind.

The gangster watched his mark, who was quickly becoming winded. It was late and the streets were deserted.

"Let me help you with your package, professor," Lev said from a distance as he closed in on the struggling, hard-breathing man.

"I have no money. Stay away from me. I will scream for help if you come any closer."

"Go ahead, scream," Lev said as he set down his own case and stopped to light a cigarette. "I'm sure the police would be very interested in what is in your package."

"Who are you? Are you FSB?" The scientist prayed that his worst fear wasn't coming true. His breath was pounding out of his lungs and the cold was instantly turning it into a frozen mist.

"I am The Lion," Lev answered calmly as he picked up his case and walked closer to the breathless old man who reminded him of a scared rabbit.

The professor got a good look at the man approaching and was sure he didn't know him. The patch over one eye made him look sinister and partially masked his face. If someone intercepted one of his Internet communications, they could have picked up the code name Lion from it. The old man was suspicious of a trap.

"I don't know anyone going by the name 'The Lion'! Please leave me alone."

Lev was almost next to the hard breathing old man when he said, "I'm afraid I can't do that professor." The mobster looked around carefully, making sure they were alone. "I need to see the bomb you are building for me."

"I am building no bomb. You are a crazy person." Once again the rabbit tried to run, hoping for a miracle.

Lev raced up to the old man and grabbed the handle of the carrier. With some effort, Lev wrestled the package away.

"Let it go!" the scientist demanded. "It is of no value to you. I have some rubles, take them and my watch. Here look!"

Ignoring the pleas and the bribes, Lev lifted the box over his head and walked to the river's side. "If this is of no value, you will not mind me throwing it into the river then?"

"No, please don't, you don't know what you are doing."

"I know exactly what is in this box, you fool. I put it there." Lev placed it back on the ground carefully. "If you don't take me to the bomb now I will have no choice but to throw you and the package into the river." He displayed the shiny handgun and pointed it at the trapped rabbit.

The scientist didn't know what to believe. This could be a clever trap by the FSB, but regardless, he couldn't admit to making an atomic bomb in his basement.

"I will take you to my workshop; you will see what you want." This admitted nothing, but it should make the gunman, whoever he was, satisfied that there was no bomb.

Lev took the cart and placed his bag on top of the orange box, pulling them both down the road as he walked with his partner in crime.

"I assure you sir, you will find nothing out of the ordinary." The professor tried to dissuade the man, though he knew it was hopeless.

"I assure you sir, you had better be wrong about that. I lost my eye because of your games. I better like what I see or you will lose both of yours before I kill you," Lev assured.

Most of the walk was in silence; clearly neither man trusted the other. Their shoes crunched through the fresh snow. As they walked closer to the university and the huge housing complex, their way became lit by more and more streetlights. Lev's feet were getting cold; he hadn't dressed for the unblessed weather. But he was Russian and cold ran in his blood. He could endure.

"How much farther?"

"Another two blocks," the professor was warm; in fact he was sweating. His mind was racing for a plan. He knew he couldn't and wouldn't expose Anzhela to this danger.

The professor intentionally walked past his street. He would lead the stranger to the university. His hope was that once at the university, he would be able to create a disturbance and escape. If he could begin a conversation with someone or a group, he could then walk away with them. The stranger would have no choice but to let him go. The professor had his hopes up and unintentionally started to walk just a bit faster.

Lev felt a double cross, and this walk didn't feel right. "You pull the cart." Lev pushed the handle at the professor. Then he reached into his pocket and snapped open a switchblade. "Give me your wallet."

The professor was actually relieved as he handed his wallet to the man. Maybe this was just a simple robbery after all. Lev raced through its contents, ignoring the money. When he found the identification card, he said to the professor, "You better be taking me to Barnaul Street."

There would be no way to shelter his wife from this criminal. The one-eyed thug with a gun knew his address now.

"Wait, the last street we crossed, I believe it was Barnaul." Lev was glad he had been paying attention to the roads they walked. "Please turn around slowly. The next time you try to deceive me, I will put my knife through your boot, with your foot still in it."

The professor started to shake, but not from the cold. The thought that he could be putting his angel in danger scared him much more than thoughts of his own safety.

"I will make a deal with you," the professor suggested.

"Go ahead. I'm listening. Though you don't have much to bargain with," Lev reminded.

Alan D Schmitz

"I will show you what I have made. You can have it, but you must leave my wife and me alone after that."

"You're right; you will show me what you have made. And if I don't like it, both you and your wife will die tonight."

The professor stopped. "I will go no farther. You will not find what you are looking for without my help." The professor was afraid that this man was FSB. He had worked with FSB before, and this man acted and dressed the part. If he showed him the bomb, he and Anzhela would be arrested. He would be tried and shot, and maybe Anzhela would be too. In the very least, her life would become a living hell with no apartment and no pension money.

"I admire your courage, Comrade." In one swoop, Lev dropped to his knees and stabbed the long knife through the professor's boot. Before the professor could let out a painful scream, Lev had his hand over the professor's mouth. "Quiet you fool. That was a small price to pay. Now take me to your home. The next time I use the knife it will be more painful and more permanent."

The old man led the mugger, who surely was a FSB agent, toward his home, limping forward with every excruciating step. In another block they were at his apartment house. Lev checked the address with the I.D. card. The lights were on; Lev saw movement in the apartment.

"Take me inside."

"No!" the professor insisted. "What you want to see is in the basement workshop."

"You do not want me inside your apartment, which is exactly why we are going there." His knife persuaded the scientist to comply.

Professor Kromonov fumbled with his keys and then opened the apartment door. If there was any way to protect his wife, he would do so. But for right now he was just an old man against a much younger man with a knife.

Immediately Anzhela saw Yuri and greeted him with a smile. Then she noticed that her husband didn't smile back as a man with an eye patch followed him into the apartment. It was plainly obvious that this man was no friend. Lev replaced the knife in his hand with a small handgun.

"Please sit down. I have some questions for you and your husband. I would have liked to keep you out of this, but your husband has been less than cooperative with me."

Anzhela noticed her husband favoring one leg. She looked to see why he was limping and saw the trail of blood his foot was leaving.

"Yuri!" she cried. "What has he done to you?"

106

"It is nothing," Yuri lied. "Do what he says."

Anzhela watched her husband of forty years eagerly take the weight off his injured foot by sitting on one of the old chairs around the kitchen table. She quickly sat down next to him, very concerned for his health.

Lev took a seat across from them. The warmth of the house felt good, and the smell of the cooking dinner was inviting.

"I want what your husband is making for me. He denied that he has it, yet I know that he has used the materials I supplied to him. Maybe you can help me and save your husband from unnecessary pain."

There was only one thing that Yuri was working on, and she did indeed know what it was. She saw it with her own eyes only weeks ago. How this man was involved she didn't know, but she did know that the parts to make such an object would have been hard to obtain.

"Let's start over, Yuri," Lev announced calmly as he read the professor's name off the ID still in his hand. He pulled his knife out again and set in on the table as a warning.

"Where is it?"

"I told you, I don't have what you are looking for. You have the wrong person."

Lev picked up the knife and slowly walked to the other side of the table. He then quickly thrust it against the old man's eye, the same eye that had been taken from him.

Anzhela cried out, "Stop, I know where it is. I will show you."

The professor was relieved as the knife was withdrawn, but he was also confused. *How could Anzhela possibly know?*

"I'm sorry, Yuri. I have known for some time. I saw it; I know what you are making."

The professor didn't know what to say or what to believe, though it didn't matter because his wife had already convinced the one eyed man that she would give him what he wanted.

"It's in the basement. I will show you. You can have it," Anzhela insisted.

Lev re-sheathed the knife and pointed with the gun. "Let's go."

In disbelief, the scientist watched as Anzhela motioned to the bookcase and said she needed to get the key. She did know his secret.

The mob boss followed her closely with the gun; she was much closer to death than she might suspect. Following her movements with his one eye, he contemplated what he might have to do next. Aiming his gun carefully at the man's wife, he followed from a slight distance afraid that a trap was being set. The trio walked outside and then to the locked door.

Inside, Anzhela twisted the lights on while the gunman turned the weapon away from the wife and pointed it closely at the not so cleaver little mouse he had captured.

As soon as Lev could see the inside of the basement, his stomach sank. This was positively not the type of facility he was expecting. Making a state-of-the-art suitcase atomic bomb would require much more than this basement could offer, he was certain. Now it was Lev who started to tremble at the thought of what the crazy Iranian would do to him if he ever found him. He felt his stomach quake. Life as he knew it would soon be over. From now on, he would be on the run, though his survival would be cut short if the FSB helped the Iranian find him.

"Show it to me now!" the mobster demanded angrily, shouting at Anzhela.

"I thought it was for my birthday; please take it if it is yours. We are very sorry."

"For your birthday?" Lev repeated incredulously.

Lev thought he was going to pass out. This was not at all what he was expecting. He hadn't traveled over fifty hours on that filthy, rocking, cold, shaking train to see this man's birthday present to his wife. Lev started to have doubts; maybe he followed the wrong man. But then, why did this man take his package from the warehouse.

The old woman slid something out from under the shelves. It was covered with the remnants of a bed sheet. The anxious mobster ran up to the covered device and yanked the cloth off, then stared in disbelief. For further proof he ripped at the cardboard box and exposed the entire machine. The device was shiny and meticulously built with some of the pieces Lev had so carefully packed. *Govno! (Shit!)* Lev thought as he sank to his knees. He was a dead man. In front of him was a shiny boiler kettle and copper steamer valves, there were small pipes wrapping around the unit for various uses, including injecting steamy cream into freshly brewed coffee.

The professor backed away from the obviously shocked man, afraid of what he might do. "It is an espresso machine for my wife. She loves espresso on sunny afternoons," the professor added as if that would explain everything. "The last few pieces I need are in the box you wanted to throw into the river."

"I can tell it's an espresso machine, fool," Lev said through his clenched teeth. He was as angry as he had ever been in his life. "Where is the bomb you are making?" he demanded one last time.

Professor Kromonov was more convinced than ever that this man was FSB. If they knew for sure that he was building a bomb, the agent wouldn't have been so cordial as to only stab his foot. He would admit nothing.

"I told you there is no bomb. I order parts from Moscow as I can afford them. I pay cash only because these are special parts. But take it if you want; it is yours."

"You fool," Lev said as he launched himself at the professor. "You tricked me to get parts for an espresso machine? Do you have any idea what you have set in motion? You are a dead man just like me, but first you will suffer as I have. The first lesson you will learn is what it feels like to have your eye torn out of your face."

The professor was not expecting such anger. He thought that once the FSB agent found nothing, he would storm out of the house angrily, but would leave nonetheless.

In an instant the professor found himself with his back flat on the floor and a one-eyed maniac on top of him. Adrenalin gave him strength he didn't know he had. He caught both of the attacker's wrists as one of the dangerous hands tried for his neck. The attacker's other hand thrust the long, sharp knife toward his right eye.

"You are crazy FSB! I did nothing wrong," the professor managed to wheeze out as he struggled to keep the knife away from his eye.

"You crazy old man!" Lev growled back. "I am not FSB, but thanks to you I am a dead man and so shall you be."

Then the irate Russian felt a crack on the head. Broken glass rained down on the struggling pair. The professor's angel grabbed the first thing she found and crashed an oversized canning jar on the attacker's head. The suddenness of the pain caused his head to spin. His one good eye flashed pure white and then went dark. The professor pushed the two suddenly limp hands away from his face and twisted out from under the dazed attacker.

"Anzhela!" the professor screamed, "RUN!"

Anzhela was paralyzed with fear. The stranger was rolling on the floor in pain. The big, rotund man rolled away from the "The Lion." Standing up was difficult; it took him several tries before his legs stopped shaking enough that he could walk.

"Anzhela! Anzhela!" he repeated, trying to shake his wife out of shock at what she had done to the man. Yuri pulled at his wife's wrist and dragged her past the haphazard rows of shelving. The basement door was only steps away. If he could get them out the door and into the open he could keep her safe, even though it meant making her run down the street dressed in nothing but her night robe and slippers.

A shot was fired. It hit the ceiling above them and splinters of wood flew about their faces. Husband and wife froze for a few seconds too long. The door was so close he could touch it, yet Yuri knew that even attempting to open the door would mean certain death. "One more move and the next bullet will kill your wife, old man," the gunman warned.

"Run Anzhela, run!" the professor screamed and tried to force his wife out the door in front of him. If someone were to die it would be him, not his Anzhela. He would protect his wife's escape with his wide body. There was another shot. This one just missed him and grazed Anzhela's arm putting a hole in her nightgown that quickly turned red. They both ducked behind some old boxes. The door behind them slammed shut and with a click of the gun they realized that the assailant was directly upon them, pointing the gun at Anzhela's head.

"Do exactly as I say old man or your sweet Anzhela will have her head blown off." He held the wife's thin, aged arm tightly while pointing the gun at her face. "The silly game you were playing with me cost me my eye. Soon there will be people looking for me who expect me to have a bomb for them. When I don't have the bomb that they spent millions of dollars on, they will kill me, very slowly I am sure. I think I will not give them that opportunity. I shall kill myself first. But so my life isn't a complete waste, I will kill both of you first. If you cooperate, you old fool, maybe your wife won't die as slowly as you."

The professor saw the look of rage in this man's face. No FSB agent would have been that angry at not finding a suspected bomb. This one eyed-man must be the real Lion. "I have your bomb. Please don't kill us." The defeated scientist finally relented. If this man was FSB, he had just won the bluff. If the man wasn't FSB, he would certainly kill them if he thought he had been double crossed. The little mouse wasn't that smart after all. The cat had caught him.

Chapter 10

The gun was cocked and ready, pointing at the terrified woman. He wanted desperately to believe the professor. "Where is it?" His hand clenched tighter as adrenalin pumped through him.

"If you hurt my wife, I will not build it for you; I will not finish it," the professor, feeling a bit braver, boldly threatened as he stood up.

"Where is it, old man?" Lev shouted again, pressing the gun tightly against Anzhela's temple.

"Let her go and I will show you."

"You lying bastard. You don't have it; you are trying to fool me again, aren't you?" Lev snarled through his teeth. The mobster was seconds away from shooting the frail, old lady shaking in his hand. Then he would concentrate on torturing the old man. "Say goodbye, bitch," the mob boss smiled just a bit at the pleasure he was about to have in killing this man's beloved wife.

"STOP!! It's here. I can prove it. There is a false wall over there. Don't hurt her, please don't hurt her," The professor was now crying in desperation.

Lev started to believe the professor, but it could be another trick. "Very slowly and carefully, show me. If you make one false move, I will kill her."

"I promise no tricks," Yuri pointed to more shelving. "It used to be a fruit cellar. I will need to move some things."

"Go ahead, but slowly."

"It's going to be okay, my Angel." The professor spoke softly to his confused wife. "He needs me yet; I promise he won't harm you."

That sounded promising to the gunman. Maybe the three people in the cellar weren't dead yet. Maybe the professor was the real deal after all.

The old man busied himself with moving boxes and other useless pieces about. He reached behind a concrete wall and lifted a hidden latch. It took some effort for him, but he slid open a section of wall that appeared to be shelving. Before he disappeared behind it, he turned to Lev. "I have to go in and turn on the lights and then you will see for yourself."

"Wait!" Lev demanded as he pressed closer to the opening, dragging the frightened Anzhela with him. "If you make me think for a second that you are up to something, she will be dead."

"If you harm her in any way, you will be killing yourself, because I will not lift a finger to finish the bomb. I don't care what you do to me."

He became a bit more cautious with the gun in his hand. If there was a bomb, the old man was right, he would need him. His instincts told Lev that the old man wasn't bluffing any more than he was.

Then he watched closely as the professor disappeared into the darkness. Soon, very bright lights came on. Anzhela's eyes widened as she saw the hidden workroom for the first time. There were special tools; a grinder, lathe and a small torch. Off to one side was a workbench with a huge magnifying glass mounted to it. Under the workbench was a pile of old computer housings and a box full of computer parts. Opposite to it was a larger workbench; on top of it was an old worn-out wood chest with handles. It was the size of a small shipping crate, too large for one man to carry easily.

"Over there!" Lev commanded Anzhela. He pushed her into a chair against the far wall. "Tie her up," he instructed.

"I will do no such thing."

"Take that rope and tie her, or I will. Who would you rather do it? I can't watch you both at the same time."

"She will do nothing, I promise."

Lev angrily grabbed the rope and walked toward the woman. He was convinced that the professor wouldn't run; he had too much to lose. But the old lady wasn't part of the plan and could do anything. He didn't trust her and that was a problem.

"No wait, don't touch her, I will do it.

"I'm so sorry my Angel; this is for your own good. I will explain everything to you. I am doing this for us." The professor apologized as he took the rope from the strange man.

"You are doing what for us?" Anzhela sobbed as her husband pulled her hands behind her back.

"Tie her tight, or I will tighten them until her hands turn blue," Lev growled.

"I have found a way to make money so we can retire someplace warm, my angel," her husband whispered into her ear as he tied her from behind.

"You are making a bomb?" she whispered back.

"That is what this country trained me to do. So now, because they will not take care of us properly, I have to use my talent to make the life for us that we earned."

Lev liked what he was hearing; with each passing moment the mobster was becoming more and more convinced that the man was telling the truth. "Enough chitchat, tell me about the bomb."

The professor seemed to immediately forget about his wife as he proudly walked over to his creation and started to explain its workings to the gunman.

"It is very close to being finished. Isn't it beautiful."

Many of the parts looked like the pieces that were used on the espresso machine. Lev stared at it trying to judge for himself if it was real. After a while of examining it, he had to be honest with himself; he wouldn't know an atomic bomb from a refrigerator, or an espresso machine for that matter.

"Explain it to me. Why is it so big?" Lev spoke softly.

The professor sounded insulted. "Big? Do you realize that it took a B-29 to deliver the 15 kiloton bomb called "Little Boy" over Hiroshima because it weighed over 8,000 pounds - about 3,600 kilos?"

"You told me you were building me a suitcase bomb. This, this is a huge packing crate. I cannot carry it, and it certainly wouldn't be inconspicuous." Lev argued.

"It is possible to build small bombs the size of a large suitcase. They have their purpose. Those types of nuclear devices can only deliver about one kiloton of power. Very powerful for sure and would bring down a building if delivered into the base of it. But you told me you wanted a bomb as powerful as the one that flattened Hiroshima."

Lev was confused. How could he deliver this monster bomb? "You said it was a suitcase bomb," he protested.

"It is. Like I said, the first bombs like 'Little Boy' weighed over 8,000 pounds. It was ten feet long, or three meters. This weighs only 100 kilos. Two men can lift it. Compared to the first bombs, these are suitcases."

"No!" Lev insisted. "It is too big; you must make it smaller."

"This is a very sophisticated device; I cannot just make it smaller. Would you tell a German clock maker to turn his Cuckoo Clock into a wristwatch? If you wanted a small bomb with a small yield you should have said so," the professor told his client stubbornly. "Let me explain. A nuclear device will only become a bomb when it has enough fissionable material to exceed critical mass."

"Of course, every school child knows that," Lev felt insulted.

113

"That amount of material has to be measured and delivered precisely into the explosive chamber." The professor pointed at his mechanical child. "Look, this is a very compact design for such a powerful machine. You told me that your sources have uranium 235 and plutonium 239. I have designed this bomb for specific and precise amounts of those materials.

"Think of these tubes extending away from the center sphere as shotgun barrels. At the end of each barrel will be some of the ingredients. Here and here go the Plutonium oxide and uranium oxide." The scientist was excitedly pointing and directing the mobster's one eye over every appendage. "Over here we will add just the right amount of Lithium-6, a nuclear chain reaction enhancer," The professor looked at Lev who seemed confused then continued. "Think of these chemicals as a catalyst; they make the uranium and plutonium more efficient. These other three shotgun barrels, to use the term liberally, house the plutonium and uranium. All of these outer chambers are lead lined and sealed against radiation leakage. The entire casing will be filled with a special foam mixture that I developed. Any residual radiation or the gasses created by their decay will be absorbed by the foam so the bomb will have no identifiable traits."

The professor bragged a bit. "It is amazing what an ingenious person can do with old computer parts, isn't it? This is the computerized detonation timer. I developed my own failsafe software and have it backed up by two computerized clocks. Once the foam has been poured into the container, it will cover everything, making the timer and the wires attached to it inaccessible. Once the timer is set, it cannot be stopped by anyone, so you must be very careful and very sure when you set it. When the timer goes to zero, the detonation sequence begins. The computers power up and they calibrate the timing, which has to be accurate to the thousandth of a second. Then boom!"

Lev was slowly letting his guard down; his gun hand was hanging limply at his side, a fact that was not picked up by the professor but wasn't missed by Anzhela. Lev questioned, "Are you telling me that it can't be tracked with radiation detectors?"

"Yes, absolutely! It is perfectly safe to be around and not only will it not leak any stray radiation, the explosive material that is used to propel the nuclear ingredients toward the center sphere will also be undetectable."

Lev was aware of the ultra sensitive sniffing machines that the United States had developed since their precious New York towers were decimated. These machines could pick up even the slightest remnants of the most used and dangerous chemicals that made up the majority of explosives.

The professor could tell that he was gaining the confidence of his newfound, though unwanted, partner.

"The center spherical housing is the mixing chamber. Think of it as a combustion chamber. When we detonate this bomb, each one of the ingredients is propelled explosively toward the center sphere. The sphere is lined with very dense and polished platinum, which is coated with a fine layer of Osmium. The purpose of that is to reflect all of the fissionable material to the middle of the sphere.

"The trick is to make all of the materials come together at precisely the right time and with enough force that they mix instantly without destroying the sphere first. The Lithium-6 must be injected just as the mass goes critical, as it super multiplies the critical reaction. We are talking about timing to the fraction of a fraction of a second. The center sphere will contain the fissionable material for about $1/52^{nd}$ of a second. Critical mass has to be attained within that time because if it isn't, the sphere will explode before it's designed to, and you will have a very small and very dirty bomb.

"Done right, Ka-boom, and everything within a two-mile radius is instantly vaporized. Farther out, there will be firestorms, and of course radiation will contaminate everything for years.

"You want a little bomb? I can make you a little bomb, but that will cost you two million American dollars more and another year," The professor spoke confidently, completely forgetting that his beloved wife was listening to every word.

Lev glanced at the old woman tied to the chair. She looked relatively comfortable but still restrained. She seemed equally engrossed in what her husband was saying. Then he holstered his gun back under his left side. "When will it be finished?"

"Another two months."

"What are all of these extra pieces for?" Lev pointed at a box full of specially made machine parts of all sorts of shinny metals. Many he recognized as parts he had supplied.

"Nothing," the professor said smugly.

"Because of a design change?" Lev asked confused.

"They are not needed and never were, except as insurance."

"I do not understand. Please enlighten me." The mob boss leaned back against one of the small workbenches, very interested in the explanation.

115

"They are for our protection," the professor stated matter-of-factly.

"Let me explain. If we supplied a complete and accurate schematic to whoever our clients might be, they would no longer need us. In this business, that could be a very bad thing. So I incorporated many extra pieces and design changes that would be easy for me to re-machine to the proper fit, but would be impossible for anyone to actually use to put together this bomb. The bomb housing and foam covering make it impossible to reverse engineer. If someone tries, they will have a multi-million dollar piece of garbage."

The professor said with even more pride, "The reason I added extra parts was to throw them farther off track. The espresso machine parts were for Anzhela." Suddenly the professor remembered his poor tied up wife. "I insist you let me untie my wife. She has no part in this."

"That is exactly what has me concerned," Lev reached for the holstered gun.

Anzhela realized that her life could be over within seconds. She spoke up and pleaded. "I support my husband, I always have. Yuri worked hard for the state. Many, many hours we both sacrificed. We never had children because Yuri felt his work was too important for the state to sacrifice the time. My husband is right. This is what the country taught him to do. It is time he used his talent for his benefit, for our benefit. If he doesn't make the bomb, someone else will, so he might as well prosper from it."

Lev stared at the old woman's eyes. She stared back directly into his. She knew that her life, possibly both of their lives, depended on him believing her.

"There is no decision here," the professor explained.

"I do not go on without my wife. All that I do is for her." Lev turned and realized that the professor wasn't talking to him but to his wife.

The gunman slowly repositioned himself from between the couple to an area where he could watch them both, and shoot them both if he so wished. He pondered his dilemma. The old couple had seen him. A one-eyed Russian with a Moscow accent wouldn't be hard to describe. Turning him in would mean turning themselves in. Or the old lady could turn on her husband in exchange for her safety and freedom. But if he killed the woman, the professor might not be coerced into finishing the bomb, even under the threat of his own life. One thing Lev did believe was that the old man truly loved the old lady.

The professor walked over to his wife. They both saw the contemplation in their captor's eyes and knew this was a moment of decision for him.

"What are you doing?" Lev shouted to the old man.

"I am untying my wife. If you don't like that, then you can shoot us both." The professor made a dangerous decision. But for him it was no bluff; he was serious. If it was their time, then so be it. But, they would die together.

Lev cocked his gun and held it out, pointing at Anzhela. The professor looked up at the gun barrel and began to untie his wife. Then he said to the gunman, "You shoot my wife, you will have to shoot me. Trust me on that. If you shoot me, you are also a dead man. You must ask yourself: do you want to be a dead man or a rich, live one?"

Anzhela stood up, hugged her husband and turned her back to the gunman. She didn't want to see the gun go off. She just hoped it would be quick and not too painful.

The younger man pondered the predicament, then un-cocked his gun and lowered it. He asked, "Do you know what they do to traitors and terrorists in this country?"

Anzhela turned around realizing their lives were being spared.

"Your husband will not even get a trial and will be very quickly executed." Lev answered his own question. "Then do you know what happens? All references of his existence are also disposed of, even his family. That is the price one pays in this country for being unfaithful to it."

Anzhela looked at the gunman and for the first time she realized that whether or not she had wanted to be involved in the bomb-making scheme, he was right, she now was. Even if the wife of a traitor was allowed to live, she would be forced to live a meaningless existence in some remote miserable village or possibly worse, in a gulag in the frozen north. Anzhela nodded her head slowly, signifying that she understood and agreed with the gunman.

"I will finish this bomb, but you are not welcome here. You must never come here again," the professor demanded.

"I will do what I must, and you, likewise, will do what you must. You will finish the bomb on time, because if you don't, I promise you that I will not die alone, my friend. It had better work as you say."

"You tell your contacts that they must follow my instructions exactly, no deviation. Even the slightest error on their part could render the bomb useless. The explosive material to ignite the fissionable material

117

must be pure and measured exactly. There can be no mistake. Too much or too little and it won't work properly."

Lev spoke with a simple, calm voice and in a matter-of-fact way, "We better all hope they don't make a mistake, because if the bomb doesn't work, they will blame you and me. I am not a praying man, professor, but in this case I pray for both of us. And if all goes well, I hope that we can sit down as friends one day and have some fine coffee from your espresso machine."

The professor didn't believe he would ever want to enjoy a coffee with a man who nearly took his life. He insisted again, "I will send you the rest of the drawings the usual way. Please do not ever come back here again. You must leave now."

"I can't, not yet, I must take some proof back to our clients; that is why I came. They have spent a lot of money, and I have lost an eye because of their distrust. If I do not bring back proof of the bomb, they will kill me. But before I die, they will force me to tell them about you, and they will not have to work very hard. They are very good at causing pain and I don't have much incentive to protect you."

The professor sank down on the same chair his wife had been tied to. "I don't know what they want, or what to give them. You have seen everything, but you of course can't take it with you."

"There must be something I can take besides a photo?"

The professor looked up hopefully. "We will take a photo of the bomb with today's paper, which will show the progress. I will also give you the formula for the absorptive foam I developed. It will show a degree of engineering knowledge." Then the professor went to the box of extra parts and rummaged through it until he produced a partially manufactured piece the size of his fist.

"This is an extra detonation end and shielded uranium containment capsule. It will match up with several of their part diagrams; I will tell you which. If they take it apart to see how it works, they will only learn that they have a lot to learn about making nuclear bombs. But it should convince them that what is in the picture is real."

Lev held the heavy piece in his hand. He was trusting the professor with his life, but then again, the professor was trusting him with his. "This formula," Lev asked, "is it unique?"

"The formula itself should be worth half a million dollars," the professor assured.

118

Milwaukee, Wisconsin:

Scott loved the change of seasons. In Wisconsin they were dramatic and he enjoyed the variety, but he could do without the sloppy mess of springtime. He swerved his SUV to miss another pothole. The frost was coming out of the ground and asphalt was popping out of the roadway in big chunks.

Scott's thoughts raced ahead to summer sailing on his big lake. He was certain he could convince Liz and Avery that this would be a good year to sail up to explore the islands of upper Lake Michigan again. He could already picture "My Chopper" slicing through the waters going under the majestic Mackinac Bridge. After crossing under the "Golden Gate of the North" you were sailing the mighty Lake Huron, another inland ocean to explore.

Scott couldn't miss a big pothole. The SUV bounced first when the front tire hit, then again when the back hit the same missing piece of asphalt roadway. Scott cursed. *We can send men to the moon but we can't build a decent street.*

Perhaps they would sail to Mackinac Island and bike around the huge island park. The island could easily take a person back to the 1800s because motor vehicles weren't allowed. A trip to the Grand Hotel was made with a horse and buggy, the only non-human powered vehicles on the island. Scott's mind wandered as he thought about sailing until he heard the computer voice tell him, "Turn left at the next intersection."

Scott pulled into the job site, happy for the four-wheel drive. His GPS girlfriend announced, "You have reached your destination. Route guidance is canceled."

"Thank you, sweetheart." Scott patted the dash like patting the head of a dog.

Dr. Maslow from the Milwaukee Mind Clinic managed to get Scott enrolled in an experimental drug test program. Months had passed and the special drugs that he was taking seemed to be working well to control his memory lapses. The doctor also worked with Scott on taking practical measures to help him conceal and adjust to his physical impairment.

Today, after one of his regular appointments with Dr. Maslow, Scott stopped at a muddy construction site to check on one of his company's projects. Scott looked at his IT-Tech phone for notes and messages. The high tech phone was like a portable memory device. It reminded him of appointments with a beep, it gave him the addresses and the built-in GPS would take him directly to where he needed to go.

119

Alan D Schmitz

Dr. Maslow kept hammering home to Scott that he had to develop consistent habits to get him through the day. By using his phone to record notes and messages, Scott rarely forgot anything. In fact, the people at work were impressed with how detail-orientated he was. Scott filed things in his phone according to job, so it was easy for him to brush up on the current events for a given project. The only phobia Scott had on a reoccurring basis was forgetting how to use the technology, or worse, worrying about losing it or his laptop computer, which was just as indispensable. So far this wasn't a problem. The businessman was becoming so comfortable with being able to look things up in his portable memory device that he seldom panicked any more.

This current project he stopped to check on was a tear down. By the end of the week they expected to have all the explosives in place to bring down the four-story structure. Scott was watching the weather closely. Too much wind, or wind from the wrong direction, would cancel the blow. If by chance there was a steady rain, it would be a plus, keeping the dust under control. Tomorrow he had to go to Chicago for a meeting on an even bigger tear-down. It would be one of the biggest their company had ever done and Scott was very aware that it could be personally his last. He was coping with his disease, and though the medicine and electronic tricks he used were getting him by, in his heart he knew he wasn't getting better.

Istanbul, Turkey:

The Russian mob boss walked back to his hotel feeling light as a feather. He was looking forward to taking his girl out shopping at one of the bazaars. Tonight he would take her to the finest restaurant in Istanbul. They would take an extra week and celebrate; the rest of the time he would spend enjoying the life he was just spared and even better, he would spend that time with his lover.

Natasha had not only agreed to go back to Turkey with him, she insisted. When he asked why, she said that he was obviously doing something very dangerous and shouldn't be alone. Since that time, Lev thought of her a bit differently, and he treated her differently. He was even thinking of proposing, though not until this whole episode was behind him.

The last two meetings, and the time between them, were excruciatingly difficult. He was constantly afraid for his life. During the meeting three months ago, Lev prayed that the formula for the radioactive absorptive foam, the finished part of the bomb and the picture of the bomb in progress would satisfy the crazy Iranian. If they did not, he would die, preferably fast. But thankfully the worst did not happen and the Iranian was sufficiently satisfied.

Today was the close of these dangerous chapters of his life. The last diagram had been delivered. The Iranians had time to ponder their investment decision. If they weren't satisfied, Lev would have probably been sentenced to death and the crazy Iranian would have been his executioner. If Kassim's superiors agreed that the proof of the bomb in progress was real, he would live. It was that simple. Lev walked away from what he hoped was his last meeting with Kassim, he was breathing air that was much sweeter than when he left the hotel this morning.

A huge weight had been lifted off his shoulders. He felt a renewal of spirit, a rebirth of sorts. It was a rebirth with many exciting possibilities, four million of them to be exact. Up until this moment, the money was abstract. A dead man couldn't enjoy wealth, so it wasn't real. Today he had been granted life. The mobster thought about the millions sitting in his Swiss bank account. The last of his money wouldn't be delivered until the bomb was, and then he would have four million American dollars. That amount of money can make a man take many chances, but was it worth giving up an eye for? It didn't take long for him to answer his own question - it was.

He was far from finished, the professor's bomb had to work, but there would be plenty of time to worry about these things later. On his mind was the fact that he wanted to buy Natasha the most expensive dress they could find, so that she could wear it to the most expensive restaurant they could find. Tonight they would celebrate the beginnings of a new life.

University of Novosibirsk, Republic of Russia:

Anzhela helped Yuri pack up the crate; inside it was the finished bomb. Soon the shippers would be here to pick it up. Anzhela realized that she was as much a part of the conspiracy as her husband now. She had months to tell the authorities and she did nothing. What she and the professor didn't know, was that the local authorities would have lied about what Professor Yuri Kromonov was doing and confiscated the bomb for the FSB. The FSB would have then come up with another plan to get the bomb into the hands of the Iranians as agreed.

Regarding the fate of the professor and his wife, they would have probably disappeared from the face of the earth. Most likely this would have been done by the hands of the mobsters they were dealing with. Plausible deniability wasn't just a Washington D.C. strategy; the Kremlin had invented it.

Through his friend at the university warehouse, Yuri arranged to have the large shipping container delivered to Moscow aboard the train. That way, Yuri and Anzhela's address would not be referenced in any way. The delivery was to an abandoned warehouse in Moscow, an address the one-eyed thug had given them.

It took both of the warehousemen to move the crate to the powered lift at the back of the truck. The professor cringed when they dropped one end roughly, though he was sure the absorptive foam would protect the bomb from shock and damage. It wasn't armed with any fissionable material or explosive charges yet, but still he didn't like to see his baby mistreated. The professor decided he would follow the crate to make sure it was loaded onto the train. Then he would e-mail his contact with a confirmation that the package was on the way.

Moscow Train Station, Republic of Russia:

Lev waited with two of his most trusted associates. Lucky for him they were both very big men, though it wasn't exactly luck. Lev found that when making a demand for payment, two big men were much more effective than even the most brutal of small men. Most of the time the big men just had to ask for payment; no one dared argue.

The mobster located an empty warehouse no more than a block away from the train station. The electricity had been turned off so he waited in the cold and dark for his partner. Anton was ordered to wait and watch the loading dock. The train had been unloading its cargo for the last half hour, and, so far, the described shipping crate had been unseen by him. This meant that it was hopefully still in one of the freight cars.

Lev had tipped, or, more accurately, bribed several of the cargo handlers to deliver the wooden box to the warehouse as soon as it was unloaded. Anton's job was to make sure that the bribe didn't cause any undue curiosity. Then he saw it being unloaded. The unusual markings on it were unmistakable.

Lev's cell phone rang. "Are you sure it is our package?" Lev asked.

"It looks just like he said. It has to be it. They are loading it onto a truck right now."

"Don't let that truck out of your sight. If it doesn't turn directly here call me immediately. You lose that truck and the shipping crate in it and it will be your life. Do you understand?"

"Da!" Anton answered. He was used to his boss talking like that. He had never let him down, so he didn't know if it was a bluff or not, and he didn't intend to find out today.

There were many thieves around Moscow; items disappeared from the rail yard all the time. Lev should know because often he was the recipient of the stolen item. This crate might look interesting enough for someone to steal, even if he didn't know what was in it; Lev couldn't let that happen.

Anton jumped into a cargo van and followed immediately behind the small truck carrying the nuclear bomb. "We are turning your way and should be there in five minutes."

"Open the door," Lev ordered as he stood just outside the warehouse garage.

Eduard gave the big overhead door a shove and it slid half way up its track.

"That's good enough."

When Lev saw the truck approaching, he waved to the driver as if they were old friends.

"This package is from the University of Novosibirsk," the driver announced to the waiting man to make sure he was delivering to the right address.

"Yes, it is ours, a very special machine the university calibrated for us."

"Sign here." The driver stepped out of his truck as did his helper. The summer sun felt good on their bare backs. Lev gave a false signature; no one checked it.

The two deliverymen were not overly large and they struggled a bit with the crate.

"It's heavy enough," one of the men said as the two tried to lift it off the end of the high truck.

Lev saw a picture in his mind of his multi-million dollar bomb crashing to the ground. "Please let my men help you. They are used to handling such things," Lev offered. Then he motioned silently for his people to take it.

"Place it carefully into the warehouse," Lev cautioned.

The deliverymen watched the two large men carefully move the trunk. They almost laughed because they had both seen how the package had

123

Alan D Schmitz

been handled earlier as it was unloaded from the train. Nobody likes a big heavy crate, which was why they were often mistreated. It was a sort of dockworker revenge. All the carefulness in the world wasn't going to undo any damage already incurred. For the owners' sake the workers hoped that it was well packed. But, that wasn't their problem. The package was safely delivered and out of their hands.

"Goodbye Comrades!" Lev shouted as he pulled on the heavy rope to close the door.

Lev waited for the truck to leave and then instructed, "Load it into the van, and for god's sake, be careful."

After the trunk was loaded, Lev locked the van doors and then locked the warehouse. He would check on his package many times a day until it was time to deliver it.

University of Novosibirsk, Republic of Russia:

The professor took his wife to his university one summer evening. The university was at summer break and was mostly empty. The professor's office was neatly cleaned. All of his papers, books and chronicles were packed away.

Anzhela had been to the office once or twice before but this was the first time she had seen it so clean.

"Tonight I want to show you something my Angel."

Professor Yuri Kromonov turned on his computer and waited for it to boot up. He poured his wife a glass of wine from a special bottle, which he bought for this occasion. He poured himself a glass and then with a few clicks of his computer mouse and the entering of a single password, he said, "Come here my Angel. I want you to look at this."Anzhela walked around the small desk and looked at the computer screen. She didn't understand at first what she was looking at, but she recognized the name on top of the account as theirs.

Finally her eyes settled on the account balance line, her face turned white as she whispered, "five hundred thousand dollars?"

"It is all ours my Angel. A Swiss bank account with $500,000, and soon it will have another $500,000 deposited to it. Tonight we make plans to retire to a warm place."

"Can we leave soon Yuri? Can we leave before winter?" she asked impatiently like a child going on vacation.

"We can leave anytime you wish my love. Now we can retire in luxury."

124

Gaptsakh, Republic of Russia:

The closer the van came to Gaptsakh, the more Lev's stomach started to churn. There was a good reason he was making more money than the mouse on this deal, his risks and effort were considerably higher.

After two bumpy days in the stiff-riding delivery van, Lev was tired and feeling sore all over. Eduard was with him and had done most of the driving. The mob boss felt good about having Eduard along. He was big and quick with a knife or gun. This would be his last meeting with the crazy Iranian and Lev knew that anything could happen.

Gaptsakh was about 1200 Km southeast of Moscow. Since leaving Moscow, they had seen much of the beautiful southern Russia scenery, twenty plus hours of it. Now they were beginning to climb into the mountains surrounding the town. The uncomfortable hot temperature of southern Russia was cooling with the altitude. Gaptsakh was a border town, and a very small one. Azerbaijan was directly south, a small country about the size of its immediate neighbor to the northwest, Georgia, and was known for being a smuggler's crossroad. But its size was nothing compared to the growling red bear to the north.

Tomorrow they would head into Baky, Azerbaijan. Because of its unique location, it served as a transit country for all things illegal. It was especially notorious for human trafficking of men, women, and children. The human contraband was transported to Turkey, the United Arab Emirates and even the United States for the purposes of commercial sexual exploitation and forced labor. Even for a criminal like Lev, the cruelness of the land made his hair stand on end.

But business was business and as long as he was here he would try to make some contacts. The group he worked for needed to move Asian opiates to Russia and to a lesser extent the rest of Europe. Azerbaijan, though lawless, was a perfect meeting point to give the bomb in the back of the van to the crazy Iranian.

Goods and people traveled fairly easily along its border with Iran to the south. The border to the north with Russia was a bit more restricted; however, no self-respecting Russian border guard ever turned down a reasonable bribe. They assumed it was part of their miserly pay.

Alan D Schmitz

Baky, Azerbaijan:

Workers at the dock stared at Hamid as he got out of his covered jeep.
His cold, steely eyes dared any one of them to challenge him. The stench
of oil was everywhere; the river empting into the Caspian Sea was coated
with an oily film. The harbor itself was coated with the silvery slick for as
far as he could see. The country was supposedly rich with oil, though
looking at the old, worn-out buildings one would never guess that. For
years it sold its oil to the countries around the Caspian Sea. Soon it would
have a direct pipeline through Georgia to the Black Sea. This little area of
the world was going to be a very politically busy place. No wonder the
Russian Bear was salivating at the thought of reclaiming Georgia and
Azerbaijan as its own.

Azerbaijan had a cordial relationship with Russia but also a healthy
bit of uneasiness about Russia's intentions with their small country. This
was all the more interesting because Georgia still claimed Azerbaijan as
its territory. Of course that was to be expected now that Azerbaijan was
building a major oil pipeline to the Mediterranean Sea through Georgia.

The fact was that Azerbaijan and Georgia had nothing in common
except the agreement on the pipeline; otherwise, they were about as
different as any two countries could be. Georgia was over 80% orthodox
Christian and Azerbaijan 93% Muslim. That was why Azerbaijan made
sure it kept a very cozy relationship with its southern neighbor, Iran,
whom they thought more of as their brothers than Georgia.

Hamid detested Azerbaijan, not because of its lawlessness but because
of its people. Though they were mostly Muslims, he felt they didn't take
their faith seriously enough. As far as he was concerned, insincere
Muslims were worse than the infidels from the United States. To call
oneself a Muslim and not strictly follow the Koran was heresy.

Hamid watched cargo being loaded into a ship bound for Chalus, a
port city on the north coast of Iran. He waited for an expected call from
the one-eyed Russian.

Lev parked the van along a quiet area of an empty dock. The stench of
oil was so thick that Lev thought twice about lighting a cigarette, and
decided that this filthy place would ruin a good smoke.

"I'm parked at dock number 12." Lev spoke very briefly into his phone.

"Proceed to dock 15," the voice at the other end of the phone
instructed and then hung up.

Eduard got out of the van. Though it was warm out, he wore his long
overcoat. It did a fairly good job of concealing the guns strapped to his

126

sides. His boss ground the vehicle's transmission into gear and slowly moved down the dockside past an oil tanker, then around a corner toward a small cargo ship. Lev saw the crazy Iranian motioning for them to park nearby. The Mafioso hoped to someday make him pay for taking his eye, but unfortunately today was not that day.

As soon as he parked, the side van door was opened and guns were quickly drawn on him. Hamid stepped into the van and opened the top of the crate with an electric screwdriver, unscrewing the top lid quickly. There was very little to see. He was even more disappointed when all he saw was the stiff dark foam packing. He touched the foam lightly at first and then scratched at it when he realized how hard the material was. Lev saw the anger building in the crazy Iranian's face. He was afraid this would happen.

"How do I know the package is inside this crate?"

Lev began to feel a panic. He was well aware of the Iranian's short temper.

"Let me show you a few important openings."

With guns still pointed on him, he moved to the back of the van. Then with a tool the professor had provided, he turned a couple of large wood plugs to open them and then remove them. The plugs looked like ordinarily parts of the crate and blended in well.

Pointing to the metal caps inside the crate that were now exposed, he explained, "This is where you insert one third of the ingredients." Lev almost said enriched uranium but stopped himself short. If the men surrounding him were nothing more than paid henchmen, educating them on the shipping crate's purpose might not be very wise.

Hamid inspected the cap of the smooth metal port. When Hamid started to turn it Lev cautioned, "I wouldn't do that."

"And why not?" the Iranian Captain challenged.

"Because you could contaminate the inside," Lev defended his position. "Your people were told what to expect. If they did not brief you on what to expect, that is your problem. This is what you paid for; it is all I have so you might as well take it. My partner will send you the instructions you will need after the last payment has been made and after I arrive safely back in Moscow. He assures me that without the very precise instructions, the device will do you no good."

The mob boss wasn't bluffing; he knew he needed insurance when dealing with the knife wielding Iranian, so he and the professor developed this failsafe part of the plan together. The device would do no good without knowing exactly how much fissionable material and explosives it was designed for, or what type were needed to begin the chain reaction.

"My superiors are far more trusting than they should be," was all Hamid commented. Then he instructed to his men, "Load it up carefully."

The gunmen were very uneasy as they unloaded the crate from the truck. They knew it was expensive. Damaging it would be very bad for their health, which was an excellent reason to be cautious. From the truck it was a short, careful walk to the loading bay, where it moved by conveyor belt into the bowels of the ship through a large watertight opening.

"My superiors may be trusting, but if they are disappointed, I will be given very much latitude in setting things straight again," the Iranian warned.

Hamid walked away from the van and motioned with his hand to someone Lev couldn't see at first. Then he saw Eduard with one of the Iranian guards. Eduard was holding his right hand with his left.

"We saw this one lurking about; he didn't want to give up his gun so we were forced to take it from him. His hand needs the attention of a doctor, but I would wait until I was back in Russia if I were you. The doctors in this town are not very sympathetic to your kind."

Hamid politely opened the van door for Eduard who was moving slowly. He had obviously been beaten up some too. Before slamming the door, Hamid threatened, "The next time I see you, it will be to kill you."

Lev said under his breath, "The next time I see you 'Mudak' (Asshole), you will be saying 'hi' to Allah personally, even if I have to introduce you myself."

Chalus, Iran:

Major Hamid Shukah walked out on deck in his IRGC uniform. He had changed on board the ship. It was good to be home. The trip on the Caspian Sea, from Baky, Azerbaijan was uneventful. His superiors were waiting with a convoy of military vehicles to take the bomb to an underground facility south of the port. There was a place in the mountains not very far from there where it would be safely studied and prepared. For now his job was done and he was being rewarded with exceptional military privileges. The next week off would be a very pleasant one. Being a devout Muslim didn't mean one couldn't have fun when it was earned doing Allah's work.

128

The next phase of the operation was much more dangerous. First he had to escort the bomb loaded with fissionable materials from here to Al Lathqiyah, Syria. The first part was easy. Syria and Iran were brothers and a simple air flight over northern Iraq or southern Turkey would land him in Al Lathqiyah. Even the Americans couldn't stop that. The Syrian authorities would be more than eager to help their brothers to the east if it meant a blow to the Americans or Israelis. Al Lathqiyah was a port city on the Mediterranean Sea. From there they would take a cargo ship into the heart of the Great Satan itself. *That would be when the fun would begin*, Hamid smiled as he thought of the carnage he would bring with him. His name would go down in history and it would be held in reverence by Al Qaeda and Taliban forces through the ages.

South of Chalus, Iran (Chalus nuclear facility):

Nuclear engineer, Dr. Kourosh Alavi, examined the last set of high-powered X-rays that had been delivered to him. The scientist had the highest security clearance in the Iranian mountain laboratory. He was the physicist who developed the process of using centrifuges supplied by Russia to enrich its stores of low-grade uranium into plutonium. After the process was developed, the centrifuges had been scattered about the country into several plutonium factories for reasons of security.

Dr. Alavi would be the person in charge of loading the small bomb with the various raw materials it would need to achieve a critical nuclear reaction. He wasn't at all comfortable with the assignment. Besides the radioactivity of the fissionable materials, he was worried about the unstableness of it, particularly the plutonium. When plutonium is exposed to air, especially moist air, it becomes hot. Under the right conditions it could become hot enough to explode in a radioactive mini bomb. Plutonium also had the propensity to expand and oxidize when exposed to air; if the material expanded inside the bomb, it could destroy the multi-million dollar machine. Kourosh hoped the designer knew what he was doing. The directions for loading the various compartments were extremely detailed and specific. Other members of his team were going over the instructions line by line, looking for errors. What they found instead was that there was much to building a nuclear bomb they thought. It gave him some confidence to see the precision of the designer.

What bothered Dr. Alavi was that he would be putting these expensive and very dangerous compounds into various sleeves of the contraption that he had no idea where they lead. He could guess, but that was all he

129

Alan D Schmitz

could do. The doctor wanted desperately to know what the machine looked like, but it was encased in some sort of foam product, sealed permanently in the wood crate surrounding it.

Kourosh Alavi had a doctorate in nuclear science; he had studied in Paris, a city he didn't particularly care for. He would know a nuclear device when he saw one. The only problem was that there was no way to see this device much less its inner workings. There was only one way he could think of. Dr. Alavi stared at the X-rays some more. For some reason the first sets of X-rays were blurred and he had to double the dosage to get anything worth looking at. The pictures exposed the mechanical parts inside the foam. He could see the outline of lead tubes going down into what appeared to be a sphere. The X-rays couldn't penetrate the materials, but he could tell through careful analysis that different types of materials were used for different parts of the bomb.

Dr. Alavi ordered more x-rays to be taken from different angles. He wasn't concerned about damaging the metallic insides of the bomb with the high-powered X-rays, but what he was concerned about was the timer mechanism and any computer chips that could be damaged on a molecular level. All computers processed code. If someone put enough 1's and 0's together in the right order, a computer could be told to do anything. But if the computer lost track of even one of the billions of 1's or 0's, the computer became confused and would do nothing. Though the risk was very small, he ordered very low dose, quick X-rays to be done first. He isolated potentially sensitive areas of the bomb and they used lead shielding to protect them.

The team was on a tight timeline. He was assured that the bomb was real, but the doctor also knew that Iran wasn't capable of developing such a weapon yet. That was obvious to him because he would have been the one to develop it. He desperately wanted to know as much about the large package in the laboratory room two stories below him, as possible. What the physicist didn't realize was that the foam encasing the bomb was doing its job perfectly. It was absorbing a significant amount of the X-rays that it was being subjected to time and again. Unfortunately for the Iranians, the buildup of radiation on the exterior of the bomb would prove much more than inconvenient. The foam had been designed to absorb and contain internal radiation leaks. Now it was acting much like an electric capacitor and was storing the X-ray energy on its exterior, which it would slowly release as the radiation isotopes decayed.

Chapter 11

Milwaukee, Wisconsin:

The Seavers waited together in Dr. Howard Maslow's office. The office was very comfortably decorated with warm colors and leather-wrapped, high-back chairs. It was formal but not ostentatious. The obligatory psychologist couch was nowhere to be seen. Once inside the office it was easy to forget they were just several doors away from a busy shopping mall.

Scott had been seeing the doctor on a fairly regular basis since his diagnosis, but this was the first time they visited together. Dr. Maslow helped him with the finer points of dealing with a disease that caused his memories to come and go. Scott didn't like giving up his independence, and going to the therapy sessions alone was something he had insisted on to Liz. After all, what would be the point of learning how to navigate in the real world if you couldn't even get to a therapy session?

"Scott, you are looking well. How has it been going since the last time we talked?" Doctor Maslow asked.

Scott looked at Liz and then confessed to the doctor, "I've been feeling pretty good for the most part, but I think the medicine makes me a bit dizzy sometimes."

"This sounds like it could be serious. Why didn't you tell me sooner?"

"At first I thought it was just my mind playing tricks on me. But it seems to be getting worse. We knew that we were coming in for this visit so I thought it would be OK to wait."

Liz interrupted, "He insisted on waiting. I found out about it two weeks ago, but he made me promise not to say anything. He said he was sure it would go away."

"Scott, Liz, you have to tell me right away if you notice a change in Scott's condition." The doctor scolded a bit, and then moved on with identifying the new problem. How dizzy do you get and how long does it last?"

"Not that bad, and it doesn't last long at all!" Scott minimized the effects.

"Not that bad?" Liz protested immediately. "You fell in the dining room two days ago. I had to help you up." Liz didn't consider that Scott

131

might not remember. She just assumed he was using selective memory so he didn't have to admit his fall to anyone.

Scott honestly could not remember, but there would be no use in denying it. A man whose mind was playing tricks on him would be very hard-pressed to defend his memory as being more accurate. And one thing he had learned recently was never, ever, admit that you can't remember something if you don't have to.

"He refuses to stop driving. I get so worried," Liz complained.

"I know when I'm about to get dizzy, I can feel it coming on, and I have time to pull over if I need to," Scott defended himself.

"Scott, no more driving!" the doctor said forcefully, hoping the warning would work but realizing that there was actually little he could do about it.

Liz knew that Scott respected the doctor and was satisfied that she won this small battle. Keeping the keys hidden wouldn't be a problem; Liz was already planning on how she would ground her husband.

"You say you can feel it coming. How?"

"It's like it starts in my stomach. I can sort of feel my stomach turning over as if I'm going to get sick. I have never thrown up or anything. I just feel a bit nauseous and then the dizziness starts. It doesn't last long."

"Have you noticed any other symptoms or changes?"

Scott seemed a bit confused at the question, or he didn't want to answer. Whatever the reason, Liz took advantage of the silence.

"He seems to be forgetting more," Liz started to cry; a tear escaped from the side of her brown eyes.

Scott looked at his wife and tried to comfort her by wrapping his strong arm around her.

"Scott, what do you think?" The doctor wanted to give Liz time to collect herself.

"I think I am doing pretty well yet. I know I am prone to forget things, but by using my electronic tricks, I am still getting by."

"Liz? Why do you think Scott is forgetting more? Can you give me any specific examples?"

Liz found a rumpled up Kleenex in her purse and used it to dry her eyes. The doctor reached over and handed her a few more out of a box on his desk. Liz continued, "I think people at work are becoming suspicious, if not concerned, that something is wrong. Nobody has said anything directly to me yet, but we were at a party the other night and some of the questions people were asking me seemed a bit probing. Maybe I'm being paranoid. I just don't know.

"Sometimes I am amazed at what Scott remembers about schedules and events that we had planned long ago. But at other times, I am afraid that Scott will leave the house and forget to come home, or forget where home is."

"This condition can be very subjective," The doctor coached. "We all experience short term memory loss, especially when we are preoccupied with things such as thinking about what it is we are going to buy in the store. I have tests you can use to hopefully show a trend in memory loss or improvement over time. But the truth is that everybody's memory can fluctuate from day to day. What I'm trying to say Elizabeth, is that if you can't specifically identify that Scott's memory is getting worse, then maybe it isn't.

"After all, we all forget where we parked when coming out of a grocery store or mall once in a while. But it doesn't mean we are suffering from dementia."

Liz sheepishly looked at Scott, and then at the doctor and said, "That would never happen to Scott."

"What would never happen to Scott?" The doctor was confused.

"Forgetting where he parked."

"Everybody sometimes forgets where they park." The doctor defended his position, knowing full well that Scott Seaver, especially in his condition, would from time to time forget where he parked his car.

"Scott might," Liz corrected as Scott sat back feeling a bit smug and superior because he knew what Liz was about to say, "but his GPS phone won't. Scott found a way to use his phone to mark where his car is when he gets out. To find it again, he just hits a button and it takes him right to his car. It's amazing!"

The doctor shook his head in admiration. It was another tip he could share with his other memory-loss patients. "You find the most ingenious ways of dealing with your condition. I commend you Mr. Seaver."

Scott replied with some degree of humility. "Just because I forget things, doesn't make me stupid."

"Ohh...., Mr. Seaver, you are anything but stupid. And nobody ever accused you of being that."

Scott felt very encouraged with what the doctor was saying and asked a question he was too afraid to ask before. "What are your tests showing? You know, the brain teaser tests you make me take sometimes."

"So far, they have been inconclusive, but for your condition, that could be a good thing. Are you still taking all the medications, Scott?"

Liz could have answered for her husband because she was monitoring the medications closely, but she kept silent, realizing that the doctor wanted Scott to answer.

"Yes, I take the anxiety medication three times a day, with food." Scott knew it was a test of his memory and fortunately at this moment he could remember exactly what meds he took. "I take the magic pills morning and night, but not with the other meds." The "magic pills" was what he called the experimental drug, tridroxolene.

"We need to identify which drug, if any, is causing the dizziness. I want you to cut back on the benzodiazepine. Stop taking the noon pill. Next week we will do another memory test and see if the dizzy spells have abated. It is very possible the anti-anxiety meds are causing the problem.

"What about remembering how to work your phone or computer? Do you ever forget how to work your memory aids?" The doctor continued with questions.

Scott thought for a second. "I might hit the wrong button at times, but I don't seem to forget how to do things. Most of this stuff isn't really that hard to do once it is set up. My friend Randy helps me if I have any problems. The electronics are easy; I mostly forget what I've just done or whom I was with. I might forget whom I talked to on the phone, but I don't forget how to use the phone itself. To help me remember, I programmed the phone to record every conversation. If I forget what somebody told me, or whom I was just talking with, all I have to do is play back our conversation.

"The same is true for when I'm driving, I might forget where I'm going or where I was, but I never forget how to drive the car, if you know what I mean."

The doctor nodded approvingly but also thought about patients who eventually forgot how to walk. On the other hand, it was not unusual to have a patient who forgot the names of things, but excelled at math and could do the most complex problems until the late stages of the disease.

Liz interrupted with what she felt was an important piece of information. "Scott has always been a techie kind of guy. I think that is why he likes to fly so much. It is because of all of that electronic equipment he gets to play with. He seems to be one of those people who knows how to work these complicated things without even using the directions. It just seems to come naturally to him."

"It certainly seems that way," the doctor agreed, then tried to get the conversation back to Scott's symptoms.

"Do you remember any other notable experiences?"

"That's great doc, you are asking me to tell you about the things I forgot."

Liz and Dr. Maslow chuckled at the irony of Scott's observation.

Scott smiled and then continued, glad he got his wife to laugh a bit; that always made him happy.

"Sometimes I end up home instead of wherever it is I was supposed to go to."

"Why is that?"

"If I forget to program in the GPS or I am driving and I can't remember where I'm going, I just tell the GPS to take me home and I call it a day."

"That is very prudent of you. It seems that you are adjusting and your memory tricks are keeping you safe and active. But for now, you have to stop driving until I say it is OK again. Do you understand?"

"OK, I guess," Scott reluctantly agreed. But in his heart he had his fingers crossed to cancel out the promise.

"Next week, same time," the doctor reminded and then added, "And Scott, don't forget!" He joked with his patient.

"Forget what?" Scott was always quick with a comeback. He lifted his phone out of his pocket as he stood and checked his calendar to make sure the appointment was listed and a reminder bell was set. Scott had learned from the doctor to never put off making reminders. Lately Scott realized that he was checking on appointments over and over again. He knew that he didn't trust his own memory anymore; perhaps he was making himself dependant on his electronic crutches. As Liz and Scott started out of the office, the doctor spoke to Elizabeth with a reminder.

"And Elizabeth, please call me anytime, for anything, especially if you feel something is not right. Scott's judgment may not always be the best."

"Scott's judgment has always been suspect to me, doctor," Liz shot back proving that there was more than one Seaver who was quick-witted.

Scott made a marking gesture in the air giving his wife a point for the pun at his expense.

Liz drove away from the busy mall and turned onto US45 north. The traffic was fairly light on the freeway as they headed home. She felt more comfortable driving her small, midsized sedan than Scott's oversized SUV. Scott, of course, felt just the opposite. The Friday rush hour traffic hadn't started, though soon it would be busy with people going home from work or to their summer cottages for the weekend. There weren't going to be that many days of summer left to enjoy.

"Scott, you cannot drive until we know you don't get dizzy anymore. You understand that, right?" Liz rather sternly reminded her husband.

"I heard the doctor," Scott admitted without necessarily agreeing with the new rule. Scott knew better than to argue about it, at least not now. He would have to let a few days pass before he could start to convince his wife that he was OK again. He just prayed he didn't have another one of his dizzy spells, because if Liz saw it, he knew he would be grounded for quite a while.

"We will have to tell Jerry soon. He has to make plans for running the office without you. It's not fair to him for you to lead him on like this." Liz breached a sensitive topic.

"Well, a lot of things in life aren't fair," Scott reminded her with a touch of resentment. *Do you think this is FAIR to me?* Scott thought to himself. Scott felt anger build inside of him and what he wanted to say to his wife but didn't. *Damn it Liz. This wasn't part of the deal. I could accept getting my ass shot down, or crashing during a rescue mission, even getting tortured, but not slowly dying, losing my mind piece by piece.* Scott hit the side of the car door with his fist in a semi-controlled bit of rage. "Liz, I'm not going to get better, am I?" Scott asked with fear in his voice.

The car was quiet for a few minutes. Liz wasn't upset that her husband angrily hit the car. She had punched her share of walls and pillows herself lately. Life wasn't fair and she was losing her best friend, lover, and father of their daughter a little more every day.

Liz couldn't help herself. She swore that she would be strong for Scott's sake, but she started to cry. "I'm so afraid honey. I don't want to be alone, and I don't want to be without you."

Liz answered his question in as direct a way as she could. Scott took a deep breath. "I'm sorry Liz; life isn't being fair to either of us. You're strong honey, you'll be fine. You know that if you find the right guy when I'm gone I want you to re-marry or whatever. I don't want you to be alone."

"Scott Seaver!" Liz shouted back in anger. "Don't you dare talk like that." Then she repeated herself in a much more calm but demanding voice. "Don't you dare talk to me like that, Scott."

The car was quiet for another couple of miles before Liz spoke again, "We don't know what will happen; nobody does. Scott, you have to understand that the only way I can deal with this is to assume the best, not the worst. You are right; I will deal with whatever happens, when it happens, just like we did when Brad died. But I refuse to accept a future without you right now, OK?"

"OK, I won't bring it up again, unless of course I forget. You know having a great excuse for forgetting things might come in handy from time to time," Scott joked.

Scott kept to himself the fact that he couldn't remember who Brad was. He was quite sure that was the name Liz brought up; it certainly sounded familiar. He would have to research it when he had time. Then again, maybe it would come to him. Often if he gave certain things enough time, a name or image would pop into his mind when he least expected it. *Brad, Brad, Brad,* he thought, trying to remember.

"I hate to bring it up, but...." Liz brought up another issue Scott had been putting off. "You can't stay on medical leave from the National Guard forever either. You can't expect Bob to hold your spot for much longer."

Scott didn't respond. Giving up his pilot spot would be the final gesture of being beaten by this disease. More than anything else, it would be throwing in the towel, admitting defeat. He didn't know if he could do that.

Liz answered the silence cautiously. "Scott, you did important work, now it's time to let someone else do it," Liz counseled gently. "The Guard needs to have all the pilot spots filled."

"I guess that would be the point for me to realize from now on."

Liz was puzzled. "What would be the point?"

"I did important work, past tense, Liz. I 'did' important work, but not anymore."

"That's not true. Dr. Maslow says that many of the things you are doing to cope with this disease he can use to teach others to do as well. You are helping a lot of people in ways you don't even know." Scott looked at his wife, and as he did, Liz took a brief glance at her husband's eyes and saw the glint of a thank you in them, but also the look of a false compliment accepted.

"Besides!" Liz reminded. "The Hueys are all gone now. You would have to learn to fly one of those new-fangled Black Hawks. You know they would never be as good as the Hueys were," Liz said quoting one of Scott's favorite sayings.

"Yeah, you're right." Scott took the bait willingly. "All the darn things ever do is crash."

Husband and wife laughed at Scott's joke. He had filled in Liz on all of the times he crashed the simulator during training.

137

Scott reflected a bit as he stared out the window at the passing scenery, not really paying any attention to the wooded, rolling hills in the distance. "You want to know the truth Liz?" Scott asked so quietly Liz was glad she was paying close enough attention to hear him.

"What honey?"

"I haven't flown for quite a while. I don't know if I would remember how to fly even the old Huey's anymore. Learning a completely new and much more complicated Black Hawk would be impossible for me. We both know that. I have just been postponing the inevitable. I guess I've been waiting for a miracle."

Liz glanced over at her husband whose head was leaning against the side door window. She saw a tear sliding down his cheek. Reaching out, she held his hand and said firmly, "You will never forget how to fly, I promise. And you know what I think?"

"I'm sure you'll tell me."

"I think that you should just keep on waiting for a miracle. Lord knows you have given up a lot for your country, and you and I have been through a lot already. Maybe it's payback time. Let's wait for that miracle together. Let's stall Bob for a bit longer." Liz knew that everybody needed something to hope for and Scott didn't have much anymore. She wasn't about to be the one to take his last hope away.

They were almost home when Scott announced a decision. "I think that after the Chicago job is finished I will retire. I feel tired and I need to concentrate on getting better. The preliminary work is coming along fine; I just want to see this one last project to an end. It shouldn't be long, a few more weeks. After that, I will tell Jerry I'm retiring, and as long as I'm at it, I might as well resign from the Guard too. Then I can stay home and sail with you and relax. Dr. Maslow said that would be good for me."

After a brief pause, Scott blurted, "I have an idea, as long as I can't drive to work, why don't I take off a week and we can go on a sailing vacation? There isn't much summer left; I certainly have vacation time coming."

"But your dizzy spells," Liz argued.

"I'll wear a life jacket at all times, even when we are exploring the islands if you'd like. Avery will be back in school before you know it and then it will be too late. Let's face it; soon it might be too late for me to do something like this."

"You know Avery would love it." Liz already started to agree with the idea.

That was when Scott knew it was a go. As soon as Liz started to say it was good for Avery, he knew they were headed for the water. Liz saw Scott's eyes light up at the thought. She had to admit that they were so involved with Dad not feeling right lately, they were beginning to ignore their daughter.

Al Lathqiyah, Syria:

Major Shukah sat on a pile of wood pallets next to a crate marked "Fragile." The ship that would carry him and the crate to America was already loaded with large shipping containers. In fact, the entire cargo of all steel containers was from his enemy to the south, Israel. The ISO containers lifted off a semi-trailer and stacked one on top of another on the wide flat ship deck. It was a very efficient way of moving a large number of products across the ocean and then by land again.

The air flight from Iran to Syria was uneventful; the disguised bomb was moved by a commercial passenger airline. The crew didn't realize how close they were to the makings of a nuclear bomb, and the fact that Iran owned the airline helped with the lack of documentation. Much in the same way, the Syrian authorities were equally uninterested about what was being delivered from Iran.

Hamid looked out over the busy port; his superiors had assured him that the captain of the "Damascus Star" was a patriot. The Damascus Star was owned by East Star Lines, which was in turn owned by another parent company. How his superiors knew that this captain was loyal to their cause, was of course none of his business. But, Hamid did know about the rumors of the parent company. It seems the company that ultimately owned the ship he was taking to the United States had been a large leaseholder of office space in the once mighty Twin Towers in New York. For some reason, about two weeks before the 9-11 bombing, the company decided to move out of its offices despite it costing them over $50,000 dollars to break the lease. What the Iranian didn't understand was that Israel was a majority owner of that same company.

Major Hamid Shukah didn't believe in coincidences, so how did the Israelis know about the plot to bomb the New York towers? A better question was why? And if they did, why didn't they tell the Americans, or did they? Major Shukah knew that some things were way above his rank and this was certainly one of them.

He found it truly ironic that he was going to use an Israeli registered ship, owned by an Israeli company, which was ultimately owned by Israel

Alan D Schmitz

itself, the good friends of the Americans, to carry a nuclear bomb into the heart of the United States. But what better way to fool the Americans than to take a Trojan Horse into the middle of their castle. An Israeli registered ship would be a lot less suspect than a Syrian one, that was certain. As a side bonus, the Israeli ship was carrying high tech medical imaging devices to the United States. These devices use low-grade radioactive material to create their images, which provided the perfect cover if by chance the bomb leaked small amounts of radioactive gases that could be detected. Somebody on his side knew exactly what they were doing.

As customary, most of the crew would be gone tonight, either out on the town for one last fling or spending the time with loved ones before being gone for the next month at sea. This is when the captain of the Damascus Star would help him carry his small crate onto the ship and store it in a smuggler's hold, a place on the ship that only the captain knew about. Apparently this captain was used to smuggling. Hamid just didn't know if it was always for personal gain, or more lofty goals. But for this mission, the ends certainly did justify the means.

Lake Ontario, Canada/US:

Hamid stood on deck smoking his favorite brand of Iranian tobacco. He inhaled a heavy dose of the harsh smoke as he watched a small plane fly overhead and off to the east. After a few more puffs, his enjoyment of the strong tobacco came to an end. He had smoked it down to as small a stub as possible. Hamid had a pouch of the tobacco in his cabin, but had rolled only one cigarette. Now that it was gone, his unoccupied hands felt strangely unnatural and he craved for another. In front of him was the first of the Great Lakes, Lake Ontario, half in Canada and half in the U.S.

The captain of the Damascus Star had told Hamid that the Americans and Canadians worked so closely together guarding these waters that it didn't matter which country they sailed into. The countries had developed something called the Integrated Maritime Security Operation. They had nicknamed it Shiprider, because American Coast Guard officers and the Royal Canadian Mounted Police would jointly man each other's vessels. Thus when making a stop, both countries were represented. If in Canadian waters the RCMP would be the officers in charge. In U.S. waters, the Coast Guard would be in charge.

So far, one boarding party had inspected the ship, making Hamid's heartbeat a bit faster. But all they were concerned about was an

140

examination of the ballast tanks. There were strict laws against contaminating the lakes with foreign creatures. Each ship had to have a ballast tank inspection each season on its first entry into the fresh water lakes. Other than that, nobody but the canal pilots had boarded the ship. He had been expecting some sort of search party but they were about to enter the heart of the United States unhampered. The canal pilot's job was to navigate the ship through the series of locks. Each section of locks had its own set of expert pilots to guide the giant ships. As the Iranian understood the system of locks, some were owned and run by the Canadians, infidels for sure, but not meddlers. And some of the locks were owned and run by the Americans.

Up until now they had been in Canadian waters. Now the American side could be easily seen to the south. The route this far took over a month, far longer than Hamid expected. The captain had made many stops and it had taken forever to cross out of the Mediterranean Sea and into the Atlantic. Hamid didn't know if all the stops were normal or if it was an effort to protect the ship and captain from suspicion of wrongdoing. With all the stops the captain had made, it would be impossible to know where a certain piece of contraband had come from.

The terrorist used his satellite phone to call his contact, another Mujahideen, who would meet him in Chicago. Back in Tehran, the government had a special task force that identified possible compatriots in cities across the United States. Most were found through Internet chat pages. Iran had trusted agents in the U.S. to search out and identify potential "moles." These were common, everyday people, often U.S. citizens, who were sympathetic to Islam and the Jihad against the Americans. Often these people would wait for years, living ordinary American lives, before being called upon by their handlers.

The Iranian's satellite phone had several advantages over a standard cell phone. The Iranian special operations commander could be in communication with his superiors from anywhere in the world. Even in the middle of the ocean he could make and receive calls. Another advantage the satellite phone had over a typical cell phone was that he couldn't be traced. Everyone knew that the location of a cell phone could be discovered by using cell tower triangulation. But with his satellite phone, even if someone did crack the encrypted call, they couldn't know where the sender and receiver of the message were located. A downside to this type of communication was that he had to be outside with an unobstructed view to the satellite miles above him in space.

From now on, Hamid would be using his alias of Kassim. His handlers in Iran gave him fake identification incase he was discovered. At the final meeting with his superiors, he was told that the great city of Chicago would be his target. With a population of over three million people, it was the largest city in the American heartland. And his superiors were very intent on striking the heart of the "Great Satan". A devastating strike in the middle of their country would send an important message to the infidels, they could not hide like cowards from the great jihad.

Chicago also had the second largest central business district in the entire U.S. The blow to the infidels' heart would reverberate through the country. It would take years for them to recover.

The Iranian major had studied the area around the harbor of Chicago. Delivering the large bomb would be made easier by the river that wound its way through the city's center. The Damascus Star itself would not be permitted to go up the Chicago River, the freighter was too big. But going up the river was critical to the plan so he had his contact arrange for a small private boat for this purpose.

It would be Hamid's job to make sure that when the bomb went off, it would be in the financial heart of Chicago, as near to the Sears Tower as possible. Not only would it take down the famous Sears Tower but also many of the other so-called skyscrapers built in the same area. Its initial destruction would be far greater than what the two planes did to the New York towers. But that would only be the beginning. The ensuing firestorm, power outages and radiation contamination would destroy forever the American city. This would be far different from New York; this time there would be no rebuilding. To the east of the Great City was only a huge expanse of water. If Allah prevailed on that particular day in the not too distant future, the wind would be right and blow the radiation either south, north or west, killing millions more.

Hamid stared toward the American side of the shore. He lifted the collar of his coat. It was getting cold on deck even though it was still late summer. Then he flicked his cigarette into the canal. If everything went as planned, he would ride this same ship to safety and be back home before the winter came. If things didn't go as planned, he would be one with Allah much sooner, and Allah would reward him then, also an acceptable outcome. He placed his fate in Allah's hands, which gave him peace.

Chapter 12

Mackinac (mak-in-aw) Island, Michigan:

My Chopper graced the seascape. It tilted away from the wind pushing it under the huge bridge. Her sails were full and her sleek lines made it part of the water through which it cut. The crew was in the perfect location to view the panorama of the huge suspension bridge connecting the Upper Michigan Peninsula with the Lower Michigan Peninsula. This was undoubtedly Scott's favorite spot on the lake. The five-mile long Mackinac Bridge canopied over them as My Chopper raced under it. The five-mile wide strait connecting huge Lake Michigan with the equally massive Lake Huron could be treacherous and busy with seagoing vessels that had made their way through the St. Lawrence Seaway. Today it was neither; there was only one other sleek sailing vessel, even larger than theirs, racing in the opposite direction. The crew of My Chopper waved their arms with a big greeting to the passing boat as the people on the opposite deck returned the favor. A few miles back they had waved to the crew on the deck of a container ship called the Damascus Star, but otherwise, for whatever reason, the shipping lanes were fairly quiet. It wouldn't be long before they would be at one of the family's favorite destinations, Mackinac Island. "Drop and tie the sails you two mangy deck rats," Scott yelled over the wind blowing past them. It was much louder than he had to yell, but he wanted to make sure they heard him call them the derogatory sailing term.

"Aye, aye Captain Baggy Pants," Avery teased back. She was positively in the best mood a teenager could be in.

They brought the sails down and tied them off tightly. The crew was very well trained. Scott started the engine for a much slower ride up to the dock. They couldn't help but soak up the grandeur of the island park. The Grand Hotel always took center stage for visitors to the island. It sat on a hillside overlooking the lake; the huge Victorian hotel with giant white pillars running the 660-foot length of the hotel was truly impressive.

"I'll race you to the fudge shop," Scott challenged his daughter, as they finished tying up the boat for an overnight visit.

Alan D Schmitz

The island was designated as a Michigan State Park. Motor vehicles of any kind were not allowed on the island in order to preserve its turn of the century experience. Racing down the street filled with nothing but pedestrian tourists seemed like a pretty good idea to Scott, and a race to one of the island's many famous fudge shops sounded even better.

Mom laughed as father and daughter lined up at the designated starting line. Scott cheated and started running before he said "GO." There was no question who would win the race but Scott gave his daughter a good run. Exercise was something his doctors prescribed, though they wouldn't have had to. Exercise and staying fit had been part of Scott's mental makeup from high school on. While in the military, being physically fit was vital to being mentally alert behind the controls of his Huey. Staying fit was a survival skill, not just good body mechanics. Dr. Maslow assured Scott that by keeping a healthy blood flow to the brain he could maximize its own recuperative powers.

The run to the fudge and ice cream shop was all uphill from the dock. Avery was already in line catching her breath when Scott dragged himself past the T-shirt store next door.

"You are getting old Dad; you used to be able to run most of the way."

The other parents in line smiled at Scott and everyone over forty saw their own mortality in Scott's struggles.

"Don't talk so smart, young lady; I can't wait to see how well you do against your fourteen-year-old son or daughter. You won't even make it past the dock."

"No, because I'll be pushing you in a wheel chair."

That shouted comment made most of the other tourist in line laugh out loud.

"I'm counting on it!" Scott huffed back, out of breath.

Liz wasn't too far behind, though she hadn't run. She was too busy taking in the crisp air off the lake and looking at the colorful Victorian cottages that lined the street. It didn't take much imagination for the island to take a person back to the late eighteen hundreds. There were no cars on the streets, only horse drawn carriages taking guests and cargo from the doc to the main hotel, which of course was "The Grand Hotel".

For the first time in months, Liz felt relaxed. Today and yesterday had been perfect, and she was feeling refreshed. All of their cares and problems seemed to have been left farther behind with each mile they sailed. Seeing Scott in his true element, sailing on the lake, no cares and no worries aside from which way the wind was blowing, made her appreciate the man he still was. The past few days there were no fainting or dizzy spells; in fact Scott seemed so completely normal and healthy that both of them had, at times, forgotten about his illness. That was a blessing.

By the time she reached her husband and daughter, they were next in line to be served.

"Talk about perfect timing honey, what would you like?"

"A big fat two-scoop praline sugar cone."

"One thousand calorie ice cream cone coming up; make that two." Scott decided on getting the exact same thing.

"Make that three!" Avery changed the order again and then added. "And two squares of white chocolate fudge with almonds."

"Two pieces of fudge?" Dad asked.

"Yep, because if I only get one you will eat at least half of it."

"So you mean the second one is for me?"

"That's right Dad."

"Good thinking," Dad agreed.

"After this, let's rent some bikes and explore the back side of the island. We have all day and let's not waste one second of it," Mom suggested.

"Sounds like work, but I'm game," Scott agreed.

Liz made a mental note to give Scott his medication later in the day. They were having so much fun and their daily rituals were so disrupted by the vacation that she and Scott had both been forgetting to keep his medications on schedule. This was further complicated by trying to keep Avery from noticing her father's new medication.

Lake Michigan – Off Two Rivers, Wisconsin, heading south:

"Mom, what's the matter with Dad?" Avery asked her mother as My Chopper sailed back to its homeport.

Mother and daughter were sitting together at the front of the boat. It was a hot day and not very windy. Scott had the boat under sail but it was a very leisurely pace. Every now and then if the bow hit a wave just right a bit of water would spray up and cool the two women up front.

"What do you mean?" The question caught Liz off guard.

"Well duh! He doesn't go flying anymore for starters. And how come you are always reminding him of things? You never get mad at him when he forgets something anymore."

"What do you mean anymore? I never got mad at Dad for forgetting things."

145

Alan D Schmitz

"Oh yes you did. He forgot your anniversary once and man you got pissed."

"Avery Rose! That is no way for a young lady to talk. Besides, that was different; he should have remembered."

"But it was your birthday two weeks ago and I heard you remind him twice not to forget because we were going out that night and you didn't get mad at all when he forgot completely."

"Your father has a lot on his mind. I just didn't want him to forget and make other plans."

"Then how come you have to remind him to take his pills every morning and night, and why do you count them? And why is he taking pills? Mom, I'm not a little girl any more. You can tell me. I know he is always forgetting things, then he goes to his phone to look things up, and then he forgets what it was he was trying to remember. And I've noticed when Dad leaves the house he doesn't give Brad's picture a finger kiss anymore."

"A finger kiss?" Liz asked, not understanding the term.

"Yea, you know, every day before leaving for work, Dad would kiss his finger and then touch it to Brad's picture on the wall. But he doesn't even look at the picture anymore."

Liz looked away at the distant shoreline. As soon as she did, Avery knew that she was right; something was wrong with her father.

"You're right honey; you are not a little girl anymore. And you are very perceptive."

"I'm not supposed to tell you this, and you are going to have to be very brave with what I am going to share with you. And, it has to be our secret because nobody else knows, not even Jerry."

"I promise," Avery agreed solemnly.

"The doctors don't know exactly what is wrong with Dad but he is starting to forget things. He will have to retire from work."

Avery looked away, out over the water; this was one time she wanted her mother to assure her that she was mistaken. Deep inside she knew her mother wasn't, but just the same, being treated like an adult could suck sometimes.

"Will he forget me, like he forgot Brad?"

"Dad will never forget you, and he certainly hasn't forgotten Brad."

The bow caught a bigger wave, splashing both women heavily.

"SORRY!" Scott yelled from the back of the boat.

"YEAH RIGHT!" Mother and daughter yelled back at the same time, suspecting that the pilot of the boat had something to do with the wave hitting just right.

"Sweetheart, he is still your father and always will be. He loves you so much you can't understand. He is very smart; it is just that until the doctors can figure out exactly why he forgets things, he might need our help from time to time remembering."

The depth finder was showing shallower waters. They were following the eastern coastline of the Wisconsin shore south, back to Port Washington. It was time to tack out, away from land for a while.

"Boom on the move," Scott shouted.

The two gals were nowhere near the boom, but Scott liked to keep good sailing habits. And warning all aboard that the sail was going to move was a good habit he liked to practice.

Mother and daughter talked a bit more, and as they talked Liz would glance back at her man behind the helm of the boat, smiling her approval of the ride. Then she caught something different in his eyes, she realized that Scott had drifted off to some unknown place though he was still steering the boat.

Liz didn't understand why he left the helm to walk the short distance to the main cabin door, but then she heard him shout loudly. "Brad, get up here and help your poor dad; I need a break."

Liz and Avery froze; they glanced at the confused expression in each other's eyes and then turned to look at Scott. He was still gazing down the hatchway expecting someone to come through it.

"Stay here." Liz pressed on her daughter's limp shoulders as she stood and made her way to the stern of the boat.

"Brad buddy, I need your help!" Scott shouted down the hatchway again.

Liz was so confused she didn't know how to handle this situation. She had never expected this to happen. Never!

"Honey, I'll help you. But let's put down the sails. We are almost home and I would like to go under diesel power."

"Sure honey, no problem."

Scott seemed to have been sufficiently distracted and forgot about calling for his son below deck.

Avery helped her mother with the sails; Scott kept the boat tacking true as the sails came down. With a click of a switch the diesel engine kicked on. The familiar tilt of the craft was now gone as they straightened to go into the harbor a few miles off under engine power.

147

Liz noticed Scott staring down the hatchway to the galley. Then she saw his face turn ghost white. "Brad is dead. Oh my god. Brad is dead," Scott remembered. "What was I thinking? How could I have forgotten that?"

Scott looked at his wife, then at his daughter. "Dear god, what's happening to me?"

Scott sank down to his knees as if in pain. Then he thrust his head over the side and started to puke and cry. "Brad, Brad, I miss you, I love you." He cried and threw up some more. When he finally collected himself, he instructed his wife.

"Liz, you got the boat; I have to go below."

Liz nodded in agreement. Below deck Scott cried like he never cried before. It was like he had just lost his son anew.

The accident itself was not in his memory, which was a blessing. Scott wouldn't have wanted to remember it, even if he could. Brad died because he lost control of the pick-up truck. The accident was his fault, which was all Scott needed to know.

Liz's seamanship was not as good as her husband's but she could easily handle the boat under its diesel power. As Liz was docking the boat, Scott came up still visibly shaken. He helped Liz and Avery as the family silently packed up the boat before driving home.

After a very uncomfortable and quiet ride home, Scott felt compelled to talk to his daughter about his condition. With his wife's encouragement, he knocked softly on her bedroom door before being invited in.

"Hi honey."

"Hi Dad." The early teen felt uncomfortable but not nearly as uncomfortable as her father.

"Sweetheart, I want..., I need to talk to you about today."

"You don't have to; Mom already told me that you forget things. I understand," Avery bravely offered.

"I wish I understood. The doctors think that I might have bumped my head too hard a few too many times. The injuries didn't seem so bad at the time, but lately the effects have become worse. That is why I forget things. I have medicine to help me but we were having so much fun I forgot to take it the last few days."

"Are you going to forget me like Grandma forgot who you were?"

Scott hugged his daughter as hard as he dared. "Sweetheart, I promise I will never forget you, never."

"But you forgot Brad," Avery reminded through choked back tears.

"But I didn't. We were having such a wonderful time that I started to remember all the good times we had with your brother. I didn't forget Brad, I was remembering all about him. In fact I remembered him so well I forgot he was gone. So you see, I won't forget you, and I didn't forget Brad."

"Then what kind of things won't you remember?"

"I might not remember that I grounded you for something. How's that?"

Avery smiled.

"Or I might not remember that you didn't eat your dinner so I'll take you out for an ice cream."

Avery laughed a bit as her father jabbed her in her rib cage trying to tickle her.

"Or, I might not remember that I already bought you a birthday present and get you two by mistake."

Avery hugged her father. He could always make her laugh and feel better, even when she didn't want to.

"Or, I might not remember we just had a vacation and take you on another one. Say to Yellowstone Park. What do you think of that?"

Avery looked up. "Are you serious, Dad?"

"Why not. I'm thinking of retiring and will have the time. Let's get one of those giant motor homes. It will be just like sailing on land.

"In fact, why don't we find your mother and tell her our idea over an ice cream?"

Watertown, New York:

Agent Louis Platt sipped on his coffee. The cup was still half full. He made a face at the taste of the cold coffee in it. He had ignored his coffee a bit too long as he went over the high-resolution pictures of the various ships coming down the St. Lawrence Seaway into Lake Ontario. The agent was comparing the printout of the timeline from the radiation detection equipment with the timeline from the high-resolution pictures.

Jeff, the scientist on his team, had located radiation in the atmosphere over the lake in much higher quantities than there should be, even when accounting for background radiation. Louis compared the radiation printout with copies from other flights over the same area only weeks before. He meant to get to this particular flight much earlier in the week, but the weather had been so nice and the seaway so busy that his team spent most of the time flying their modified Cessna T210 single

149

engine airplane over potential targets. He looked out his window at the rain pounding down on the cars in the parking lot. *Good plan,* agent Louis congratulated himself as he stared at the pouring rain and listened to the crack of thunder. "I love a free car wash," he said to himself whimsically as he stretched a ruler over his desk to help him compare the two documents side by side.

There appeared to be several ships that could be potential sources. Louis did a simple bracketing procedure. Two were still inside the St. Lawrence River; three had started to head out on course through the big lake. The Canadians and his counterparts at the relevant ports of entry would have to be notified. One thing he was pretty sure of right now was that one of those ships had something nuclear onboard that was leaking. That was what he was paid to find. He couldn't wait to finally write a report that had something in it besides "Nothing suspicious to report."

Milwaukee, Wisconsin:

Dr. Maslow was trying to be sympathetic to the tearful Seavers. He didn't want to lose his objectivity, but it was hard to ignore his human side. Scott was still severely distraught by the sudden revelation on the boat that his son Brad was dead. As soon as possible after the incident they went to Dr. Maslow's office for a consultation.

"How could I have ever forgotten about my son? I killed him, and now I've forgotten him," Scott sobbed.

Dr. Maslow gently pushed Scott's slumped shoulders up against the back of the chair so he could look him in the eyes as he talked.

"Scott, you didn't kill him, it was an accident that you tried to prevent. And as far as forgetting certain things, you can't help it. You know that you have a medical condition that causes your memory to lapse." Then he said more forcefully. "It is not your fault you forgot; you have no control over these things."

Liz was sobbing too; she could feel the pain her husband was going through. Yet she was angry with him. How could he have forgotten about their son? She certainly understood the situation, yet forgetting about their dead son was unforgivable. She listened to the doctor talk to her husband hoping it would help her cope too.

"The pain of realizing he was gone was horrible," Scott recanted. "It was like having him die all over again."

"Scott." The doctor talked slowly making sure he had his patient's complete attention. "You told me what you said to your daughter to comfort her. Those were some very wise words and you were right. You didn't forget about your son, your memories never died, you were remembering him in the way we all like to remember someone dear to us who has passed on. You were remembering him as vibrant and alive and part of the family. It is just that your mind made the memories very real. And now we might have an idea as to what is happening when you blank out, you may be regressing to past memories."

Scott thought back on the moment when he had called to Brad. That moment was wonderful; he could see his son in his mind's eye. Brad was there with them on the vacation. That was why it was so painful when he realized the truth; it was as if Brad had died then and there. The idea that he hadn't forgotten his son was comforting to him. He thought back to that fateful Christmas when he was going to give Brad a .22-caliber semi-automatic rifle. Brad never saw the gun. To this day it was still in its gift-wrapping in Brad's room. Scott tried to visualize his son's face and the smile that was often on it. He could see it right now. Scott concentrated on that smile. He never wanted to forget his son again and never wanted to have to re-experience the grieving process or suffer the initial shock of realizing that his son died.

Liz was as shaken by the episode as Scott. "I didn't know what to do. Poor Avery, she had to experience such a terrible scene."

"Elizabeth!" the doctor continued gently. "From what you told me, you and Scott handled it exceptionally well. I think that I should talk with Avery soon. Unfortunately this disease affects the whole family, and obviously you can't protect your daughter any longer.

Elizabeth remembered something else the doctor had just said and asked. "What about if Scott is regressing as you suggested?"

Doctor Maslow looked at Scott when he answered. "It could be your mind going back to those painful memories that you think you forgot. Yet your mind can't accept the pain from those memories, so when you wake up from the daydreams, everything is conveniently forgotten again. It seems to me that you may have found a way to cope with all of the terrible things that happened. But this worries me; I don't think your mind can do this tug of war with itself much longer. I would like to try hypnosis at one of our next few sessions."

"What for?" Scott asked.

"To see if we can make you consciously remember these incidents."

"But doc., I don't want to remember them."

"I think you have created a wall in your mind to protect you from those awful thoughts. But that wall is getting bigger and stronger, blocking more and more memories. It could be that your physical injuries are nothing compared to the emotional scars. I, of course, can't know for sure, but what if breaking down that wall starts the healing process that you never let happen. What if you could eventually be made whole again by accepting the memories back into your life?"

"Doc., I can't. I just can't."

Elizabeth suggested, "What if it helped, what if it made you better? Wouldn't that be worth it?"

Scott was starting to perspire and was visibly shaking. Then he folded his arms across his chest as if in pain. He looked at Liz, "You don't understand..., I..., I am afraid to remember them with every fiber of my being. I think the memories will kill me, that's how afraid I am of them. Even if I could remember, I know I mustn't. I don't want to feel that pain and see the results of my actions. I just couldn't bear it."

To the doctor, it was obvious that he struck a nerve, a very tender and delicate nerve. That made him more convinced than ever that it was a direction worth pursuing. He only hoped that it wasn't already too late.

"Please think about it Scott, it could be important," The doctor urged and ended the session. His patient had already been through enough for the day.

Chicago, Illinois:

Dr. Michael Stark watched the equipment in front of him to make sure it was recording properly. The helicopter was bouncing from low air turbulence, but Michael had learned long ago to ignore it. The only time it bothered him was when he tried to adjust a sensor and his hand would bounce away from the controls, like it just did. So he tried again with success. He checked the high-resolution camera; it was clicking away at the rate of one picture every five seconds. The camera downloaded the images to a computer as it took them. Mike liked to watch out the windows at things happening in real time, though the truth was that he could study the high-resolution pictures on the computer in front of him and probably learn much more. But the pictures could be looked at forever, and the human eyes scanning the entire area would only happen now. He double-checked the equipment making sure it was working properly as he scanned the harbor and ships below.

The doctor of nuclear science worked for the Office of Emergency Response at the National Nuclear Security Administration. When introducing himself, he would say that he worked for the NNSA. Of course most people only heard the NSA, or National Security Administration. That gave him a bit more street credibility so he usually didn't correct anyone regarding their assumptions.

They were scanning ships in the Chicago Harbor. Their job was to help the Coast Guard and Dock Patrol. More specifically his job was to detect weapons of mass destruction before it was too late.

All ships had to submit copies of their shipping manifest before entering the United States, so Michael had a pretty good idea of where each ship came from and what it was suppose to be carrying. Of particular interest was the ship "Damascus Star." An interagency e-mail from Agent Louis Platt had advised the team to be particularly concerned with the freighter. He warned that the Damascus Star was giving off signs of radiation when their plane flew over it, but the readings were very minor, likely false.

However, the shipping manifest did contain a possible explanation. The ship was carrying high-end medical scanners from Israel. They shouldn't leak, but the scanners used electromagnetic radiation similar to the gamma radiation that the NNSA high tech pictures were monitoring for, and that made Michael suspicious. On the other hand, the NNSA equipment was so sensitive that it would flag someone as being radioactive if he or she had been a recent patient examined by such a machine. Michael and his team wouldn't ignore it. He looked at such coincidences as an opportunity to use their training and break the boredom of months of no activity.

The scientist and the rest of his team didn't mind being paid to be bored stiff though, because their job was the last hope of staving off a catastrophic attack. If they found something serious, that meant it had already passed through many layers of defense against such nuclear smugglers. Michael was just one scientist of two thousand who were recruited by the United States to use their expertise to detect minute quantities of plutonium or highly enriched uranium.

Because of an earlier call from an NNSA team near the St. Lawrence Seaway, Michael had the background of the ship, its cargo, and its captain and crew with him already. The other teams suspicions proved correct, his instruments were picking up the same thing as his counterpart who flew over the ship as it entered into Lake Ontario. The helicopter he rode in was piloted by agent Mitchell. While Mike was a scientist by training, Agent Matthew Mitchell was FBI through and through. Mitchell was well trained by the FBI and had been a field agent for twenty years. Matt learned to expect the unexpected and always

153

carried his gun, which to Michael was comforting. The group worked well as a team, but if push came to shove, there was no question that Matt Mitchell was the agent in charge. Another member of their small team was a bomb expert. It sounded a lot like Hollywood to Michael, but if they ever found a bomb, somebody had to disarm it. You couldn't just toss a nuclear bomb into a nearby sewer and run for cover.

Michael and the entire team had already come to terms with the fact that if they found a bomb they would either disarm it or die trying. The lives of thousands of other people would depend on their skills. Michael and Matthew both considered themselves lucky to have Detrick Hans Krier on their team, someone they considered one of the best bomb diffusion experts in the program. If Dieter couldn't disarm it, then nobody could. And if he couldn't, there wouldn't be time for Dieter to say "oops..," they would all disintegrate in a matter of microseconds.

On the ship, the Iranian terrorist watched the small helicopter fly over head, assuming that it was a sightseeing ride of some sort. The Iranian major soaked up the sunshine. His associate on the small pleasure craft commented earlier how this was a beautiful September day for the Great Lakes. Hamid's associate was a young man named Behrouz Golzar who had rendezvoused with the freighter the prior evening.

The freighter Damascus Star was not unloading its cargo yet. Hamid and Behrouz could see the ship from the marina where they were docked, but the only thing that had been transferred off it was a delicate shipping crate, and even that had been done from the middle of Lake Michigan. It was a dangerous operation, especially to be done at night, but it was a risk that had to be taken.

Captain FarzAm Zarin had slowed his ship down as much as he dared while most the crew was asleep. Captain Zarin, a now bearded Major Shukah and another trusted crewmember took the special crate out of its hiding place in the hold and carefully lowered it to the boat below. The major left the perpetual stubble on his face grow into a full-grown beard to help to disguise him as well as to better match the fake passport he was carrying. Besides the large crate, the new visitor to the United States carefully handed an oversized canvas satchel to Behrouz, the young operator of the motor craft. It contained special weapons and tools he might need for his mission. In fact, the pack itself was also a type of weapon as it was lined with a highly flammable mixture of phosphorous. If in trouble he could pull on a hidden tug ring which activated the phosphorous, igniting the backpack into an extremely bright and hot fireball. That fireball would disintegrate everything inside the pack

154

except for the thick steel gun barrels of his weapons, hopefully leaving very few clues behind. From now on, the pack and Hamid were to be inseparable.

After the bomb was secure, Hamid and Behrouz left the freighter and docked before daybreak in the small boat marina. The major in the Revolutionary Guard Corps had a fake passport just in case, but thought it best to avoid a formal entry into the United States. The Americans had facial recognition software that might be able to identify him despite the beard, it was best not to take that chance.

After his young accomplice left him, the Iranian went down into the spartan quarters below the bow. It was comfortable enough for Hamid to get some badly needed sleep. Later that afternoon, Behrouz left his work in time to show his new friend the city. "It is time I show you Chicago," he announced. "First I will take you to an Iranian neighborhood; there you will find many familiar foods."

Hamid didn't want to see his displaced countrymen, people who would soon be dead by his hand. They had to be sacrificed and Hamid had no problems with that. His countrymen had no business living in the human cesspool of the United States, but that didn't mean he wanted to fraternize with the walking dead.

"Please take me up-river. I wish to see the city by boat first."

"You are the boss, Kassim." Hamid had given Behrouz his Alias, the less the American born compatriot knew, the better for everyone.

Behrouz Golzar was American born; his parents were both Iranian by birth and moved to the U.S. over twenty years ago. As far as Behrouz was concerned, his parents were traitors to their country. The nineteen-year-old detested the Americans for how they treated his country. Just because he was born in this foreign land, didn't mean he would forfeit his heritage and his religion as his parents had done.

The young freedom fighter started the engines. "My boss thinks I love to fish. I have been using his boat all summer since I was given this mission. If you want, I will take you fishing. It is very enjoyable. If I catch something I have the fish smoked by my friend in little Iran. I always give my boss a fish for letting me use his boat, even if I have to buy it."

Major Shukah realized that this lad was risking his job and life for nothing more than gratitude, so Hamid gave it to him. "Your country is proud and honored to have you on our side against the infidels. You should be proud of your work. I will tell my superiors how you have helped me."

155

Behrouz felt as if he had suddenly graduated into manhood. His own father couldn't have said anything to him that would have meant more to him. "My friends call me Beez," Behrouz felt compelled to add proudly, because today he was important to his adopted homeland.

The big shipping crate was on the small deck of the boat. It was exposed to the weather but Hamid had been assured that all sensitive parts were protected. "Is there a tarp on board?" Hamid asked as he stared at the big crate. He wasn't about to take any chances. He and the bomb had come so far and were so close to finishing their mission.

"Yes Kassim, there is a canvas cover. We could use that. What are we smuggling?" the young man asked as if he should be told the whole plan.

"My young friend," Hamid explained, "you should not ask questions that cannot be answered. It is best for you to not know more than you need to."

"Yes sir, I understand. Sorry, I just want to be of help to my country."

"And your country trusts you, but in our line of business, knowing too much can be dangerous, and your country wishes to protect you."

"Of course. Thank you Kassim."

The boat slowly made its way up the Chicago River.

"Where are the guards?" he asked.

"What guards?" Behrouz was confused.

"Where are the guards who protect the river and the city?"

"Oh, you must mean the Coast Guard. They have a small boat that patrols the harbor and the river a bit. I don't see them too much. I'm more afraid of the DNR."

That sounded quite sinister to Hamid. "Who is this DNR?"

"They are the Department of Natural Resources. They check on fishing licenses, floatation devices and safety equipment on fishing boats. They are a real pain."

"A real pain?" Hamid was puzzled by the term.

"Yeah, a pain in the ass," Beez said as he pointed to his backside. "If everything isn't just right, they will give you a ticket."

"So the people guarding the fish are more of a problem than the people guarding the people?"

The younger man laughed at the observation. "I guess you could put it that way. I've never been stopped by the Coast Guard, but I have been stopped plenty of times by the DNR boat."

"And did you get arrested?"

"Arrested? Hell no! I got a $50.00 ticket for having old flares on board."

"Do they check papers?"

"You mean like passports? No, they only want to see your fishing license, and what kind of fish you caught, how many, and what size."

"The Americans pay people to look at fish?" Hamid was further puzzled.

Behrouz laughed again at his friend's ignorance of the U.S. way of doing things.

Hamid didn't really understand, but he realized that it wasn't important. He looked at the skyline of the great city.

Behrouz was careful to keep his speed down to the posted limits or his friend would meet the DNR for himself.

This would be the first of several scouting missions Hamid needed to do. He had studied the satellite pictures from the American firm "Google." Views of the city that would have been otherwise impossible for him to get any other way were now free on the Internet. But he needed to see streets and alleys and shipping areas for the big buildings. *Stupid Americans. No military, no machine guns, no guards, no police, instead they have their police count fish. Besides that, they provide high definition satellite pictures of their major cities and infrastructure.* He had even studied street level views, as if he were driving through the city itself, from the same "Google" company. And he did it all from the comfort of his office in Tehran. Here pleasure crafts, like the boat they were on, could go anywhere they wanted. It was pure insanity, especially when a country had as many enemies as the United States. This mission would be far easier than he ever imagined. Hamid chuckled as he wondered if he could find a couple of officers to help him carry the bomb into the Sears tower.

Deck of the Damascus Star:

Captain Zarin shook hands with Michael Stark, Matthew Mitchell, and Detrick Michael Krier.

The captain didn't know exactly who the V.I.P.s were, but what he did know, was that he was being forbidden to unload his cargo.

"Why can't I unload?" the captain asked in broken English with a Turkish accent.

"As we said, we are from the NNSA and the FBI," Matthew Mitchell said quickly as he flashed his FBI badge and replaced it in his pocket again.

Alan D Schmitz

"I do not know why you are here. This must be a mistake." The captain became instantly nervous about having the National Security Agents on his ship. He wasn't expecting this.

"We need to go over your shipping manifest and inspect some of your cargo," Matthew continued, his hand not far from his gun handle, which was already unstrapped from its holster.

Michael started to walk around waving a type of wand in the air. He paced the deck listening to his headset, which was plugged into the equipment contained in his backpack.

"What is he doing?" The captain became agitated.

"This is an official Port of Entry into the United States; until you are cleared by us, you, your crew, your ship and your cargo are being detained."

"What does this 'detained' mean?" The captain didn't scare easily; he had been in foreign ports around the world and had been threatened by the best. Most the time a well-placed bribe was all that was needed. Though for some reason he didn't understand, he was warned that he should not try to bribe American soldiers or police. Americans didn't take bribes, and offering one could further one's difficulties with the authorities.

"You will not be allowed into the United States until we say so."

The captain was dumbfounded. He certainly knew geography. "I am already inside the United States; I could not be farther into the United States if I wanted."

The agent understood the captain's perspective, but just like an airplane must land someplace to enter the U.S., so must a ship. For an airplane that someplace could be Denver, Colorado. For this ship it happened to be Chicago, Illinois.

"No sir, you are at the Port of Chicago. If you do not clear customs, you will not be permitted into the U.S. and must return home without entering," Matthew tried to explain the technical aspect.

The captain understood clearing customs and certainly didn't want to leave without delivering his cargo. Though what the agent didn't know was that the most important cargo had already been delivered into his country, with or without his permission.

158

Chapter 13

Port of Chicago:

D etrick Krier had been with the Marine Special Forces and was trained in demolition. Blowing things up was his specialty back then; now his job was to prevent things and especially himself and his team, from being blown up. After twenty years in the armed services, he took a job with the FBI and learned how to use his training to disarm bombs. It was the FBI that led him to the special assignment with the NNSA. So far he never had to test his training on a real bomb, and it was all right by him if he went the next twenty years without that kind of challenge. He was also trained in surveillance. As he stood on the deck of the Damascus Star with his two partners, he thought that the captain of the ship seemed a bit too nervous, so he kept his hand close to his sidearm.

"I'm picking up something here!" Michael yelled back to his partners.

Dieter and Matthew immediately drew their weapons, Matthew pointed his at the captain and Dieter swung around looking for other dangers.

"Captain, I'm afraid I have to ask you to call your crew together. Can you do that for me?"

It was stated like a request but the captain knew an order when he heard one.

"Yes, of course. But we have done nothing wrong," he began to protest.

"We are not accusing you of wrong doing; this is just a precaution."

"Do you always point guns at people who have done nothing wrong?" the Captain dared to question.

"Only when we think our own safety might be in jeopardy. Please do as we asked so we can settle this quickly."

"I must go to the bridge to call the crew."

The team knew that in a situation like this they were on their own, there was no back-up waiting in the wings to help them if needed. The local police could not board a vessel which was not technically in the U.S. yet. The NNSA had special authority to inspect foreign vessels, but even that authority was limited. Matthew knew he could phone in a request for

Alan D Schmitz

police to stand by on the dock, but the local police may or may not oblige. They had their own problems to deal with, he would be reminded. The Coast Guard could be called. If the crew were lucky, a boat would be nearby, otherwise it could be hours before help would arrive.

The captain was cooperating. Matthew reasoned it was very unlikely that he and his crew were involved in some sort of mass conspiracy. In fact, the most likely outcome was that Michael was picking up stray radiation residual from a shipping container with a faulty medical scanner. Matthew assessed the threat level as minimal, so he didn't call for further assistance; he hoped he was right for the sake of his team.

The captain called the crew over the ship-wide intercom and assembled them in the mess hall toward the bow of the ship. Dieter stayed with the captain and crew, and called out names from the crew's list to make sure that everyone was accounted for. While he was busy rounding up the crew, Matthew and Michael inspected the ship. The NNSA team warned the captain that inspecting the ship and its cargo could take hours. This was a job best done slowly and carefully by trained people, and they were the only ones in the area with that type of training.

Michael started to pick up higher levels of radiation; it was still minute but getting stronger. The trailer-sized, steel shipping containers were all locked shut, a very typical precaution against theft and tampering.

"I need to get into this one." Michael pointed to one of the large containers.

"We better go get the captain," Matthew suggested. Agent Matthew Mitchell was the ranking officer, which was fine by Michael because he was just a scientist, persuaded by the government to work part-time looking for radioactive weapons of any type. He still considered himself more scientist than law enforcement officer.

The captain wouldn't have the keys to the cargo containers either, but he should be a witness to their break in. Matthew looked around for something that might break the lock. "I'll get the captain, you keep scanning. I'm sure this ship has a machine shop. I'll have the captain take me there and help find something to open it."

Michael used his sniffer wand and continued to scan the area around the container box for radiation. There were some radioactive gases but they all seemed to be emanating from the same place. So far only the one steel box appeared to be contaminated.

The scientist had nothing to do while he waited for the captain and his boss to return, so he walked a precise pattern around the deck. A small

160

camera attached to a head strap recorded everything Michael saw, while the laptop computer in Michael's backpack synchronized the video with the radiation counter. The video and radiation counter together could be used as court evidence. Eventually he became convinced that there was only one source of radiation, and that source was emitting at extremely low levels. He could analyze it later. All radiation gave off a type of fingerprint and, with the proper equipment and database of signatures, he could determine exactly what type of radioactive material he was registering. In some cases, with the right information, the origin of manufacture could also be determined. The United States, along with other countries, tried to keep their database of these signatures up to date so that if radioactive material was found someplace it wasn't supposed to be, they could identify its source. Identifying the source of radioactive material was called "nuclear forensics," a new field of expertise developed since the attack on the New York twin towers on 9-11.

Nuclear forensics was a lot like collecting fingerprints at a crime scene. With that fingerprint it was highly likely nuclear forensic scientists would be able to match the type of radioactivity to a specific country's processing methods. Part of the United States' plan for stopping an enemy from using a clandestine nuclear weapon was letting their enemies know that after a nuclear blast, they would be identified and retaliation would be swift in coming. The hope was that if the enemy knew they would be discovered and attacked, it would deter them from initiating an attack in the first place.

Michael Stark walked to the stern of the ship listening for the sound of radiation contamination to come through his headset. The only sound he heard was the slow click of random background radiation. That was until he thought he heard a deep but distant metal on metal sound. Michael focused on the clanking sound, and despite the headset blocking external noise, he was sure he heard it again coming from a staircase. Nobody was supposed to be left wandering the large ship, so he went to investigate. He took his headset off to better hear. He was now positive that someone was approaching; he could hear footsteps. Though Michael was issued a gun by the NNSA and had some training, this was the first time he thought he might actually need it. Michael stepped through the hatchway; the gun felt heavy in his hand though it was only a light side arm. *Shit!* Somebody was in the lower hold. If it wasn't Matthew, the individual could be dangerous. He always thought of the gun as a useless weight on his hips. Right now it felt exceptionally reassuring to have.

Everyone but the captain and Matthew were supposed to be confined in the mess hall. *Maybe it was Matthew?* Michael felt his heart beating faster and his hands starting to sweat as he gripped the gun way too tightly. *Maybe it wasn't!* He was sure they wouldn't be this far away from the mess area. Michael stepped farther into the wide stairwell and very quietly descended a level to listen to the conversation. There were rustling sounds. Michael's heart beat even faster; he slowly descended a few more stairs to a blind corner and listened closely. He could hear voices now. The scientist held his gun tipped up, his entire arm a spring ready to point and aim the gun as he had been trained.

In broken English he heard, "I don't care who you are, you cannot break into the containers. I am responsible for theft. It will cost me my job if you break one of those expensive machines."

Michael felt relieved; it was the captain coming up the stairs from below deck. He was undoubtedly protesting to Matthew. Feeling a bit foolish, the doctor of science went to re-holster his gun. *Shit!* He still had the gun on safety. Had he tried to use it for self-defense he would probably be dead. The scientist climbed the stairs quietly, then stepped outside the stairwell and waited for his boss and the captain. More importantly he waited for his hand to stop shaking. The kind of fear he just experienced was new to him. The adrenalin rush was also a new phenomenon. When the two men emerged at last from the dark hold, he saw the captain of the ship carrying a long bar and Matthew carrying a sledgehammer.

"You will have to explain to the hospital why their equipment was broken into. I will take no responsibility for this," the captain kept protesting. "I will not break it open for you."

Matthew took the big bar out of the captain's hand and looked at Michael, "You sure about this?"

Michael put the headset back on and listened for the audible response to the sound of deteriorating atoms. "Something inside is giving off radioactive gasses, not hazardous, but steady. Yea I'm sure about this."

Matthew was a fairly big man. He gave a pull on the bar he had wedged between the box and the locked chain sealing it. After a few tries it popped open with a loud snap. Michael stepped through the open doors of the shipping container, recording the view inside. The other agent peered into the shadows, watching his partner, but keeping a close eye on the captain at the same time.

"Are the levels high?" Matthew asked, a bit concerned about being exposed to radiation contamination.

"It's not the amount of radiation. It's the type that concerns me."

"This is a computerized axial tomography scanner and its leaking radiation. It's giving off gamma rays, which is making the DAC concentration inside this container on the high side. This CAT scanner was manufactured incorrectly or it was damaged in transit. Either way this unit needs to be quarantined."

"How bad is it?" Matthew asked.

"I probably inhaled a couple of years' worth of natural background radiation already; luckily the watertight crate contains the radiation fairly well."

DAC concentration stood for derived air concentration. It was a measurement of the concentration of radioactive material in air. Everybody breathed in radioactive air every single day; radiation workers measured their exposure to percentages of a year's worth of natural radiation. "If my calculations and measurements are right I have probably been exposed to enough radiation as an airline pilot might have in a year of flying at high altitude. You can imagine this would not be a good thing in a hospital setting with the same workers around this thing day in and day out," Michael finished.

Michael walked out of the dark trailer. As he came into the daylight, he could see that Matthew was visibly upset and in a hurry to close the wide doors again, as if to quickly seal in an invisible monster. In contrast, the captain didn't seem to be upset at all about carrying a leaking ultra-high tech X-ray machine.

"Customs will have to decide what to do from here," Matthew told the captain, before asking Michael, "What are your recommendations?"

"I would recommend that this trailer and the ones right next to it are all quarantined and scrubbed. The manufacturer of the CAT scanner needs to be contacted immediately to find the leak and seal it."

"That's it then? We're finished?"

"Looks that way to me."

"Captain, you can tell your crew they are free to go about their business. The customs officials will be in contact with you very shortly. I would tell your company what is going on. I am sure this is going to delay your return. I suggest you section this area off so your crew keeps its distance." Matthew gave the final instructions.

Michael examined his radiation badge closely; it hadn't changed colors yet and neither had Matt's, so the danger to the captain's crew would be minimal, especially if they kept their distance.

163

Alan D Schmitz

"Thank you gentlemen, I appreciate your concern," the captain graciously accepted their advice.

As Dieter, Michael and Matthew walked down the gangplank off the ship, Dieter commented, "We saved the world from another dangerous terrorist attack; we are fucking superheroes."

"The truth is that the radiation leak would have been detected by customs and if not by them, then by the hospital setup staff. We got there first. That is a bit reassuring," Michael consoled himself and his partners.

"You will probably be taken off the team," Matthew said seriously to Michael.

"You mean because of a little radiation exposure?"

"You said you probably had more than a year's worth of exposure. That is enough to put you on injured reserve for a year."

Michael didn't say anything at first. Instead he thought about his options. The scientist knew that someone in some office somewhere would make that decision; he would have to minimize his report if he wanted to stay active and he did. He liked these guys and this was more exciting than staring at numbers on a computer monitor all day, every day.

"I may have been exaggerating my exposure; I will have to calculate things carefully for my report. I was not in the trailer for more than a minute, I am sure. How long do you think I was in the trailer?"

Matthew Mitchell looked quizzically at his friend. "I can't remember. Maybe if I see a copy of your report it will refresh my memory."

Michael realized that his exposure had suddenly been dropped by at least half.

Chicago small boat marina:

Hamid and Behrouz came back from their assessment cruise and tied up in the same slip from which they left. Hamid had a close up view of the Damascus Star when they entered the harbor from the river. There was no doubt that something was wrong. The Damascus Star hadn't even started to unload its cargo yet. He could call the captain with his satellite phone, just as the captain could call him, but the less communication the better Hamid decided. If the captain thought he should know what was going on, he would have called. So the terrorist had to assume that the plan was still a go.

"Do you have access to a vehicle?"

"Yes of course, Kassim. Where do you want to go?"

164

"I would like to get something to eat, someplace simple, but downtown near where we boated today."

"I know just the place." Beez was eager to please his new boss. Then he thought about his rundown Toyota. "My car is very modest, Kassim, if you do not mind."

"A modest car will serve Allah well. Will our package be safe?"

"Absolutely!" Beez confirmed. "Only boat owners are permitted beyond the gate, and the area is patrolled by a private security company. Boat owners respect each other's property; I can guarantee that nobody will disturb it. I have left a cooler full of beer on the boat over a weekend and nobody stole it."

"This is not a cooler full of beer!" Kassim was a bit upset at the analogy and scolded the young man.

"Yes of course. I could pick up a chain and lock from a store, and then we could secure it. Too bad it is too big to fit inside the lower cabin."

Kassim nodded his approval and waited for Beez to return. He was uncomfortable waiting out on the open deck of the boat so he descended into the small cabin. Better to keep out of sight, he decided. With little to do inside the small cabin he picked up a magazine to read. Hamid cursed at the immoral decadence of the Americans as he scanned the old Playboys tucked into the magazine rack. Though he was proficient in reading English, the magazines he was looking at required very little reading and he shook his head in disgust as he paged from picture to picture.

As soon as Behrouz was back, they headed out in his small wreck of a car. To Hamid, who had grown up in the countryside of Iran, such a wreck was commonplace in the poor farming community. In fact, a person who owned such a car would be considered somewhat important.

The short ride from the harbor took them past several beautiful, huge old buildings.

"What are these?" Kassim quizzed.

"These buildings house giant museums, world famous," Behrouz added. "I am sure you have heard of the Chicago Museum of Science and Industry. It is very important; it even has a German World War II U-boat that was captured. The building over there is the Museum of Natural History. There are many important artifacts inside it. Some of the best examples of dinosaurs in the world are kept there. There is an important planetarium and aquarium. School children from the entire Midwest come here to visit them every year."

165

Kassim kept his thoughts to himself, but if any parts of these building were still standing after the blast, they would not be visited again for many, many years, if ever. The loss of important museums would be a terrible waste, but it was necessary. Often in war, civilians and important buildings had to be sacrificed.

The city quickly grew around them; tall buildings had sprouted everywhere. The names on the buildings reflected the significance of them all. Hamid recognized many of the names because they were international in their stature.

"I can park here. Do you have any change? I'm all out."

"What kind of change are you talking about?" Hamid was unfamiliar with the term.

"We need change for the meter," Beez pointed to the steel column in front of them.

"I assure you, I have no change."

"Then I cannot park here or we will get a ticket." The young man gunned the accelerator and the car gave off a puff of blue smoke as he drove around the block. He remembered a construction site that was nearby. He could park there. The walk would be a little longer but he was sure he wouldn't be ticketed because the police would think his car belonged to one of the workers.

"What is this?" Hamid asked as Beez slid his shifter into park.

"This building is going to come down soon; we can park here. My friend George sells coffee and cigarettes to the workers here, but he said they are done working for a while until another building close by comes down."

"What does this mean, to come down?" Hamid was perplexed by the term.

"It will be taken apart somehow, probably blown up. Then another building can be built here."

"I see," Kassim nodded apprehensively. He didn't understand why the Americans would take down a building just to rebuild it again. *Why didn't they just fix the original building? Certainly that would be cheaper. The United States was a wasteful country*, he concluded.

Walking along the busy sidewalk was so much different from the leisurely and peaceful ride on the river. Cars were honking horns, and everybody seemed to have a cell phone permanently attached to their ear. More than once Beez saved Kassim from inadvertently running into another pedestrian as he scanned the tops of the tall buildings. The young man chuckled at his older friend with his nose in the sky; this city had a way of doing that to a newcomer. It was impossible not to stand out in a crowd as someone who didn't belong.

"Do you have money?" the young man asked. "I won't get paid for another week."

"I have American twenty dollar bills." Hamid's superiors had provided him with U.S. currency, completely clean money, untraceable and positively not counterfeit. It would not do to have your agent arrested for passing forged currency, even if by accident.

Beez felt entitled to a good lunch and picked a corner diner that was two blocks from the giant Sears Tower. "I will take you past the tallest building in the United States and then we will eat."

Kassim felt overwhelmed, he had never seen so many huge structures in his life. Each building contained thousands of people. The bomb had to go off during working hours, he committed to himself. So many easy targets could not be wasted. Each person who died would be one more strike against the infidels' economy. The heathens would learn to worship through the one true religion, or they would die. He prayed silently for the soldiers of Islam who would also die. He promised to Allah that tonight, and every night of his life, he would pray for them as martyrs of the cause.

Beez asked Kassim what he wanted to eat and ordered for both of them. "I have to be back at work. If I get fired we will not be able to use the boat anymore."

Kassim looked up and assured his associated that he should make sure that didn't happen. What he didn't say was that the boat was critical to his plan. Kassim ordered some coffee and was very disappointed. They called it coffee and it was dark, but instead of the thick syrupy mixture he typically enjoyed, it was just weak, coffee-flavored water.

The lakefront wasn't that far away. The walk would do him good and he would be able to study the city better without the young man watching his actions.

"How will I get back to the boat? The guard will not let me through the gate at the marina." Kassim was already planning his next moves.

"This is the dock key; tell them you are staying at slip twenty-six. It will be okay."

Kassim took the key and nodded then asked, "I may need your help tomorrow. How do I contact you?"

On the back of a napkin Behrouz wrote a number. "This is my cell number. Call me if you need me. My mother wants me to take her to the doctor and I said I would. She will really be pissed if I don't, but Wednesday I can take you wherever you want."

Kassim was disappointed that his country couldn't have found a better contact in this city of millions than this Beez. Hamid had another slang name for this young man but he didn't quite know how to translate it into English. What he did know was that it wasn't a compliment to him.

NNSA Offices, Chicago:

Michael Stark was filling out his paperwork. The sad reality was that the paperwork took three times as much time to do as the actual surveillance. Unfortunately, as exciting as the surveillance was, the paperwork was equally as boring. The whole time Michael worked on the Damascus Star file, his mind kept returning to the image of Matthew nervously anxious to close the door to the contaminated container. This didn't bother him, but the calm in the captain's eyes did, it was as if the captain knew about the contamination and the negligible risk.

Michael stopped the computer-generated timeline at the point of the door opening, and saw the immediate spike in radiation and gas contamination. He verified it against the video running just below the radiation graph. He ran the video in slow motion until it showed him coming out of the container. At the point of his exit from the container box, he froze the video and examined it more closely. The graph of the radiation was within the limits he first reported; still, something was bothering him about the frozen images on the screen. Not only did the captain appear unconcerned, he actually had a small smile on his face. It was more of a smirk than a smile, but nonetheless it was there. The scientist played the same section of video over and over again. The smile was real enough; it only lasted for an instant, but it was there. Then Michael began to understand what he had discovered. The captain knew something about this contamination, Michael was convinced of it.

He pressed the play button again and watched the video of him scanning the rest of the aft section of the ship. During an uneventful moment in the video he took a quick glance away from the computer toward his holstered gun draped across a chair behind him. Michael shook his head in disbelief at the critical mistake he made when he didn't take the safety off. Looking back at the video he watched himself enter the stairwell. Then in real-time his heart started to pound. Something was wrong, very wrong. He played the video over again. *It couldn't be.*

The radiation detector graph on the computer was spiking just as the video showed him entering the stairwell on the ship. The radiation the graph depicted was even higher than inside the container. "Shit!" Michael cursed to himself.

The scientist realized he never heard the sound of the radiation because he had taken the headphones off when he was distracted by the sounds from below deck. With his gun drawn and the headset off, he never would have heard the clicking sound the detector produced when in a contaminated area. "Shit!" Michael cursed to himself again. The captain's smile came back to mind. The captain did know something. Something else on board the ship was giving off contamination, but what was it? Michael printed out a copy of the stairwell radiation and a copy of the container contamination and compared them. They were definitely from two different sources.

Next Michael went to the original flyover records. He paused the video from the helicopter at the point where it was directly over the cargo ship. He printed out a copy of that reading and compared it to the others. It was inconclusive and didn't seem to match either source. What Michael did know was that it was of the same type of radiation as the CAT scanner, definitely different fingerprints, but of the same type. The good news was that it didn't seem to be uranium or plutonium. It was more like another leaky X-ray machine, though that didn't make sense to him. Why would another machine have been stored below deck? It would have been much too big for the stairwell. Matthew would have to be notified immediately. The scientist picked up the phone to call his partner at home. The ship would need another inspection.

First thing the next morning, Matthew, Dieter, and Michael huddled around the computer printouts and the computer screen. If Agent Mitchell was going to insist on another inspection of the Damascus Star he would need to be convinced it was absolutely necessary. Dieter listened to Michael explain, in some very technical language, what was upsetting him about the radiation. Dieter was quickly bored by the technical jargon and didn't even try to disguise his boredom by pretending to understand. He walked to another computer. Dieter thought it amusing that Matthew was doing a much better job at pretending he understood the scientist. Matthew and Michael took the wide printouts to an empty desk and tried to make some sense of them. Dieter had missed out on the original helicopter flyover, so he played it again and again on the computer, giving it a halfhearted look for some sort of clue it might hold. The copter's downward pointing camera

169

Alan D Schmitz

showed the edge of dock -A- then the water and soon dock -C- came into view. Dock -C- was for container removal and the big crane dockside was idle. The Damascus Star was tied against the side of the dock waiting for permission to unload. Dieter watched the radiation counter increase in activity as the copter came in lower and scanned the ship. Dieter took note that the heavy steel deck door to the aft stairwell was closed.

"Hey professor," Dieter asked using the title more as a slang expression than of respect. "These outer deck doors on ships are pretty heavy and solid. Would they stop radiation from being detected?"

The professor was also familiar with the heavy bulkhead doors. They were made to withstand the worst pounding giant waves could possibly give and so was the structure around them. He thought about his partners implied suggestion. "They're heavy enough alright, and water tight. I would guess that if the doors were closed tightly, not much of anything could escape in or out, including radiation.

"I don't know much about all that other crap but my vote is we go see the captain again. Let's check out the stairwell and the lower hold," Dieter volunteered and then played the flyover video again.

"You are positive it's not bomb making radiation?" Matthew asked again.

"I'm positive of that."

"Then it is a job for customs. Our job is to look for weapons of mass destruction, not leaky X-ray equipment."

"I have a bad feeling about the ship's captain. I think we were being purposely misled to the container," the scientist argued.

"I respect hunches, but why would someone who is doing something illegal, intentionally lead us to their ship with a leaky X-ray machine?"

Michael couldn't come up with any good reasons. Just one came to mind and it was not very selling. "So that we would get a convenient answer if by chance we discovered any radiation."

"Hey professor?" Dieter asked again in his folksy way. "How come this meter thing went crazy when you guys flew over the small boat marina?"

Matthew and Michael immediately shot over to the computer. Dieter was right. The low-flying helicopter was recording some sort of radiation well away from the large ship. Michael played the same footage over again two more times and then printed out a copy of the radiation spike. It matched perfectly with the stairwell radiation.

"Whatever was or is in the stairwell, was or is at the marina. We need to find it."

Port Washington, Wisconsin:

"Scott, why don't you let Jerry do this? I don't want you going to Chicago tomorrow and especially not with a truck full of explosives," Liz pleaded.

"Liz we've gone through this, I remember, see." Scott wasn't being facetious; he was frustrated that his wife thought him incapable of doing his job because of his illness. He angrily went to the walk-in closet and took out some clean trousers to pack.

Coming back out Scott stated flatly, "Just because I have some short-term memory problems doesn't mean I can't remember how to do my job."

"But you could faint; you could crash on your way to Chicago."

"I haven't fainted in weeks, ever since I stopped taking the benzodiazepine three times a day. I even remember that too. And the wonder drug that neither I nor you can pronounce is working; I can feel it. And my truck isn't full of explosives, I just have a few boxes of RDX in case we need more than we thought. Somebody has to transport the extra explosives to the site, and my name is on the paperwork, so I am responsible for it. Paxton has the detonator caps with him, and as long as the detonator caps aren't on the RDX, it is perfectly safe. Liz, I promise that this will be my last job, and you know that nobody can place these charges like I can. Jerry's success and our future depend on this job going off right."

"Scott I'm so worried that you'll forget something, something important. You could be killed, or you could kill someone else."

Scott was becoming angry, he wouldn't be talked out of this, and his wife should know that.

"Yes, I admit that I forget things, but I am not stupid. I know how to do this better than anybody else in the company. I have been studying this building and its structure for a year now. I did the test blast on it. This is my project Liz. If I don't do it now, Jerry will have to start over from scratch, and that would happen only if a very pissed off client gave him the chance, which they wouldn't."

Scott lowered his tone, taking the anger out of his voice and remembering his need to stay calm. "I wouldn't attempt this if I didn't know I could do it. In a few days you will see this building come down as straight as an arrow, on television."

"On television?" Liz quizzed.

"Didn't I tell you? One of the local stations is going to make a big deal out of it. They're doing a countdown and everything. I am supposed to do an interview before and after. I wish you could go with me; it's going to be quite a show. Are you sure you can't get your sister to watch Avery for a few days?"

"Avery has tests this week and you know my sister, she would let Avery stay up all night long if Avery wanted to. Besides, I know how focused you get. I would be sitting in a hotel room day and night while all you did was go over blue prints again and again."

Scott realized that his wife had thrown in the towel; it didn't happen often so the least he could do was honor her request.

"Please Scott, listen to me closely." He stopped packing his clothes and sat down on the bed.

"Promise me that you will concentrate on this job like none other. And if anything doesn't feel right, you will call it off. Promise me that!"

It was hard to stay angry at his wife. He knew that she loved him and that was why she worried. Scott took her hand and agreed. "Of course I will. It's all about risk management, and I promise that if something isn't right, we won't blast. It's that simple."

"I won't be able to sleep until you're home again."

"I'll be back home before you know it. Then I'll retire, I promise. Besides, you, Princess and I are going to the Packer Game in Green Bay this weekend. I bet you thought I forgot."

"Forget a Packer Game? Not a chance. I know you better than that."

"They're going to cream the Bears."

Liz gave her husband a quick hug and peck on the cheek. Before leaving the room she whispered in his ear. "I love you Scott Seaver and you better come back home to me ASAP."

Scott sat on the edge of the bed lost in thought, he didn't remember for how long. He looked at the alarm clock, it was almost eight. Glancing outside he saw that it was dark, so he reasoned it was eight PM. He looked at his half-packed suitcase and assumed that he just came home from a meeting, so he continued to unpack, hanging his trousers up in the closet. Then he realized that his socks were all unused. He looked at the date on his phone and then at his appointment calendar. That was when he figured out that he was packing for a trip to Chicago, not unpacking. Scott looked around. He was lucky Liz didn't see this. He wondered where she was. He hadn't seen her for a while. Scott tucked his packed suitcase in the closet and put a post-it note on it: "Chicago blast." Better safe than sorry, he reasoned.

Chicago Lake front:

Feeling well rested from the night's sleep, Hamid piloted the small fishing boat out of slip twenty-six. He tried to memorize each turn of the river and the buildings along it. It could be very soon that he would need that information to take the small craft on its final voyage. The day before, while on reconnaissance of the city, he had spotted a potential tie-up area for the small boat and wanted to check it out from the river. His hope was that after the Damascus Star left port, he would be able to pilot the small boat up river for the last time. The area he had in mind would be close enough that its blast and concussion wave would bring down many buildings, including the huge Sears building.

Hamid made sure to keep his wake to a minimum. Apparently that was important to the DNR police. As he passed other boats he would wave and smile as if he did this trip every day. He was pleased with his trip up river. He saw another boat tied to the unofficial dock area he wanted to use. The DNR police didn't bother that boater, so Hamid guessed that he would also be allowed to use it unhindered.

His complaints to his superiors about the need for someone else besides the idealistic young man had paid off. They located a much more qualified and experienced operative for Hamid to work with. This man would pick up the Iranian at a location not far from the floating bomb. Hamid would set the detonator for two hours; even with bad traffic he was assured that his contact from Milwaukee would have enough time to get them both out of the city.

The Iranian piloted the boat back towards the big lake and under a drawbridge that connected a very busy lakeside thoroughfare to its north and south sides. Higher vessels, often sail boats, needed to have the bridge raised so that they could proceed to their berths up river. Once under the bridge, Hamid could see that the Damascus Star had unloaded all its cargo and was in the process of loading different containers for the trip back to the European side of the world. That meant all was on track. Tomorrow or the day after, a bomb would go off and change the world forever.

The plan was for the Damascus Star to leave port hours before detonation. His contact from Milwaukee would take him north to a small town along the lake from which he could boat out to the waiting freighter. The ship would then smuggle him back out of the United States in the same way he came into the country. After the fiery destruction of this city, he would be welcomed as the hero of Islam and Iran for his bravery.

Alan D Schmitz

The small fishing boat turned a corner. Hamid piloted it past the Damascus Star then turned it into a much smaller harbor area that would take him to the small boat marina. That was when he noticed a man waving a small wand device in the air on one of the piers. They were searching slip twenty-six, he was sure of it. "Koft meekonam roo toh" *(I shit on you),* he said to himself as he cursed at the three men. He had been found out somehow. Hamid pulled the fishing boat over at the transient dock some distance away and pretended to dispose of trash as he watched the three men. It was obvious that he couldn't return to the dock or the slip. From the looks of things, they were detecting a radiation signature. Hamid swore some more, this time at the Russian for giving him a bomb that didn't conceal the radioactive material inside of it. What he didn't realize was that it wasn't plutonium or uranium that was giving him away, it was the excessive exposure of the bomb to X-rays during inspection in their own laboratory.

Hamid jumped into the boat and headed back up river. He needed to find a place to dock and hide the boat. He thought back to his night's sleep and accepted the fact that from now on, he would certainly get very little rest.

Small Boat Marina, Chicago:

"There is no doubt that this is the spot the radiation came from. The water is not currently affected, but it certainly was. The wood on the side of the slip absorbed quite a bit of the second-hand radiation. The wind isn't helping the situation, but something was here all right. We need to get the harbor master to tell us who rents this spot," Michael reported to his boss.

Matthew and Dieter were looking for clues next to the slip. Nothing but the radiation was unusual. "Dieter, you ask other residents if they saw anyone or anything here. Maybe they know who rents this area. I'm sure these guys share fishing stories all the time. I'll go check with the guard who let us in. Somebody has to know something."

Michael suggested, "From the helicopter, we might be able to trace where the boat went. I can't know how strong the radiation leak still is, but it is as if something or someone was X-rayed a hundred times over."

Matthew had never thought of that and then asked for clarification. "I thought we were looking for a something, not a someone?"

"I've never recorded someone who has been through radiation treatment for cancer but the agency has, though not very often. A person

174

given high doses of radiation could potentially give off radiation residue for a while after."

"Let me get this straight. We know for sure that this isn't plutonium or uranium signatures. But it could be somebody who was X-rayed recently?"

"High energy X-rays, but yes," Michael corrected.

Michael saw the look of disappointment; they could be on a wild goose chase.

"I know what you're thinking, but this is the same source as the freighter. Whether it is a person or an object doesn't matter; it came from the freighter before it was cleared for unloading. I'm telling you, something is up."

Matthew shot a hard look at Michael. "Your hunches got us this far and you're right. Either somebody is trying to hide from us or they are trying to hide something from us. Let's find out what we can here and then get the copter."

Alan D Schmitz

Chapter 14

Chicago, Illinois:

Scott had already checked into his hotel. His spirits were high with the expectations of a successful outcome of his final project. He decided that for his last company trip the InterContinental Hotel wasn't a bad choice. It was a grand old hotel from the 1920s, restored magnificently in the late 1980s, keeping as much of the historic value as it could. The Holiday Inn Downtown had been his hotel of choice for the last several months whenever he needed to stay in Chicago. It was convenient and comfortable, and most of all, considerably less expensive than the luxurious InterContinental, but Scott knew this was going to be his last stay in Chicago; he would treat himself to the best. The InterContinental was east of his project, along the river and had secure parking, which was especially important considering his cargo. The hotel was situated in the middle of Chicago's Magnificent Mile of shops and restaurants. *Liz would have had way too much to do here*, he mused.

The ride to Chicago was uneventful, or at least that was what he remembered. Scott chuckled at his strange situation. The truth was that he couldn't remember the ride to the city at all. At least it appeared that the GPS had delivered him to the busy downtown area without incident.

Proper procedures meant he should have gone to the site first and unloaded the RDX into the guarded, secure trailer, but he reasoned that nobody knew he had explosives in the vehicle and the parking area was also guarded. Besides, without any way to detonate the explosives they were as harmless as apple pie. It wasn't like him to take shortcuts or ignore safety protocol, but he was in a hurry, actually anxious to get settled in his room. As he drove the SUV through the hectic city streets, he could feel himself becoming more and more agitated. He didn't remember the drive downtown upsetting him so much on previous trips. This ride was different, the noise of honking horns and the constant activity of moving cars, trucks and people everywhere made him feel uncomfortable and confused. This made him feel upset and anxious, which usually led to bad things. By the time Scott reached the Intercontinental, his nerves were raw. After a quick check-in, he took the mirror-lined elevator up to his room. Scott dropped his cases on the floor

176

the second he entered. The businessman felt so drained from the three hour ride that he crashed his frame onto the bed and was soon asleep.

By the time he awoke, Scott realized that several hours had passed, but he felt better after the rest. In fact, at the moment, he was much less apprehensive about being in the noisy city, even a little excited.

He was running a little behind in his schedule. A two-hour nap hadn't been part of his plan, so he rushed out of his room and took the elevator down to the parking level. Captain Seaver didn't trust his SUV to a valet and insisted on parking the vehicle himself, but now he didn't remember where it was. When he opened the door to the parking structure he turned on his IT-Tech and pressed the button on the parking application program; his phone started to talk to him. It gave verbal, turn-by-turn directions to his car. Scott knew that his memory was failing him more often, and he had to check and double check almost everything. To other people it appeared that he was just an extremely industrious businessman, constantly talking into his phone. The truth was he used his phone to make notes to himself frequently. He didn't trust himself to remember anything. Scott even used his phone to take pictures or short videos of places he was or where, for example, he hung his coat. He realized that he was leaning on his technological toys more and more for his daily survival, and soon they would fail him.

With the help of his phone, he found his SUV in the huge structure, and soon he was sliding into the front seat of his vehicle. Scott was ready to shift into drive when he realized that he couldn't remember the location of the jobsite, even though he had been there many times before. Its location had always been relative to the Downtown Holiday Inn, the hotel he usually stayed at. Staying at a different hotel was impairing him in a way he hadn't anticipated. There was no doubt any more in his mind that his memory was rapidly deteriorating.

The GPS in his SUV suddenly announced, "You have reached your destination."

Scott realized the GPS was still programmed to take him to the InterContinental, but this reminded him of a quick technological fix to his current problem. He punched in a few commands on the GPS and found the address of the doomed building. After a few more entries, his SUV was ready to direct him once again.

As a last item of habit, he reached over to touch his laptop computer, that's when a small panic set in. Scott quickly glanced over at the empty passenger seat. Where was it? He couldn't remember. In a full panic he unstrapped his seat belt so he could look more closely. It wasn't on the floor either. His computer was his lifeline. It was his memory even more than the IT-Tech, and it held important company information. Scott felt the panic coming on that he knew he couldn't afford to have right now. Remembering Dr. Maslow's instructions, he took a deep cleansing breath, and then exhaled slowly. The breathing technique started to calm him. He still remembered what caused his panic but he stayed calm. He didn't lose his computer; he just didn't know where it was. He would find it, he reminded himself. Maybe it was in his room. Soon he started to feel better. The panic was gone and he felt back in control. Before getting out of the SUV, Scott turned to see if anyone was near and saw the computer in the back seat. With a sigh of deep relief he reached back, moved the computer to the front seat and plugged the camera on the dash into it. Why it had been in the back seat he couldn't remember. Normal everyday tasks and habits that had served him well the last year were eluding him.

Captain Scott Seaver had always been a logical, steady and pragmatic man; soon he would have a big decision to make. He always knew the day would come, and this incident reminded him that it would be sooner than later.

Scott toyed with the bottle of pills in his pants pocket. It was an extra bottle. He didn't know why he had them, just that he did. His wife and doctor also didn't know he had them and that sometimes he would take extra doses. He had been doing this since shortly before their sailing vacation as a precaution. Taking an extra pill a day seemed to help at first but he only had about five extra now, and he knew his memory was getting worse even with the extra pill.

Scott wanted to see this project through to completion; it would be his last hurrah in life. After that, he reasoned it would be time to take his own life. He would do what he could to make it seem like an accident for everyone's benefit. That is, everyone's benefit except his life insurance company's. Scott knew that he couldn't let this disease kill him slowly and unmercifully. He would have to plan his suicide before he was a burden to his family and incapable of even remembering how to kill himself or why.

The SUV headed out toward the job site. The little voice in the GPS said, "Turn right at the next intersection. You are one mile from your destination." The next synthesized voice recording he heard was, "You are at your destination; guidance canceled."

Scott pulled into the demolition site over a mound of broken ground and waved to the project foreman.

"Hi Paxton. Are things secure?"

"Hey Scott, welcome to the windy city, and I mean that literally. The weather is a bit iffy, the wind is picking up. The city won't let us blow the tower if the wind is greater than five miles per hour. They don't want the dust to blow all over."

"Yeah, I know, I got your e-mail. I don't blame them. Who knows what's in these old buildings. But the problem is that we need to have the fire department here to keep the dust down with the water hoses and they need twelve hours notice, and even then there are no guarantees. What do you calculate as the latest we can make the decision?"

"Tonight before five, if we want to do it tomorrow. That gives us a little wiggle room."

Scott did some simple math in his head. "I agree, so let's not worry about it until then. We'll check the weather at four-thirty and then make the call."

"Sounds like a plan, Captain." Scott's co-workers often referred to their boss by his Guard rank. It had started out as a tease, but the fact was, they were proud of him and trusted him.

"Like I said, the charges are all placed as we discussed, but I want to make sure the timing is set up like you want," Paxton suggested.

"Let's walk the building exactly in the order that the charges are timed to go off," Scott insisted.

Scott and Paxton had to go through security to enter the inner jobsite. Security was extremely tight and cost a bundle for each day they were needed. Making or losing money on a job of this size could come down to the weather and other unforeseen delays. Each day of waiting and guarding a building loaded with explosives cost thousands of dollars.

The lower part of the old apartment building was gutted and looked like a war zone. All the walls were gone and only the concrete pillars supporting the upper floors were visible. Each of the pillars had been drilled with huge concrete drills and charges pressed inside each hole. Then the pillars were wrapped in protective blankets to contain the blast. The blankets would only last for precious seconds when the RDX detonated, but by then they would have done their job.

As they walked around the debris-strewn building, Scott felt very comfortable. This was what came natural to him, this and flying his Huey. Here he didn't need any memory aids. After years of doing these blasts he could sense how the building would fall. It was a lot like an experienced logger who knows instinctively which direction a tree will fall and exactly where to cut it to make it happen.

Alan D Schmitz

"Did Liz come down with you to see the blast? It's going to be a big one."

Scott heard his co-worker's question but he couldn't remember if Liz came along or not. He stalled for time, something he had gotten pretty good at.

"Pax, this is the center area, right?"

"Almost there; it starts at the next set of pillars." Then Paxton added, "These two rows will be the first to go. If your calculations are right, and they always are, these two rows won't start the building collapsing on their own. We'll give the building thirty seconds and then the inner columns go, then twenty seconds later, the set just inside the perimeter will blow. The building should already be caving in by that time."

Scott had already forgotten Paxton's question as he was deep in concentration. He was trying to visualize exactly what each brick and block was going to do. For some reason it wasn't coming to him like it usually did. Something wasn't right, but he didn't know what.

"Pax?" Scott asked cautiously. "This doesn't feel right; what are we forgetting?"

"Nothing I can think of Captain, unless you mean the charges on the eighth floor?"

Scott needed time. Things weren't as clear as he imagined they would be.

"Let's take a look."

"Yeah sure boss, but it's a simple layout, just the inner columns to help with the implosion."

"I would feel better seeing it myself."

"Let's go, I only climbed it a million times the last few days. One more time won't kill me."

They started climbing so Paxton asked again, "Is Liz here with you or are you alone this trip?"

Scott still couldn't remember, but he couldn't stall again either. "Are you wondering if the real boss is going to be watching you?" Scott kidded.

"Something like that. It's going to be one hell of a show. I'd hate for her to miss it."

"So would I," Scott agreed while he tried not to let panic set in. He needed time to think, time to relax. "I have a call coming in, could be important."

"I didn't hear any phone ring."

"I have it on vibrate. You can keep going; I'll be right behind you."

"Sure Captain! See you on eight."

Scott played back the last few voice messages to himself. He heard his own voice remind him what floor he was parked on and what hotel and room number he was staying at. *Would he have left those messages if Liz was along? Possibly.* He quickly looked through the photo album feature. *Maybe a picture of him and Liz in Chicago would be on it.* Scott quickly checked the day's date, but there were no recent pictures. Next Scott looked at the calendar for notes he might have made. Today's date was highlighted. There were notes about meeting Joe at the Chicago site. But tomorrow's date said "Call Avery about test." *Test.* Scott repeated the word. *Test.* He repeated it again. Something about a test sounded familiar. *Of course, Liz stayed home to help Avery with her tests.* Suddenly it seemed very clear to him. He remembered their conversation. She didn't trust her sister to watch Avery. He reached into his pocket, found one of the Tridroxolene pills and took it. No sense letting them burn a hole in his pocket, right now he needed every bit of help he could get. This job had to go off right. Scott raced up the stairs trying desperately not to forget the question or the answer.

"Sorry Pax!" Scott apologized as he reached the eighth floor landing, puffing a bit.

"You asked about Liz. She had to stay at home with our daughter. I wanted her sister to take care of Avery but Liz didn't think that was a good idea. Her sister is a bit of a flake, if you know what I mean."

"You don't have to tell me about that. My sister-in-law is an absolute loon."

The run up the stairs had actually done Scott good. Though he was out of breath, it had taken the panic away. It seemed that the hard physical exertion made him focus on activity, rather than the lingering feeling of despair. Scott made a mental note to try to remember that trick. The doctor might be interested in it also. Unfortunately he couldn't make a voice reminder in his phone while the foreman was standing right in front of him.

The eighth floor was nowhere near as gutted out as the first. The inner set of columns was exposed and wrapped like the lower, but the rest of the floor was intact since only the support columns that were to be destroyed needed to be exposed.

"This set goes off at the exact same time as the first set downstairs."

"If you did your job right, like you always do," Scott knowingly repeated his foreman's words from earlier.

Alan D Schmitz

Paxton laughed a bit at Scott's quick wit; it also made him feel a bit more at ease. He began to think that maybe the guys were wrong about Scott not being able to even remember to tie his shoelaces.

"It all looks good and ready to go. I'm going to go over the blueprints one more time, but I'm confident we're all set," Scott slapped his coworker on the back heartedly. "Once again, Pax, you're the man."

"No, you the man!"

"No, you the man!"

The two grown men kept saying this to each other all the way down the stairs.

Chicago Harbor:

The Iranian terrorist cautiously proceeded back up river; he needed to hide the boat. But how does one hide a boat? Previous to this, Major Shukah and his young friend had always taken the south branch of the river. It was a highly populated area, perfect for bomb placement because it was close to the financial center and the huge skyscrapers. Now he needed to vanish from sight. Hamid decided to use the north branch this time, hoping for the opposite result.

The Iranian tried to put the pieces of the puzzle together. If the government police found the dock, they would soon find the owner of the boat, and then of course they would find the young compatriot. That young idiot would certainly tell them about his friend Kassim and the midnight rendezvous with the freighter; maybe he had already. By tonight the entire place would be swarming with government policemen. *"Golole,"* he swore out loud.

Hamid saw an empty, untended dock. It seemed pretty dilapidated, but he needed time to think this through. He pulled next to the small pier and tied the boat up. Walking carefully off the rotted wood pier, Hamid went ashore; he needed a place to walk, to pace, to think.

After a few minutes he realized that the problem broke down into several solvable pieces. First, the young man Behrouz had to be silenced forever, and this needed to be done quickly. Second the bomb had to be hidden. The plan, so diligently conceived, was falling apart rapidly. Major Shukah desperately wanted to use the power of the bomb, but his first priority was not to let his country become involved in a scandal that would be considered an act of war. This was a difficult situation. He had come so far. His country had worked so hard on this plan to strike at the enemy of Allah, he couldn't let them down. Finding a way to use the

182

destructive power of the bomb was his sworn duty. He would not let God down. Hamid dropped to his knees in prayer and spoke out loud, "Please help me God, I need your guidance. There must be a way to strike down the infidels."

After a short prayer, Kassim rubbed his beard, tugged on it lightly and then made a telephone call with regret in his heart. He would take no pleasure in luring the young man into a death trap.

The young man answered after a few rings. "Hello, this is Beez."

"Behrouz, I need to see you today, very soon. I need your help."

"I told you man, I'm at the doctor with my mom today," the young man scolded a bit, annoyed about the intrusion.

"When can I see you?" Hamid persisted.

"She should be done in an hour, I think. But she wants to take me shopping with her after that."

"You must meet me at three o'clock at the same place we parked the car yesterday," Kassim insisted. "Your country needs you very much," he added as extra incentive. "And do not talk to anyone. Do not return to your home. Just drop your mother off and go to the meeting place."

Everything was becoming much clearer to the Iranian. He contemplated setting the timer on the bomb and taking it down river toward the giant tower and the business area at this very moment. He would gladly become a martyr for a cause as great as this. The reward awaiting him in the afterlife would be great. There was only one problem with doing it now. That problem was a nineteen year old who knew too much. The only thing more important than not wasting the nuclear bomb was the paramount condition that such a bomb absolutely could not be linked to Iran in any way. There would be no guarantee that the young man would be killed by the nuclear explosion. And if the blast didn't kill the young man, he would be able to piece everything together for the police.

Behrouz would tell the police about the midnight rendezvous with the Damascus Star and the large crate he helped load onto the fishing boat. Then he would tell the authorities about his Iranian contact, a man called Kassim who he helped sneak into the United States, and that this man needed to find a spot close to the Sears Tower to dock a boat with a large crate on it.

Taking even a small chance that Behrouz would escape death was not an option; he needed to be assured that Behrouz would be at the construction site at three o'clock. The major came up with a simple plan. He would pilot the boat up river toward the old building where they

Alan D Schmitz

parked the previous day. A telephone call to his accomplice at precisely three P.M. would assure him that he was at the meeting place. Then he would detonate the bomb, killing himself, the young man and thousands of infidels.

Hamid still wondered how the police found the slip where the boat was docked. Maybe his young friend was already talking to the police and perhaps they already knew the entire plan. *"No!"* Kassim contained his paranoia. The young idiot wouldn't have sounded so calm on the phone. Hamid was sure that at this moment, Behrouz had not talked to the police. There was a buzzing sound coming from the boat. His satellite phone was ringing. Captain Shukah ran for the boat, almost falling through the rotted dock.

"Salam!" *Hello!*

"Kassim, the police were on my ship again." The ship captain sounded panicked. "The special police suspect something; they went up and down the stairs at the aft of the ship, but didn't find the hiding place. There are three men, the same men who found the broken machine. They know something is wrong, but seem confused. They asked me if any of my crewmembers were ill with cancer. It seems the police think someone is suffering from a possible overdose of X-rays."

"I know the men you are talking of; they were at my dock also. Luckily they didn't see me. But that means somehow the device can be tracked." Hamid didn't tell the captain what he had in mind. The less he knew the better. The captain and his men, if they survived the blast, would probably die a painful radiation death. *Allah, help them*, he prayed.

With the new information, Hamid realized that he could probably be tracked. If the police found the slip where he was docked the last few days, they would certainly be able to eventually find him. The bomb must be giving off telltale signs of some sort. The Iranian pounded on the dash of the boat and cursed "Golole," *SHIT*. He had to hide the bomb soon or he would be found, but that meant that sooner or later the bomb would also be found by their machines. The more he thought of the cascade of events, the angrier he became.

"Captain, when will your ship be ready to depart?"

"God willing we will leave first thing tomorrow morning; you must rendezvous by tomorrow noon. If there are further complications, I will call you."

"Good luck to you Captain. May the grace of Allah be with you."

In all probability, the bomb itself was giving him away. He didn't know how. He didn't understand such things. But the IRGC captain did

184

understand evasive maneuvers; if the bomb was traceable, he could potentially use it to confuse the officials and lead the police away from the real target. Captain Shukah decided that he had time to go further up river. He would traverse north as far as he could, then while the police were chasing the radiation from the bomb up the river he would double back and strike the heart of Chicago.

Timing would be critical; he had to turn the boat around and head back south toward the giant tower at just the right time. Too soon and Behrouz wouldn't be at the old abandoned building yet. He needed to have enough time to arm the bomb and get the boat close enough to his young associate so they could die together.

Helicopter over Chicago River:

"Whatever the source is, I'm still reading it. I wish we knew what we were looking for. There are thousands of small boats, it could be anyone," Dr. Michael Stark told his partner over his headset.

Matt was piloting the small copter. He asked over the constant thumping of the rotor blades, "The river forks off to the north and south up ahead; which way?"

"Hell! Your guess is as good as mine."

"More targets south. Is the camera rolling?"

"Everything seems to be working fine. If you could go lower and slower that would help."

"Roger that!"

"I'm still picking it up. Same radiation source; that's for sure. But it seems weaker. It's being diluted. Head out west over the city a bit; I want to calibrate the sniffer over relatively clean air."

Matthew banked the chopper and pulled back on the collective. The chopper lifted itself high enough to clear the cityscape

"Just as I thought, away from the river the air is clean of radiation. Whatever it is, it's on a boat, or was."

"I don't mind telling you I have a bad feeling about this Michael. Are you sure this radiation isn't dangerous?"

"I'm with you boss. Something is very wrong here, but the radiation itself is not dangerous, at least not at this level. It's possibly some sort of dirty bomb we haven't contemplated, but I can't understand what it could be with this type of radiation. I think it's time we notify the agency. Something has been giving off dangerous levels of radiation for too long. Head back south until we lose the trail. It has to end sometime."

The copter banked again. Once they were over the river, Agent Mitchel dropped the chopper down as far as he could.

"OK Matt, let's turn around. The radiation stopped somewhere between Union Station and the Sears Tower. I really don't like the way this is going."

"Now what?" Matthew shouted into his mic.

"Head north, the readings were a bit stronger on the main branch."

"Whatever you say, Professor."

Michael took his IT-Tech phone out of his pocket and checked for messages. I wish Deter would get us a picture of the boat. He should have contacted the owner by now.

Chicago River:

Captain Shukah turned his boat around and had gone as far up the north branch of the Chicago River as he dared. It was time to start heading south again. Hamid breathed deeply, trying to remember each breath. Soon the senses of this world would be forgotten to him as he celebrated in the paradise of the next.

Off in the distance, the Iranian could hear the unmistakable sound of a helicopter. He had seen many helicopters the last few days, His young friend assured him that they were mostly news people and traffic copters. As Hamid boated south, the low flying copter flew over him going north.

Helicopter over Chicago River:

"The radiation seems stronger in this direction. That makes me feel a little better." Michael spoke into the mic, though the thought was mostly for his own benefit.

"I don't know as much about this stuff as you do, but this isn't ghost radiation. Somebody is moving something up and down the river, that much is for sure, and that makes me very nervous."

The copter went another mile up river when Matthew confirmed the trail had ended. "Might as well turn around. I want to try to mark a location on the GPS where the radiation starts to drop off. We will probably have to search the area by foot, but that could take us days unless we get damn lucky."

Michael felt his phone vibrate in his pocket. A text message just arrived from Dieter.

"Talked to owner, he hasn't used the boat for weeks. But he does lend it to an employee from time to time. Young man, nineteen. I believe him. Sending picture of boat. Will locate employee. Owner's name Ismael Bartimeus. Employee is Behrouz Golzar."

"Hey Matt, I got a text from Dieter. He's talked to the owner who says he hasn't used the boat, but he lends it out to an employee. He's sending a picture. Dieter is going to try to find the employee."

Michael anxiously waited for the picture of the boat to download to his phone as he marked the probable northernmost position of the radiation.

"I've got the picture," Michael passed his phone to his partner who took a glance at it in between scanning the gauges in front of him.

"I think we flew over a couple of boats that looked about that size," Matthew added.

"I think we flew over more than a couple of boats that looked something like this. This will be like finding a needle in a haystack. Hold on. I've got an idea."

The scientist sent the picture on his phone to his computer using a bluetooth connection, and then with a few clicks on the keyboard he had what he needed. "I'm going to search the video for a match as we fly south again. Maybe I'll get lucky."

They had flown over a few marinas and private docks. Many of the upscale apartments and condo projects along the riverfront had private slips for their occupants. Michael scanned the computer well aware that as long as he was using it to view past history it couldn't record what they were presently flying over.

"Michael!" the excited pilot shouted. "I think I've got it, dead ahead."

From Michael's position in the back of the chopper he didn't have as good a forward view as his partner, so he couldn't see it yet. Michael pressed a few buttons on the computer and soon he had a large screen view of the picture Dieter had sent. With the large picture in front of him he should be able to confirm the target.

"I'll circle it on your left."

"Rodger"

The startled captain of the small cruiser below them slowed his boat down, staring up at the circling copter.

"I can confirm that it's not our boat. Let's move on."

The small four-person copter was soon at the main fork heading back toward the harbor. The scientist was studying the computer-generated video again.

Alan D Schmitz

"Anything?" Matthew asked.

"Nothing! You?"

"Nope, not a thing."

"Wait, I think I have a match. Head back north."

"We only have fuel for another fifteen minutes, and then we have to head for base."

"Copy that," Michael responded dryly. Then with excitement in his voice he said, "I have a confirmed match. Let me check coordinates." A few more minutes passed. "About halfway up the river, we passed it on the way up. It was headed south. I'm sure we didn't see it coming back but it's a positive match."

"It could be anywhere by now. What about the radiation?"

Michael was so busy going over the video he hadn't paid any attention to the sniffer.

"Nothing special; more of the same. My gut says go north."

Hamid could hear the sound of the small helicopter as it chopped through the air. He had no doubt in his mind that the chopper was looking for him. Just minutes earlier he had watched it circle a small lake cruiser that was heading south. For the time being he was safe because when the low flying helicopter had zoomed over him on its way north, Hamid decided to search for cover. Luck or Allah provided the same dilapidated pier he had been at earlier. The overgrowth around the abandoned pier concealed him well enough. The police were getting closer to finding him and the bomb; that he was certain of.

To take the boat back out on the water now would be like surrendering. He imagined U.S. Coast Guard and DNR police patrolling the river looking for him. He had to take action to protect his country from discovery and that meant making sure the bomb was not found and that he was not captured.

"Golole," he swore again. "If it wasn't for the one loose end of the American teenager, he could try to get as close to the downtown area as possible and detonate the bomb. Then the terrorist thought of another potentially devastating problem. *What if the bomb didn't work?* The fact that it was obviously defective in some way bothered him. Even if he killed himself, the unexploded bomb would be too big of a clue to give up. Hamid realized he needed two things. He needed to kill the young man, and he needed to hide the bomb so that it was safe and he could retrieve it if it failed to go off. "Golole," he swore again and then asked Allah to forgive him for his improper language.

188

Hamid sunk to his knees to face the direction of Qublah, the shortest direction to the holy land and prayed. When he was done, he looked up. Then as if by divine guidance the solution quite literally presented itself. In his desperation he had docked at the same decaying pier as before. But what he didn't see before was an abandoned building. It was weed choked and nearly invisible from the river. The terrorist inspected it more closely. There were padlocks on the doors but they were rusted. He had a plan, but he had to work fast.

"Captain, I need you to pick up a large package for me."

The ship's captain wasn't expecting a call from his secret passenger before tomorrow, but he immediately knew what package was being talked about.

"The ship will be leaving tomorrow morning. I do not have a vehicle to use to get the package."

"I am disposed. You must pick up the package, and you are the only one that I can trust. You will find a way."

The ship's captain took a moment to consider the circumstances. He didn't know how he would do it on such short notice, but if the IRGC Major needed him to retrieve the bomb, he was desperate.

"Where is it?" the captain of the Damascus Star asked.

Hamid looked at the coordinates displayed on his satellite phone, and gave the latitude and longitudinal numbers.

"Once you have the package, call me and I will give you directions to the delivery destination."

The captain of the cargo ship couldn't help himself as he warned his Iranian countryman. "If I am caught with the package there will be no denying our involvement."

Hamid cursed to himself. The captain didn't need to tell him the obvious and he certainly didn't have to say it in English. Sometimes he thought that the old man just enjoyed hearing himself speak the foreign tongue. He really hoped that nobody was listening to their conversation as he pressed the "End" button and broke the satellite connection.

The bearded Iranian dragged the bomb off the boat, not an easy task but doable. Hamid lifted his pack of weapons and espionage tools off the boat. Once he had the bomb hidden in a good spot, he scuttled the boat by shooting it full of holes with his powerful magnum .44. Walking to the nearest hotel, he found a taxi to take him back toward the downtown area.

Chapter 15

Chicago, Illinois:

Scott and Paxton went step by step through the exact sequence of events. It was as much a dress rehearsal as they would get. If things went right, tomorrow, Friday, would be the opening and closing night of the show. Captain Seaver was feeling more like his old self and was confident he hadn't forgotten anything. The magic pills seemed to be doing their magic.

"Pax, the last check on the weather makes this a go. We are ready. The fire department and the police are ready. Tomorrow is going to be a blast," Scott smirked as he looked at his coworker.

Paxton gave his boss a thumbs up. "Is Jerry going to be here? It would be a shame for him to miss it."

"I'm calling him right now; he wouldn't miss it for the world. Which reminds me, I have to find a place from which to record the implosion."

"Are you kidding Captain? The TV stations are going to be all over this thing. I'm sure they will give you a copy. And don't forget; tomorrow you have an interview with the media."

"Thanks for the reminder on the interview; I'll have to put on my Sunday best."

"Hope you break a leg, as the movie stars say," Paxton teased his boss with an actor's customary mantra. "I have to make quite a few calls myself, and then make sure that security and the police are coordinated. We know that nobody is in the building now, and I want to make sure it stays that way," offered the foreman.

"See if you can get them to beef up security in the whole area. It wouldn't be impossible for some homeless person to come in the back way; it's wide open."

"Point taken. I'll try to sweet talk the Chicago Police Department."

"Good Luck with that."

Scott walked up a few flights of stairs in the building that would be coming down tomorrow. He would be the last person to walk these steps and halls. Scott wanted to use the height of the building to try to find the right vantage point outside to place his camera and laptop. *Paxton was right. Getting a copy of the building going down would be easy.* Hell, he was sure that Liz would record it if it played at home. But he wanted to make his own small video from a very unique perspective, if he could find the right place to set it up.

On the third floor, Scott walked the perimeter of the building, looking out each of the glassless windows. Exactly what he was looking for, he wasn't sure. But he was confident he would know it when he found it. And suddenly there it was.

The new building was going to take up several existing lots. Across an empty field was another building being prepared to come down. If he could set up the camera there, it would get a shot of his demolition project from the back side as it went down. It also was close enough that the tremendous dust cloud would eventually engulf his camera and computer. The shot would look totally cool, but would probably wreck his camera and laptop; it was a chance he was willing to take.

It didn't take long for him to drive his SUV around the corner to the abandoned demolition site opposite their project. He parked on the street, glad to have found a spot. Parking spaces were as coveted in Chicago as Green Bay Packer season tickets were in Wisconsin. As he left his vehicle, he remembered to hit the "parked" button on his IT-Tech phone to record the exact position of his vehicle. He was becoming a creature of habit, which served him well.

Though the building, or rather the land it was on, would be part of the new construction, this site wasn't part of Scott's responsibility. That didn't stop the captain from making a note on his IT-Tech that the police should secure this building too. Scott didn't want anyone injured or killed at one of his blasts. He had a perfect record for safety and didn't want it tarnished.

Scott planned his camera placement; the old building would work perfectly. Tomorrow's sun would be coming up on the front side of the old building, so it wouldn't blind the camera as it faced out the back. He looked toward the sun, which was starting to get lower in the sky. He checked his watch. It was almost three o'clock and sunset would be in about an hour.

As a precaution, Scott set his video system up today, to make sure the camera and placement worked. He also wanted to make sure that he could get good reception for a wireless, high-speed Internet connection. Though he wouldn't risk leaving it sitting out all night, tomorrow morning he would have no time to make adjustments. First thing in the morning he would have to quickly place the camera before he was needed at the demolition blast site.

Alan D Schmitz

Scott saw an old garbage bag being blown in the breeze across the floor and that gave him an idea. He wrapped up his laptop in the bag; it would give a little added protection from the dust of the blast. Tomorrow he would bring tape and secure it better, but it should work. There was an open staircase that would serve as a platform. If the shot turned out like he hoped, the large missing window would frame the destruction of the building across the wide open lot as it went down in a swirl of dust and debris. It would be a unique gift for their client.

Scott turned on his computer and checked the camera angle. All in all the camera angle and height looked pretty good. Then Scott had an idea. Maybe a higher viewpoint would be better. He left the camera and computer behind, if he found a better viewing angle he could come back for them.

As he headed up, Scott looked over his competition's prep work for blasting the building and approved. They certainly had more work to do, but they were off to a good start. Then he took notice of the old building's architecture. It wasn't just another old factory; it had been something much more interesting at one time. The structure was solid brick on the outside; he recognized it as what was known as Chicago Cream Brick. It also had arched walls and some of the ancient, ornate wood molding was still in place. This made Scott wonder what it had been originally built for. Its architecture was beautiful if you got past all the trash and wreckage lying around.

Scott cautiously walked up the stairs, being careful of dangerous demolition debris lying around. He was eager to get a look at some of the floors that hadn't been torn apart. The second floor was in better condition but it was still ransacked by the demolition team. If his guess was right the third floor would have been left largely intact. When he got there, the third floor didn't disappoint.

Scott used his IT-Tech to take pictures of the more interesting features. *Too bad the old girl had to come down; they just don't build 'em like this anymore,* Scott thought to himself and whistled softly in approval as he ran his hand down some of the intricate carved woodwork.

With his IT-Tech in hand, he checked to make sure the computer and camera on the floor below him were working properly. If they were, he should be able to use the Internet to see exactly what view was being captured. So he accessed the company website over his high-tech phone and with the right login password, he was soon looking through the eye of the camera two floors below. That gave him a degree of comfort,

192

knowing his plan should work. Tomorrow morning the camera and laptop would send the video wirelessly to the Internet world, which would send it to his office's secure server. If the laptop computer was damaged by the dust from the blast, the video would be safely stored on their company's server back in Milwaukee. *Technology was wonderful when it worked*, Scott mused. Jerry and their client should be happy with the unique up-close, ground-floor view of the building going down.

Scott felt refreshed and at ease; taking the time to relax and enjoy the old architecture was calming. He had come to terms with the fact that soon it would be time to end his life. The experimental pills helped, actually they helped quite a bit, but he knew that soon there wouldn't be enough pills to postpone the inevitable conclusion. Scott tried to be pragmatic about it; he had one hell of a life, and soon he would be with his son Brad. He was a lot like the old building; he served his purpose and now it was time to move on. There was one problem to overcome. In order for Liz to get the life insurance proceeds, his death would have to appear accidental. Arranging a fatal accident would not be easy. There was no doubt that if he died suspiciously there would be an investigation.

It was just starting to get dark. He didn't want to be caught in the dangerous building after sundown, so he found the stairs again and started down toward the ground floor and his equipment.

Along the north bank of the Chicago River:

Dr. Michael Stark, Matthew Mitchell and Detrick Hans Grabowski from the Office of Emergency Response at the National Nuclear Security Administration rode together in the small, government-issued SUV. Michael had the backseat loaded with equipment that he used to continue sampling the air as Detrick drove. Matthew's job was to try to spot the young man's car. Finding nineteen-year-old Behrouz Golzar's vehicle was their best chance at getting answers to the puzzle. Dieter was doing whatever he could to get the vehicle as close to the river's edge as possible. He picked his way through the back alleys and explored behind offices and factory buildings. The task was daunting.

Agent Mitchell had called his superiors as soon as they landed the chopper and urgently explained the local situation. Dr. Stark had electronically sent the supporting information to be further analyzed by experts at the main bureau. It took their superiors several hours to collect the facts and analyze the data, only to come up with the same conclusion. Something very suspicious was going on along the Chicago River. In fact

193

it had become suspicious enough that it was now the priority issue in the country for the NNSA.

The Chicago Police Department was notified to keep an eye out for suspicious activity. The problem was that nobody knew what the suspicious activity might be. Dieter's efforts to find the young fisherman named Behrouz had been unsuccessful. His mother told him that her son had a date with a girl; she seemed proud of that fact and mentioned it more than once. But the old lady didn't know who the girl was or where they might go. However, the agent was successful at identifying the make and color of the car he was driving. With a records check they came up with a license number too. That was probably their most solid lead. Officers throughout the city were put on high alert to find that vehicle. There was no doubt in the team's minds that the young man held the key to what was going on.

The picture of the boat and its name were passed on to the police, the coast guard, and the department of natural resources. The boat should have been relatively easy to find; there was only so much river area in which it could be, but so far the boat seemed to have disappeared.

There was some good news for the team and the populace of the city. The stray radiation was still being tracked by the team. The ground trace was working exceedingly well, mostly attributed to the calm weather not dispersing the gas that they were measuring. Often, in order to proceed to the next property down river, they had to take the SUV away from the target area. So far, each time Dieter found a way back toward the riverbank, the gaseous radiation detector would become active again. They weren't chasing a ghost; whatever it was, they were hot on its trail.

The sun was setting and the last vestiges of light would soon be gone. Dieter turned down an abandoned drive, overgrown with weeds and scrub grass. Halfway down it, a heavy rusted chain stretched across the drive, blocking the way to the river and the neglected property.

"It sure doesn't look like anybody was down this way for quite some time," Dieter said as he slipped the small SUV into reverse.

"No wait!" Dr. Stark shouted excitedly. "Let's walk in farther; this is the strongest signals I've registered yet."

The three got out of the car. Matt and Dieter checked their weapons and slipped off the safety. Michael busied himself with the equipment. After adjusting the equipment-laden pack across his back, he proceeded on with his partners. He trusted them to protect him if needed, so he could concentrate on the sounds he was hearing. With each foot closer to the old building the detector clicked faster.

"Whatever it is, it's here," Michael spoke assuredly.

"Do we wait for back-up?" Sergeant Grabowski asked his boss.

"We don't know what we are looking for. If it is a bomb, we need to find it now. Call in before we proceed. Tell the police exactly where we are and what we think we found. E-mail this location to our office as well. If something does happen to us, they need to pick up where we left off."

Michael knew that this was the real deal. The tone and stress in his partners' voices were very convincing. They could be walking into a trap, or be surprising the terrorists, people who would think nothing of killing them to succeed at their mission. But he agreed with Matt. If there was a bomb, it was their job to find it and to find it now.

There wasn't much time left. The sun would soon be down. Matthew and Dieter took point, with Dieter taking an occasional look back. The clicking sound was steady in the scientist's headset and becoming stronger.

"It's in the building, I'm sure of it," Michael whispered.

This was going to take all three of them. Matt motioned to Mike to put down the equipment and ready his gun.

If Michael thought his excitement level was up before, the knowledge that he was going to be part of a siege on the building tripled it. This time he remembered to take the safety off his pistol. Matthew and Dieter knew of Michael's apprehension about using his firearm, but they also had confidence in his ability to use it for defense if he had to.

The three stuck together canvassing the outside of the building. Matthew very carefully looked into any opening or window they found. The old warehouse seemed deserted, but they wouldn't know for sure until they were inside.

Dieter saw that an old lock on the side door was recently broken into; the rusted steel was still shiny where it was severed. The agents had been trained over and over again on how to enter a hostile building. Matthew would go in low, Dieter would take the opposite high, and Michael would watch their backs and also be additional forward firepower if needed.

As Matthew gave the count and swung the door open, they both slid into position. The sun was low but still provided some light through the broken windows. All was quiet. Special agents Mitchell and Grabowski shone their flashlights into the corners. Without letting their guard down for an instant they entered the building.

Dieter made a quick motion toward the floor with his flashlight. The dusty floor was recently scuffed with footprints. The agents continued to search the building as Michael guarded the door from the outside so that nobody could double back and ambush them.

After about ten minutes, Matt gave the all clear sign to Mike. The scientist rushed to his equipment and took it inside. "This is all hot, even hotter than the container on the ship."

"Dangerous?" Dieter asked.

"Getting there!" Michael admitted. "It was here, I'm sure."

"Dieter call in; get the local HazMat team here. This building needs to be contained. Contact the office. Something is going down. We need help, now!" Matthew knew it was time for some command decisions.

"No sense hanging around inside here without HazMat equipment," Michael suggested and he didn't have to say it twice. Outside, he continued his search as Matthew and Dieter lit his way with their flashlights and drawn guns.

There was no doubt that the contaminated item or person came from the river. They saw the old pier but there was no boat. Michael was picking up strong signals of radiation from the old wood dock; Matthew shone his light into the river next to the pier. The murky water revealed little, but there was something sticking up from out of the shadowy depths. Carefully Matthew walked out onto the dilapidated pier and took a closer look. It was the navigation light on the end of an aluminum pole. Dieter joined his partner on the pier and between their two lights the outline of the small cabin boat took shape.

"We found our boat, I'll bet," Matthew said confidently and then asked, "Is it safe to handle?"

"I won't know how contaminated it is until we get it out of the water. We need a HazMat team NOW."

Dieter was already calling the local police; he explained the situation as best he could and then passed the phone to the scientist to further explain.

"Shit!" Matthew swore. "We gotta find that thing, whatever it is. My gut says we have ourselves a bomb of some sort. Is there any way to trace it back out of here?"

"I'm sorry, but we were lucky as all hell to find this spot. To track it out of here would be a miracle."

The first squads were already arriving. Matthew identified himself and filled the officers in on what was needed. He reminded them to guard the place but not enter it. With all the authority he could muster, he demanded that the boat be pulled out of the river by the Hazard Materials Team ASAP.

Agent Matthew Mitchell took time to remind his two partners that they would have to make their own luck. He was more convinced than ever that they were looking for a bomb, and that bomb had to be found.

Downtown Chicago:

Hamid paced back and forth nervously inside the old building, constantly rubbing and tugging his beard out of nervous habit. The bomb was on its way, but by the time he started the initiation sequence it would be too late. By then the downtown would be emptied of its thousands of high-value targets. His chance to become a martyr this day would have to pass. He would live to see at least one more sunrise with the possibility of seeing many more as a hero of Islam if he planned his escape properly. Tonight he would stay with the bomb through the evening. No sense in detonating it today in the relatively deserted downtown. He would set the timer for the bomb to go off at 10:00 A.M. tomorrow and try to escape before it took half the city down. If by some chance it didn't go off, he would return with a vehicle to remove the bomb from the city. If his plan worked, he would escape the blast and then be able to meet up with the freighter off the Port of Milwaukee. Hamid took out a long, sharp knife from his bag; he would need it soon. He hid it under his light jacket. Sliding it into the small of his back, the carved ox bone handle would be easily accessible. Tonight the boy who called himself Beez would become a man in the eyes of Allah. With his martyrdom would come the reward of seventy-two virgins. It made Hamid jealous.

His young accomplice was late. That could mean many different things, and the IRGC Major didn't like surprises. One of the reasons Major Shukah had picked the inside of the old building, was that the open back and missing windows would give him a means to escape if needed. There were many exits. Once he crossed the field, he could disappear into any of the buildings across the street.

Finally, a noisy car pulled up next to the building. A car door slammed. Kassim peered cautiously out a window. It was Behrouz, and he appeared to be alone. The young man tentatively entered the ruins through a broken door.

"Where were you? I expected you hours ago."

"Sorry Kassim. We had to pick up mom's medicine, and then she saw her friend Alice. Alice's husband just died and she was crying and needed some comforting."

"Yes, yes, but you are late, but never mind," Kassim was going to reprimand the young man and realized that it would be a waste of breath.

"Has anyone contacted you from the police?"

"No, I did just as you said. I told my mom that I had a date. Then I left and didn't even get out the car to help her with the groceries."

"You went grocery shopping too?"

"Mom is going to make spaghetti and meatballs for supper tonight. Want to come over? I'm sure my old man and my mom won't mind."

"I'm afraid not. I am also afraid that you won't make it either."

"Do we have a mission tonight?" Beez asked anxiously.

"Your service to your country is over. Allah and your countrymen will be forever grateful. You will go down in Iran's history as a great hero and warrior."

Hamid wanted to make the death quick. Though the young man was inept, he didn't want him to suffer needlessly. Lucky for the younger terrorist, Major Shukah was as good at killing quickly as he was at making it painfully prolonged.

As the IRGC major talked, he casually made his way to the backside of his co-conspirator; no need frightening the young lad. Hamid drew his long knife out from behind his back and thrust it expertly under Behrouz's ribs and into his beating heart. The major twisted it in deeply as blood spurted over his knife and hand. Behrouz immediately felt the stabbing pain inside his chest. He wanted to turn around to look at his hero and ask why, but it happened too fast. The last thing he felt was his head twist around quickly as his friend Kassim snapped his neck, finishing the job in less than five seconds. His death was mercifully quick.

Hamid held the young limp body in his arms as he prayed to Allah for forgiveness, though he already knew that he would. All he did was for God and his country; he took no joy in killing a young believer.

Scott stood on the landing in shock. He thought there were voices coming from the story below, so he cautiously approached not wanting to be a surprise guest at a drug deal in progress. The exposed stairwell opened his view as he descended and peaked around the corner. *Oh my god*; he had just witnessed a murder. Scott instinctively froze in place, staring at the assailant's bearded face. His heart immediately started pumping harder as adrenalin pulsed through his system preparing his body for fight or flight. The murderer didn't see him yet and Scott had no intention of letting him. Captain Seaver tried to stop breathing because he felt that every breath was shouting out his location. His heart was beating so hard that he was sure it could be heard across the room.

Kassim held the slumping, bloody body in his arms, looking down at it and praying for the young lad. Destroying the beating heart first, was a learned technique that prevented a bloodier mess. A non-beating heart wouldn't pump the body's life fluid out of his victim any more than necessary, though there was no way to stop the blood completely. The terrorist looked around inside the old trash-strewn building for a place to hide the corpse. He wouldn't have to conceal it for long because after tomorrow the entire area would be disintegrated anyway. Under the stairwell seemed like a good enough place. He could bury it under a pile of trash.

Scott held his position; the killer was coming closer to him, dragging the body under the staircase. If the killer looked up at the right time, Scott realized he would be completely exposed. Hamid stuffed the body deep into the far crevice, then rushed around finding lose pieces of drywall and construction paper to toss over the body.

Major Shukah's phone rang. Scott almost lost his footing, startled by the noise. *Crap, what if my phone rang?* Scott slowly reached into his pocket and lifted it out to turn off the ring tone. When he did this, it automatically went into vibration mode as he held it steady in his hand.

"Where are you?" Hamid asked the ship's captain.

"We have the bomb, we are a block away."

Fool, Hamid thought. *And why does he insist on speaking English?* "Wait where you are. I will meet you soon. I have some unfinished business to take care of."

The ship's captain parked the small truck and waited patiently with the lights out.

In the eerie quite of the building, Scott could hear the conversation on the phone below. The bearded, dark-skinned killer spoke in a foreign, Middle-Eastern tongue. He wasn't quite sure which, but there was no doubt that the language was not Arabic. Throughout his time as a pilot during operation Desert Storm, he listened to many hours of taped conversations. It was both a hobby and for survival to learn the native language. The sound of it was something he would never forget because during his captivity, he strained to hear every word his captors said. It had given him comfort during those difficult times to know what his captors were saying.

If the language wasn't a form of Arabic, it could be Persian or more specifically, if the killer was from Iran, it could be Farsi. Some words sounded familiar. Farsi was based very loosely on English. From his study of the region, he knew that Farsi was from the Indo-European language family. He didn't understand the language, but he did know that it was only spoken in a few countries, such as Iran. He was fairly certain that the person on the phone was speaking English and said they had a bomb. Right now though, it didn't matter what was said. Scott knew he was going to be the next one dead if the killer spotted him.

Slowly he tried to back away. If he could go up about three steps, he would be out of sight around a corner post. It was starting to get a bit darker as the sun began to rest lower in the sky. Scott was grateful for the help from the setting sun, casting deep shadows inside the old building.

Hamid carried several handfuls of garbage and threw them over the body until he was satisfied that a casual look under the stairs would reveal nothing. He picked up his satellite phone to call the ship's captain and tell him to bring the truck with the bomb to the building.

Scott started to feel clammy and cold as he slowly slipped his heel up another step. His heart was pounding; his hands were wet with sweat. *Breath Scott, breath,* he told himself. *Don't pass out or you will never wake up.* Without realizing it, his life had become very precious to him.

Suddenly the phone that was still in his hand started to vibrate. *Shit.* It was his partner Jerry. When the phone vibrated with the incoming call it also lit up to show who was calling. In the darkened stairway it seemed like a beacon just turned on. He hid the light as fast as possible by stuffing the phone in his pocket. Scott could no longer see the killer, so he didn't know if the man with the knife heard the phone vibrate or if the light caught his attention. Captain Seaver froze in place, listening for approaching footsteps.

The distraction helped him forget about his panic attack for a short while, but now Scott felt the panic coming back. Slowly he breathed in and out, trying not to think about the dangerous man just a few yards away. When Scott heard footsteps moving away from the stairwell, he slowly lifted one shoe to the next stair. Cautiously he put his weight on it and lifted his body one more step. Then a rat scurried between his feet. It ran down the stairs making what, to Scott, seemed like a horrendous sound as it ran through the scrap paper lying about.

The terrorist, because of years of special operations work, was suspicious of any sounds. Now there had been two. He replaced the satellite phone into its holder and watched the small rodent leap from the stairs a few feet from him and down a hallway. Hamid decided that he should secure the upper floor before the ship's captain delivered the bomb. Something startled the rat. Instinct told him to use caution as he proceeded slowly up the steps. He was also suspicious of a flash of light he thought he saw. It might have been a car or some other reflection, or not. He would soon find out.

The killer took a step. His boot crunched on broken glass near the first landing. He looked down at the step for more glass, and then his eye caught the end of a two-by-four flying toward his face. His hand blocked the worst of the blow, but the thick stick of wood still hit the side of his head with a smack. The three-foot piece of lumber clattered as it bounced off the stairs. Hamid glanced up, but didn't see the attacker, though he did hear footsteps running up the staircase. It took him a minute to collect himself. His left hand wasn't broken but it hurt like hell. Soon he would have to commit another murder in the old building. Hamid proceeded up the stairs even more cautiously. Time was on his side. Whoever he was after, would be no match for him. If he had a gun, he would have used it already. In hand-to-hand combat, even with a knife, an indignant alcoholic would not make a contest. Hamid had made one mistake already that could have cost him his life; he wouldn't make another.

Scott scrambled farther up the old building; he didn't know why he kept going up floor to floor. All he knew was that he was putting distance between him and the killer. The IRGC major took out his gun. He disliked using guns in close contact situations. Knives were much quieter. But inside the old building a shot should be sufficiently muffled. Emerging with a burst onto the next floor, the captain knew he was trapped. There were no more stairs to climb. He ran away from the open door of the stairwell and hurt his knee as he bumped into an old barrel; the half-full barrel rang like a bell, giving away his position.

The upper floors hadn't seen the demolition crew's destructive hammers and the floor plans were pretty much like the ones below it. This helped Scott, because in the darkening sky he could still feel his way around. The sound of footsteps coming up the last section of stairs was getting closer. Hiding wasn't an option; the killer would search each room until he found his prey. The frightened architect found another broken off two-by-four; he would have to make a stand. Then he had an idea borne in desperation. He ran to the old barrel of solvent and used all his strength to pick it up. In a blind rage he raced down a half flight of steps with the barrel in front of him. At the bend in the stairway, Scott looked into the eyes of death as the man started to aim the gun at his head. The two men locked eyes for an instant, during which, time stood still. The terrorist pointed his gun at the man, shot and fired. The big barrel took two hits. Luckily the solvent didn't set fire but the liquid did absorb the bullet's energy. Scott lifted it in front of his face for the throw of his life. With all his might, he sent the barrel flying. It bounced on the steps above Hamid. Scott never saw what happened; he was already running up the stairs. Another shot rang out.

Captain Seaver had another important piece of information. The killer had a gun. Scott picked up the two-by-four realizing he was at a huge disadvantage. "shit!" He cursed in a whisper.

Hamid saw the barrel take a bounce as it sprayed its contents through the large bullet holes his .44 magnum had made. The bounce landed it squarely at his feet. When he tried to jump over the rolling barrel, his finger accidentally pressed the trigger and a bullet shot into the wall next to him. The rolling barrel caught his feet and dragged him down the remaining stairs. The Iranian stood up slowly, bruised and pissed. He wouldn't miss again, he promised.

He climbed back up the steps, gun drawn and ready. The IRGC agent felt the adrenaline pumping him up. *Good,* he thought. A little fear would sharpen his reflexes and senses. The sound of footsteps had gone up to the next floor and he followed them cautiously. The floor above him was eerily quiet; the racing footsteps had stopped.

The last rays of the day's setting sun glowed through the back windows; the inner hallway on the other side of the wall was very dark. Scott carefully picked his way across the barely lit room, trying to silently make it to the opposite side of the building. He was sure that there would be a way out into the dark hallway at the far end. Another stairwell on the other side of the building was his hope. He prayed that the last of the sun's light would allow him to make it through the debris noiselessly, and that by the time his pursuer got this far, he wouldn't have that advantage.

Hamid suspiciously stepped around the corner; he wouldn't be caught off guard again. There was rustling in the shadows of the first room he came upon. Carefully he pushed the door open all the way, then entered. This room was much darker, but the open door let in some of the dimming light. He saw movement. Hamid shot twice; two rats died. Three more ran across the room and disappeared into a hole.

Time was running out. Without a flashlight, he realized it might be difficult to find the squatter. Somehow he would have to make the man reveal his position. Then Major Shukah heard a faint sound coming from down the hall. There was a small glow; it was the light of a cell phone and somebody talking. The terrorist approached slowly. His target was talking to someone, no doubt calling for help. Hamid quickly kicked the door open and shot three times. The first shot was just a good guess but it lit the dark room; the second and third shots hit the slouched over victim.

Scott bounded out the door opposite the doorway where the killer stood and cracked him over the shoulder; the old two-by-four broke in half. In his eagerness he missed his mark, which was to be the man's head, but nonetheless the assassin was down. The captain had used his phone to play a recording of his voice to lure the killer. And the bag of garbage had looked like a body in the dwindling light, just as he hoped.

The terrorist fell to the ground; his shoulder was in excruciating pain, but he held tightly onto his gun. Scott lunged over the downed man and into the dark room; he grabbed for his phone and tossed it into his pocket out of instinct to protect his lifeline. Then he turned to run. The Iranian was lying on the floor, still recovering from the blow, though he still had the strength to point his gun at his next victim. The Revolutionary Guard major's training took over. His actions were automatic. He aimed and pulled the trigger in one practiced move. Hamid couldn't see the face of his target but his body was clearly silhouetted by the last vestiges of the setting sun. At this distance he wouldn't miss.

The professional killer made a rookie mistake. He forgot to count the one shot that was fired by accident. The gun made a slightly audible click and nothing more. He had fired his eight shots. His clip was empty. The shot that went off by accident when the wino threw the barrel at him had saved the drunk from certain death.

Scott instantly knew his life had somehow been spared. He tackled the downed man and in a split second they both were fighting for their lives. Hamid tried to ignore the pain in his shoulder, as he fought off the desperate madman on top of him; he reminded himself that soldiers in the elite Iranian Revolutionary Guard Corps do not feel pain.

Scott was too scared to think about anything but punching the killer in the face over and over again. The Iranian blocked many of the punches with his arms and knew that he needed to go on the offensive quickly. For a man who Hamid thought was a homeless wino, he was very strong and quick. With his good arm, Hamid grabbed at the knife still tucked into the belt under the small of his back. He paid for that move with a very solid right cross. That would be the last free shot he would give the alcohol-deranged man on top of him. He swung the ox handle knife around and the only thing that stopped it from puncturing Scott's side was the left cross that was already in motion. Instead of hitting Hamid across the face once more, his fist slammed into the hilt of the knife and the knuckles holding it. The force was enough to jolt the knife loose, but the killer was already reaching for it. In another instant, the knife was back in the hands of its owner. Scott knew he would lose in a wrestling match with an armed man, so he jumped up and ran to the stairway in the darkness. Seeing the room earlier in the thin light helped him. He knew exactly where to go. The fact that his memory was working so well was lost on him completely, not that he wouldn't have been thankful.

Hamid grabbed his gun and took a chance running down the dark hallway toward the same stairs as his prey. "Golan," the terrorist cursed as he realized the rest of the clips for the gun were in his pack several floors down. But then he got lucky. The hall was mostly free of trash and he made it to the stairs at the same time as the soon-to-be-dead man.

Scott slammed a heavy old wood door across his attacker's path. That only gained him seconds but he used them wisely to turn around and buy a few feet of space between him and the killer. He ran across the dark room again. This time his attacker wasn't so lucky. Hamid tripped over an old filing cabinet that was tipped on its side.

Captain Scott Seaver was as scared as he had ever been in his life. If his guess was right, there would be another set of stairs at the end of the building. He bet his life on it. If he was wrong, he would have to find a weapon in the dark very quickly, because he was sure that the killer would be coming at him with the knife again.

He didn't know if the man trying to kill him was a drug dealer, or street punk, or gang member. But, if whoever he was had more bullets, the dilemma of how Scott would die would soon be solved. Right now, the thought of departing this world at the hands of the gunman wasn't part of the captain's plan. He intended to fight until he couldn't.

Scott thought of his phone. He pulled it out of his pocket and clicked it on. It served as a pretty good flashlight. He found the exit for the stairs and opened the door. Inside, the stairwell was strewn with debris; apparently it was being used as a demolition chute. Scott had no choice. He stepped inside and closed the door again. Maybe the killer would give up the chase or be misled. With so much construction trash lying about, the stairwell looked like a stacked garbage heap. The down staircase seemed impassable, so Scott looked up.

Soon he had another plan. He used his phone's light to help him climb between the piles of debris, safely finding one step after another. When he was up to the first accessible landing, he picked up a heavy, broken piece of a cabinet top. Scott carefully dropped it between the opening of the spiraling staircase. As it fell, it hit the lower landing and caused even more debris to fall. With his phone safely back in his pocket, he waited. If the attacker was still out there, he would hear the noise and hopefully try to follow it down. If the murderer had given up, the doorway would remain closed. Scott listened in the absolute darkness.

It didn't take long. Scott heard the door open. The killer rushed into the darkness and immediately fell painfully against the sharp edges of broken off drywall and wood pieces with exposed nails. The falling garbage from below was still making rustling sounds.

Scott heard a scream of frustration and then some terrible swear words. Scott didn't understand them, but in any language it was fairly obvious what was being said. The killer's phone rang. There was some more swearing before it was answered.

"Yes! What is it?" Hamid asked in Farsi sounding very irritated.

"Police are surrounding the building; they must know you are inside."

Major Shukah thought about it for a minute. *How could they know? Of course, the young man's car. The police had tracked the car down looking for Behrouz.*

"We are leaving this area. It is very dangerous to be here. We will take the bomb with us. They won't suspect that it will be departing on the same ship that brought it into the country."

"No!" Hamid protested in English. "You must deliver the bomb to me." It was Hamid who had, under stress, reverted to speaking in the same tongue as the person on the other end of the phone.

The ship's captain answered back with a firm voice. "My orders are clear. We cannot be connected with the device. I will take it with me and drop it into the deepest depths of Lake Michigan as soon as I can."

"Listen my friend, we will find a way. It is not too late. I am in the building still. I will call again," Hamid pleaded for more time.

"Be careful Kassim, and if you are to be captured you know what you must do."

"I am aware of my duties, Captain." Hamid angrily acknowledged the potential need for his suicide. "I will do my duty, but you must do yours too. Do not destroy the package unless you do not hear from me by noon tomorrow. We can still do this!" Hamid assured.

There was a click; the phone was dead.

Hamid cursed the unknown man he was chasing. The wine drinking bum had ruined years' worth of planning and risk taking. A lone drunken bum had done what the entire United States Homeland Security Department had failed to do. He saved Chicago. The bum would have to die for his insult to Allah.

Alan D Schmitz

Scott heard the killer's side of the conversation and wanted to record it on his IT-Tech but didn't dare. The killer was only a half flight of stairs below him. There was no doubt about what he heard this time. "You must deliver the bomb to me! We will find a way. It is not too late." The captain realized that the man wasn't just a murderer; he was a terrorist.

Hamid realized that his priority was to escape the building before being captured. He climbed back up the half flight of the stairwell and went out the open door. Then he wedged a piece of wood against it on the outside. At least his prey wouldn't escape out this door. Even more carefully than he came up the main stairs, he went down them; on each floor he took the time to wedge the door to the trash-strewn stairwell closed. The scarred rabbit inside wouldn't have come out yet, he was sure. Once a scared rabbit finds a hiding spot, it will never leave it. Hamid had an idea to finally kill the witness, a witness who could identify him. The IRGC major could still picture the man's face just before the barrel came tumbling and bouncing toward him. It was the face of a very frightened rabbit.

After the door had closed, Scott felt his knees start to shake. His hands were trembling. It didn't take long for a cold sweat to develop. He knew it was a panic attack and then things went even darker for Captain Scott Seaver.

Hamid peered out the upper windows when he had a chance. The police were guarding the front of the building. He could see the old car his accomplice brought; the police seemed to be ignoring it. In fact, the several police he could see were casually smoking cigarettes and joking with each other. There certainly was no sense of urgency being displayed.

When he reached the floor with the barrel that had been thrown at him, he came up with a plan. He sniffed at the solvent leaking out of the holes pierced by his gun. Whatever it was, it was definitely flammable. Carefully and quietly he poured what was left in the barrel out onto the floor and on top of the garbage strewn about. Hamid made sure to soak the area where the far stairwell began. He knew that the wino couldn't have possibly exited here because it was packed solid with debris. A nice fire would provide a distraction, and kill the man still trapped in the staircase.

Chapter 16

Chicago, Illinois:

It didn't take long for the fire to spread. The old building was built mostly out of very old and dry wood. It caught fire quickly, and burned hot and fast. Major Shukah ran to the lower floor and waited until the police in the front of the building saw the fire. When they did, activity of all sorts broke out. There was shouting and pointing, police cars were being moved to make way for the fire trucks. Everyone was too busy to notice as the terrorist grabbed his pack and slipped out a hole in the wall where a window used to be. He stayed in the shadows and cautiously made his way to the next building over, and then the next, until he was down an entire block. He turned and started walking back toward the burning building just like the rest of the gathering crowd.

Police cars zoomed by while safety tape was stretched around barricades to keep the crowd at a safe distance. It didn't take long before several fire trucks, with red lights flashing in the darkness and sirens blaring, to pull up a safe distance from the building. A tow truck moved the vehicles out of the way of the firemen. The first car moved was the one closest to the burning building. It was the old car that belonged to Behrouz Golzar, whose body now laid in a crumpled heap under the flame-engulfed stairs. The police paid little attention as the tow truck lifted the old car and dropped it off a few blocks away. Then the truck came back for the next vehicle, a full-sized black SUV. The tow truck continued to move cars until the street in front of the building was clear.

Because it was an abandoned building, no heroic efforts were employed to stop the blaze or to fight the fire from within. The fire fighters were smart enough to keep their distance and use high-pressure hoses to control the flames. They saturated the building with water. One pumper concentrated on the rooftop while others pumped into the blown-out windows. The building would burn. They couldn't stop that, but the water would keep the blaze from turning into an intense inferno. Their goal was to contain the blaze and prevent it from spreading to adjacent structures. What they didn't know was that a lone occupant was passed out inside a stairwell that would soon act like a chimney, sucking smoke and fire from the lower levels through it.

Alan D Schmitz

Hamid was certain that the one man in this country who could identify him was still trapped in the treacherous stairwell. If the man wasn't already dead from smoke, he soon would be. The two bodies would burn to a crisp inside the building. Eventually their burnt bodies would be hauled to a trash site just like the rest of the charred ruins. Kassim didn't have anywhere to be, so he waited to make sure the fire fighters didn't find any survivors. The old drunk still inside the building proved to be more resourceful than he expected, and the major didn't want any more surprises.

Maybe the bodies would be discovered eventually, but even if they were, he would be long gone by then. Even better, if he had his way, he would get the bomb back off the ship and by tomorrow afternoon half of Chicago, including whatever was left of this building, would be vaporized.

The Iranian knew where the blaze started; the fire had already climbed two floors, and was consuming the fifth floor and growing stronger each minute. The terrorist winced in pain when he moved his shoulder. He didn't think it was broken, but it sure hurt like hell. He hoped that Allah would punish the man in the stairwell and have him burn to death slowly for causing a mujahedeen such pain.

Captain Seaver slowly opened his eyes still feeling dazed. A buzz coming from his pocket drew him out of his sleep. He tried to sit up, realizing in his efforts that he didn't feel well at all. His stomach felt nauseous. He wanted to lie back down to rest, but something was poking him painfully in the back. Scott knew his eyes were open, though he couldn't see a thing. Nothing was making sense to him. He felt totally disoriented, though he registered the fact that whatever had been making the strange sound had stopped. He thought about his breathing exercises, tried to take a deep breath and started to choke. The strong taste of smoke triggered a survival reflex. He stood up, which relieved the pain of whatever was pressing into him but immediately made his breathing more difficult. Though he couldn't see it, the smoke was noticeably thicker, so he crouched down, coughing the smoke out of his lungs.

He felt the vibration again and reached into his pocket for his phone. Lifting it out of his pocket he looked at the lighted screen, it said, "Jerry's cell." Feeling terribly confused, Scott stared at the device, as the phone continued to buzz in his hand. He tried to make sense of things. What did that mean? Who was Jerry? What was he supposed to do? Where was he?

Scott was too confused to know he should feel panicked. Eventually the phone stopped vibrating in his hand and the screen suddenly turned brighter. That was when he saw the smoke billowing around him.

Something from his flying career struck him, he was trained to recognize the symptoms of hypoxia, which is the effect on the mind from the lack of oxygen. He had taken many rides in altitude chambers to simulate cabin decompression. A feeling of euphoria as your mind became starved for oxygen would be the last feeling you would have if you didn't get the aircraft to a lower altitude immediately. Scott knew that he wasn't to that point yet, but the feeling of confusion meant that it wasn't far behind.

Captain Seaver struggled to stay focused; he used his phone as a flashlight to see the staircase and realized immediately he wouldn't be able to go that way. Then he saw the exit door and rushed to it. He turned the handle and pressed against the door; it wouldn't budge. Scott got more aggressive and pushed on the door harder; it still wouldn't budge. In desperation he kicked the door as hard as he could, which caused him to break into a coughing fit from the exertion. The door still wasn't open, so he pointed his phone at the door to see what was blocking it; he saw smoke pouring in from underneath. With his hand, he felt more carefully. The steel safety door was hot. The fire was just on the other side. Good thing it didn't open or he could have been engulfed by flames.

Scott was thinking more clearly now. Adrenalin was apparently doing its job. He didn't know where he was, but he had to get away, and the only direction he could go was up. He thought about making a call. Whom would he call? Nobody outside could help him; and even if he did contact someone, he couldn't even tell them where he was. Time was critical; he maybe had only minutes before the fire broke through the safety door and he would find himself in the middle of an immense fireplace filled with kindling.

As he climbed cautiously up the stairs, he found a torn up cloth and used it to protect his lungs as much as possible. The smoke was getting thicker and the room hotter, meaning the fire below him was getting closer. Scott knew that stairwells were built to be sealed systems so that they didn't act like chimneys, drawing smoke and fire up through them. This one was doing the opposite. *Why?* Scott wondered. Then he had it. The answer was obvious; there must be an opening above him somewhere. To create a draft, the stairwell had to be open to the outside. If he could find that opening in time, he could make it out. Scott worked his way upward as fast as he dared, praying the light from his phone wouldn't quit on him. The smoke was starting to become unbearable; it was burning his throat. He approached a landing and saw a flash of light; all he had to do was go another half flight when he saw his next problem.

209

The last section of stairs had been replaced with a chute. That was how all the debris had been tossed into the stairwell in the first place.

Scott crawled into the opening on hands and knees, blinded by the smoke; he carefully tried to move up the slippery chute. About half way up, a small pack of escaping rats crawled over him. Startled, he lost his balance and slid all the way back down to the stairs. The heat was becoming as unbearable as the smoke. He would have one more try. He was barely conscious and focused his entire being on one thought, *LIVE!*

Crawling up the slippery chute, he pressed his knees into the sides of the tube. He was tired and out of breath. Scott tried not to breathe the poisoned gasses but that was impossible. He had to exert to climb out, and to do that he needed air, even poisoned air.

Scott didn't remember the rest of the climb out of the tube. What he did remember was the wonderful clean air as his head poked through the top of the chute. Gasping and coughing, Captain Seaver cleared his lungs and then with a great final push he dropped the three feet from the top of the chute to the floor of the roof. There was smoke and fire pouring up all around him. He crawled across the rooftop to what appeared to be a safe area, spitting dark smoke residue out of his lungs all the way. Then the rooftop started to spin around him. Scott Seaver, exhausted and confused, collapsed on the roof of the burning building.

Jerry and the job foreman Paxton sat in the hotel bar at the Holiday Inn Downtown, watching the fire on the evening news. Paxton assured Jerry that he had told the police to guard that building; in fact he had talked to the sergeant in charge that very evening and was assured that the CPD was protecting the entire block.

It was unusual that neither of them could get in touch with Scott. He always had his cell phone with him. Possibly Scott was at the fire scene. It would be like him to be in the middle of things to make sure that the fire at the old building didn't hamper the implosion planned for the next day.

He woke up just in time to see a helicopter hovering above him. The cool and relatively clean air had refreshed his lungs. The copter was shining a bright spotlight, searching across the building top.

Scott rolled himself under a piece of huge ductwork from the air conditioning unit. *I won't be captured!* Captain Scott Seaver promised himself. He couldn't remember crashing in enemy territory but evading enemy capture was critical. The Iraqi's didn't follow the rules of war; he could be beheaded on the spot or dragged through the streets and torn limb from limb as a symbol of defiance.

The spotlight passed over his position. Scott tucked in his arms and legs as much as possible. The roof was hot beneath him; he smelled the smoke around him. It was obvious that the bastards were trying to burn him out. To his right a section of roof caved in, and as it disappeared with a sickening crash, flames shot up and took its place. He had to move to a safer location, if there was one.

The copter's light came back toward him. The television news crew couldn't resist filming the line of flames as it shot out the top of the building. Scott used the distraction to move down the roofline. Two more helicopters with searchlights approached the building's top; on tonight's news the main local stations would all have identical coverage of the burning building.

Damn! Scott thought. *I must be a high profile target for the enemy to spend so much capital finding me.* He had to get off the roof of the burning building, and he had to do it undetected. They might easily shoot him on sight. Scott reached down into his flight suit. He never went flying without a flashlight in his pocket, and it would be helpful here.

His flight suit was gone; he was wearing a pair of civilian slacks and shirt. If he was caught without his military uniform on, the Iraqi's would have every right to shoot him as a spy. He couldn't remember how he had got here, but that didn't matter now. All Captain Seaver cared about was that he had to escape.

Another section of roof caved in twenty feet in front of him. He had to get off this rooftop and he had to do it now. Scott saw the helicopters swing around for the new footage. Quickly, he slid under another section of ductwork. The lights from the choppers were concentrating on the new section of collapsed roof, but they were close enough that they lit up the area around where Scott was hiding. The ductwork went over the edge of the building. He peered cautiously over the top and saw that the duct went all the way to the ground. Scott had a plan. If he could find a way into the duct, he could use it as a ladder down and it would keep him completely out of sight.

Driven by the fear of capture, the flames shooting up around him became little more than a distraction. Scott shimmied under the ductwork, making sure to keep hidden at all times. Then he found what he was looking for. Directly above his head was a service hatch, it opened into the sheet metal ducting. He carefully moved himself until his foot was in just the right place. One good thing about the helicopters was that they were creating abundant noise. No one could possibly hear his foot as he kicked at the cover repeatedly until it opened.

211

There was another explosion. Scott never looked back. He climbed into the pitch-dark opening, feet first. Soon he was over the edge of the roof. Like a mountaineer he pressed the tips of his shoes and his fingertips onto any corner to keep him from falling six stories down. It was impossible to see anything inside the rectangular duct, so he warily felt his way down inch by inch. It was hot inside, even though the Chicago Cream Brick was protecting him from the worst of the heat inside the building. Cool fresh air was rising from the bottom of the shaft further cooling him. Without that help, he would have been cooked by the extreme heat just several feet away. Scott worried about what would be waiting for him at the bottom. If he couldn't find a way out of the duct, he would no doubt die a miserable, slow death. When he looked earlier, he didn't see anything connected to the duct at the bottom, but it was so dark that he couldn't be sure. And even if he did escape the ductwork, there could be armed guards surrounding the building. With only one way to find out, Scott continued to climb slowly down, his fingertips cut and bleeding from the sharp metal edges he used for handholds.

Finally he reached the bottom; he was standing on some sort of mesh screen, no doubt used to keep debris and small animals from finding their way into the duct. Scott took a deep breath; he was sure he could kick out the screen and escape the tin coffin, but what would be waiting for him? Scott heard another loud explosion. The captain pictured the confusion and panic that the bombs hitting the building might be causing. He hoped the distraction would cover his escape, so he kicked out the mesh panel below him. It was now or never.

Scott inched his way carefully out of the duct. As soon as his head was in the open air, he carefully looked around. He was in the shadows and nobody was near. So far he had gotten very lucky. Staying in the shadow of the burning building, he crawled his way to the far edge of it, flattening against the ground whenever a flash of flames lit his escape route. When he was at the farthest corner, Scott had to cross a small open area to reach the concealing shadows of the next building over. It would be a risk but he had to take it.

Scott looked back along his path and witnessed the entire middle portion of the building's back crash to the ground in a fiery mess, taking the ductwork he had just been in with it. The helicopter's searchlights were soon dancing around the debris. Again he used the distraction from the fire, this time to dart across the section of open space between the buildings until he was hidden in darkness again. Only an hour before, the Iranian agent used the same section of building to shield his escape also.

Scott, though exhausted, crawled along the length of the next building. Then he ran across another open area to the back side of the next. The burning building seemed distant to him; the shouting voices were muffled. He took a deep relaxing breath; he was safe for now. Captain Seaver found a protected covering and slouched behind some overgrown brush to rest. It was time for him to analyze his situation. Where was he? How did he get here? Why was he dressed in civilian clothes? He reached into his pocket and in the darkness he found his wallet; it was too dark to look at it now, but it was comforting. Then he reached into his other pocket and felt a set of keys and something else. He pulled out what felt like a solid piece of metal. He looked at the strange device and felt it gingerly. Though it had been in his pocket, he didn't recognize it. There was a button on its side and he pressed it. The phone lit up. "TO UNLOCK, SLIDE BAR," it said.

He used his fingers to move the graphic bar like it told him. Then the phone said, "ONE MISSED CALL, JERRY'S CELL." Scott felt the world around him spin once again. *How come I don't understand?* was his last thought as he lost consciousness and slumped to the cold ground.

On the Chicago River Front:

It didn't take the NNSA team long to realize that the suspected bomb didn't move farther up river. After spending an hour searching north of the old factory, Mike could confirm that the telltale radiation gasses weren't present. The object, whatever it was, must have gone in the other direction. At least they knew what side of the haystack the needle was buried in.

"It will take us all night to run up and down these streets looking for traces of radiation," Matthew said angrily to his partners. "If my hunch is right, there is a bomb on the move and whoever has it, is in a panic to use it because they know we are on to them. If you were a terrorist and had a dirty bomb, where would you go with it?"

"Downtown!" Michael and Dieter answered at the same time.

"And if you had a choice, when would you set it off?"

"After everybody is back at work tomorrow morning," Dieter guessed at what he would do.

Matthew came up with a plan. "Let's start a search pattern from the middle of the business section. We'll cross over the Sears Tower; it would be a high profile target."

"We could cover more area from the air," Dieter suggested.

"Too many high buildings. We can't get low enough to get samples from the road. Whatever it is, it's pretty hot and if the radiation traces are fresh, we should know fairly quickly if we cross its path," Michael said.

"We need more help. When will the other teams get here?" Matthew was trying to coordinate the arriving teams in his mind.

"If we're lucky, we might have them on the street just before dawn. The local police have been instructed by Homeland Security to give us their full and unconditional assistance. They have raised the threat level for the city to orange," Dieter added.

"What are the odds of us convincing them to shut down the downtown area before tomorrow morning?" Michael asked.

This time Matthew and Dieter said simultaneously, "Zero!"

Matthew further explained, "We have nothing, a sunken boat, radiation in an old building that could have been used for who knows what. Some stray radiation on an old container ship. And, best of all, it's X-ray radiation, not plutonium or uranium."

"But that could very well mean a dirty bomb is on the loose," Michael protested.

"Sure, or somebody who had a few too many X-rays, some sort of hypochondriac who gets his kicks out of being X-rayed over and over again," Matthew reminded.

Dieter said, "The cost of closing down Chicago for even a day would be hundreds of millions of dollars. We need more evidence, so let's get it."

The three agents sped to downtown Chicago hoping that their hunches would lead to the needle in the haystack.

Downtown Chicago:

It had been several hours since fire in the burning building was brought under control. Scott woke up cold and shivering. What was a beautiful, pleasant fall day had become cold with the darkness. Scott looked around, confused by his surroundings. Why was he crouched over behind a bush with his back up against an old building? In the darkness he didn't realize how tattered and dirty he looked.

He reached into his pocket, took out his IT-tech to check the time. It was almost midnight. He crawled out from the hiding place and tried to get his bearings. It didn't take him long to recognize the large building across the empty field. The security lights lit it up nicely. Now that he knew where he was, he felt a bit better, though still cold. He rubbed his arms with his hands and realized that his fingertips were cut and bruised.

His whole body felt beat up. He needed to get back to his hotel. But where was his car?

Scott pressed a few buttons on his phone and soon the GPS directed him from his present location to a few blocks up the street. *You really did it this time!* He thought to himself. If there was any doubt before about his ability to function normally, it was now settled. Scott knew that he couldn't trust himself anymore. He wanted to talk to his wife and hear her comforting voice. He knew she could help him even though she was miles away. But he also knew that his comfort would be her unsettling. The cold of the evening kept him walking. He convinced himself that once he found his car he would be safe. In his car was his jacket and then the car's GPS would take him back to his hotel.

Scott assured himself that he would be okay; he didn't need to worry Liz more than she already was. She was right. Scott remembered their last conversation. He should have stayed home.

He watched the dot on the map of his IT-Tech get closer to the spot where the hi-tech gadget thought the vehicle was. Scott saw the red police tape wrapped around the sidewalk and street area in front of him, warning that entry past the line was forbidden. He smelled the smoldering ruins of the building in which he nearly died.

Scott's GPS pointed the way to his SUV just another block up.

"Officer, Officer!" Scott shouted.

One of Chicago's finest, though not necessarily most athletic, walked over to Scott about as slowly as a human could walk.

"What do you want?" he said angrily, tired of answering stupid questions from civilians all night.

"Officer, my car is parked down there. I need to get it. My jacket is in it," Scott added as he shivered and rubbed himself a bit theatrically for the officer's benefit.

The officer looked at the poor dirty bum in front of him. The man's cloths were torn and he was soiled from head to toe, with dirt, grime and filth. The officer didn't even want to guess what it was that stunk so bad on the man. "Your car? Yea right. More like your bottle that you had stashed up the street."

Scott saw the officer look at him with disgust and for the first time he examined himself under the streetlight. The officer started to walk away and Scott realized his predicament. Quickly he pulled the keys out of his pocket. "Officer!" he shouted again.

"Beat it! I'm telling you." The officer didn't want to threaten arrest for the fear that he would be forced to actually touch the filthy bum.

Alan D Schmitz

"Look, I have the keys for my car just down the road," Scott pleaded.
The officer heard the keys jingle and turned to look.
"How did you get those keys?" The officer became suspicious.
"These are my keys, my car. I can prove it."
"That I would like to see." The officer seemed amused.
Scott reached into his wallet and took out a business card. "I work for the demolition company that is going to take down that building over there." Scott pointed to the lit up building across the open field.
"Here is my ID officer."
The policeman examined the photo with his flashlight, slowly becoming a believer.
"So you are Mr. Scott Seaver?" the officer asked with suspicion still in his voice. "How did you get so dirty?" The officer was still skeptical.
"I don't remember, I must have fallen and bumped my head."
The officer took a deep sniff through his nose, expecting the strong odor of alcohol, but all he smelled was smoke and trash.
"I haven't been drinking officer," Scott offered, though after he said it he realized he couldn't be sure of that himself.
"You smell of smoke. Were you by the burning building?"
"I can't remember officer; I woke up two blocks down that way." Scott pointed in the opposite direction.
"Hey Charlie!" a voice shouted.
"What!" the officer quizzing Scott shouted back, sounding annoyed at being disturbed.
"Our shift is over; they want us out of here. Let's go. It's been a long night and tomorrow we have to babysit the demolition blast. I want to get some sleep."
"Look, buddy," the officer gave some advice. "You should go to a hospital and get checked out. Your car isn't down the street; they moved all the cars for the fire trucks. I think most of the vehicles were towed down Randolph. I would look over there."
Then the officer shouted back to his partner, "Ralph, bring me a blanket out of the trunk will you?"
"Look buddy, I'd help you but you heard my partner. We gotta go. Whatever you drank or took tonight, I wouldn't take it again. Find your car and go home."
Officer O'Keefe handed the cold bum the blanket and both officers walked away.
"Man..! was that guy in tough shape," Ralph said to his partner.

216

"Tell me about it. And he's in charge of blowing up the building we are babysitting tomorrow."

"You're shitting me?"

"Nope! Better be prepared. It might be a very interesting morning."

From a distance, Major Hamid Shukah watched the police give a blanket to a dirty old wino. *These people are not without passion but someone who abuses alcohol does not deserve Allah's forgiveness. It is a shame that this country condones and breeds such decrepit behavior.*

****

The team from the Office of Emergency Response at the National Nuclear Security Administration was cruising through the emptying streets of Chicago. They already searched the four streets surrounding the Sears Tower. The team was both relieved and disappointed with the lack of results. They were relieved, of course, that they didn't find a bomb in the vicinity. On the other hand, they were disappointed they didn't find the bomb that each was convinced was in the city someplace.

Matthew took the responsibility for the search pattern. Neither Michael nor Dieter had a better idea so the team looked for anything suspicious along their route. Michael kept the electronic sniffer out the window as Matthew drove; slowly through the search area. By morning a few more search teams would be available, but for now they were it and they would be working all night and into the next day. The device had to be found before whoever had it decided it was time to use it.

Two blocks north:

Scott Seaver took the blanket from the officer and wrapped it around his shoulders. It shielded him from the cold but made him look all the more like a homeless person. He covered his face slightly with it out of embarrassment as tried his best to walk through the gawking spectators. Hamid stepped back, as did most of the thinning crowd while the bum headed through the throng toward his car.

The captain was cold, hungry and confused. Why couldn't he remember how he got so filthy? Why did he wake up lying on the cold ground hidden behind a bush? He tried to stay calm and concentrate on what he did know. He was physically OK and he had his keys, wallet, and phone. His pride prevented him from calling Jerry or Paxton for a ride. He didn't want them seeing him this way, nor did he want them to ask questions he couldn't answer right now.

Scott continuously pressed the panic button on his key set, hoping to make his SUV's horn and lights go on. He looked at his watch; it was nearly midnight.. At last, he saw an SUV respond to his remote button. *Thank god,* he thought. It was parked on a slant, rather haphazardly next to a beat up old compact. But it was his vehicle and that made him feel safe. Scott slipped on the jacket that he had inside and then instructed the GPS to take him back to the hotel. At the hotel, Scott let the attendant park the vehicle and once he was up in his room, he threw his clothes into a plastic bag because they stunk like smoke and who knows what else. Then he refreshed himself in the shower, took his P.M. medications and went to bed feeling very tired and sore.

Chicago downtown:

It was just before dawn when Michael's tired ears thought they heard a familiar sound. Throughout the night, the team expanded its search. Now the search grid covered four city blocks in all directions. It was a wide pattern, and now Michael thought their persistence had finally paid off. He patted Matt on the shoulder and signaled him to slow the SUV. Matthew crept down the nearly empty street. The signal was fleeting but Michael was sure of it. They decided to make the hot spot the center of a new search pattern.

Intercontinental Hotel:

Scott groaned when he heard the phone go off. He had not slept soundly; strange surreal dreams bothered him all night. He twisted his body to answer the electronic wakeup call and he groaned again. He felt as if he was in a prizefight the night before.

Something wasn't right this morning but Scott couldn't identify what it was. He looked at his appointment calendar for the day. "8:00 A.M. TV channel 23, 9:00 blast detonation."

The time was 6:30; he might have time for a quick breakfast if he didn't laze around. Scott pushed his sore body out of bed and into the shower. His medications were sitting on the top of the dresser as a reminder; he took an anxiety pill and one of the Tridroxolene pills.

On his way out the door, Scott noticed a bag on the floor. He picked it up, not remembering why it was there or what was in it. The bag might hold a clue to the evening before. When he opened it, his nose cringed at the odor. *No wonder it was in the plastic bag.* The strong smell tried to jog his memory. It was as if a familiar name was on the tip of his tongue but just out of reach. Scott opened the bag and let another dose of the smoky smell assault his nose. Maybe another whiff would help his mind connect the dots. It didn't.

Scott realized that the customary weight of his laptop case over his shoulder was absent. He searched the obvious places in his room but didn't find it. It wasn't that unusual for him to have forgotten if he carried it with him into the hotel or left it in the car. Still, it continued to haunt him, not being able to remember the previous evening. What time did he come back to the hotel? Scott looked at the bottle of Tridroxolene and though he wouldn't or shouldn't need another pill until tonight he slipped the bottle in his pocket. One more at breakfast couldn't hurt. Today wasn't a day to take a chance with his fading memory.

His phone started ringing. "Hello! This is Scott.

"Oh! Hi Jerry, good morning. I was just going out for a quick breakfast. Sure, I would love to have breakfast with you. How about we meet at Lisa's Corner Café?"

"I know the place, just down from our demolition site, right?"

"That's the place. See you then."

****

"I was worried about you last night," Jerry said as he sipped his coffee.

Jerry noticed the puzzled expression on his partner's face.

"You never answered my call," Jerry reminded.

Scott pulled out his phone and checked it. "I see that you called. Sorry, the battery must have been out of power. I was using it an awful lot yesterday."

Jerry accepted Scott's excuse at face value and asked, "Did you see the fire yesterday? I never saw a building go up in flames like that in my life."

Scott thought about his clothes in the bag up in his hotel room. He sipped on his coffee slowly, trying to remember. He must have had one of his blackouts last night. Quickly Scott put two and two together and answered, "Sure did, you should smell my clothes. They are full of smoke."

"Then you were close?" Jerry asked.

"As close as the fire department would let me."

"What happened to your hands? They look like you were in a fight."

Scott examined his hands, and for the first time he realized that they didn't just feel sore, they were cut up and badly bruised.

"I fell last night." Scott didn't know what happened but took a good guess.

"Fell into what? A barrel of nails?"

Scott laughed, "Yea, something like that. There was a lot of debris at the fire. I didn't see it and before you know it, I was lying right in it."

Jerry looked at Scott's eyes suspiciously not necessarily buying the explanation.

"It's a shame that we have to postpone the implosion because of it."

Scott was shocked and the look on his face showed it.

"Didn't you know?" Jerry asked surprised.

"No, I didn't. When did that happen?"

"I'm sorry. I thought Pax told you."

"He may have tried, but like I said, my phone was dead. What happened?"

"The fire team that was trained for the blast and assigned to us was the same one out all night on the building fire. The fire chief tried to call you, when he couldn't reach you, he called Pax and cancelled. We have to plan for tomorrow and hope the weather cooperates."

"Crap, I told Liz I would be back ASAP," was all that Scott muttered. What he was really thinking was that he didn't know if he could keep up the charade for another day.

Scott ordered some scrambled eggs, toast and sausage; he was strangely quiet as he tried to remember the previous evening. Captain Seaver concentrated on what the good doctor had told him. *If you don't remember something, don't dwell on it. It won't help you remember and will only upset you more. Think about what you do know and remember. Live in the present, not in the past. If you are safe, there is nothing to really worry about, is there?*

"Now what?" Scott asked his partner as he picked at his breakfast.

"We have ample security, even more police around since the fire last night. So our site is secure. They must suspect arson, but nobody was hurt as far as the papers say. I guess we just wait and enjoy the fair city of Chicago for one more day. Jean came down with me, so I'm going to bet she will want me to take her shopping on the magnificent mile."

"Lucky for me, Liz is safe back home, away from those expensive stores," Scott joked and then added in a more serious tone, "I will probably drive by the site; I will have to tell the reporters that the implosion has been postponed. Then I'm going to my room for a nap. I feel as though I was in a prizefight last night. I woke up this morning sore as all hell."

"Your hands look like you did more than fall on some construction garbage. Did you get into a fight last night?" Jerry asked probing.

"Not that I remember," Scott joked. Though Jerry didn't realize how serious his partner was.

Jerry and Scott parted ways. Scott got in his car and realized it too smelled sickly of smoke. The GPS guided him to the demolition site. Everything looked under control and Scott never left his vehicle. He decided instead to go toward the burned out building. It seemed to be calling him toward it. The road was blocked off; a fire safety vehicle was parked in front. Scott parked and got out; he looked around and had a déjà vu experience. He was here before. He was sure of it, though he couldn't remember any specifics. Even the awful smell of smoldering garbage was reminiscent. The captain felt the uneasiness of not remembering as he watched one lone fire truck continue to pour water onto the smoldering remnants. He tried to imagine the intense activity that must have accompanied the huge fire the night before. Scott was trying to will his memory back; he closed his eyes, trying to picture the scene from the night before. He opened his eyes and stared for a while at the activity around the charred mess. Nothing seemed to help. The goings on were now subdued. Officers and safety personal joked as they drank coffee and ate donuts. Scott's IT-Tech phone chimed an alarm. He pulled it from his pocket and looked at the message. "CHANNEL 23 NEWS INTERVIEW." It was time to go back to the demolition site.

****

During the early morning hours, the terrorist had convinced the captain of the Damascus Star that he shouldn't dispose of the bomb yet. The captain of the container ship assured the terrorist that he would wait, but that the bomb was ready to go over the side of the ship in an instant if anything suspicious happened. The great lake covered over twenty-two thousand square miles. The bomb had a footprint of maybe six square feet. It would be nearly impossible for the Americans to find one small crate, one thousand feet under the water.

Hamid had a plan in mind; soon he would be on his way to Milwaukee, Wisconsin. The Damascus Star would be leaving port sometime today and they would rendezvous two miles off the Port of Milwaukee the following day. The terrorist swung his pack over his shoulder. His identity was again safe; after a night without sleep, it was time for a generous breakfast.

Alan D Schmitz

****

True to her word the television station reporter was setting up for the scheduled interview. Scott parked at the edge of the demolition site, walked up to the reporter and introduced himself.

"Hi, I think you are looking for me. My name is Scott Seaver of Wells and Seaver Company. We are the company that is in charge of the implosion."

"Hi!" came a very chipper young voice. "I'm Cynthia Rosan, Channel 23 news."

Scott explained. "I'm sorry to report that the building isn't coming down until tomorrow. That is, if the weather cooperates."

"Why is that?" she asked off camera with disappointment in her voice.

"It seems that the fire from last night kept the fire department out too late. The firemen need to rest up."

"I would still love to interview you. This is great background, with the added hook about the fire last night." Cynthia Rosan sounded excited.

"I'm game if you are," Scott agreed.

****

Hamid found the restaurant his young accomplice had taken him to. It was called Lisa's Café. The terrorist watched the news and ordered a large breakfast. The Revolutionary Guard major had convinced the captain of the Damascus Star to delay his departure and then sail at minimum speed. With luck he could still be able to catch up to the ship and retrieve the bomb. If he couldn't ruin Chicago, the city of Milwaukee would still make an acceptable target. His commander granted the time and resources to make another attempt at destroying the infidels after Hamid explained his plan to him. All did not have to be lost.

The major glanced at the large television hung in a corner of the diner. The local news was broadcasting. The terrorist nearly choked on his toast when he saw the face on television. It was a face that he would never forget, the face of the madman who stared back at him from behind the heavy barrel that brought Hamid painfully to his knees. The terrorist leapt to his feet and turned up the sound on the TV.

"Good morning Chicago. This is Cynthia Rosan for channel 23 news, and this is Mr. Scott Seaver of Wells and Seaver Company," the pretty television reporter introduced her special interview guest.

"His company is in charge of bringing down the old Wentworth Building to make way for The River Walk Civic Center. When is the big blast going to happen?" she smiled into the camera, only half looking at her guest.

"Originally the implosion was scheduled for an hour from now. But because of the fire last night it has now been postponed until tomorrow."

"Can you tell our viewers why the fire changed your plans?"

"As I understand it, the fire department worked very late last night to contain a fire not too far from here. This is the same fire station that is responsible for keeping watch over our implosion area. The chief decided that the men needed some well-deserved rest. Better safe than sorry," Scott added and tried to smile into the camera.

"So now when is the blast scheduled for?"

"We are hoping that the weather cooperates and the fire department is ready for the implosion tomorrow at nine AM."

"There you have it folks. The city is anxious to get working on building the new River Walk Civic Center, but it looks like we will all have to wait at least one more day. Tomorrow is forecast to be a beautiful day. So folks, come on down and watch this unique event in your downtown.

"This is Cynthia Rosan, wishing you a great day from channel 23 news."

Hamid's jaw hung open; he now knew who his nemesis was. His name was Scott Seaver and he worked for the company that was going to bring down the building two blocks away.

****

Scott was glad the interview was over and the bright light on the camera turned off.

"Thank you, Mr. Seaver. I will be looking for you tomorrow and you can comment on the hopeful success of the blast."

"Implosion," Scott corrected as Cynthia Rosa walked away.

Hamid smiled. Allah had provided the answer to his prayers. Allah was indeed watching over him; how else could you explain that in a city of millions, the one person he needed to find would be delivered to him over the television. Armed with his name and the name of the company he worked for, it would not be difficult to find this Mr. Seaver again.

Hamid wrote down the name that he heard. The man who had ruined his plans for the destruction of Chicago still lived. This man had to die; Hamid swore to Allah he would avenge him.

Hamid thought about his target. This Mr. Seaver was a pretty ballsy character. Last night he was shot at and nearly burned to death, yet today he was on the television like nothing happened. Apparently he didn't tell the police about the murder he witnessed. Hamid was at the scene of the fire all night; there were no attempts to retrieve a body. *Why?* He wondered. Then he understood. The capitalist dog was afraid that if he was involved in a murder and fire investigation, they wouldn't let him blow up the building. And if he didn't bring down the building, he wouldn't get paid exorbitant amounts of money. Maybe this Scott Seaver wouldn't tell the police about the murder, or maybe he would wait until after he collapsed the building. But Hamid couldn't take that chance.

****

It was late Friday morning before the team from the NNSA was convinced they had identified the trail of the radiation. According to all the readings, the westerly path of the bomb was at their current position. They had faint readings along a few blocks in this area, but then they converged again onto a single boulevard.

Detrick Hans Krier, bomb specialist, was on the phone, constantly coordinating with the other two teams that had finally landed to assist them. Matthew looked at a map of the city. Then he had another hunch. The shipping docks were due east of their position; Matthew turned the SUV to the east. Three blocks later Mike gave a thumbs up. Matt's hunch was paying off. The closer to the dock, the stronger the radioactivity sniffer clicked.

"The bomb was either moved back onto the Damascus Star or it was recently unloaded from it," Matthew verbalized his hunch. "We need to get back on that ship to find out."

The group raced toward the pier and the cargo ship. When they reached the dock, the Damascus Star was gone; the ship had already left port. Dr. Stark took out a pair of binoculars and scanned the freighter leaving the harbor. "That's it all right," he confirmed.

"Shit!" Matthew and Michael shouted.

"Dieter, try to get the Coast Guard on the line. I'll get Homeland to give us authority to board it." Matthew was making a series of decisions.

"Mike, you call the other teams. I want this boulevard, from the dock west, scanned for two blocks on either side. If the bomb is back on the ship, we need to know where the bomb was. And if it came from the ship, we need to know where it is now."

Slowly the team members made their way back up the boulevard, trying their best to follow the radiation residual. Having a starting point was extremely helpful. Michael was able to pull up a map of the city and superimpose the GPS signals from the other two teams. Michael felt that it would only be a matter of time now. The question was, would it be in time? If there was a bomb, it would probably be timed to go off after most people were at their offices downtown. After all, bringing down the tall skyscrapers would be disastrous, but killing the people, and the combined knowledge they held, would be an unrecoverable catastrophe. The optimal time was right now, before lunch scattered the lawyers, bankers and accountants.

The teams eventually ended back at the burned-out building. With a magic marker, Agent Mitchell drew lines along the points of strongest radiation readings. He was so sure of what route the bomb had taken over the last twenty-four hours that he felt it was blinding him to other possibilities. He wanted to stay objective but the facts told him that there was only one explanation. The bomb was back on the freighter.

Michael looked up the road from where they parked; he stared at the activity going on a block from their location. A lone fire truck was spraying down the street in the final efforts to clean up the scene from a spectacular fire. Gut instinct was guiding him; he couldn't help but suspect that the fire a block away wasn't a coincidence. The police had the building sectioned off with yellow caution tape, but it wasn't being treated like a crime scene. Though the entire area was being guarded by the police department, most of their concentration was on another old building. Apparently the building scheduled for implosion to make room for a new civic center and condo project, had most of their attention.

Something about the location and timing of the fire made Michael very suspicious. Dieter declined Michael's offer to go with him as he walked toward the smoldering mess. Agent Krier saw no reason to take the risk of entering the dangerous, charred remnants and warned his partner to be careful.

Michael ignored the police caution tape and very carefully stepped inside the burned-out hulk of a building. The few police guarding the street didn't see him enter. The nuclear scientist didn't take any equipment with him; he didn't need a one hundred thousand dollar machine to tell him that all he had was burnt and charred debris. Still, there had to be something about the coincidence that linked the building burning down to the radioactive materials in this same vicinity. Something was drawing him into the remnants of the building.

The entire back of the brick building had collapsed outward, so light was not a problem. Michael stared at what was left of the stairway going up to the second floor. He wasn't a fire inspector and didn't have a clue as to what he was looking for, yet he suspected that something was there to find.

Michael heard his partner Dieter mock him in a loud voice, "Say Inspector Clouseau, did you find anything but charcoal yet?"

Michael chuckled at the reference and brushed off the comment as lighthearted ribbing. That was when, without warning, a board gave out from under his left foot. The floor was much weaker than he thought, his foot fell through the suddenly open floor. As he fell, his hands grabbed for the closest thing they could find. Thankfully, the half-burnt stairway brace held his weight, because the opening below his feet was now large enough for his entire body to fall through.

Michael cursed himself for being stupid enough to take the risk of going inside the burnt building. He had no idea how dangerous it was, but the fire department and police did, and that was why they stayed out.

"Inspector Clouseau, you OK in there? I heard some noise."

"Yea, I'm OK. I'm coming out. This was stupid," Michael yelled back.

"No shit Dick Tracy!" Dieter invoked the name of another famous detective.

As Michael pulled himself up, hoping the board would hold his weight for a few more seconds, he saw the most ghastly sight in his life. Charred black bony fingers seemed to be grabbing for his throat from behind the remnants of stairs. If he wouldn't have fallen, the black fingers would have looked like the rest of the debris. But at this close angle there was no doubt.

Dr. Stark tried not to panic. He held on to the blackened board for dear life, though he really wanted to run out of the charred building as fast as he could.

"Dieter! Dieter!" he screamed. "Get the police. There is a dead body in here."

"You sure?" Dieter yelled back, though he could tell his partner was serious.

"You're god damn right I'm sure."

Michael pulled himself up much more slowly than he would have preferred and managed to escape the building unharmed, though his entire body was shaking from his find.

"What was it? What did you find?" Dieter asked concerned.

Michael was as white as a ghost. "Somebody was in the building when it burned; the body is by what's left of the stairs."

Chapter 17

Chicago, Illinois:

The team was still at the burned-out factory waiting for a possible confirmation on the identity of the body Michael found. Matthew got a call from another NNSA team that was stationed at the old abandoned factory by the river. The sunken boat had finally been pulled from the riverbed. "Are you sure?" Matthew asked.

"It was sunk on purpose all right; the bottom is full of holes; big ones. I can't tell you what kind of gun did it, but it was powerful."

"What about radiation?"

"The water washed most of it away, so the signal was weak, but when we amplified it electronically its fingerprint matched the radiation in the building. My guess is that the boat was used to transport the object here."

Matthew concurred. "I'm sure of it. Whatever is emitting the radiation signal originally came from the freighter, and then was somehow transferred to the boat you are looking at. It was taken from the old factory to our location at this burned-out building. We have a dead body being recovered by the fire department. Unfortunately the building is too dangerous to investigate further than that."

"I am going along with your assessment that it's a bomb of some sort. So what happened to the object after it left your location?" the female at the other end of the phone questioned.

"I can't imagine what else it could be. What else would someone go to these lengths to conceal? My best guess as to its current location, and I know this sounds crazy, but I think its back on the freighter." Matthew knew how this must sound to his coworker.

"Why would it be back on the freighter?" Sarah Beth Weber didn't quite follow.

Matt knew Sarah Beth and respected her. They had worked together for a couple of years out in L.A. So he gave her his reasoning, hoping to have another persuasive tongue on his side.

"The radiation trail leads from here to the dock. I think that they took it back to the dock from here."

"That doesn't make any sense. Why go through all the trouble to find a small boat, risk unloading the bomb from the freighter to the boat, sink the boat, stash the bomb in an old factory, find another vehicle and take it from the factory, just to put it back to the freighter again and risk having someone see you move it so many times?"

"That's pretty much what Dan Price said back at headquarters. I want to search the freighter again but no one is buying my story."

"Matthew, I'm sure you have your reasons but I'm not getting it," Agent Weber explained her doubt.

"I think we spooked them. Whoever it was, tried to sneak the bomb up river. They scouted out a few places along the south river near the downtown center, which was where they hoped they could set off the bomb. At some point they feared we were on to them, so they tried to misguide us up the north trunk. When they thought we were getting too close, they sunk the boat, and moved the bomb by land back to the city center, where it would do more damage to the financial hub."

"Okay!" Sarah Beth followed along with more than a little doubt. "It takes quite a few leaps of faith to look at it that way, but go on."

"Whoever it was, picked up the bomb from your location and brought it to the old brick building here. There was some sort of scuffle and somebody ended up dead. A fire was started to conceal the body, but now they were afraid the bomb would be found, so they took it back with them to the ship that they all came from in the first place. That's why we found the same radiation signature on the ship."

"Matt, it isn't a bad theory, but I could give you about ten other ones by tomorrow morning with equal probability. Where is the ship now?"

"By now I'm sure it's out of the harbor. It could be setting sail any time, and then in a couple more days be on its way across the ocean. I need to get to it now. Only I can't unless you help me convince Dan Price, so he can convince Kara Johnson of Homeland Security to give us boarding authority.

"Sarah, if I am right, the body we found will be the one person in Chicago who knew what was going on. Will you add your clout to mine and demand that we stop the ship immediately?"

"I can't promise you anything Matthew; I need to think this over. Whoever the John Doe is, he/she isn't talking."

"Well, if I can prove it's who I think it is, then he'll be telling us a lot."

"Who do you think it is?"

"A young man called Behrouz Golzar. The boat pulled out of the river belonged to his boss. We know that the young man used the boat quite often with the owner's permission to go fishing. His mother is very worried about him because he hasn't returned home, something she claims he's never done before."

"You are connecting an awful lot of dots together," Sarah conceded. "Let me know when you get a positive ID."

"That could be a problem," Matthew sighed into the phone. "The body is very badly burned."

Agent Weber was interrupted, "I have to go Matt. Just keep me posted. If I get a better idea than yours, you'll be the first to know."

"Oh, I have no doubt about that." Matthew acknowledged the healthy competition between them.

Uptown, Chicago:

Detrick found the apartment belonging to the parents of Behrouz Golzar. The badge he flashed to the mother looked very real and impressive, so she let him inside. He talked to her with concern for Behrouz's safety, which was clearly on her mind. He suggested, "Perhaps if I search your son's computer I might find out who his girlfriend is, then maybe we can call her and find your son."

"I don't know about those computer things, but if you want to look, go right ahead," the mother agreed with a great deal of worry in her voice.

Dieter wasn't quite sure what legal rights he had to look at the young man's computer, but he was being given permission by the owner of the house, so he decided that he would worry about the legal ramifications later. He couldn't pass up this opportunity.

Dieter turned on the computer and found her son's e-mail. Nothing special there. Then he checked the web browser to see what type of websites Behrouz had visited. He clicked the history button and the last two weeks of browser activity showed up. A quick scan of the web pages showed the a list of pornography sites the young man visited, much to the embarrassment of his mother. Dieter quickly skipped passed these hoping that the mother didn't change her mind about letting him see into her son's life.

There were many websites connected to what Dieter would consider radical Islamic anti-American sites. Many of the sites were written in a language Dieter didn't understand.

"Do you know what language this is Mrs. Golzar?" he asked.

"Yes, it is Farsi."

Dieter didn't understand, and the old lady repeated herself.

"It is written in Farsi, it's what we speak in Iran. My husband and I are both from Iranian families. But this is talking about doing bad things to the people of the United States and to all people who do not agree with the teachings of the Koran. My husband and I are Muslim, but these are radical teachings. Most Muslims do not believe in these things."

"I understand Ma'am."

Dieter went to the deleted file section and searched it. He then searched the deleted e-mails. That was where he found the smoking gun so to speak. Dieter printed the e-mail without asking the old lady if it was okay. There was no time for a philosophical debate about her privacy rights vs. the rights of the residents of Chicago to live.

****

Right after Major Shukah recognized the man he thought he killed in the fire, he paid his bill at diner, left the building and started to make phone calls on his secure satellite line. Hamid needed to know exactly who this Scott Seaver was. Where did he live? Where did he work? But most of all, the terrorist needed to know how he could find this man; he needed to make sure that Mr. Scott Seaver knew that it was in his best interest not to report the murder to the police. If he had to kill him again, there would be no more mistakes.

The major explained the situation to his superiors. They were not too happy with the major, and it was not like him to compromise himself or his country like he had. It wasn't a minor threat when they told him to clean up the mess and make sure he did it right this time. The bombing of Chicago had become a miserable failure. That was also the major's fault, but for now he was to concentrate on tying up loose ends.

Hamid cursed. Why was Allah testing him? Hadn't he always served him well?

A morbid curiosity drove the major to take the long walk back to the burned-out building for a final look, a last postmortem of his handiwork. The large fire had been exciting to watch, even more so because he had created the monster.

Hamid turned the corner to find extraordinary activity going on at the front of the charred wreckage. The major was a half block away from the smoking building and stopped to light a cigarette. That gave him some temporary cover for his surveillance. Casually leaning against a no-parking sign while he smoked made him look unsuspicious to anyone who might care. It was just a coincidence that his commander chose that particular time to call him. Talking on what appeared to be a typical cell phone only served to further protect him from suspicion.

"Yes, go ahead," he said in Farsi. It was his commander back in Iran.

"We have an asset in Milwaukee; he will be at your disposal and standing by for my orders. Here is what I know about your Mr. Seaver and his family."

Hamid listened to his commander and watched with great interest as a body on the street was covered with plastic. The police were taking pictures of it from different angles. A police photographer was also taking pictures of the inside of the burned-out building. There was no doubt; somehow they had found his young friend. Possibly Mr. Scott Seaver had already talked to the police, or perhaps it was just by chance. Maybe the police of this country weren't as inept as he imagined.

Major Shukah cursed Captain Zarin. If the ship's captain had any balls and delivered the bomb to him as planned last night, it would have gone off by now and half of Chicago would be gone in a giant cloud of dust. Hamid cursed his luck; he would have been one of the greatest martyrs of all time. A line of virgins would be waiting for his affections at this very moment.

The terrorist turned his back and walked away; with the information he had, he would find the businessman and kill him. If he did it quickly enough, the bomb could still be retrieved and used.

****

Using ladders and safety equipment, the police and fire department entered the charred building to look for clues. It was dangerous and slow work. At one point, a fireman handed more charred wreckage to the crime scene's lead inspector. "It's a laptop computer, or what's left of it. Nothing salvageable, that's for sure," the fireman commented.

The inspector turned it in his gloved hand; charred pieces fell off. The metal tags on the bottom of it were somewhat intact. "Maybe forensics can make something of these tags."

Several hours passed since the remains of the charred body were first found. The three teams of federal agents responsible for detecting and disabling weapons of mass destruction felt completely helpless. They had mapped out the route of the radioactive device; they knew where it had been, or maybe where it still was. The only problem at this point was that they still had not found a device or any convincing evidence of its existence. Nobody at homeland security headquarters felt there was near enough evidence to warrant searching the ship for the third time.

231

Michael, Matthew and Dieter along with Sarah Beth Weber sipped coffee around Sarah's red Jeep Cherokee.

"They don't even believe it's a bomb," Matthew complained.

"They don't think there is enough evidence to call it a probable bomb detection," Sarah corrected.

"Isn't that what I just said?" Matthew argued back sarcastically.

"They are not as emotionally tied into this thing as you are. You have to respect their opinion. Besides, they weren't up all night chasing ghosts and might be thinking a bit more clear-headed."

Mike felt insulted by the comment. "We weren't chasing ghosts all night; this is very real and potentially very dangerous."

"But the point is we don't even know what or who we are looking for. Even if the body is identified as that of the young fisherman, it won't prove anything," Sarah reminded.

"It will prove that he was murdered because he could identify the people involved," Matthew argued.

"Or," Sarah conjectured, playing the devil's advocate, "he died because he was stoned and in the wrong place at the wrong time. He might have even been the one who started the fire."

"What did the big cheeses say about the e-mail letter I got off his computer?" Dieter questioned.

"You mean besides the fact that the mother could sue us for misrepresentation, searching her property without a warrant and taking private property," Matthew reminded his partner.

"I told you, she gave me permission."

"Your word against hers; won't hold up if push comes to shove."

"But the e-mail gave instructions and times."

"Sure, instructions to meet his fishing buddies at some coordinates on the lake where the fish were biting," Sarah Beth added. "Look, I know I sound like the bad guy. I'm just thinking like the big wigs; we need more evidence."

Then Sarah Beth came up with a plan and asked, "Dieter, if we plugged those coordinates in the computer, would it be possible to match them up with the exact location of the freighter at the time suggested in the e-mail?"

Dieter thought for a moment. "It might be. We still have enough pull to get some help from Homeland Security. They could get help from military satellites and check for any eye in the sky that might have some pictures of that area, at that time. I know just the gal to call to get it done; I don't think she's pissed at me anymore."

Sarah rolled her eyes at the last comment; Matt just laughed guessing his friend was just kidding. *Then again*, Matt thought, *knowing Dieter, he probably wasn't.*

"If the coordinates in the e-mail turn out to be the same location as the freighter at that precise time, then that would tie our young friend to the freighter. If we can prove his death was a murder, we might be able to persuade someone that the murderer of a U.S. citizen is on the freighter."

Matthew liked the plan and added, "If we can't prove a bomb is on board, maybe we can prove a murderer is. Either way, we get to board it again."

****

The terrorist called the office of the Wells and Seaver Company. It was Friday afternoon and the receptionist was still at her post. "Hello," Hamid said graciously, trying to conceal his Middle-Eastern accent. "I am in Chicago and have a delivery for Mr. Scott Seaver. It is very important that he receives it before tomorrow's implosion. Could you tell me what hotel he is in?"

The receptionist, Mary Linden, had been with the company for fifteen years and knew more about what was going on at the office than her bosses usually did. If a package was sent to one of her bosses, she would know about it. "I don't remember a delivery scheduled for Mr. Seaver."

"I am a courier from the current owners of the Wentworth Building. It is important that Mr. Seaver gets these diagrams before tomorrow."

Mary felt on the spot. She wouldn't normally give out this kind of information, but this project was extremely important to the company and she couldn't take the chance that she screwed something up. "Please hold the line; I will have to call Mr. Seaver."

Mary pressed the speed dial button for Scott's cell. It rang and rang and there was no answer. *That's strange.*

Scott's phone was set for vibrate only. He didn't hear it as it bounced lightly on the countertop near the window. After the television interview he went back to his hotel and called Liz to tell her about the canceled blast and that he had to stay another day. Shortly after that, he crashed on his bed, taking only his shoes off. Though he intended on only a short nap, he quickly fell deep asleep. As he slept, his body and mind healed from the ordeal the night before.

The receptionist clicked back to the caller on hold. She realized that she would have to make a decision. "I haven't talked with Mr. Seaver so I

233

don't know what hotel he is in, but he usually stays at the Holiday Inn Downtown."

"Can I get his cell number so I can alert him that I am on my way?"

Mary knew better than to give out her boss's cell number but this certainly sounded like an emergency. Since she couldn't get hold of Scott and would be leaving soon for the weekend, she didn't want to take any chances. "I don't usually do this, but you sound desperate and I am going home for the weekend."

Hamid wrote down the number and repeated it to make sure there were no mistakes. "I am sure your boss will be very glad that you helped me. I appreciate your help so much." Hamid had what he needed and hung up before more questions were asked.

The Iranian terrorist called his support team back in Tehran. Could they determine which room Mr. Seaver was in?

Major Shukah went to the Holiday Inn Downtown and booked a room. He was fortunate that it was Friday evening and the business travelers had gone home for the weekend. He slung his pack over his shoulder and went up to his room to plan his attack. It would be a simple operation once he found what room his target was in. Slashing the man across the throat would both silence him and bleed him out quickly. Then the major would get a good night's sleep and check out as any guest would. With a DO NOT DISTURB sign on the door, nobody would find the body until late afternoon at best.

It was 5:00 P.M. Chicago time when the commander finally called back. "We hacked into the hotel's computer. We are certain that Mr. Seaver is not registered. Either Mr. Seaver is going under an alias or he is not there. We were able to trace his car make and license number; I suggest you search the parking area for his vehicle."

Hamid had to wonder if the police suspected Mr. Seaver's life was in danger and moved him to another hotel. "If I give you his cell phone number, can you trace his phone?"

There was a pause on the other end of the line as the commander researched the question.

"It is possible; it depends on what type of phone he has and if the GPS locater function is turned on. We have successfully hacked into the U.S. telephone system; our people will give it a try."

While the major waited for further assistance, he checked the parking structure for the Seaver vehicle, not finding it. Then he waited in his room. At 7:00 P.M. the call came.

"We traced his cell; apparently he is at a hotel east of your location called the InterContinental. I will give you the address. Unfortunately we cannot tell you what room he is in. Our people tried to hack into the InterContinental system, but their private system is more secure than the American power grid. You will have to find his room on your own."

"Thank you for your help; may Allah bless you."

Hamid wasn't too worried about finding Mr. Seaver's room. He had been doing his job for many years and wasn't used to the luxury of being handed his information through compromised computer systems. He would have to do this the old fashioned way, his way.

****

Dr. Michael Stark was at his apartment catching some much-needed rest, as were his teammates at their respective homes, until agent Matthew Mitchell woke him up with a phone call.

"Good job Mike, the body you found was positively identified as that of Behrouz Golzar. He was stabbed and his neck was broken. We have part of our smoking gun."

"What about Dieter? Did he come up with the location of the Freighter the evening our murdered fisherman was out?"

"So far we don't have an answer; this is strictly on-the-side work, no priority."

"That is such bullshit! We could have a bomb in a major city."

"I'm tired of hearing excuses too. But I have Price prepped. He agrees that if we link the freighter and the sunken fishing boat to the murder of the young man, he will back our request. We had better be right on this. Dan told me that when he contacted Homeland Security about the radiation traces, they called the Secret Service. It appears that the president was going to go back to his hometown for a few days. His coming to Chicago was strictly hush hush, but he agreed to cancel it based on our findings. If we're right, we may have saved the president."

"Yea, and if we're wrong we'll be lucky to be guarding an outpost in Antarctica," Dieter complained.

Michael couldn't fall back to sleep after the call. He was confident that there wasn't a bomb in the city any more. That was comforting, but he also felt strongly that there was a bomb somewhere close, possibly on the ship on the Great Lake. That was extremely unsettling. They had stopped a catastrophe in Chicago only to move it to kill Americans elsewhere. One way or another they had to get to that ship to find out.

****

Hamid left his hotel with the backpack full of lethal tools swung over his shoulder. He might need it tonight. The taxi picked him up in front of his hotel and soon he was a block away from the InterContinental.

This would be more of a challenge than he anticipated. The landmark hotel was obviously very upscale and the staff was undoubtedly trained to protect the privacy of its guests. Hamid looked around him and realized the assets he needed were surrounding him on the street called the Magnificent Mile. There was a flower shop across the street as well as a fruit vending company. A few blocks away was a Bloomingdales; he would find whatever else he needed in there.

****

Captain Seaver was plagued by strange nightmares as he slept. He awoke startled more than once, his own voice shouting "help" with a sleepy rasp. He had to try to force his petrified body to move from the danger, but it wouldn't or couldn't. The only thing stronger than the nightmares was his insatiable tiredness. Each time he woke, he soon fell back asleep, only to be trapped by his dreams again.

Scott woke a final time, his arms flailing at the air as he fought the bearded man in his dream. He was drenched in sweat; the dream seemed so real. His body ached as he got up to relieve himself. Even his fingers and knuckles ached as he tried to open and exercise them. Scott remembered what his grandmother told him when he was little. *"If you die in a dream, you will never wake up again."* These dreams were so real he felt that his grandmother might be right; thank god that he awoke before being burned. The captain dragged himself into the shower, which made him feel better as the warm water streamed over him. By the end of his shower he was feeling hungry. He hadn't eaten since breakfast. A look at his watch gave him hope that the lobby restaurant was still open.

Scott dressed and took his medication. He couldn't remember if he had taken his morning dosage but was sure he hadn't taken any of his meds since returning to his room. Then he dropped his freshly charged IT-Tech into his pocket along with the half-full bottle of pills. It was time to call Liz, but that could wait until after he ordered some dinner.

Downstairs, in the elaborately appointed and expertly restored lobby, the sign at the entrance of the restaurant let him know he was in luck. It was open until 9:00 P.M. Though he still felt a bit weary, he ordered a beer, soup and a sandwich. His ice cold beer came in a tall frosty mug and went down quickly; he ordered another. There was a half wall between him and the elevator that had a rippled lighted glass built into it with lazy water falling over it. The water was soothing and peaceful. Scott started to finally relax while he more slowly enjoyed his second beer.

The call home went uneventfully. Liz and Avery were enjoying a girl's night in together. The movie they were watching wouldn't have been Dad's choice but it made them both cry; so they were happy with it. Avery complained about her tests and how she didn't do so well. Scott took it with a grain of salt. If he knew his princess, she had done just fine, though she liked to hedge her bet with him just in case. She did have to tell her dad that the phone he gave her was the talk of her class. "It was so way cool!"

Scott sipped the tall frosty mug of beer and laughed at his daughter's jokes. His soup came so he gave both his love and hung up. Scott realized how lucky he was, or had been. His luck had finally run out, but he had to admit it was one hell of a run. Many of his war buddies never made it back; he was truly the lucky one.

Thirty feet away, but shielded from him by the restaurant wall, the front desk of the InterContinental Hotel suddenly became extraordinarily busy. The telephones were demanding attention. Even the manager from the back office came forward to help. People were trying to book rooms. Others were checking on existing reservations. Guests started calling to get directions from the hotel to downtown destinations. Besides all the calls, a florist stopped with a full bouquet for a Mr. Scott Seaver and demanded it be delivered to his room immediately. In between calls and putting people on hold, the manager tried to assure the florist the flowers would be delivered promptly. At the same time a fruit vender with a full basket of colorful, ripe fruit insisted that his basket for a Mr. Scott Seaver deserved even more immediate attention.

The craziness just got worse as a clothier came between the two vendors and demanded that he needed to see Mr. Scott Seaver to deliver and fit a new shirt, which he carried carefully in front of him. The desk manager was trying to keep some degree of dignity and control, though it seemed impossible. He waved his long skinny finger at the three to be patient as he put another caller on hold. The phone was still demanding attention from yet another caller. The manager answered it.

"Yes, Mr. Seaver, there is a gentleman here with a shirt for you."

"How can I give a speech in thirty minutes if my shirt is down in the lobby?" Mr. Seaver quizzed sarcastically. "Did he bring ties with him?"

The nervous desk manager quickly asked the man with a backpack over his shoulder, "Did you remember to bring ties?"

"Yes, several," he answered.

"Mr. Seaver, he assured me that he has several."

"I have to get back to practicing my speech. Send him up immediately. I need to be fitted. And no more interruptions please. I only have twenty-five minutes now." The phone went dead.

"You are to go up immediately. I will have our people take up the fruit and the flowers as soon as possible."

"What room?" the clothier asked impatiently.

The manager quickly looked it up and wrote it down on a piece of paper as he took one of the other calls that had been on hold.

Hamid walked toward the elevator, trying not to laugh at the predicament and commotion his countrymen caused the hotel desk with a handful of well-timed international calls. But the ploy worked. The fake Mr. Seaver, an agent in Iran, demanded that the clothier be let up to his room. That caused the frazzled clerk to bend the rules a bit under the hurried conditions and give the vendor Mr. Seaver's room number. That was all Hamid needed, soon the American would be executed.

The terrorist walked past the half-wall of streaming water, concentrating on making a beeline for the elevators. That was when a look of pure terror shot through the eyes of Captain Seaver. The hair on the back of his neck stood up. In an instant he broke out in a cold sweat and his hands started shaking. On the other side of the sparkling half-wall was the man from his nightmares. The face, the beard, it was the man from his nightmares. The horror of seeing the face in his dreams caused Scott's body to prepare for flight or fight with adrenaline pumping through his veins.

The elevator doors closed. Scott tentatively moved from his table and willed his legs to carry him toward the devil himself. It took all the courage he could muster to stand in the same spot the evil had stood. Scott watched as the restored 1920s style elevator rose through the floors. The arrow above the door showed exactly what floor it was passing. He felt another chill race down his back when the elevator stopped at his floor. Scott didn't know why he was so afraid of the stranger. His hands were shaking as he walked back to his table to collect his thoughts. When asked if he wanted another beer, he politely declined but used the empty mug on his table to calm his hands as he gripped it with them both. Was he imagining things? How could he be so frightened of a man he didn't know? How could he be so frightened of any man?

The elevator door opened again. Scott peaked around his empty beer mug as he held it up to shield his face. A young couple exited the elevator.

It now stood empty with the doors open as it waited for its next passengers. He wondered if his acute, sudden fear was another effect of the disease, something that the doctors hadn't expected. Now, besides his forgetful nature, he was becoming intensely paranoid. He remembered reading that intense paranoia was not an unusual symptom for dementia patients, nor were delusions. "Damn," Scott cursed as he pressed his forehead against the glass he was holding. The disease was getting worse.

In a fit of confusion and anger Scott left the restaurant and stormed out the beautiful brass double doors of the hotel.

"Good evening, Mr. Seaver." The doorman remembered the name of the new guest. George, the bellman, made it his hobby to try to remember the names of guests as they checked in. It was a mental challenge for him and helped the day pass more quickly; it also helped with his tip income. He learned many years ago that everyone likes to hear their own name. Scott didn't even glance back at the doorman; his mind was already a block away.

****

Hamid approached the door for the room number in his hand. Opening his pack, he took out a simple electronic device. He slid the wired card into the electronic key slot and turned on the attached mini-computer. Nobody was in the hallway, and in a minute the machine would send the right combination of 0's and 1's to the key's electronic chip and the door would open. The code wasn't difficult to break and soon the door light went green. He flicked the safety on the pistol in his hand off, the silencer had already been securely screwed on. One more glance down the hallway and he turned the knob of the door slowly. The room was dark, a sleeping Scott Seaver would be temporarily blinded by lights so Hamid flipped the switch and aimed his gun toward the bed.

Mr. Seaver's luck had saved him once again, but only temporarily, the room was empty. Hamid took the time to verify that it was Mr. Seaver's room by checking his luggage tag. It was. All Hamid had to do now was to make himself comfortable until his prey returned.

****

The cool night air didn't faze Captain Seaver as a very slight breeze brushed through his hair. Michigan Street's stores and restaurants were still bustling. His eye for architecture stopped him in front of the Tribune Tower. He looked at the corner stone; it read 1923. He stared up at the huge lighted news building. Its gothic design reminded him of a scene

Alan D Schmitz

from Batman. It seemed so out of place in the modern world, yet completely at home in the middle of Chicago. The gothic building fit his mood, dark and ominous.

Is my mind completely untrustworthy? He wondered. If he couldn't trust that what he saw was real, then what was real? Maybe he wasn't looking at this ageless building. Maybe, right at this moment, he was in a room being cared for by assisted living personnel. Possibly his entire trip to Chicago and his job of imploding a building were all fabrications of a confused mind. He pinched himself hard and only stopped when he was convinced that it hurt. Scott chuckled ironically at his predicament; he didn't know what was real and what wasn't. But the hard pinch sure felt like it hurt, and that would make it real he surmised.

Walking farther south, he stepped onto a long bridge over the Chicago River. The bridge was well lit, lining the sides were turn of the century motif pole lights lining shining down on the wide concrete walks. The river lazily flowed under him, going east into Lake Michigan. Something about water was a calming influence and he stopped to contemplate his situation. Scott wanted his wife; he wanted to hug her so hard his arms ached. A tear formed and dropped down to the water, catching the light like a solitary rain drop. He leaned slightly over the railing to watch it flow away from the bridge. He didn't want to die, yet he didn't want to live; not like this. He wanted to be the perfect father to his perfect daughter. He wanted to protect her from high school boys and college men. She needed him. He couldn't die and he couldn't lose his mind.

The cold evening breeze was refreshing at first. Now it was becoming cold as he collected his thoughts. Scott knew his family needed him, but more than that, as much as they might need him, right now he needed them even more. Lazily he started back up the street. Passing the gothic Tribune Tower gave him a bit of an added chill with its foreboding nature. It seemed to warn him that danger was lurking.

"Welcome Back Mr. Seaver," George spoke regally but friendly. He stood stiffly and opened one of the large brass doors.

Scott took time to look at the man's nametag. "Thanks George."

"A bit cool out tonight to be without a jacket, sir."

"Yes, but just the same, it felt good."

"Yes sir, good for you sir."

As he walked toward the elevator, on some primitive level the hair on his body became stiff and reminded him of the danger from the bearded man. Scott had to know if he was completely mad or if something he didn't consciously remember was endangering him. There was only one

240

way he knew to find out. He had to find out if the stranger was in his room or not.

The captain pressed the up button and immediately the doors of the elevator opened. Next stop was his floor. He would look the demon in the eye if he had to, but the demon or its myth had to be dispelled tonight. Scott had an unusual feeling of paranoia.

As he came to his room in the long empty hallway, he considered that he could be walking into a trap. He knocked on the door and shouted, "Maintenance!"

After thirty seconds nobody had answered. Inside Hamid was alerted; somebody was outside the door. It wasn't for the flowers or fruit, they had already been delivered. Possibly if he didn't answer they would go away.

Scott knocked again and spoke loudly through the door. "Maintenance, Mr. Seaver. I'm here to fix your television." Again nobody responded. If there was somebody in the room, he would soon find out. He pulled out his key card from his wallet.

Then, just as he was about to slide his key card in the door, he thought he would try one more time. "If you don't answer, Mr. Seaver, I will assume the room is empty and I will enter to fix your television. So if you are in the room, please answer me sir."

Hamid felt he had no choice. Maybe this man knew who Mr. Seaver was, and if Mr. Seaver did come back the repairman couldn't be allowed to see either of them together. Hamid answered back, "I am sorry, I was in the bathroom. The television seems to work fine now, but thank you very much."

Scott never actually expected to hear a voice; he fell against the wall in terror.

"I am sorry for the inconvenience, but I am quite busy and the television works fine. It seems to have been a loose cord."

Scott pulled himself together enough to answer, though it was subdued. "Yes sir, thank you and good evening."

The captain somehow knew that the man inside was dangerous to him, the way a squirrel knows a circling hawk is after its life. What he didn't know was why. He felt himself becoming disorientated; he saw an exit sign and ran toward it. He opened the door and felt more panic when he entered the stairwell. Certain memories tried to surface. An image of a smoky stairwell came into his mind. Adrenaline flowed through his body along with his fear.

Scott knew that his pounding heart from the claustrophobic reaction wouldn't allow him to linger, so he raced down the stairs barely touching the handrail. For some reason he felt terror all the way down the staircase. He had a strange premonition that he would be trapped inside. When the outer door opened at ground level he felt a tremendous relief as he burst out the stairway exit and into the wide, brightly lit hallway. The captain was shaking, his lungs grasped at the air in the hallway. He felt as though he had been under water while in the staircase and had finally come to the surface, again able to breathe life-giving oxygen.

Hamid thought about the maintenance man at the door. The man had said the television didn't work. The terrorist turned on the television; it came to life and lit up the room. He checked the sound and used the remote control to change the channels. The set seemed to be working perfectly to him. "Gohla," he swore, realizing that he had been somehow discovered. With a click, he turned it off again to wait in the darkness.

The maintenance man was probably his target. It was just a hunch, but in his line of work a hunch was often as close to fact as he could get. Mr. Seaver must have left some sort of sign to alert him if there was somebody in his room. Hamid had underestimated the businessman once again.

The Iranian stood by the window hoping that his phone would find a satellite to connect to. Luckily for him, from Mr. Seaver's room he was high enough that no other building blocked the line of sight to the sky. One of many orbiting satellites found his phone through the glass of the window. He called his commander. "My guest has not come home yet. Can you locate his telephone?"

It took at least five minutes before the commander gave him the unwelcomed news. "Either his phone is off, the battery is dead or it is unable to communicate with the GPS system. We do know that earlier he was inside the hotel. He called his wife from the lobby area."

"What time?" Hamid was curious.

"About 8:30 P.M."

That was about the same time Hamid created the commotion in the lobby. He was more certain than ever that Mr. Seaver had identified him then, and that was why he was suspicious of a visitor in his room.

"How soon can you have the asset in place at Mr. Seaver's home?"

"I can have him at the home in thirty minutes, if you need him."

"I may need his assistance yet. I will keep you apprised of my situation. Again, thank you for your help, my friend."

Hamid decided to vacate the room in case Mr. Seaver reported to someone that an intruder was in his room. Major Shukah decided to play out another hunch. He went down the wide hall to the ice and vending area next to the emergency stairwell. There he waited; if Mr. Seaver was going to the police he would do it now. It was a risk for Hamid but he would know shortly. If nobody came to the room to check out Mr. Seaver's story, then for a reason he didn't fully understand, Mr. Seaver didn't want to involve the police, at least not yet.

As Hamid waited and watched, Scott had the valet retrieve his SUV from the parking garage. It was a busy evening and it took a while for the valet to pull up to the front doors. Scott had just pulled away from the curb when George opened the big brass door for a Middle Eastern looking gent with a pack slung over his back. The terrorist had waited for fifteen minutes, more than enough time for the police or security. Nobody showed up. The businessman had told no one.

Scott was tired and scared; fear drove him to the only familiar place he knew in Chicago. He got lucky; the Holiday Inn Downtown was not completely booked. It only took a few minutes for him to check in using his express check-in card. His room was on the second floor. He didn't have any luggage, so he made his weary legs climb the wide winding staircase from the lobby to the second floor.

Hamid was the third guest in line waiting for a taxi at the busy hotel. From there he went directly to the Holiday Inn Downtown. After entering through the main doors he saw only one guest. A man with his back toward him was at the top of the staircase looking very tired. Hamid thought it strange that on this cool night the man didn't have a jacket. The Iranian took the elevator back to his room on the tenth floor. He felt as tired as the old man walking up the staircase. In the morning he knew where to find Mr. Seaver; tonight he would get some needed rest.

Chapter 18

The Following Morning:

Scott woke up in familiar surroundings. His clothes from the previous day were draped neatly over a chair. He slept in his underwear and was terribly confused by the fact that he didn't have any of his bags or toiletries, not even a toothbrush. He called down to room service and requested a guest service pack of the items he was missing.

He knew he was in the right hotel. Maybe he somehow entered a wrong, unoccupied room. He thought of a few other plausible answers, but none of them were probable. He checked that his room card unlocked the door, he had the right room. *This not remembering things was turning into a real pain in the butt,* he mused to himself.

Scott used his phone to get the latest Chicago weather. "Wind is calm, that's a good thing."

Scott called the job foreman, "Morning Pax, what's the good word?"

"Looks like everything is a go. The fire trucks are pulling in now and setting up. If the wind doesn't pick up, we should be in good shape." After discussing a few more details they hung up. It was only a minute later when his phone rang.

Jerry called Scott. "Want to meet for breakfast again, same place as yesterday?"

"Sure, ahh.., could you remind me of the name again."

"Lisa's Diner, just down from the construction site."

"I know where it is, I just couldn't remember the name," Scott lied.

Scott took two of the Tridroxolene pills and one benzodiazepine for the stress he was bound to feel today.

The terrorist, nine stories above him, was also awake, going over his equipment and preparing his weapons for use. Today Mr. Seaver had to die. There could be no more excuses. He had talked with Captain FarzAm Zarin who assured him that he was sailing as slowly as the propulsion system and rudder control would let him. It was lucky for both of them that the lake was calm and easily navigated at the slow speed. He estimated that the ship would be off the Milwaukee coastline at 2:00 P.M. If Kassim couldn't be there at that time, there could be no transfer of the package.

"Did you forget your jacket?" Jerry asked as he sat at the dining table.

"It's supposed to warm up." Scott made up an excuse.

All during breakfast Scott didn't say a word to his partner about the scary series of events from the night before. He seemed to remember bits and pieces, like a dream or in this case, a nightmare. But so much of the evening was nebulous that he knew he wouldn't be able to explain much of it, and would look the fool if he tried. The last thing Scott wanted to do was plant seeds of doubt into Jerry's mind before such an important project. With so much he couldn't explain, it wouldn't take long before his friend would question everything Scott had said or done in the last months. Today it was Scott's job to blow up a building in the middle of Chicago. Today was not a day for doubt by his partner.

Captain Seaver was beyond questioning his memories or lack of them. Whatever happened, or whatever was happening, would have to take a back seat to one of the most important days of his life. Today he would concentrate on the here and now, and nothing else.

A final call came in from Paxton; the project was a go.

Scott confirmed with Pax, "I'm with Jerry; we'll be there in fifteen, twenty minutes."

"See you then, bye."

"It's looking good Jerry. Let's go watch the show."

"Scott," Jerry said seriously, "you know the future of the company depends on this going off without a hitch. We can't afford a screw up."

Scott thought about the job and building for a moment. Each floor was crystal clear in his mind. "Pax and I walked each floor and studied each charge two days ago. I'm confident we did it right. I don't want any surprises either."

"What I'm trying to say, is that, if you aren't sure, don't be afraid of pulling the plug. We can do it another day. The old expression of 'it is much better to be safe than to be sorry' takes on a whole new dimension when you are talking about destroying an entire building."

"Jerry," Scott said as seriously as he could, "trust your old friend one more time. We're good."

"I trust you Scott. It's just that this is a big job, and you haven't exactly been yourself lately."

Scott hesitated and then replied, "I have been preoccupied a bit. I'll admit that, but trust me, we're good to go."

"OK Scott, I'm with you, sink or swim."

245

Alan D Schmitz

"You just sit back and enjoy the show. You did your part, now let me do mine. Besides," Scott joked, "blowing up a building isn't rocket science you know. If you use enough explosives anything will come down."

"Now you have me worried again." Jerry chuckled and slapped his partner on the back.

"Riding with me?" Jerry asked.

"I better take my own vehicle, in case I have to make a quick getaway," Scott joked again.

When Scott jumped into his car he automatically looked for his laptop. He started to panic. His laptop was as important as his phone to him. Scott took a couple of deep breaths. He shouldn't need it today, and he didn't have time to go back up to his room to look for it. Scott accepted that, today he would have to leave without his security blanket.

Cynthia Rosan searched out and found Mr. Seaver again. "Mr. Seaver, what is the plan for this morning?"

"We don't want to wait too long because the winds might pick up as the day goes on. Right now, if all things stay a go, in about a half hour we will detonate the explosives."

"Is the blast going to create a lot of dust?"

"We can't eliminate all the dust, but the Chicago Fire Department is standing by and they will be using high pressure fire hoses to water down the site immediately after the blast. Our company has used this technique very successfully in the past."

"As our regular viewers know, there was a spectacular fire just down the road from here two nights ago. Did the fire at the nearby building create any problems for your company?"

"It could have, but the fire department did an excellent job of containing it. The chief assures me that they are ready to go."

"How much dynamite do you need to explode this building?" she asked.

"We don't use dynamite anymore; it's a bit more sophisticated than that. And the amount of explosives we will be using is proprietary information." Scott didn't want to make the young reporter look bad to her audience, so he tried to respond to her questions as diplomatically as he could. "The technique we are using is called imploding. We will make the building collapse inside of its own footprint, more or less straight down." Scott hoped she wouldn't ask him what a footprint was.

She had used the two minutes of her allowed air time allowed, so she wrapped things up for the audience. "There you have it. In about half an hour from now, Scott Seaver of the Wells and Seaver Company will be

246

exploding this building with dynamite to bring it straight down. The fire department is standing by in case the dynamite lights the building on fire. We expect to have the explosion live, so stay tuned in to channel 23, your accurate news source." She gave the channel signoff expression.

Scott tried not to show his exasperation for how badly the reporter screwed up the information he had given her.

Off camera she asked, "Thank you Mr. Seaver. Will I be able to interview you after you explode the building?"

"That would be great, if we can find the time for another interview." That was Scott Seaver code for- *If you can find me, but I'll bet you won't.*

****

Jerry, Paxton and Scott stood together. Even without his jacket, the excitement was keeping Scott warm enough. The day was starting out beautiful, and if the implosion went as planned, it would only get better. Each was holding his breath and crossing his fingers when Scott pressed the one button on the panel that started all the action. Though it took the fire department a bit longer to get into position than originally planned, the explosions from the RDX came off exactly as predicted. Scott and Paxton counted each explosion; they had them memorized down to the exact second. After the last loud boom, there was an eerie silence. The building didn't fall. It hung in the air for what seemed like an eternity. Then, just as Jerry was about to say his favorite cuss word, the building started to collapse into itself on the top three floors. Next, it cracked in half, right up the middle along the entire structure, from the ground to three floors shy of the top, just as it was supposed to do. The two sides fell into each other as the top floors buckled. The building fell straight down.

In another ten seconds, the entire building had collapsed with a thundering roar and clouds of dust. Every fire truck started to pump tens of thousands of gallons of water over the structure. The dust looked like some sort of opaque monster trying to spring from the collapsed building, but it was being drained of its life by the water. The blast was a success, a complete unadulterated success. Not a brick fell out of the containment area. Everybody was congratulating everybody else, but most of all, everybody was patting Scott Seaver on the back for a job well done and for securing the future of Wells and Seaver Company.

Back in Port Washington, Wisconsin, another viewer stood with pride and relief. Elizabeth Seaver had found a news channel on the satellite TV that carried the blast. She had the recorder going. She realized that she was actually jumping up and down in their living room along with her daughter. They were cheering for joy as if they were both front and center at Lambeau Field after Green Bay scored a touchdown. Her husband could come home now; he could retire with his head held high. She couldn't have been more proud.

The reporter lady from channel 23 attempted to get near Scott for another interview. Scott felt his phone vibrate in his pants pocket and motioned to the reporter that he had a phone call he had to take.

"Did you see it Liz?" Scott said sounding out of breath.

"Yes, yes I did. It was beautiful." Liz realized that she was nearly out of breath herself from the excitement. "I got it all on the recorder so we can watch it together."

"Did Avery see it?" Scott asked excitedly.

"She sure did. She is right here with me, we are both so proud." Then Liz added, "I love you honey; come home as soon as you can. I miss you so much. We miss you so much."

"I will. I have to inspect the site after the dust has settled, and sign an awful lot of paperwork, but then I'll be home."

Liz walked to a more private area of the house, away from the ears of her young teenage daughter. "When will that be, because I have a very special surprise for you," Liz added in the sultriest voice she could muster.

"I'm afraid you'll have to keep the surprise wrapped up until tomorrow. But then I'll be home to unwrap my present as fast as I can." Scott wanted to hold his wife more than she could possibly imagine.

"You had better be; you wouldn't want your surprise to get cold."

"You are way too hot to ever get cold. I love you honey, but I have to go. There is a pesky reporter I'm trying to avoid and if I don't get out of here, she is going to have me cornered."

"By love, see you soon." Liz hung up feeling light on her feet. She loved her man, and even though things were bound to get a bit tough for them, she still wanted him with her. Soon he would be home where he belonged.

Scott hung up and turned around with a wide happy grin on his face. Standing right in back of him was his coworker Jerry. Embarrassed, Scott explained, "That was Liz, she saw the blast on TV and was calling to congratulate us."

"Really? Is she going to have a surprise for ALL of us?" he kidded. "Sorry for overhearing. I just wanted to give you your car keys back. I placed ten detonator caps under the front seat. You're the only one going back to the office with the secure storage area. Paxton is going south from here, and I will be supervising the cleanup for at least a week.

Scott had forgotten about the fact that he had some RDX in the SUV too. Safety procedures would mean keeping the two separate. Carrying the two together was against protocol, but to be dangerous, the caps had to be manually placed on the RDX. Even in the worst accident, the RDX couldn't explode.

"O.K., and thanks for everything. Couldn't have done this without your help," Scott complimented Jerry.

Just blocks away:

Killing his foe would be the only way to avenge himself, his country, and Allah. He never dreamt the pleasure of killing one man could be so great. As the IRGC major rushed to the implosion site, he had to remind himself not to get so excited at the prospect of killing Mr. Seaver that he would make mistakes.

Hamid approached the implosion site. The crowd of people was being kept a block away and he saw no way to get closer to the site or his target. He watched like all the other onlookers as the building came crashing down and the dust billowed up. The sound was deafening, and then came an eerie silence as all of Chicago held its collective breath. Now the crowd erupted in cheers and car horns honked in congratulations.

It took quite a while for the crowd to quiet down again. That was when he made his next move to kill his nemesis. Hamid punched a telephone number into his satellite phone.

"Hello!" Scott answered.

"Hello Mr. Seaver," Hamid said in a friendly tone. "You do not know me, but I have a business proposition for you. I saw the demolition of the building and my partners and I also have a building that needs to come down."

"I did not catch your name."

"I apologize; my name is William Hampton." Hamid consciously worked at hiding his Iranian accent and sounded very continental. He had positioned himself near a very identifiable landmark so his target could find him.

"As you can imagine, Mr. Hampton, this is a very busy time for me. If you could call back next week we could talk then?"

"I understand Mr. Seaver. Perhaps you have time to take my card from me. I am across the street from your location. The police will not let me get any closer. I am sorry."

"Let me give you the number to my office. You really want to talk to my partner Jerry." Scott tried to dissuade the gentleman.

"I would like to take the opportunity to introduce myself and to congratulate you. If you cross the road to the west you will see me. I promise to keep it short."

Scott saw the television reporter trying to coral him again, so he shot across the empty street, which had been closed to traffic. "Okay, I'm headed your way. Do you see me? I'm in the middle of the street."

"I see you Mr. Seaver. If you go to the right toward the television truck I am quite close to it."

"I see it. I'll meet you there Mr. Hampton." The dangers from the previous two evenings were not even distant memories to Scott. As the crowd of people cheering and congratulating an obvious VIP from the implosion site made him feel like a celebrity.

Scott approached the equipment truck looking for someone to be waving at him. Hamid kept a low profile. He didn't want his target to recognize him until the last instant.

Scott walked to the security tape, and the officer on duty waved to him and said something very strange. "You are looking much better today Mr. Seaver, congratulations. Hey Ralph!" He yelled to his partner. "This is the guy I was telling you about the other night."

The other officer was busy with crowd control but took the time to shout out congratulations just the same, and then something about keeping the blanket as a souvenir.

Hamid didn't hear the exchange, but he saw Mr. Seaver stop and wave to the officers. The crowd was still whistling and clapping loudly. Some of the crowd who recognized him from the TV interview started to pat Scott on the back in congratulation.

Ducking under the security tape, he hoped that he would be equally as well recognized by the police when he wanted to go back to the job site. He didn't understand the comment about looking better today. The police obviously recognized him from somewhere. Scott would have to go back and ask them how. It was possible that they could help him remember the missing hours. He looked around for anybody who might be waving a hand in the air at him; he saw nothing as he stumbled deeper into the crowd. Then he felt something sharp poking him in the side.

"Do not turn around. I have a knife and I will use it. Do not say anything. Walk straight ahead, away from the crowd. One wrong move and you will be a dead man. We have your family and they will also die if you do not cooperate."

"You can have my wallet. Just take it. It's in my back pocket."

"I don't want your wallet; I just want to talk to you someplace quiet."

"Mr. Seaver, Mr. Seaver!" A lady's voice shouted over the crowd.

Hamid pressed the knife harder into Scott's side as a warning not to move, and then he twisted his head and saw a lady with a microphone coming toward them. Behind her was a cameraman aiming his shoulder camera directly at them.

Hamid immediately withdrew and melted into the crowd. Scott never saw who was attempting to accost him.

The reporter took her place beside Scott and without asking for permission began talking to her imagined fans. "I am Cynthia Rosan and this is Mr. Scott Seaver. Scott was the driving force, or should I say, explosive force behind today's excitement." She smiled into the camera at her own cleverness. "Please give us your impression of how successful the explosion was, Mr. Seaver."

Scott was looking around to see anyone who might be looking suspicious or familiar to him. The light from the camera blinded his vision some. Ms. Rosan saw that her interviewee was a bit distracted and started again.

"I am Cynthia Rosan and this is Mr. Scott Seaver. Scott was the driving force, or should I say, explosive force behind today's excitement. "Please give us your impression of how successful the explosion was, Mr. Seaver."

Scott collected himself some and gave a short summary of the implosion, and then he quickly excused himself. He crossed under the security tape, ignored the officers who had recognized him earlier and rushed back to the safety of the secured area.

Scott was visibly shaken; there was one face that stood out. There was a Middle-Eastern looking man who seemed to be watching him very intently. The man watched him from behind the cameraman. He could have sworn he saw the face before and it made his skin crawl, but he couldn't place it. Scott's phone rang; it was an unregistered number again.

"Hello!" Scott said casually.

This was the second call Hamid had made in the last two minutes. The first was to his commander, ordering the Milwaukee asset to kidnap and contain the Seaver family.

"Listen to me very carefully Mr. Seaver. If you value your family's life, act naturally. If you don't, I will kill your family. Do you understand?"

"Yes, I hear you," Scott acknowledged quietly.

"If you care about your wife Elizabeth and your daughter Avery, you better listen very carefully. Walk to a more private area along the front of the property. Good! I am watching your every move."

Hamid had to make sure that Mr. Seaver did not say any more than he already had. Hamid also had to stall for time to give the Milwaukee agent time to do his work.

"What did you tell the police about the night of the fire?"

"I don't know," Scott insisted strongly.

"Maybe if we made your wife scream a bit your memory might improve?"

"No, don't. I'll tell you what you want. Don't hurt them please. Who are you? What do you want? I will do whatever you want, just leave my family out of this," Scott begged.

"I will ask the questions, Mr. Seaver. What did you tell the police?"

"Look, whoever you are, I don't remember. All I know is that I woke up in my room this morning sore as hell. I didn't have my bags, my computer, or even my toothbrush. I don't remember anything else."

Hamid was now confused. Certainly someone who was threatened with injury to his wife and child wouldn't have the balls to continue lying. And if he was lying, why would he claim to remember nothing but yet talk about missing clothes?

"What hotel were you at?"

"I was at the Holiday Inn Downtown, where I always stay. Why?"

Was this man toying with him? Did he know that he was checked in at the same hotel?

"What room were you in?"

"I can't remember. It was on the second floor. I can't remember. What is this all about? I think you have the wrong guy mister."

"I assure you Mr. Seaver, I do not have the wrong guy. And if you do not tell me what I want to know, I will hurt your family." The bewildered terrorist had a flash back. He remembered the old man walking up the stairway of the hotel with no bags. From the back side he looked like a very tired old man. And the old man wasn't wearing a jacket but had the colored shirt that Mr. Seaver was wearing now.

"I don't know. I don't remember last night. Look, I forget things." Scott tried to explain but was abruptly cut off by the caller.

"If you are lying to me, I will find out, that I guarantee you. If you go to the police, I will find out, and your family will pay the price. My suggestion is that you forget everything that you saw the last two nights. If the police contact you, you better tell them you saw nothing. If you understand me, nod your head slowly."

Scott nodded his head scanning the crowd across the street. He didn't have to be told to forget anything, he already had. Except now it was critical that he remembered.

"Very good. I am watching you closely. Do not use your phone for anything. Hang up and slide it into your pocket. I will call back in ten minutes. Look at your watch. Good! Do not take your phone out of your pocket for any reason until it rings again in ten minutes."

Scott slowly did exactly as the mysterious assailant said. He made sure that the crowd across the street could see him slide his phone into his pocket; he even held his hands up and made an empty palm signal when he was done. Scott felt panic coming toward him. It was a building wave of confusion. He fought it and took a few deep breaths. He reached into his pocket, took out his bottle of medication and made a point of not hiding what he was doing. Then he took one of the Tridroxolene and a benzodiazepine for calming him. He had to remember what happened last night. This time the doctor's advice of not worrying as long as you were safe didn't apply. He wasn't safe. His family wasn't safe. And he couldn't remember why. Maybe his phone held a clue, but he couldn't take it out of his pocket without endangering his family.

Jerry approached Scott with a few details that needed attention. Scott did his best to pretend as if nothing was wrong, though Jerry could see the agitation in his friend's demeanor.

"Is something bothering you Scott?" his friend asked concerned.

Scott gave a smile to his partner, making a point to keep his face toward the street. Scott wanted to make sure that the assailant realized he wasn't communicating for help.

"No nothing at all." Scott kept smiling. "Things couldn't be better." He patted his partner on the back. "It was a great success. Thanks for your support. I couldn't have done it without your help."

"And I, yours, congratulations again."

Jerry had his partner sign a few documents and guaranteed him there would be more.

"I'll be here," Scott assured.

Hamid made some more calls as he kept an eye on his target. So far, it seemed as if Mr. Seaver was behaving himself, but he couldn't tell what he was saying to the man who had approached him. "I will need the leverage of the family to neutralize Mr. Seaver," He told his commander.

"I will call you back with a message when it is done; the asset is at the home now. You cannot fail us my friend," the commander warned.

Hamid also needed to start going north if he had any hope of retrieving the bomb from the freighter. Time was running out. Hamid had to start for the Port of Milwaukee if he wanted to have enough time to steal a boat and rendezvous out on the lake with the passing freighter.

Ten minutes went by amazingly quickly; Scott had just managed to satisfy all of Jerry's questions in time.

"This will be my last warning. Your wife and child are no longer at your home, but, if we see the police go to your home, they will die. We are watching your home to see if you betrayed us. For their sake, I hope you haven't." It was a bluff, but for now that was all Hamid had.

"I didn't say anything to anybody; tell me what you want from me," Scott begged.

"I want to know what you told the police."

"I already told you. I didn't tell them anything."

"You are playing a very dangerous game if you think I'm a fool."

"What do you want me to do? Just tell me. I will do anything to save my family, so just tell me. But I swear, if you hurt them in any way I will find you and kill you."

Hamid thought that it was very possible that the businessman was stalling for time. Maybe the police were using him to find the killer of the young man. If that was the case, then they could be setting a trap. Hamid had to find out. "I will call back in ten more minutes with further instructions." Then the phone went dead.

Scott swore at the phone and then slipped it back into his pocket. He had to know if Liz was OK. He decided that at the next call, he would insist on talking to Liz. If he couldn't, he would have to assume it was a bluff. He'd then call Liz and have her take Avery some place safe, away from the house. Then he would go to the police and play back each of the phone calls that were automatically recorded on his IT-Tech.

Port Washington, Wisconsin:

Mohamed Jones pulled up to the address given to him. He was at work when the call from Iran came. It was a call he had waited over a year for. It was finally time for him to help his adopted country. He rushed to the address given.

Mohamed Jones was still legally named Russell Jones; he changed his first name to Mohamed in prison. While doing his time for robbery, battery and intent to sell narcotics, Russell had taken to religion. Many of the inmates found religion while incarcerated, all for different reasons. Russell Jones soon learned that he needed to be associated with some group for protection. What he liked about the brotherhood of Islam was that the group wasn't known for its violence, yet it had a reputation of being brutally protective of its members.

Inmate Jones accepted that he initially joined only for the protection. But during his incarceration, and after many hours of prayer, he was converted. After ten years of hard prison life, he continued practicing his Islamic faith and was adopted by an Islamic community. They helped him get a job and stay mostly out of trouble. The five daily prayer times seemed to help him control his anger and other temptations. It was difficult for him to pray to Allah and then commit a crime against his people.

Now at last he would be able to repay Allah and the people who had helped him. When he was called to duty by his Iranian master, he was honored to become a soldier for Jihad. As a mujahedeen, he would give his life to fight against the non-believers.

Mohamed didn't have to wait long outside the house; soon another call came from his Iranian handler. "Hello! This is Mohamed. I understand. I will not fail my brothers."

Making sure that his gun was securely hidden in the small of his back and covered by his loose shirt, he walked up the concrete sidewalk, past manicured lawns. He parked a few houses away. It took him only a few minutes to walk past several two-story houses to the Seaver home. It was an impressive home with a winding circular drive; brick pillars guarded both sides of the drive from the street.

The Seaver's brick-faced house was set back from the street a little more than the others on the block. Mohamed was counting on his everyday work clothes to serve as an appropriate disguise as someone servicing one of the homes.

He walked to the front door. As he rang the doorbell he noticed the rough tattoo on his forearm and quickly tried to roll down the sleeve of his work shirt.

"Hello?" Mrs. Seaver said suspiciously through the partially opened door.

"My car broke down and I was hoping I could use your phone?" he asked politely.

Mrs. Seaver was never one to turn down someone in need, but this seemed way too suspicious to her. "I will call the police for you; they will be here shortly to help you with whatever you need." But when she attempted to close the door, it held firm.

With his left hand Mohamed grabbed the door and held it open with his powerful arm. Then he forced his gun through the opening, pointing it at the woman trying to close it. Liz backed up immediately and started to run for the garage, thinking that maybe she could get to the car.

"Stop or I will shoot," came a calm warning. "I don't want to hurt you, but I will if I have to."

Liz stopped. She realized that the gunman was right behind her. She would never get to the car much less start it, open the garage door and back out.

"What do you want? My husband will be home at any minute."

"I doubt that. Your husband is away on business."

Liz now knew that this wasn't a random break-in, she quickly assessed the situation. *He knew Scott was out of town. He must have been studying their house for a while, but why their house? The Winstons were out of town all week; any professional burglar would have picked up on that easily.*

Mohamed waved at Mrs. Seaver with his gun. "Sit!" He pointed at a kitchen chair. Mohamed was surprised at how easily he reverted to his old ways. Having a gun in his hand always made him feel at ease and in control; this was becoming fun. And the woman wasn't hard on the eyes at all. It had been a long time since he had a bit of ass. *Maybe he wouldn't get in too much trouble for enjoying himself a bit before killing her.* He thought as he quickly became aroused with the idea.

He came terribly unprepared, "time was critical," he was told. He rushed from work to the house. So that not a moment was lost, his handler guided him turn-by-turn using an internet mapping tool. Just because the person on the other end of the phone was in Iran made it no less easy to use the American map engine to guide him.

Mohamed went to the blender and ripped out the electric cord. "Put your hands behind the chair," he ordered.

"No!" Liz refused. "Tell me what you want. I have some money; I'll give it to you if you leave."

"What makes you think I want money? I'm not here to rob you." Mohamed felt and sounded insulted. He didn't know what his mission was, but it was much more important than being mistaken for a common thief, that much he did know.

"It's a lot of money; I've been saving it so I could leave my husband."

Mohamed Jones thought about the money again. He should be compensated for his work; it would be only right. "Let's see the money, and then we'll talk." *A few extra dollars would be nice,* he thought.

"It's hidden downstairs where my husband wouldn't find it."

"Where is your daughter?" Liz became more concerned about his intentions. How did this man know about Avery and why? Liz was thanking God that she had agreed to let Avery play video games at a friend's house.

"She is gone for the weekend, up north with friends," Liz lied.

"If you are lying to me, I will kill you both."

"I'm not lying; she isn't here."

"First we will search the house. If I find her, you will pay dearly."

"Start walking and if you try anything at all, I have an itchy finger," Mohamed bluffed. His instructions were to not harm Mrs. Seaver or the daughter until told to, they were needed healthy.

The search of the house for the daughter was unsuccessful. Mohamed made Liz walk down the stairs. Liz Seaver knew there was no money in the basement, but there were plenty of tools and closed-in areas. This man wasn't acting like a thief. That frightened her. Avery would eventually come home, which made Liz desperate to put this to an end. There was no way this monster would touch her daughter.

Mohamed was more concerned with the shape of Mrs. Seaver's ass in the tight-fitting jeans than where she was taking him. The laundry area was next to Scott's workshop. She walked past the clothes dryer and then the washer. On top of the washer was an opened box of detergent. Liz grabbed the box and swung around, throwing the dry powder in the face of her captor.

"Ahhh!! You bitch," he swore as the powdered soap blinded him.

The gun started going off in all directions. Liz was already headed for the workshop door. Bullets were pelting the wood and concrete around her. She was desperate for a hammer to swing or a screwdriver to stab with; anything she could find that would inflict injury. Inside the room, she closed the door. Angry cussing was still coming from the other side.

Mohamed tried not to let his anger get the better of him. The bitch would pay; her tight little ass was going to get pounded for sure. But now he had a problem. He had to recapture her without hurting her, at least not severely. His eyes watered and burned, but eventually he could see well enough to pursue. Years of lifting weights in prison made him firm and muscular; it was a hobby he kept up after he was released on parole.

He kicked at the workshop door. It held, but another two or three kicks, and he was sure it would open. The first hard kick against the door frightened Liz. She gasped and jumped away from the door as it shook. The latch held, but it was never intended to keep out intruders. Scott had made the door to help keep noise and dust inside his workshop. The door shook again. Liz noticed screws starting to pop loose. The next kick might be the last it would take.

Liz had her weapon ready; she wouldn't go down without a fight. This madman would never touch her daughter. Another hard kick and the door swung open. In the next instant, a gun poked through the door, ready to shoot in whatever direction necessary.

Liz hit the switch of the Sawzall power saw. The long, sharp reciprocating blade sprung to life and came down on the extended hand. It could have easily cut the hand off at the wrist, but Mohamed pulled back against it. His gun took the brunt of the saw but not before his right wrist and thumb became very badly knurled. His thumb was barely hanging on. The gun dropped to the ground. Immediately blood started to spurt out of the exposed, raw skin. The pain hadn't hit him yet, just anger at what she did to his body.

Now he knew where she was. He bolted through the open door, facing her direction, this time ready for anything. She could come at him again with the saw but he would kill the bitch with one kick of his foot before she touched him with the machine again. Liz wasn't ready for a full body attack; it took her an additional instant to twist the saw for a wide swipe to the attacker's side.

Mohamed stuck to his game plan, even when the saw came toward him. Instinct made him block the saw with his left hand, even though he knew what it would do to him. His kick was swift and his heavy work boots hit Liz squarely in the chest. The saw dropped to the ground as Liz flew backward with tremendous force. She caught his left arm with the saw blade for just an instant. But at the high RPM of the tool, an instant was all it took for it to rip a wide deep cut.

Liz wasn't moving, and Mohamed took the time to look at his left arm. The pain was becoming real. He found an old shop-rag and wrapped it around the deep cut of his left arm. It was impossible to tie off with his damaged right hand, so he tightened it with his mouth and carefully stuffed the loose end into itself. Then he found another rag and used his wounded left arm to gingerly wrap the rag around his right hand. He had been in knife fights before and the clean cuts from a sharp knife were nothing like the ragged deep cuts from the saw. If his thumb was to be saved he needed immediate medical attention. The old shop rags were quickly becoming saturated with blood.

Elizabeth Seaver was out cold on the floor. His lust for her evaporated; killing her would be much more rewarding. With his left hand he took some laundry rope that was on the workbench and tied the woman's hands behind her. She was still breathing. Then he wrapped rope around her ankles and using the rope, he roughly pulled her out of the tool room and toward the stairs. He considered pulling the bitch up the stairs. But why? She was secure where she was, so he left her lying on the cold concrete floor, as he walked up to the first floor.

Mohamed Jones dripped blood up the stairs and down the hall into the kitchen. His right hand was throbbing. He went into the bathroom and found some Tylenol in the medicine cabinet. He swallowed a handful of the capsules. The badly injured man realized that he was suddenly very thirsty. Back in the kitchen he filled a glass with water, sat down at the kitchen table and gulped it. Water never tasted so good.

Chicago, Illinois:

Scott Seaver's phone rang again, exactly ten minutes since the last time. "Mr. Seaver, go to your vehicle and drive south along Clark Street, then take the freeway back to your home in Port Washington."

"Fuck you! I'm not doing anything except calling the police unless you let me talk to my wife right now, right this fucking instant."

"That would not be very wise; your wife's life is in your hands. If you call the police we will be forced to dispose of her and your daughter."

"I think you are bluffing, asshole. I don't believe you have my wife."

"Then Mr. Seaver, you will lose your most precious assets in a very risky gamble."

"Either I talk to my wife immediately or I go to the police. I assure you, I am not bluffing."

"I will set up the connection. Wait ten more minutes, I will call you back and she can tell you how serious we are."

"You bastard," Scott swore through the phone. He knew he had to wait. He couldn't take the chance. The phone went dead.

Alan D Schmitz

Port Washington, Wisconsin:

A cell phone rang; it was the commander in Iran. "Mohamed, you were to call me when you had the Seaver woman restrained."

"Yea, well, she's restrained all right," he said flatly, not letting on about the serious problems he had.

"Good, listen carefully. We need her to say a very limited number of words to her husband. As soon as she says anything, I want you to take the phone away and hang it up; she must not be permitted to talk very long at all."

"She may not be available," Mohamed warned.

"What do you mean? You were not to injure her."

"She hit her head or something. She passed out. I can try to wake her."

"You were told we needed her unharmed. We need her to talk."

"Hold on," Mohamed said dryly. He took his glass of water, walked down the stairs and splashed it into the face of the passed out victim. Liz awoke and, as soon as she saw the face of the attacker, she tried to run. That was when she realized that her feet and hands were tied. Roughly, Mohamed lifted her to a sitting position on the floor.

"The bitch is awake, and you should know she hurt me real bad. I need a doctor."

"Listen carefully, my friend." The commander spoke calmly and delicately but with firmness in his voice. "When I tell you, put the phone up to her face, but don't let her talk long. I just need someone to know she is alive and that is all."

"Can I kill the bitch after the phone call?" Mohamed asked casually but sincerely.

"No, she may still be needed. I repeat, do not harm her."

"What about me? She nearly cut my hand off. I need a doctor."

"You may go to the doctor when your replacement gets there; he is not far away," the commander lied.

The commander punched a few buttons and soon had a conference call going with Major Hamid Shukah. "We have the woman on the phone; the conversation must be very brief."

Chicago, Illinois:

"I understand. Hold while I connect to her husband."

"You wanted proof; say something."

"Liz? Liz can you hear me?" Scott nearly shouted trying to contain his concern.

"Scott, help me. Don't let them hurt Avery." Scott heard a click on his phone.

"Do you believe me now? If you do not want them hurt, do exactly as I say. Calmly get into your car and drive down Clark Street south, then onto the freeway and I want you to drive toward Milwaukee without stopping for anything."

"If you hurt my wife or daughter, I will kill you, so help me god."

"Your God will not help you, that I am sure of. If you cooperate with us, they will be fine." It was a lie of course. There could be no witnesses. "What kind of vehicle are you driving and what color?"

"It's a black SUV, a black Ford Expedition," Scott said angrily.

There was another click on his phone and the caller was gone. Scott felt the world spinning around him. *Not now, I can't panic,* Scott said to himself as he took a deep breath trying to slow things down. *Please God, don't let me forget.*

"Scott, are you okay? It looks like the color has gone out of your face."

Scott looked up, happy for the distraction. It seemed to bring him around a bit. "Actually Jerry, I'm not feeling well. I need to go back to the hotel. Can you take care of things here?"

"Well of course, but maybe I should take you to a doctor."

"No, please don't. If Liz found out, she would get all upset. I'll be fine; I just need to lie down for a while."

"Tell you what. I'll have Paxton drive you back to the hotel."

"No Jerry!" Scott said angrily. "Sorry, I was up late last night. This was a big day, lots of pressure, and I just need a nap; that's all."

Jerry could see the color coming back already. "I guess you are right. I'll check on you later."

"Thanks Jerry, I'll talk to you later."

Scott found his SUV. He started it, and then programmed the GPS to take him back home which was also the way to Milwaukee. Before taking the SUV out of park, he played back the voice recording of his wife begging for help and the stranger's instructions one more time. "Don't let them hurt Avery!" *The bastards must have his daughter too,* Scott assumed. *This couldn't be real.* Why couldn't he remember the last two evenings? What didn't the man want him to tell the police?

Two men in a car waited for the black SUV to pass them. "That's him," Hamid announced calmly. We know where he's going, no need to follow closely. Stay here and look for cars following him." Scott was a full block away when Hamid told Jafar Raad to pull onto the roadway and start following the big black SUV. From Clark Street, the SUV turned onto the freeway entrance for highway 290.

Hamid and Jafar followed from a respectable distance. The businessman's SUV was speeding down the freeway. As the SUV approached an exit, Hamid called Scott once again. At the last second, he instructed, "Turn off at the next exit, right now, and keep listening for more instructions."

Scott swerved into the right lane and just barely made the exit ramp. The dark green Chevy stayed on the freeway, watching the erratic SUV in front of it abruptly turn toward the exit. More important was that no other car followed the SUV down the ramp.

"He looks clean," Jafar announced from the driver's seat.

Hamid gave his next instruction. "Get back on the freeway, NOW!" he ordered and then hung up.

Scott had to make a dash through a yellow light; it turned red just as he entered the intersection. Scott followed the onramp and soon was heading back toward Wisconsin and his wife and daughter.

Scott realized the turn off the freeway was a test of some sort. He picked up his IT-Tech and looked at the recent caller list. When he tried to access the last number called, it gave him an error. Whoever this person was, he had used some sort of telephone number block. Scott looked around at the vehicles next to him. If he found something or someone suspicious he considered ramming it. What he didn't know was that the green Chevy was now about a quarter mile in front of him, though it was very slowly falling back in traffic.

Scott listened to the recent messages on his cell phone again, looking for a clue to what the stranger wanted from him. He heard the sounds of Liz pleading for help. His palms started to sweat and then his forehead. Captain Seaver turned on the radio. In order to stay on task, he had to relax. It was very important that he not panic. His family's lives depended on it. A song came on the radio, "The ship was the pride of the American side, Coming back from some mill in Wisconsin." Scott knew the tune or thought he did and tried to sing along. He couldn't remember any of the lyrics and gave up trying. But, focusing on the song helped him calm down. "And later that night when his lights went out of sight, came the wreck of the Edmund Fitzgerald."

Toward the end of the song Scott had a thought. *What had happened to his laptop computer?* Scott didn't panic. In his rush it could be anywhere. Still, if it was in the back seat there could be a clue on it.

Maybe one of the e-mails contained something, or there was something recorded by the camera. He couldn't know if he was being watched. Any one of the cars around him on the four lane highway could be watching his every move. But Scott also knew that if he didn't come up with a plan of some sort, the odds of him and his family escaping from the mad man's clutches would be very low. Then his cell phone rang again.

"Keep driving Mr. Seaver. You are to keep driving toward Milwaukee. If you try to contact anyone, your wife and daughter will die," Hamid reminded.

Hamid's plan was to have the wife and daughter brought to Milwaukee as bait. And with the right bait, he could finally kill the one man who could identify him and link the bomb to his country. Of course the two women would have to be killed too. That neither pleased nor saddened the IRGC major; it was just a fact of war that sometimes women and children had to die.

The driver of the green Chevy thought he knew where they might find a boat to use. There was a large marina in Milwaukee; stealing one of the hundreds of boats shouldn't be too big of a problem. Hamid called the captain of the Damascus Star.

"We are on time; the mission can still be a success if you do not panic, Captain."

"I am cruising as slowly as I possibly can. In a couple of hours I will be three miles off Milwaukee. Don't be late."

If they didn't waste too much time killing Mr. Seaver and family, there should be time to rendezvous with the freighter. In fact, a good place to kill the family would be in the middle of the giant lake. The bodies could be disposed of with weights taking them to the bottom of Lake Michigan. Hamid recalculated the time it would take to get to Milwaukee, steal a boat, motor out to the passing freighter and intercept the bomb. There was ample time, he assured himself. His plan was to bring the bomb back to shore in Milwaukee, and using the Milwaukee River he could more or less accomplish the same task. Though Milwaukee was a much smaller target, the same effect could be accomplished. There would still be many deaths and much disruption to the Americans.

Chapter 19

Highway 94 near the Wisconsin, Illinois border:

Scott tried to maintain his calm as he drove north. He used his analytical skills to remain as emotionally detached from the situation as possible. To say it was difficult was a huge understatement. He had come to several conclusions, none of them comforting.

He had to assume the kidnappers had his wife and daughter, and that the reason they were being held was because the kidnappers wanted something he had or knew. The only fact he did know, was that there were at least two kidnappers, one in Chicago and one that had his wife and daughter. He assumed more were probably involved, but unfortunately, he didn't know why they wanted him so badly. Scott also concluded that kidnappers very seldom leave witnesses. So, if he wanted to save his wife and daughter's lives, he had to come up with a plan.

Scott had been driving for about an hour; he cautiously studied his IT-Tech for clues to his whereabouts last night. He kept the phone in front of him by the dash, but low enough that nobody could tell he was concentrating on the small screen. There were no clues in his e-mails or voice records. Scott thought about the camera function of his phone. Maybe he took some pictures. So he scrolled through the photo album application on his phone.

Scott saw detailed pictures of intricate wood molding and old-country craftsmanship on doorframes and window ledges. He had been in an old building somewhere. The pictures looked familiar, though he couldn't place them. He did his best to drive as he worked his phone, but a couple times came dangerously close to the car next to him when he focused his attention too long on his IT-Tech. The photo application automatically kept track of where and when pictures were taken using the built in GPS. Scott scrolled to the properties page of the pictures he had taken. It told him where they were taken in latitude and longitude; it also told him when. At last Scott felt he was getting somewhere. The pictures were from two nights ago, though he still couldn't remember where he took them. Simply by pressing a button on the picture application, the question of photo location was immediately answered. A map popped up on his phone and a location was displayed. He stared at the map; he knew exactly where it was pointing to, but couldn't remember being there. It was the building right across from the remnants of the one he had just destroyed. It was the building where there had been a large fire.

Traffic in front of him was coming to a stop, but Scott had been too intent on looking at his phone to notice. The last of the Illinois toll stops was approaching. Scott glanced up just as he was about to rear-end a green Chevy. With no time to stop, he swerved to the right. Luckily the toll area widened to eight lanes, all of them filling rapidly with slowing vehicles. Scott hit the brakes just in time to squeal to a stop behind a gold Cadillac. The car directly behind Scott also had to screech to a stop, also managing to avoid an accident. Then there was the noise of a series of tires burning rubber against pavement and the crunch of metal and broken glass. The same green Chevy that Scott had so narrowly avoided was hit by another car. Hamid cussed and looked off to his right at the SUV that caused the accident. Scott heard the screaming tires and the crunch of metal, and looked back toward the accident. Hamid and Scott's eyes locked; the hair on Scott's neck stood on end. It was the man in back of the cameraman. It was the man he had seen in his nightmares. It was the man who had his wife and child.

Port Washington, Wisconsin:

Mohamed's hand was still throbbing; he had lost quite a bit of blood through the open gashes on his hand and left arm. The last time he dared to look at what was left of his thumb, it was turning black. Mrs. Seaver was sobbing in the basement. She had been pleading with him constantly since the phone call to untie her or at least loosen the tight bindings some. She insisted he needed to see a doctor. She was right, but he couldn't leave. It was his duty to stay.

Mohamed Jones felt tired, very tired. His eyes were drifting shut when he was startled by the sound of a door opening. "Mom..., Mom, I'm home." Avery walked from the side door into the kitchen. She was ready to swing her backpack full of video games to the floor when she noticed the red stain covering it. "Mom, where are you? Are you hurt?"

From deep in the basement she heard her mother scream, "Avery, run, run! Go to the neighbors! Get the police!" Avery ran for the basement and the sound of her mother's voice.

"Mom, Mom, what happened?" she hollered as she opened the basement door.

"No honey, leave me. Run to the neighbors. Get the police."

Avery stared at the sight of her bound mother and froze for an instant at the top of the stairs. Without any further thought she raced down the stairs.

That was when the door at the top of the steps slammed closed.

A very mean and angry looking man glared down at both of them. "Don't touch your mother little girl," Mohamed threatened as he flashed the long, shiny blade of a butcher knife he had found in the kitchen. Slowly he walked down the stairs. "Tell her to do as I say."

"Honey, listen to me. Do exactly as he says. He will hurt you if you don't." It pained the mother to tell her daughter to let the monster touch her. But Liz needed to believe that if he wanted them dead, he would have certainly killed her by now. Using the large knife as persuasion, Mohamed walked the daughter away from her mother. Mohamed had just a fraction of the strength that he had when he first came to the house. Even this little girl might get the best of him if he gave her a chance. He didn't intend to. There was just enough rope left to tie her hands behind her. Soon his help would be here, and then they could do as they wished with them while he went to the hospital.

"Put your hands behind you," he ordered gruffly.

Avery looked at her mother who was still bound hand and foot. Liz cried as she nodded her head for Avery to cooperate. Mohamed's right hand was near useless, but he was still able to tie the cord around the teenager's tiny wrists tightly by wrapping it over and over again with his left hand. He couldn't knot it with only one hand but the wrapping was tight and wouldn't come apart easily.

Mohamed knew he was too weak to subdue them if they somehow got loose. He prayed the promised help arrived soon. Too tired to worry about much else, Mohamed walked back up the stairs and closed the door. Even if he passed out, the two women wouldn't know it, or dare to come up the stairs even if they got out of their bindings.

Mohamed Jones made one last call. "I have the daughter too. I need to get to a hospital soon."

"You have done an important service for your countrymen and Allah. We will see to it you are well taken care of," the commander promised.

I-94 Illinois:

Horns were honking. People were cussing and swearing. The cars in front of Scott were oblivious to what had happened behind them and continued through the tollgates.

266

Scott looked back again; the driver of the Chevy and the driver of the car that hit it were in serious discussion. Scott got out of his vehicle; he would confront the man in the car right here and now. It was time to face his nemesis. Scott's anger at what this man was doing to his family empowered him. There was no fear in his body, he only envisioned pummeling the fiend. This was the break he was looking for. He would beat the man until he called his friends to free his wife and daughter.

Hamid saw the businessman get out of his car and run toward him. This was no place for an altercation. He could easily kill this Mr. Seaver, but once again his luck would prevent it. If he killed the man right here, he would have no place to run, and every driver on the freeway would be a witness. There were probably video cameras on him at this very moment. Still, he had to do something because Seaver was almost upon him. And unlike him, the businessman wouldn't care about consequences of a public display of violence, in fact, he would prefer it.

Hamid slid over into the driver's seat and stepped on the gas. The car sped forward into the coin collection gate, leaving the perplexed owner of the green Chevy standing foolishly behind. The terrorist tossed the required coins into the large hopper and took off down the freeway. An angry Scott Seaver ran after the speeding car until he realized his attempt at catching the vehicle was futile.

Scott looked back at the now stranded driver who immediately ran in the other direction. Scott ran toward his own car; he had to somehow catch the green Chevy if he wanted to save his family. Scott slid into the driver's seat and slipped the gearshift into drive.

"Hold on sir!" An officer stepped in front of his vehicle.

"Officer, I don't have time. I have to go," Scott pleaded.

The officer moved her hand over the pistol holster as a warning. "Yea! Well so do all the people in back of you. Now give me your ID and tell me why you were out of your vehicle."

Scott peered down the busy highway; the green Chevy was long gone. Telling the officer the truth could be deadly to his family. Reluctantly he reached into his back pocket and withdrew his driver's license. "Sorry officer, I thought somebody was hurt in the crash next to me. I went to help, but the driver of the other car took off before I could help him. You can ask the people in the car that hit him."

The officer scanned Scott's license. "I am going to take down this information; we have the entire thing on video so you can be sure that I WILL sort this out." The officer emphasized the "will." Then she looked over at the vehicle with the damaged front grill and bumper. The driver was standing outside of his car looking very confused. "Stay right here," she ordered as she walked to the other driver and instructed him to get back into his vehicle and wait.

After checking more licenses and piecing together a very unlikely scenario she decided to let Mr. Seaver go. Scott pulled away cautiously and proceeded down the freeway, not sure of what he should do next. Speeding into a trap wouldn't help his family; his only leverage was that they wanted whatever he knew or had. He kept up with traffic, not in a particular hurry to rush to his or his family's death.

Scott pulled off the freeway at the first exit a few miles down the road from the toll stop. There wasn't much there but a rundown gas station. An old man was raking up the last of the fall leaves and had a small burn-pile going. Captain Seaver pulled up to the pump and filled his near empty SUV with gas. As he picked up the pump handle, he noticed his hand was shaking badly. An urge to urinate came fairly abruptly once he stood. He started the pump and trusted the auto shut-off enough to walk away and relieve himself. Out of habit, Scott pressed the "find location" button on his IT-Tech. He certainly wouldn't have lost his car in the small gas station, but habits were hard to break once developed.

Back at the car he slowly, tiredly replaced the nozzle into the pump and turned his gas cap back on. He had to do something to save his family, but what? His phone rang again showing an unlisted number.

"What do you want with me and my family?" Scott shouted into the phone.

Calmly, Hamid explained again. "You will do exactly as I say. That is all I require." Hamid chuckled to himself as he thought about the question literally. How would you tell a man that *What I want, is for you and your family is to die.* "Where are you?"

"I got stopped back at the toll gate by the police. I'm still in Illinois, and I didn't tell anybody about you or my kidnapped family."

"Yes I know. We were watching you. Mr. Seaver, I want you to think about something. If I have to kill your wife and daughter because you tried to be the hero, I will let you live. That way, every day for the rest of your life you can think about what would have happened had you listened to my instructions. For now, I just need to talk to you Mr. Seaver, and when you tell me what I need to know, you and your family will be free to go, I promise. Continue to Milwaukee. I will call with more information when it is needed." The line went dead.

Scott slumped against his car confused; he dropped his IT-Tech back into his pocket. What did he know that this man needed so desperately?

Scott smelled the scent of the burning leaves as a puff of smoke wafted in his direction. The smell of the smoke brought back some buried memories, memories of danger. He felt panic and his heart started racing. The world felt as if it was closing in around him and he suddenly had an uncontrollable fear of dying. He saw flashes of fire and explosions, explosions so close he could feel the heat. Scott saw the pained faces of soldiers, faces he seemed to know. There were deadly screams blasting in his ears and a collision of glass and steel. There were sirens and flashing red lights. The gas station started to spin and Captain Seaver could feel a cold sweat breaking out. He looked at his trembling hands as he curled up into a frightened ball of flesh.

"Mr.? Mr.? You all right?" the old man who had been tending the burning leaves asked repeatedly. He bent over the man lying on the concrete next to the SUV. He tried to wake him with a gentle tapping on his shoulder. "Pete, Pete," the old man shouted, hoping to get the attention of the attendant inside the station.

Scott started to come back to consciousness slowly. "Pete, Pete," the old man shouted even louder.

"What do you want?" Came a disinterested reply from the door of the gas station.

"Call 911. This guy fell or something."

Pete, the 18-year-old attendant, suddenly became excited, rushed to the phone and explained the situation to an overly calm emergency dispatcher.

Scott started to sit up. "Don't get up, Mister," the old man insisted. You must have bumped your head. Scott opened his eyes as the world in front of him spun. His stomach felt nauseous and his body very weak.

Scott looked at the concerned gentleman for the longest time, and then asked, "Where am I?"

"You're safe buddy; there is an ambulance on its way."

It didn't take long before the sound of a siren was heard. To Scott it seemed as if it was only a moment later before an officer was standing in front of him.

"Mr. Seaver, can you hear me?" she asked. It was the same officer from the toll area.

Scott looked up at her, she looked familiar. "What happened?" Scott managed to ask through a very parched mouth.

"There is an ambulance coming. I want you to stay calm and stay right where you are. I think that whatever happened at the toll stop caught up to you."

Alan D Schmitz

Another siren could be heard. It didn't take long for it to pull up next to the officer's car. Seconds later a man was taking Scott's vital readings, and two more were retrieving a gurney from the back of the ambulance.

"His pulse and blood pressure are very low. We'll take him to Center Hospital." Scott didn't argue, he was way too weak. "Mr. Seaver," the EMT explained, "we are going to take you to a hospital. You are very sick." Scott nodded like he understood, though most of the words were blurred to his mind.

The officer moved the SUV to a safer area, locked it and gave the EMT the keys.

Port Washington, Wisconsin:

Liz was completely immobilized; the tight ropes around her wrist and ankles had long since numbed her hands and feet from the pain. Soon her daughter's hands would be equally numb.

"Mom, Mom," Avery sobbed. "My hands hurt; they're starting to tingle a lot."

"Listen to me honey. You have to be brave. I can't walk, but he didn't tie your feet, so I need you to do something for me."

"What!" Avery sobbed more, trying to hold back the tears.

"His gun is on the floor by Dad's shop. I need you to pick it up and bring it here. Can you do that?"

"Yea, I think so. I'll try."

"That a girl. Listen to me carefully, honey. You must be very careful when you pick it up. Make sure you do not touch the trigger. You have to pick it up by the handle only and touch nothing else."

"OK, I'll be careful."

"Be very quiet, and don't touch anything else but the gun handle."

Avery nodded bravely and found her way to the shop. She saw the gun on the floor and the ample amounts of blood on and around it. Kneeling down, she pressed her body backwards as far as she could to grab the gun. It took a few tries but finally she had it in hand.

Avery walked back to her mother whispering that she had the gun.

Liz rolled to her side. "Now I want you to slip it inside the front of my jeans." Liz gambled that she wouldn't be searched. "Mom, I'm scared. I can't feel my hands."

"You can do this honey." She encouraged.

"What if it goes off?" Avery cried a bit, concerned for her mother's safety.

"If you don't touch the trigger, it won't," the mother assured her daughter, wishing she was as confident as she tried to sound.

Highway 94 northbound to Milwaukee:

Hamid was on the phone with his commander. "I need the two women brought to Milwaukee. Tell your agent to put them in the trunk of the car and bring them to the dock."

"I haven't been able to reach our man at the house," the commander reported as he sensed a bad turn of events. "He said something about being badly injured, but that he had the women tied up in the basement."

"Damn!" Hamid realized that once again he was without local support. His plans were falling apart more and more by the minute. "I will go to the home myself. Is the agent traceable to our cause?"

"Not directly."

Hamid raced to formulate a new plan. The two women were forty minutes north of Milwaukee. By the time he went there and back to the Port of Milwaukee, he wouldn't have time to steal a boat and reach the freighter. But there was still a chance; the city of Port Washington was also along the coastline of the Great Lake. Hamid called Scott.

In the hospital, a groggy Captain Seaver heard his phone ring. He lifted his head and then dropped it back to the pillow, too tired to hold it up. A male nurse asked, "Do you mind?" Scott nodded an OK and then the nurse took the phone out of Scott's pocket and answered it.

"Mr. Seaver's phone. Can I help you?" Nurse Donahue asked politely.

Hamid was confused and hung up immediately. *Why would someone else answer that phone*, he wondered? If it was the police, they would have had Mr. Seaver answer as they listened. Hamid called again.

"Mr. Seaver's phone; can I help you?"

"I need to speak to Mr. Seaver; it is very important."

"I am sorry, Mr. Seaver is unavailable."

"We were supposed to have a very important business meeting. I really need to talk to him now."

"Look mister, I probably shouldn't be telling you this, but Mr. Seaver has been admitted to the hospital. He was in a car accident. Please do not call back. When he gets better who should I say called?"

"Tell him his friend from Chicago needs to talk to him."

"Sure, but right now he has bigger problems." The nurse thought the man was an ass and hung up.

Alan D Schmitz

Then the nurse looked through the phone address book for any "In Case of Emergency" numbers. People were encouraged to place one or more ICE numbers into their cell phones. ICE #1 Liz Seaver. The nurse pressed the call button and soon was dialing the Seaver home phone.

Liz heard the phone ringing through the closed stairway door, but could do nothing. Eventually the answering machine picked up and encouraged the caller to leave a message, but Liz only heard silence.

Troy, the nurse, found ICE #2. It was Liz's cell phone. Again there was no answer. The last number ICE #3, said Dr. Maslow. This time there was an answer. It was Dr. Maslow's receptionist. Troy explained the situation and soon the doctor was on the line insisting on talking with the attending physician.

****

Hamid's mind raced. The very reason for kidnapping the man's wife and daughter was to keep Mr. Seaver from talking to the police. He was confident that had worked, but now Mr. Seaver could be severely injured. The man on the other end of the line did assure him that WHEN Mr. Seaver improved, he would notify him of his call.

Even Mr. Seaver's bad luck turned out to be good luck for the businessman and his family. He had managed to postpone the deaths of his family and himself because of the accident. None the less, Mr. Seaver still had to die, and the sooner the better.

The bomb was safely on the ship; his duty to God and country was to contain the situation. He would no doubt be reprimanded severely, but his duty right now was to make sure that nobody could connect the murders, or the radiation that had been found, to his country. Then it came to him, the hospital would try to contact Mrs. Seaver. It was clear that he needed to contain the situation at the Seaver household more than ever. He needed the man's wife to locate the hospital and location of this Mr. Scott Seaver.

Port Washington, Wisconsin:

Since the phone call, the upstairs had been very quiet, not even the sound of footsteps. Though both of their hands were bound so tightly that they were numb, Liz thought that she might be able to use her teeth to unwrap her daughter's bindings.

It took quite a bit of effort, but finally Liz had undone one wrap of the rope. If she could do one, she could do more. Though it would take many

272

more turns to unwrap enough of the rope to free her daughter's hands, they were both encouraged when Liz announced success.

****

An hour after Scott was admitted to the hospital, Hamid entered the south side of Port Washington. His commander guided him to the Seaver household using Google Maps from his office in Iran.

****

Liz was exhausted; her neck was in a continuous cramp from being forced into an unnatural position for so long. Instead of becoming easier, unwrapping the rope around her daughter's hands became harder. It was nearly impossible to unwind the entire length of the rope using only her mouth.

****

Hamid drove past the Seaver home at a normal speed. If the home was being guarded by the police, he didn't want to give himself away. His trained eye would spot the police if they were watching the property, but saw nothing suspicious. Hamid continued past the Seaver residence and drove around the block to casually glance at the backyard of the Seaver home. If a number of neighbors were outside raking leaves, cutting grass or working in their gardens, he would know the home was under surveillance. Nothing seemed out of the ordinary. Hamid parked up the block, across from the home and walked past it one time. When he was confident that there was no trap being set, he walked up the concrete drive and toward the small service door on the side of the garage. The door into the attached garage was locked, but using his large knife like a pinch bar it swung open. Once he was inside the garage, he closed the door behind him. Hamid took note that a car was still in the garage. Its hood was cool, meaning it hadn't been used lately. Carefully he checked the door going into the house; it wasn't locked. Hamid replaced his knife and drew his gun, ready to die in a gun battle if that was what Allah desired.

Liz and Avery heard the door squeak open and then what sounded like lone footsteps walking across the floor. Liz didn't know if they should stay silent or shout for help. She decided that if it was help, the rescuers would search the house until they were found. She prayed that if the single person above was an accomplice, God would protect them. So she stayed silent and listened to the footsteps.

Avery was too frightened to pay attention to the footsteps. Having her hands tied so tightly bothered her at a primal level. In a last act of desperation, she strained her hands until she thought her thin wrist would break. The rope moved. She did it again even harder, and the rope moved even more.

"Mom, I'm free," Avery whispered.

"Take the gun and hide. Don't be afraid to use it. Do not let anyone but the police near you. Do you understand?"

Avery reached for the gun and carefully took it in her hands.

"Avery honey," Liz whispered, "no matter what they do to me, do not give up the gun. They will kill both of us if you do. When you shoot, don't aim for the head, aim for the chest area. That is your biggest target. Keep shooting until the gun is empty."

"Mom, I'm so scared."

"Me too honey. Now hide someplace where you can see me but I can't see you."

The door above them creaked open. Avery darted off.

It didn't take long for Hamid to realize that the first agent had bled to death. If the information was correct, the women would be tied up in the basement. Hamid looked for the proper door. After a few bad choices he opened the right one.

When Hamid saw the bound woman, he assumed that the police had not been called. "Do not be alarmed. I am not here to hurt you."

"Then untie me and call the police."

"I am afraid that I can't do that. Where is your daughter?" Hamid queried as he walked carefully down the stairs with his gun ready.

"She's at school."

"Do not lie to me, Mrs. Seaver, or I will have to punish you. Where is your daughter?" Hamid asked again as he stood over the woman.

"I told you. She is at school."

The terrorist didn't want to do it, but he felt he was forced to display some resolve, so he kicked the prone woman in the shins with the hard edge of his boot.

Liz screamed from the pain, but she didn't want to entice her daughter out of the hiding place, so she quieted herself as quickly as she could by taking huge gulps of air.

"I know she is here, now where is she?" he demanded more forcefully.

"You're wrong, she's not here," Liz replied with equal force.

Hamid kicked the woman again, this time in her side, very painfully.

Liz screamed out in pain once again and then for a few minutes lost her breath. She couldn't keep from sobbing as she insisted that her daughter wasn't there.

The terrorist saw a bloodied section of rope and picked it up. The young girl had gotten loose somehow; the daughter could have gone for help and the police could be on their way here at this very moment. Hamid realized he had to work faster. If the young girl was in the house, he had to find her quickly. If she had gotten away, he might only have minutes to escape the home. "If you tell me where she is, I won't harm her. But if I have to find her, I cannot guarantee her safety."

"What do you want with us?" Liz demanded.

"That is not important right now. One more chance. Tell me where your daughter is."

"She's getting the police. If I were you, I'd start running now. They are going to be here at any moment."

Hamid prided himself on knowing people. Very seldom was he wrong when interrogating someone. It was what gave him such confidence when he tortured. He knew that eventually he would get the answer he was looking for. In this case, he was sure Mrs. Seaver was lying. The daughter was still here.

"Little girl, I know you can hear me. If you don't want me to hurt your mother, you must come here. I won't hurt you, I promise."

Avery cringed in the corner, partially under a blanket thrown over an unused piece of exercise equipment. She could see her mother's legs.

"Tell your daughter to come out, or I will have to hurt you."

"I told you, she went to get the police."

Hamid bent over, grabbed the woman's hair and twisted it roughly." Liz tried not to scream but the pain forced her to.

"I don't want to hurt your mother, but you are making me do nasty things to her."

The terrorist pulled and twisted her hair, tightening it and making her scalp feel excruciating pain. Liz tried not to let the pain control her actions, but she couldn't help it and she cried out again.

"She's not here," Liz insisted.

"I have a knife," Hamid announced as he unsheathed it and turned it in his hand slowly, convinced that the daughter was watching. "If you do not come out, I will have to cut an ear off of your pretty mother's head, and it will all be your fault."

Liz couldn't contain herself any longer. "Baby, don't come out for anything; he's going to kill us both anyway!"

Alan D Schmitz

"You lied to me. I'm afraid you will have to be punished for that. And if your little girl doesn't come out, I will take off your other ear as well."

Avery silently climbed out of her hiding place. "No don't, I'm here."

"No Avery, No!" Liz sobbed. She was afraid what the sadistic man might now do to her daughter.

"Come out here where I can see you," Hamid demanded.

Sheepishly, with eyes down, Avery walked toward her mother's tormentor.

"Come HERE!" Kassim demanded more sharply at the dawdling teen as he pointed with his gun to the floor in front of him.

Avery took another couple of slow steps toward the man, then she raised the gun and fired. Hamid was already aiming his gun at the girl. He could have got off three shots in the time it took the girl to fire once. But once again, the Seaver family had caught him unprepared. The bullet from the small Saturday night special hit his shoulder just as he was aiming. The force made him drop the gun.

For her first time shooting a gun, the young girl's aim was pretty good, but what she didn't expect was the recoil that tossed her hand backward. Before she could re-aim, the big man was upon her, and with one swipe of his hand the small girl was thrown to the ground and the gun slid across the floor. Hamid cursed wildly in Farsi as he kicked the small teen.

"Stop it, stop it!" the mother demanded through her tears.

The fact that he needed the young girl alive was the only thing that made him stop. He retrieved the small pistol and with the same rope as before, he retied the young girl. The small caliber bullet had gone right through him. It missed bone, and he could still use his arm and shoulder, but the wound would hurt and bleed.

"Listen lady and listen well. If you don't do exactly as I say, I will hurt your daughter in ways you can't imagine. I will make you watch what I do to make her scream," Hamid threatened as he held the long, sharp knife up to the young girl's face. "It would be a shame to see such a pretty young face scarred for life, wouldn't it? I am going to call a number and you are going to ask for your husband. He was admitted to a hospital, and I need to know which one."

"What did you do to my husband?" Liz demanded.

"You have your own problems right now, just do as I say."

****

It was over an hour since Scott had been admitted. After he was given something to calm him, he felt much better. Dr. Maslow and the

276

emergency room doctor had agreed on treatment, which they were giving to him intravenously. Dr. Maslow also left a caution that Scott had to be kept at the hospital until he could locate Elizabeth Seaver.

Scott's phone rang; it was on the table next to his bed. "Hello!"

"Scott, are you all right?"

Scott immediately recognized the voice. "Hi Honey, I'm fine. They think I bumped my head in a car accident but I don't remember."

Hamid was holding the sharp knife against the throat of a very frightened teen. He held the phone up to the lips of the mother with his other hand as he listened in on the conversation. Liz was warned: one false act and her daughter would bleed very badly.

"Scott?" Liz asked trying not to cry. She knew she may be trading her husband's life for her daughter's immediate safety, but she didn't have a choice. "Scott, what hospital are you in?"

Scott looked at his wristband. "It says Scott Seaver. Wait, that's my name. There is another name on it; it says Central Hospital, Gurnee Illinois." Scott sounded drunk to Liz. "Gurrrneee, that sounds funny doesn't it," Scott slurred. "Lizzy baby, I'm fine, they got a hold of Dr. Maslow, and he talked to the doctor here." Now Liz was quite sure her husband was being seriously sedated. "I talked to him on the phone. I don't remember much, but I think he said I must have fainted again because I don't even have a bump on my head. He wants me to wait here overnight for observation and you are supposed to pick me up, I think."

"Scott?" For an instant Liz forgot about her own terrible situation. "You don't sound all right."

"I'm a bit sleepy; they are putting something into me to make me relax. I don't know what it is, but I am really feeling just fine. I mean I am really feeling good, real, real good," Scott repeated proudly as he held up his arm with the solution dripping into it and stared at it for a minute.

Hamid whispered into Liz's ear. "Tell him he has to come home tonight."

"Honey, I need you to come home right away. It's very important."

"Oooo Kaaay..," Scott answered, dragging out both syllables. Then he repeated them again exactly the same way and giggled. "Oooo Kaaay. You know honey, that is a silly expression. Oooo Kaaay. I wonder what it stands for? Maybe Okee-Doky," Scott giggled again.

"They put me in one of those skinny little machines and told me I didn't have a concussion. I don't think I bumped my head and neither does Dr. Maslow. I talked to him," Scott repeated.

Alan D Schmitz

The Iranian lifted the phone to his own mouth. "Don't think your family is safe, because they are not. I expect to see you at your home, within three hours. And once again, I warn you, if you get the police involved, I will kill your family."

"Scott, help us; they have Avery!" Liz couldn't help but shout out a plea for help.

The phone went dead; Scott stared at the TV, though he wasn't paying attention to it. He was trying to comprehend what he just heard. Scott felt strangely calm despite the fact his wife had just told him she and their daughter were being held hostage. Scott replayed the phone call, but it was hard to concentrate on touching the right buttons. He was becoming so tired, he needed to rest. After trying to listen to the message, he fell asleep. His phone dropped to the floor.

****

Hamid cursed as he checked the bindings on both women. The man he needed to kill had more lives than a cat. The husband was safely in a hospital, miles away, and though Hamid now knew where Scott was, he couldn't leave the women alone to go kill him.

The bindings were cruelly tight. Liz had long ago lost the feeling in her blood-starved hands and feet. Her daughter would be going through the painful process of having the circulation in her hands cut off very soon. The terrorist left them alone to tend to his own wounds.

Back upstairs, he took a medical kit out of his pack. In it was standard issue emergency medicine. He took off his bloody shirt and gave himself a shot of morphine for the pain. Then he pressed another needle into his shoulder area and squeezed a syringe full of antibiotics into it. Pressing gauze into the small caliber entry hole was painful but relatively easy. The gauze would stop the bleeding on the front of his shoulder, but he couldn't reach the larger exit hole. For that he would need help. The Revolutionary Guard Corps major thought about his options. No doubt the older woman would be more capable of doing the job right, but she would also be more dangerous untied. Hamid decided on using the young girl. She was the one who shot him; she would have to help him. And with her mother tied up, the young girl wouldn't dare try anything.

As he waited for the morphine to ease his pain, he walked the house searching for clues about who this Mr. Seaver was. He found the master bedroom and a fresh shirt hanging in the closet. He would put it on when the bleeding stopped. In the hall there was a picture of a young man by a boat, proudly holding a stringer of fish. There was another picture of the

278

young boy kneeling next to a soccer ball. On the same wall area was another picture of the lad piloting a sailboat. Tucked into the corner of one of the pictures was a small religious card. On it was a prayer to their God, trusting him to take care of a Brad Seaver. They had lost a son, not important information, but information just the same.

The terrorist looked at more pictures and realized that the sailboat was in many of the photos. They were all family photos, most with four Seavers in them, the son, daughter, mother and father. A perfect family! He would soon send them all to hell. There they would be united with their son. Just as interesting were the photos of Mr. Seaver in front of various helicopters. It appears that Mr. Seaver was a military man, a helicopter pilot. Several medals were displayed behind glass in picture frames. This information would make killing him and his family all the easier. This man wasn't an innocent bystander, he was a hero in the desert war; he had undoubtedly killed many true believers. They may not have been from Iran, but he had attacked his brothers.

It was time. Hamid walked down the stairs. "I need your daughter to help me."

"Leave her alone, you animal," Liz hissed.

"I will not harm her if she does as I say," the terrorist said calmly to the mother. He turned to the teenager and untied her feet. "And if you don't do exactly as I say, or you try to run away, I will hurt you and your mother very badly. You can count on that."

"Please don't take her, take me!" Liz pleaded. "I will do whatever you want. Leave her, please leave her."

"If she cooperates, I will bring her back unharmed. Up the stairs," he commanded as he took hold of the girl by her thin upper arm and roughly forced her up the stairs.

The tugging on Avery's arm hurt her and she cried a bit, then bravely told her mother, "I'll be OK Mom. I'll be back soon."

"Just do as he says." The mother coached loudly and then threatened, "You hurt her and I will kill you, I promise. I will find a way."

As the two walked up the stairs, Liz had hope. The gaping hole in the kidnapper's back was bleeding profusely. This made her wonder about the other abductor. There had only been the sound of one set of footsteps, she had never heard his voice again. And that made her think that he was probably very weak from his injuries or dead. If she could only get free, they had a chance against the man Avery had shot.

Upstairs, Hamid took the young girl into the bathroom and retied her legs just loose enough so she could stand. He then untied her hands and

Alan D Schmitz

gave her a stern warning. He used a small hand-mirror to watch the reflection of his back in the big wall-mirror. Avery had trouble at first because her hands were numb from the tight rope. Hamid calmly encouraged the young girl and instructed her how to stop the bleeding.

Avery Seaver cried softly through the entire ordeal. The sight of so much blood sickened her and she had to use her fingers to press the gauze into the hole that was left from the bullet. She didn't realize a bullet could do so much damage, nor could she understand how the man could stand the pain.

True to his word, Hamid took the young lady back to her mother when she was finished. He retied her hands and feet. Without saying a word, he left the mother and daughter alone. He needed time to think. He was running out of time. Mr. Seaver had better not be late to his death or the bomb would be past Milwaukee before he had time to boat out to it.

Chapter 20

Chicago, Illinois:

Detrick Hans Krier, from the NNSA team in Chicago, took a call from his friend at the National Security Administration. "Dieter, when are you going to be back in Washington?"

"I don't know, Angel." Dieter wasn't being romantic; the woman's name was Angel.

"You can do better than that. I have the information you wanted and I want you to thank me personally," Angel said seductively. "And I want you to give me an apology in person."

"Angel baby, you know I'm sorry. I had an emergency assignment. That's why I had to stand you up. I called as soon as I could."

"Save it Dieter. Rebecca saw you at Mitchell's with a blond."

Dieter didn't know why Angel Raye put up with him. She was smart and sexy. He was the proverbial bad boy, always jumping the fence for greener pastures but eventually returning to the same side Angel was on.

"I forgive you sweetheart; but if you want this information, you will promise me a night out on the town I won't forget."

It wouldn't exactly be a punishment to spend a few evenings in D.C. with his sometimes girlfriend. And he did need the information. "Baby trust me, I will run into your arms next time I'm in Washington."

"I need better than that, love."

"If you give me what I need, I can be there in two weeks. I'll take a week off. Just you and me baby. I promise."

"If you don't baby, you will wish you had, trust me!"

"How can I resist charm like that, Angel."

Angel got what she wanted and became all businesslike. "I am e-mailing the infrared photos to you. Not only did we confirm the location of the freighter, but we have a smaller boat docking up to it for about fifteen minutes. I have the series of images time stamped."

"I'm pulling up the first image now," Dieter confirmed.

"Can you identify the smaller boat?"

"Not with the infrared. It only picks up heat signatures. It's obviously a small boat, but that is about as good as it's going to get. It is interesting that while approaching the freighter, there is only the heat signature from one person, but going away there are definitely two people on board the smaller vessel."

"Angel baby, I love you. You're an angel." Dieter thought through the implications now that their theory was confirmed.

"There is one other strange thing," Angel pointed out. "If you look at pictures numbered five through nine, you can see a crate being moved from the freighter to the small vessel. On the last picture it is clearly resting on the back of the boat."

"Yes," Dieter confirmed that he saw it.

"If we see it on infrared, it means that the box is hot. It could have been in a warm place on the ship, or it could be generating heat internally. Do you want to fill me in sweetheart?" Angel knew the silence on the other end of the phone meant some serious thought was going on.

"Listen baby, I can't, but you might get a medal for this." Dieter thought about the seriousness of the situation. He also realized that he might not make it to Washington ever again. Angel was the closest thing he had to a steady girlfriend, and often she was just a friend when he needed it. Suddenly he missed her more than he thought he could.

"Angel I never told you this before, but I want you to know that you mean more to me than I have ever told you. If I don't see you again, I just want you to know that I truly love you. No bull shit."

"Dieter stop, you're scaring me."

"Baby, I think something big is going down, I have to go. I love you." Dieter hung up before he said more than he should. The team had to be informed ASAP.

Port Washington, Wisconsin:

The hours passed; Hamid gave himself another injection of morphine to control the pain in his shoulder. The bleeding had stopped and he didn't feel like he was in any immediate danger. He was tired; it had been a long day and the pain was wearing on him.

The kidnapper was gracious enough to allow the two captives a bathroom break, one at a time of course, making sure that they both realized the life of the other depended on her actions. He even shared some water with them.

The woman's husband was late. The ship was moving into the vicinity of Milwaukee. Time was running out. Another call had to be made.

Nurse Donahue heard the phone ringing in Mr. Seaver's room. He searched the room and eventually found it by following the sound of the musical tone. The phone said "ICE #1." The In Case of Emergency number meant that it was probably the man's wife or closest relative.

"This is nurse Donahue, Mr. Seaver's phone."

In his best Western accent, Hamid asked, "I am Mr. Seaver's brother, how is he doing?" It was obvious to the terrorist Mr. Seaver was still in the hospital and not on his way to save his family.

"I am sorry, but medical privacy dictates that I cannot share medical information with you. I can tell you that he is sleeping comfortably now."

"When he wakes, could you please have him call his wife; she is very worried."

"We are expecting her, is she still at home?"

"Yes, she is indisposed at home. We are trying to make alternate arrangements, but please, it is very important that he call her cell phone as Mrs. Seaver may not be at her home much longer."

"I shouldn't tell you this, but Mrs. Seaver needs to know that he is OK but out cold for now. The doctors prescribed some serious sedatives. His family physician wanted to make sure that Mr. Seaver stayed sedated. His wife should get here as soon as possible."

"I understand, thank you sir for your help." Hamid clicked the phone shut. He could kill the women, then go to Milwaukee and still get to the freighter in time to retrieve the bomb. But Mr. Seaver would eventually wake, and when he learned that his wife and child were dead, the police would be told everything. Even as Milwaukee went up in a mushroom cloud of dust, Mr. Seaver would be safe in the hospital, miles away from the blast and able to help the police piece together the chain of events.

The terrorist paced the home, searching his mind for a plan. Mr. Seaver had to die and so did his family. At this moment, killing them was more important than using the bomb to destroy the infidels. Hamid pounded on the wall near the pictures of the smiling Seaver family. *What in the world was the businessman doing in the old building in the first place? Why had Allah made their paths cross? What was the reason? Allah always had a plan, though I don't always understand his ways.*

Hamid starred at the picture of the family in front of a docked sailboat named "My Chopper." Then he looked at the picture of Mr. Seaver in his uniform in front of a helicopter. It dawned on him that helicopters were often referred to as "choppers;" the sailboat belonged to the family.

Hamid raced to his pack and took out a map of the area. Port Washington was also a coastal town along the giant lake. If the sailboat was still in the water and docked at a local harbor, retrieving the bomb was still possible. Hamid raced down the stairs, and using the knife

283

Alan D Schmitz

against the throat of the daughter, it didn't take long for him to get the facts about the sailboat. It was still docked at the local marina. With a little more prodding, Liz admitted that if she had to, she could sail it. It had a powerful diesel motor and was quite fast even without its sails up.

The sun was going down, Hamid needed a bit of luck to get the woman's husband home in time to die. And then if the captain of the freighter cooperated, he could still retrieve the bomb.

Reston, Virginia:

Mr. and Mrs. Johnson said goodbye to the sitter as they left their suburban, red brick, colonial two-story home. Their two young boys barely noticed them leave; the video game they were competing against was too captivating. Mr. Lamar Johnson clutched the two coveted tickets firmly in his hand. The night for them to see the all-star production of "The Phantom of the Opera" had finally arrived. The last hurdle was crossed when the sitter showed up on time. The couple was excited about the upcoming evening. The sitter and the children were on their own from here on out. Nothing was going to disturb this particular evening.

Lamar gave his wife a quick, romantic kiss on her lips just before he opened the car door for her. She looked stunning in the powder blue, delicate chemise. Once he was in the car, Lamar seductively slid the lacy skirt up farther along her thigh. Kara scolded her husband, but didn't press her skirt down again. It made her feel sexy when her husband of ten years exposed her shapely thighs. *A little eye candy for her husband on the way into the city couldn't hurt the evening any,* she mused.

South of Milwaukee on Lake Michigan:

"If I go any slower the crew will become suspicious. I am afraid that you have run out of time, my friend. Tonight when the crew is asleep I will throw the package over the side. I will not go to jail for the rest of my life on some American island prison."

"Just wait until morning, Captain. I have a boat. If I haven't accomplished my goals here by then, you can do as you wish."

"NO!" The captain of the freighter was emphatic. "I have wasted enough time already; I will take no more risks."

Hamid pleaded for more time but failed, the call ended abruptly.

But Hamid wasn't about to give up so easily. He made another call to a well-placed associate, someone whom he had trusted his life to many times. Nassir would not fail him.

If the businessman didn't come to his family, Hamid would have to abandon the bomb, and kill the woman and child. Then he would have to go to the hospital and kill Mr. Seaver before using one of his planned escape routes out of the United States. The mission would be a failure. He would be a failure. But, he would protect his country. Hamid would return to be judged by his peers and the president. He might pay for his failure with his life. Hopefully his countrymen would kill him quickly.

But Hamid saw something in the pictures hanging on the wall that encouraged him. Mr. Seaver didn't strike him as a coward who would turn his back on his family. He clearly loved his family. Hamid was sure that if there was a way, the man wouldn't shirk his responsibilities. Hamid was confident, if the copter pilot woke in time and wasn't injured too badly, he would return to his home to save his family.

Hamid checked his gun. It was fully loaded and the safety was off. He would sleep in a chair hidden from the windows and the doorways. When Mr. Seaver comes through the door, he will be killed instantly. After that, Mrs. Seaver will help him sail the boat to get the bomb, or the same fate would befall her daughter. The evening was out of his hands at this point; Allah must bring Mr. Seaver to him. The one other loose end was also out of his hands. Hamid prayed that his friend and associate, Sergeant Nassir Azodi, had successfully commandeered the freighter. If the freighter was now under his control, Hamid still had hope of retrieving and detonating the nuclear device on American soil.

Hamid had become used to watching the American television news channels. It was always interesting what the Americans thought newsworthy. He picked up the remote and turned on the small flat screen TV on the kitchen shelf. Weather would remain calm, which was excellent news for boating on the giant lake. The weather lady promised a fine day for football. The news anchor solemnly spoke of several killings in Milwaukee the previous night, probably drug related. The food pantries were stocking up on supplies for the winter and he encouraged everybody to donate at their local grocery store. Looking into an opposite camera, he announced that unnamed sources report that the president of the United States was going to make a surprise stop in his hometown of Chicago but his visit was canceled at the last minute for unknown reasons. The news announcer continued. "Stay tuned Wisconsin; you might be surprised at his new destination." He added a teaser.

285

Alan D Schmitz

Hamid thought it very interesting that the president had canceled his trip to Chicago. Was it possibly because of him? The thought that it potentially was because of the threat, made Hamid feel self-important. It was empowering to think that his efforts caused the President of the United States to change his plans.

Sports came on next, with a very excited announcer. "Big day in Packerland!" he started. "One of the Chicago Bears' most notable fans is going to be in Green Bay for the big game. It has been confirmed that the president will be coming to Green Bay Wisconsin to watch, in person, the football game between his favorite team the Chicago Bears and their fiercest rivals, the Green Bay Packers. The sports announcer promised it would be a terrific game with over 73,000 people in attendance. "That's right folks, the city of Green Bay Wisconsin will almost double in population for tomorrow's afternoon game. Mr. President, hope you have a ticket and parking pass, because if you don't, I don't know anybody who will give theirs up, even for the President," he kidded.

"Allah be praised!" Hamid whispered. The reason Allah was testing him, was to prepare him for his greatest challenge. The President of the United States, along with over a hundred-thousand infidels would die by his hand tomorrow. "Allah!" Hamid prayed out loud. "I will not fail you."

Opening a map of Wisconsin he saw an immediate plan fall into place. The huge football stadium was very close to the waters of Green Bay, which were part of Lake Michigan. There was even a river inlet and small marina that would get him that much closer. His advantage over what was sure to be increased security, was that he only needed to get into the vicinity. The huge nuclear blast would do the rest. Allah in his wisdom had provided everything he needed.

Chicago, Downtown:

The results were finally in. Dental records proved that the young man was Behrouz Golzar. The unofficial autopsy report said the young man was dead before he could inhale any smoke. A wound in the side of the corpse seemed to have been caused by a large knife. A burned, charred body was difficult to assess post mortem, but the importance of this particular body was impressed on the coroner. The broken neck made it much easier to see that the young man had been murdered.

An hour later, Matthew Mitchell looked at the forwarded e-mail of the infrared satellite photos. As far as he was concerned, he had ample circumstantial evidence to re-board the ship. Agent Mitchell composed an e-mail with the photos attached. In the e-mail to his boss, he tried to piece together the chain of events that tied into the photos. He couldn't be positive the bomb was back on board, but the ship needed to be searched carefully and the captain needed to be questioned thoroughly.

Dan Price, the area chief for the team, read the e-mail closely and studied the pictures. The team in Chicago might be on to something. The box giving off the one hundred degree heat had him concerned. Maybe it was just the personal belongings of the man making an illegal entry into the U.S. And if the personal belongings were stored in some hot area of the ship, the trunk would contain residual heat. Unfortunately, the team did not have in its possession any more photos of the private fishing boat. There was no way to tell if the box eventually succumbed to the cool night air or if it continued to radiate heat. The connection between the young dead man and the freighter was also suspicious, but not condemning. The jurisdiction of the NNSA over a potential murder investigation was muddy at best. Tying a murder in an abandoned Chicago building to a potential weapon of mass destruction, via nothing more than a heat signature and residual X-ray isotopes, was a stretch.

It was time to have faith in his field officers, so Division Chief Price called his immediate superior at home. For whatever reason he couldn't get Kara Johnson to answer her phone. That was unusual but it was late on Saturday night. Unfortunately, his team on the ground in Chicago didn't have time to waste, and he had to go through Kara in order to convince Homeland.

Chicago, Illinois:

It was ten P.M. in Chicago and field agent Mitchell was waiting for a call back from Dan Price. It was driving him crazy, waiting for his next instructions, but there seemed to be little else he could do. It was getting late and he was sure the rest of his team was having the same jitters. Matthew used his cell phone to arrange a conference call among the team members. He included Sarah Beth in on the call; he trusted her insight.

"There must be something we can do?" Mike insisted. He wasn't used to the "hurry up and wait" aspect of the government chain of command.

"My contact at the NSA did another status check on the freighter with the last satellite pass. For what it's worth, the freighter seems to be going as slowly as it possibly can. I can't even begin to guess why it would choose to move so slowly, but it is due east of Milwaukee. If it stays at this pace, by tomorrow morning it will still be in Lake Michigan. If during the night it decides to speed up, it could well be east of the Mackinaw Straits and into Lake Huron by then.

"When do you expect authority to board?" Dieter questioned.

Matthew Mitchell also understood the issue of the government chain of command, which was why he was a field agent. "I don't expect anything. Who knows what goes on in the minds of the politicians and bureaucrats?" Then Matthew had an idea.

"Dieter, how fast can you get us up to Wisconsin in the chopper?"

"How far north are we going?"

"I want to get as close to the freighter as possible. If a decision comes down, I want to be able to jump on its deck one minute later."

"What if we don't get a go ahead?" Tony questioned.

"Sarah Beth and her group can handle things here if the freighter turns out to be a bust. But at least we will be ready to move."

Dieter did some quick calculations. "Depending on winds, in an hour and a half, to two hours, I can get us well north of Milwaukee."

"Do you think you can land that thing on the freighter?"

Dieter didn't have to think about the answer to that question at all. "You bet I could. But, I will have to stay with the chopper. I can set it down on the top containers, keep it at hover, and you and Tony will have to jump off."

"Fair enough. We can't do anything until daylight, so let's meet at the airport at daybreak. We'll fly as far north as we have to, to stay close to the freighter. Let's hope that we get the okay while in route. I want to surprise them with the helicopter. I'm afraid that if they see a Coast Guard cutter, any evidence that might still be on board, will immediately be lost into the lake. Sarah Beth, you'll take command of the remaining teams here. If we have reason to suspect the bomb is still here, it will all be up to you."

They all agreed to the plan and also agreed that, despite how difficult it might be, the best thing they could do right now was to get whatever sleep they could.

Gurney, Illinois:

Scott woke up slowly. He listened to the noises around him. Machines were beeping quietly; somebody was outside the door talking in hushed tones. It took him a few minutes before he remembered where he was. His mouth and lips were parched. Scott pressed the service button; a small light went on behind his bed, which he didn't see.

It didn't take long for a young female attendant to step in. "Yes, Mr. Seaver. I see you are awake. What can I do for you?"

"I'm very thirsty. Can you get me some water?"

The nurse picked up a cup with a straw in it. "There is water right here waiting for you. You couldn't see it in the darkness."

"Thanks! What time is it?"

"It's one A.M."

"How long have I been sleeping?"

"You had a very strong sedative; you've been pretty much sleeping for the last ten hours."

"Is my wife here?" Scott felt ready to nod back to sleep, but he needed to see Liz.

"No, but your brother called. They are very concerned and he said that your wife is unable to come to the hospital."

Scott looked at the nurse confused.

"Is there something wrong Mr. Seaver?"

"No, I just wish my wife was here," Scott said a partial truth. He didn't remember having a brother. But in his current state, not remembering he had a brother didn't mean he didn't have one.

"You need to try to get more sleep. The doctors have more tests for you tomorrow morning and they don't want you to sleep through them," The nurse's aide gave a comforting smile.

"I'll check back in a while. Try to get some sleep," she encouraged.

Scott could have easily drifted off to sleep, but he became worried. Something wasn't right, he could feel it. He had just woken up, yet he felt a sense of panic. The nurse's aide left the room. The light from the hallway lit up his room and he saw his phone.

Scott still didn't remember having a brother. He picked up his phone and paged through the listings. The only Seavers listed were his wife, daughter and his parents. Then he thought to look up the number from his received calls list. If his brother called, it would be listed. Only his wife's number was familiar. He was seconds away from calling his wife's phone, but an uncomforting feeling persisted. Maybe if he heard the recorded conversations, memories would come back, so Scott played back the recorded messages.

Scott started to replay all of his recent messages, even the one the nurse intercepted for him. Slowly Scott put together all the pieces, except the why. With each piece of information he remembered more and more. He was still very groggy, but now he remembered that he didn't have a brother and his family was in terrible danger. Images of the previous day came to mind. One image he couldn't get out of his mind was the face of the man at the toll stop. It was the face of a man he knew he had to kill to save his family.

Scott had to get to Port Washington; it was clear that Liz wasn't going to come to the hospital for him. The longer he concentrated, the more Scott started remembering. In fact, he felt that he was starting to think unusually clearly. Scott looked at the solution dripping into him through the IV and wondered what was in it that made him feel so good. He was in a hospital gown, but the nurse had assured him his clothes were in the closet.

Scott wished he could take a short nap, though he knew he didn't have time. His wife and daughter needed him. His mind was ready, but his body wasn't in a rush to get out the bed; he was very comfortable and relaxed. Scott played with his IT-Tech some more. Memories continued to come back to him. Then he remembered the implosion of the building from earlier, or at least he thought he did. He connected to the Internet through his phone and went to the company web page. If his memory was accurate, he would see a video of the implosion.

After searching the company's web site, Scott couldn't find any link to the most recent success of their company. That was strange; normally it would be posted immediately. Then Scott chuckled to himself. He would have done the posting, and if he didn't do it for one reason or another, it wouldn't have been done. His partner Jerry was great at a number of things, but the company website was not one of his fortes. Scott typed in the password for his personal web backdoor. That was where he would have sent an unedited video before releasing it to the public.

There it was. He found the video, but the strange thing was that the video was from the day before the demolition event. Scott played the video. Suddenly his world opened up and things were starting to make even more sense. Scott played the video again and then again. For the first time since the nightmare began, he understood what was happening to him and his family. He laid back in his bed thinking. It all began to come together. The video showed the man from the toll stop using a knife to kill a young man. It showed the same man going up the stairs. Scott remembered chasing him and trying to kill him. It showed the man starting the fire and leaving the building out a back opening. The last thing the video showed was the fire and smoke consuming the laptop.

Scott smirked. At least now he knew where his laptop was. He looked at the big clock on the wall and tried to calculate how long it would take him to get to his home. It was hard to concentrate for some reason, though he assumed he had better get going. Scott sat up in bed, which immediately started the room spinning around him. With a wide grin, he realized just how good he felt. He was definitely bombed on something. It took a couple of tries, but eventually he disconnected the IV from his arm. Too bad, he was sorry to separate himself from the bag of liquid medicine.

Getting dressed was no picnic either. Putting his socks on seemed particularly difficult, so he said the hell with it and slipped on his shoes without them. He was ready to walk out the door when he patted his pockets and felt his car keys, but realized that he didn't have his phone. "Woops!" he said to nobody but himself. "Can't leave without my little friend." Finding his phone on the bed, he slid it into his pocket and then walked out the door of his room. Lucky for him there was a green line drawn on the floor of the hospital hallway. Green was for "go," he assumed, stating it out loud. He tried to follow the line, making a game out of trying to stay centered on it.

The female nurse on duty looked up and saw the back of a silly man pretending to tightrope walk the line on the floor with his hands out for balance. She thought it funny and laughed a bit as he turned down the hallway out of sight.

Outside Scott looked for his SUV, then pressed the car icon on his phone. The phone drew a map and a flashing pin showed where his car was. It clearly wasn't near. Out of the darkness came a set of car lights. A young man drove by him and Scott vigorously waved him down. "Can I help you sir?" the man asked politely.

"I was in an accident and bumped my head," Scott explained.

"Yes sir. You are at the hospital. If you go into the emergency entrance they will help you." Jeremy Logan was just finished with his night shift and was anxious to go home and get some sleep.

Scott laughed, "No, no, you don't understand. I was already helped. See..." Scott swung his arms open and turned himself around in a circle almost falling. Then he said. "I'm all better, I feel great, but!" Wagging his finger at the young man Scott tried to sound sober and serious without much success. "My car is not here, and I have to get to it so I can save my wife and daughter from kidnappers."

The young man knew a drunk when he saw one and said, "Sorry sir, maybe you should go back into the hospital. I have to get home and get some sleep."

"I need a ride son, I need it real bad. I'm sure I seem a little relaxed because they gave me something to make me feel better and it worked great," Scott explained again as he nearly fell backward while swinging his arms around to demonstrate how good he actually felt. "Look!" Scott said excitedly as he showed the IT-Tech to the young man. My phone knows where my car is. It's at the end of the yellow line. We are here." Scott tried to point to a little spot on the screen. His finger was not capable of staying in one place. "And this is where my car is. I'm not going to drive; my wallet is in it and I have to get my wallet, they want my insurance card," he repeated. "Then I'll come right back to the hospital, I promise."

That was something the young man understood. The insurance card was very important to the hospital. The orderly wasn't used to turning down those in need and this man was clearly in need. After looking again at the map on the IT-Tech phone, Jeremy saw that the end of the yellow line was on his way. "Sure, OK, get in. But promise me you won't drive."

"Of Course not." Scott sloppily crossed his chest with his right hand and made the promise while keeping his left hand behind his back with fingers crossed. Jeremy took the phone and followed the voice instructions until they were at the old gas station. Before leaving, the orderly made the older man promise again that he wouldn't drive. Scott lied again and made another promise.

Scott went into the gas station and bought one of those heavily caffeinated power drinks, the kind over-the-road drivers use to keep awake. The seriousness of the situation was never forgotten. It was just hard for him to concentrate. Scott knew he had to start to focus if he was to be of any use to his family. An hour later he was on his way, doing his best to keep the car centered between the lines. It wasn't as easy as he remembered.

Chapter 21

Somehow Scott managed to keep his car more or less centered in his lane. The cover of darkness helped to hide his slow, erratic driving from the few cars that shared the freeway with him. As time went by, Scott became more and more cognizant of his surroundings and started to feel mentally alert again. Whatever had been in the IV solution was wearing off.

An hour and a half later he was entering Wisconsin. Scott kept his window open; the night air revived him. It was time to play his trump card. Earlier he had pulled off to the side of the road to rest his eyes from the night and the glare of headlights. During that time he played back the video of the murder on his IT-Tech. His mind was much clearer now and his next move became apparent.. It was time to play his one card.

Scott called his wife's cell phone, assuming that the kidnappers had it. He was right. The ringing phone startled the terrorist from a rather deep sleep. "This is Elizabeth Seaver's phone, may I help you." Hamid was polite and to the point; it could be the hospital calling.

Scott wasn't as congenial. "Listen asshole, you harm my family and I will kill you very slowly. Trust me. I won't tell the police anything until after you're dead. I wouldn't want them to ruin my fun."

"You are not in a position to threaten me, my friend."

"Don't be so sure, asshole; maybe I am. I assume you are at my home, waiting for me. I want you to go to the computer in my office. There is a web video you need to see before you call my bluff."

Scott knew the best he could hope for was to create a stalemate, one that he could eventually use to save his family. Scott's tough talk was intended to cause the kidnapper to reconsider the notion that he was in complete control of the situation.

"I am at the computer. What is it you want me to see?"

"I want you to see a nice little movie I made. It shows you killing somebody with a knife and dragging the dead body away. It also shows you starting a fire to destroy the evidence."

Hamid clenched his fists. Without even seeing the video, he was fairly certain it wasn't a bluff. There would be no purpose in that, because he would know for sure in a few minutes anyway. Hamid typed in the web

Alan D Schmitz

address the angry husband and father gave him. There was a single video file. He double clicked on it. "Golole," he swore. The man wasn't bluffing.

"It seems you have something I want, Mr. Seaver."

"And you, asshole, have something I want. Here is the deal. You give me back my family unharmed and I will not distribute the video."

"And how will I know that there aren't copies?"

"In fact, you can bet there are copies, many copies. But I don't want trouble or to ever see you again. I know that if I release the video to the police, you will have nothing to lose in killing me or my family. So, if you leave my family alone, nobody ever needs to see it. On the other hand, if I or any person in my family dies from suspicious causes, you had better be ready to run for your life because the video will automatically be posted to the Internet for everybody to see."

"I need some time to think about your offer." Scott unexpectedly heard his phone go silent.

"Shit!" Scott swore. He didn't think there was anything for the kidnapper to think about. He apparently was wrong and that scared him into thinking maybe he was too late. Scott decided not to call back immediately; if it was too late, it wouldn't matter. If his family was still all right, then he couldn't afford to let the kidnapper know how desperate he was. In the meantime, Scott pressed on towards his home. The morning sun was starting to climb into what seemed to be a beautiful day weather wise. A prayer slipped through his mouth. "Dear Lord, please take care of my family. I'm yours anytime you want, but please spare them."

Chicago, Illinois:

As the sun was making its appearance over the lake; Matt, Mike and Dieter climbed into the small chopper waving goodbye to Sarah Beth. There was no decision from Washington on boarding the freighter yet. Dan Price indicated that the Israelis who owned the ship were not too keen on the idea of the captain and crew being harassed for a third time. Their ambassador insisted that as close allies of the U.S., the idea that they would harbor terrorists and murderers was insulting. Price took the intense reaction as a sign that possibly the Israelis were up to something secret–something the Israelis were particularly good at.

Agent Matt Mitchell didn't tell his boss what he was up to. His boss didn't ask. It was another government procedure. Don't ask and don't tell. Certain things had to get done in the field; you won't find the operating procedures for all the grey areas of fieldwork in any book. Dan

Price knew it and agent Mitchell knew that his boss couldn't condone his current actions. What his boss didn't know would protect him.

Green Bay, Wisconsin:

The United States Secret Service was scrambling. The president had done the unimaginable. At the last minute, he decided to throw himself into the Lion's Den of public exposure. When they insisted the president change his itinerary because Chicago was close to being flagged as a severe risk, they had no idea he would insist on seeing, in person, the major rivalry he had enjoyed since childhood. It was their job to protect the president's life, but they didn't have authority over where the president went. The Secret Service had unwittingly taken their boss out of the frying pan and into the fire.

Was the president brave or foolish? It was a question that went through each agent's mind. Surprise was their only ally in this mission, code named "Operation Football." Normally, for a security task of this magnitude, the agency would have weeks, if not months to prepare. Bulletproof glass was being erected at a special secured seating area. Many fans would be terribly inconvenienced; security into the stadium would be much stricter than normal.

The president was trying to maintain an image of being the "Average Joe"; only he wasn't. As he flew into Green Bay's Austin Straubel International Airport, a not so small army of security people, favored reporters, financial backers, key senators and congress persons flew in with him on Air Force One. And of course, there were the other support planes and helicopters with even more personnel on them.

The truth was that his appearance was bound to be a big hit on the national news. Ninety-nine point nine percent of the American public wasn't going to be inconvenienced in the slightest; it would be priceless free publicity for the most public figure in the world. Not priceless for the taxpayer, but the president was entitled to live his life, despite being the leader of the free world. The free publicity would undoubtedly help him in the next election, if it didn't kill him first.

Port Washington, Wisconsin:

Hamid woke and looked at the wall clock; it was morning, the sun was just breaking and it was time to call his compatriot on the Damascus Star. "Do you have the boat secure?"

295

Alan D Schmitz

"The captain suddenly is being very cooperative," the sergeant assured his partner on the land. The captain of the Damascus Star nursed a severe limp and a broken nose.

Hamid and Sergeant Asodi had been through many campaigns together in the Islamic Revolutionary Guards. When possible, they prayed together at the same mosque. They were closer than brothers. If Hamid had to trust his life to someone, it would be Nassir Asodi, and if the sergeant had to do likewise, it would be Hamid.

"What is your location Hamid? I am in a little town on the shoreline called Port Washington."

After a moment the sergeant replied, "We passed your town about an hour ago; we are about two miles from shore and ten miles north."

"Nassir, we have been granted a great gift from Allah. Is the package secure?"

"It is. The ship is at your command."

"I will be seeing you soon, my friend." Hamid didn't dare say more.

Hamid was so energized that he didn't feel the soreness in his shoulder. He rushed down the basement stairs. It was time to go. He cut the rope from the women's ankles and made them walk up the stairs and into the garage. The blood rushing back into their feet burned as the circulation pumped through their aching feet once again. On their way out the house, Liz saw the body of the first attacker lying on the floor, just like Avery said. Hamid marched the women out to the attached garage.

Hamid held the long bladed knife against the daughter's throat to make sure that the mother did exactly as she was told. When all three of them were inside the car, he commanded. "Drive us to the boat. If you try to contact anyone, or do anything suspicious, I will be forced to kill you and your daughter instantly. Any sudden movement of the car and your daughter will be cut severely."

"Why do you want our boat?"

"That is none of your business. Now drive," he demanded.

At the Port Washington marina there was a fair amount of activity. Fishermen and sailors were an early rising group. Hamid pretended he was hugging the young girl by the shoulder when in fact his knife was pressing against her jugular vein ever so slightly. Lucky for all three of them, the other sailors were too busy prepping their boats to notice.

After years of sailing on "My Chopper," Liz knew the pre-sail routine by heart and started the diesel engine to warm it up. She hoped that the kidnapper didn't insist on using the sails, because she wasn't skilled at sailing. Even with Avery's help it would be difficult to control. Scott

296

enjoyed the challenge of single sailing, but she was much less experienced at it. Soon My Chopper was slowly moving through the inner harbor and out between the breakwater, into the open lake.

The teenage girl's fragile neck was never far from his knife blade. The diesel engine moved the boat along smartly and Hamid decided not to press his luck by insisting on sails, though it would be faster. They set a heading of 035 degrees. The northeasterly direction would intercept the freighter in due time. Hamid pressed the knife blade just a bit tighter and warned the girl to stay quiet while he placed another call.

Hwy 43, just south of Port Washington, Wisconsin:

Scott listened to the voice recordings on his IT-tech. The messages he left to himself were keeping him focused and that was what he needed. As he traveled north towards his home, every half hour Scott would add another recording, filling himself in on the latest developments in case he started to forget. As he was reaching for his phone to leave another voice note it started ringing, he listened to the caller say. "Mr. Seaver, I have a proposition for you."

"Nothing doing until I talk to my wife and daughter to make sure they are OK." Before the kidnapper could argue back, Scott added. "If you don't let me, I will assume you have killed them. Deal off."

"That is not a problem, Mr. Seaver." Scott was relieved.

Hamid placed the call on hold and told the frightened teenager, "Tell your father that you and your mother are OK. Say nothing else!" Hamid pressed the sharp tip of the knife into the girl's neck enough to make it bleed. Though Liz was busy steering the boat and was too far away to hear what was being said, she could sense what was happening when her daughter lifted the phone to her lips. Liz was pained by the expression on Avery's face; she looked extremely frightened. Yet Liz dared not do anything about it.

Soon Avery was on the phone. "Daddy?" she asked.

Her voice was music to his ears. "Princess, are you OK? I'm so sorry this happened honey." Scott tried to reach out to his daughter.

"Daddy, I can only tell you that Mom and I are OK." Before Hamid could take the phone away again she managed to add, "I am so scared Daddy; he has a knife."

"Here is my proposition Mr. Seaver. I want you to meet me in the city of Green Bay. I want to do the handoff at the football stadium. There will be plenty of people there, so I will have protection from any tricks."

Alan D Schmitz

Scott thought about the offer. It made sense. If he were a kidnapper he would want the same. Snipers or an ambush would be hard to plan with seventy-thousand people around.

"Fair enough. What time and where?"

"Just before game time. I will call and tell you where. I will be watching. If I sense that you are leading me into a trap, I will kill both of them. I would rather take my chances running from the police than walking into an ambush."

"If you don't deliver my family unharmed, I will release the video, and I will spend the rest of my life finding you."

Hamid didn't doubt Mr. Seaver's sincerity, but it wouldn't matter. If things went as planned, husband, wife and daughter would all die, instantly incinerated from the sun-like heat of the nuclear explosion. Mr. Seaver would never see his wife and child again. Hamid would never need to see Mr. Seaver again. All Hamid needed was for Mr. Seaver to be in the vicinity of the blast and he would die with the one hundred-thousand other people in Green Bay.

Scott had no choice; he bypassed his hometown and headed for I-43 north. In two hours he would be in Green Bay.

Hamid was a bit distracted as he made the arrangements on the phone. It was the first time he had let his guard down even a little, and the teenager took advantage of it. Her hands were still untied from the ride to the marina, allowing her hand to slowly slip into her hip pocket and take out her phone. She couldn't believe the kidnaper didn't notice. With the dangerous man sitting right next to her, making a call was out of the question. The teen slipped the phone in between some deck roping, concealing it. If the kidnapper didn't move her, she might be able to make an emergency call if the right opportunity presented itself.

"I am sorry little lady, but it is time to tie you up again."

"No!" Avery protested. "I won't do anything, I promise. Please, please," Avery cried.

Hamid looked for rope on the deck; he saw the coiled rope right next to the teen. It was a bit thick, but it would do. The terrorist kept one eye on his captive as he reached for the rope. His hand was inches away from the cell phone before he remembered that he had stuffed the original rope in his back pocket. It was a much more appropriate size and would be easier to work with. Hamid wasn't gentle in taking the thin, young wrists and tying the rope tightly around them. The girl's wrists started to bleed again, and the rope bit into her open skin. Liz cried as her daughter

298

winced in pain. A flash of the long knife blade reminded Liz that her daughter's life depended on Liz staying calm.

****

Scott continued north, driving away from his family, and unknowingly driving into a trap that would kill him, his family, and about one-hundred thousand residents and visitors of Green Bay, Wisconsin. Hamid never intended to let the husband and father see his wife or daughter again. All he needed was to have Mr. Seaver in the blast zone at the time of detonation. His family was just the bait.

Scott felt the sunshine against his arm. He left his side window open to keep him awake. For a reason Scott didn't understand, he felt very tired and the open window revived him a bit. The sunshine felt amazing on his skin; the cool morning air was warming up fast. A better fall day in Wisconsin would be hard to imagine. The radio was playing one of his old favorites, Ottis Redding's, "Sitting on the Dock of the Bay." The song always reminded him of his youth, when he would sit out on the long pier in the harbor, watching the gulls dance through the skies, looking for scraps from the fishermen's lunches. Those were the days; nothing to do but watch the birds fly and hope a fish would bite on the line. His mind wondered a bit, taking him back to his youth. He remembered a time when he and a friend hiked the beach up to a spot not far from here. They camped out overnight next to the calm lapping waters. In fact, that particular section of beach wasn't far from his current location. Now it was part of a state park. It had been quite an adventure for two young boy scouts displaying a bit of independence. Scott began to smile as he relived those simple times. He had definitely been blessed in his youth.

It had been awhile since Scott drove on this particular road. A blue sign flashed as he passed by, announcing the entrance to a state park at the next exit. Scott remembered that park, he had camped there as a youth; it was very clear in his mind. During the late 1800s it was a limestone quarry. Years ago, the huge limestone blocks were cut or blasted out and then moved the short distance to the lake to be shipped to Chicago or Milwaukee. The quarry was long abandoned and had filled with ground water. The steep white cliffs of the quarry were a beautiful contrast to the blue water of the small lake that had since formed in it.

Scott didn't remember why he was on his way to the park but the beautiful weather was the only excuse he needed. He took the freeway exit and turned into the park entrance. He wasn't far from home and a walk through the serene settings would be helpful as he contemplated his retirement. Besides, his legs felt a bit wobbly and a walk would help revive them before he went home. He parked the SUV and watched a young man playing with his dog, a rather large yellow Labrador. A quick stop to use the bathroom and he would be ready for a small hike.

A short walk through the woods took him past the quarry. Thousands of silvery leaves of the white birch trees that lined high bluff fluttered with each gentle breeze. Scott felt his stomach relax and his nerves unwind. The park always had that effect on him. It rejuvenated him and gave him an extra bounce in his step. He continued down the well-worn path from the small quarry lake to the great lake. Leaves were falling all around him, like giant red and yellow snowflakes. It was a wonderful fall day, one he intended to enjoy completely. The path he was on soon diverged. Scott took the upper trail; he knew exactly where he was going.

At the top of the bluff, Scott looked out over his lake. He could hear the sound of waves splashing lazily, even though they were far below the bluff he was standing on. Because it was so late in the year, the park was nearly deserted. A safety chain with a warning wired to it separated him from the edge of the steep bluff.

Far off in the distance was a sailboat heading north. The sails were down as it took a leisurely pace. Scott felt peacefulness settle upon him. There was only one thing more relaxing than watching a sailboat and that was sailing on one, he thought. But yet, the more he stared at it, the more he realized there was something about the craft. There was something vaguely familiar about the sailboat in the distance he couldn't quite place.

The back of Scott's neck bristled. He thought back to the awful moment when he was sailing and called out to his son, only to be reminded that he had caused his son's death. Those thoughts made him think of his wife and daughter, and that was when he remembered that his family was in danger.

Scott ran down the old path back to his SUV, trying to remember his plan to save them. At the parking lot, out of breath, Scott turned on his phone looking for answers. As he rushed through the various applications for anything that might help him remember, he accidently pressed the locate icon on the touch screen. Before he knew it, a map with a flashing yellow dot appeared.

Instantly Scott knew what it meant, it was the location of his daughter's cell phone. But something was wrong, the location of her phone was somewhere on Lake Michigan, that was impossible.

Scott grabbed binoculars from his car and ran back up the high bluff. When he got there, he had to lean against a tree to rest because he was so out of breath. He lifted the binoculars to his eyes and trained them on the sailboat now even further off in the distance.

There was almost no doubt in his mind that it was My Chopper. It appeared as though there were three passengers, but because of the distance, he couldn't make them out.

Scott ran back to his SUV and soon was speeding towards the Port Washington Harbor. He still couldn't believe his eyes, maybe he was wrong, but he had to know for sure. Scott cursed his failing memory, though in this case it was a blessing. Instead of being led farther away from his family, he now knew exactly where they were, if his boat was indeed gone from its slip.

West Bend, Wisconsin:

The NNSA team landed at the West Bend Municipal Airport to refuel the helicopter. Dieter's friend at the NSA was giving them updates on the position of the freighter. It was moving north at a very slow pace. The ship was only a couple of miles off the coast, tracking north. That would be a plus if they got the go for their mission. For the time being, there was nothing to do but wait and be prepared for departure on a moment's notice. Mathew cursed a bit. With each moment of indecision by the politicians in Washington the freighter moved farther away.

Michael asked the airport receptionist if any restaurants were nearby. As long as they had to wait, they might as well catch some breakfast. Soon, they were walking into the diner across the street from the airport; it would be their new home until the call came, if it came. The three knew that they could also be ordered back to Chicago at any time.

Andrews Air Force Base, Maryland:

Air Force One departed Andrews Air Force Base for the flight to Green Bay, Wisconsin. The President of the United States of America didn't want to miss one minute of the game or the pre-game festivities. The highly modified Boeing 747 would easily do 500 knots; its actual airspeed was classified, but at that rate, it would take the plane just over an hour to get to Green Bay. That would give the president plenty of time to pose for pictures and local television shots. He made sure that his aides brought along several footballs for him to sign and throw out to the crowd. His brand new, presidential looking, Chicago Bears shirt, looked both casual and dignified. Photo ops were not to be wasted; the current election year was just starting.

301

****

The instant Scott reached the marina, he leapt out of his car and down the wood walkway toward his boat. In another minute, Scott had his answer. His hunch was right; the kidnapper had stolen his boat. What was he to do now? He looked at the boats surrounding him; most were chained to the piers. *Stealing one might be possible*, he thought. With a feeling of hope, Scott lifted his IT-Tech out of his pocket and rechecked the current location of his daughter's phone. Scott estimated that their location was probably at least ten miles away and growing. The reality was that even if he was successful at stealing a boat, it wouldn't help. None of them would be fast enough to catch another moving craft, already that distance away. The sad fact was, he was already too late.

He needed something fast and he needed it now. What he needed was a helicopter. That was when Captain Scott Seaver realized what he had to do. He was a Huey pilot and fifteen minutes from the dock was his helicopter, his Huey. It was his family's only chance.

Scott ran back to his car and raced west toward the guard base. Maybe, just maybe, his friend Major Robert Allen would be there. He might listen; he might help if he saw the video of the murder and the recordings of the man's threats against Scott and his family.

Fifteen minutes later, Captain Seaver tried hard not to appear nervous or agitated as he pulled out his military ID and presented it to the guard at the main gate. When the guard saluted him with approval, Scott thanked him and waited for the chain fence gateway to slide open.

Scott parked his car and scanning the parking lot for his commander's vehicle; it was not in Major Allen's reserved space. "Shit" he wasn't here. Scott glanced at his watch and then at the moving dot on his phone's screen. He didn't have time to find Bob and explain the situation. Besides, there was no guarantee that the base commander would give him a multi-million dollar government vehicle without mission approval. Just because Scott was sure that the small dot was his daughter's cell phone didn't mean that anyone else would accept it as fact.

Scott sat in the car for a moment and thought about his predicament. He was quite a distance from the flight line, but he could see two helicopters ready for flight as usual. He couldn't just rush into the base and demand the officer in charge give him one of them. The choice was fairly simple; he would have to steal a Huey.

Scott knew the base and the routine of the guards. From the number of vehicles in the parking lot, it seemed like the base was busy today. He recognized many of the cars as belonging to some of the other pilots. This would be much more difficult than he imagined.

Captain Seaver started to think like a military man. He needed a diversion, a big one, but what?

He studied the base from the front seat of his car. *There has to be something I can use to create some confusion?*

He slowly scanned the area, looking for anything that he might use. *"Nothing"* disgusted, he turned his head toward the back of the SUV and the guard shack, hoping for some inspiration. Then, out of the corner of his eye, he spotted the unmarked box of left over detonator caps in the back of his SUV. *Of course, that's it, the RDX in the back and a timer fuse. Nobody would get hurt, but the explosion would draw everyone, including the guards, away from the helicopters on the flight line.*

Scott tried to avoid being spotted as he entered the officer's flight building. He already set the timers on the RDX packs. In ten minutes all hell would break loose opposite the flight line and the waiting helicopters. The heavy coat he wore helped conceal a few extra sets of RDX and detonator caps for another diversion. Scott quickly walked by the technician's center and the pilot's ready room. The ready room was where the pilots on call could relax until an emergency call came in, and. this Sunday in particular, everyone hoped that the only event needing their attention would be the football game. It was only three hours to kickoff and the television was already on, with the volume turned way up. Some of the more dedicated sports fans didn't want to miss one word of the pre-game hype. Everybody at the base seemed to be enjoying the extra energy surrounding this game. It looked to Scott like most of the residents of the base were gathered together in the same small room.

Scott was very nervous by the time he got to the pilot's changing room. He fumbled with the combination lock on his locker but couldn't remember the combination he had used for years and years. Nervously, Scott fumbled with his phone, trying to remember the one code that protected the electronic list of all his passwords and security codes, for some reason that too was escaping him. What was happening to him?

Scott sat on the changing bench behind his locker. He felt tired and worn out, his mind wondered. What was he doing at the base anyway? He thumbed through the photo album feature of his phone; the hi-resolution photos made him long for his family. There was a picture of Liz and Avery making funny faces with their tongues stuck out at him. Another was Liz and Avery sitting on a park bench, licking their ice cream cones. Scott remembered the next photo, it was of him steering the

Alan D Schmitz

sailboat, complete with his sea captain's hat that Brad and Avery bought him. The next photo was a bashful smiling Brad, taken on his 14th birthday. The corner of the photo contained the date. Of course, that was it, the combination. Ever since Brad's first birthday he had used that date as his combination. Scott also remembered why he was at the base, he had to steal a helicopter. A quick look at the IT-Tech showed that his daughter's phone was still located somewhere out on Lake Michigan.

Captain Seaver jumped up and entered the digits. The door swung open. It didn't take long for Scott to change into his olive green flight suit and military issue boots. Just before he slammed the locker closed again, he grabbed his lucky helmet and tucked it under his arm. It was time to steal a Huey from the United States Army.

****

Elizabeth Seaver guided "My Chopper" next to the large freighter and Hamid tied the small craft up to the east-facing hull. Elizabeth prayed for help from the captain and crew of the freighter, but her heart told her that the kidnapper knew exactly what he was doing. She and her daughter could expect no help from the ship's occupants.

Sergeant Nassir Azodi was standing-by topside, and made sure that the women onboard the sailboat saw the machine gun in his hand. He had also instructed the captain of the Damascus Star to hold a crew meeting below deck to keep all crewmembers oblivious to their new guests. When the sailboat was securely tied to the huge freighter, a rope ladder was dropped down to it.

"Climb up," Was all that Hamid said, pointing his gun at Liz.

Liz didn't move. "I will go nowhere without my daughter."

"Fine, have it your way." The terrorist took his knife and cut the binding around the teen's wrist. "You first!" He turned the gun and pointed it at the young girl's head. She and then her mother climbed the dangling ladder. Hamid held it as tightly as he could so the women didn't have to struggle as it twisted and swung against the hull of the big ship. He followed, his shoulder aching with each move he made. Soon all three were on the deck of the freighter and Hamid gave his friend a great hug.

"Please, my friend, tell me of the great gift Allah has given us," Sergeant Azodi grinned. He could wait no more.

"The American president is going to be at the great football game in the town called Green Bay. It is only a few miles from us at this very moment."

The sergeant fell silent; it took him a few moments to realize what his friend was suggesting to him.

"Praise be to Allah!" he finally said. "We will be the most famous martyrs for eternity."

"My friend! Who said we have to be martyrs? The bomb can be delivered on this small vessel. There is an inlet and a small marina near enough to the stadium that the nuclear bomb will be able to incinerate their president and the thousands of decadent, unfaithful souls attending the sporting event.

"We will change the United States forever. We will kill their president, and in the process destroy the Americans' feeling of security for all time. All gatherings across their country will be stopped. The decadent sporting industry will be ruined forever. The cowardly Americans will be too frightened to attend football, baseball, and basketball events. Their stadiums will stand empty. Their overpaid heroes will have no one to play for. They will realize that they are not safe from the jihadist anywhere; and we can strike anytime, even killing their president if we so wish."

Liz's heart sank as she now knew that they were a reluctant part of a much more sinister plot than she could have ever imagined. These men were rejoicing at the thought of killing thousands of innocent people. *Killing Avery or me wouldn't take a second thought. Why had they kept us alive this long?* she wondered. *Certainly they didn't think that I would help them kill fellow citizens or the president. And why did they want Scott?*

"Sergeant, we do not have much time. Lock these two in one of the containers. Where is the bomb?"

"It is close," the sergeant assured. He then pointed his gun at the head of the young girl and pointed down the deck. The two terrorists marched their captives at gunpoint to an empty steel box. Once the captives were inside, the men closed and locked the airtight container. Mother and daughter cried as they hugged each other in the blackness. It was darker in the container than any darkness either of them had ever experienced. A hand in front of their eyes was invisible.

After sobbing for a while, Avery asked, "Do you think anybody will save us? What about Dad? He'll save us." She had faith in her own hero.

"I hope so baby; these are some very bad men. Do as they say."

"Are they really going to kill the president?" she asked.

"They are going to try. I'm sure of that."

305

Chapter 22

Army National Guard base, West Bend, Wisconsin:

Captain Seaver walked past the technician's office on the way to the flight line. He held his IT-Tech in his hand, staring at the yellow dot depicting his daughter's phone location. Scott prayed repeatedly that he would not forget his mission, he couldn't.

Lieutenant Randy Schmidt was the one person Scott most wanted to avoid. Schmidt would certainly want to talk, and he was more than aware of Scott's no-fly status. Scott peeked around the corner into the office. It was empty. He saw the lieutenant's desk and Randy's IT-Tech on the desktop, but the officer wasn't around.

"Is that you? My god! Captain Seaver, it's great to see you around here again." Randy popped his head up from behind his desk, where he had been hooking up some sort of new gadget to his computer. "Why are you in your jumpsuit? How come you have your helmet?"

Scott turned around, forcing a big smile, and walked toward Schmidt in a friendly manner. "I just wanted to take a look at my old bird."

Randy walked up to his friend. He heard the rumor about the captain's failing memory. "All the Hueys are gone sir. Your copter is being donated to a museum in Idaho; it's gone sir."

Scott never heard a word Randy said as he planned his next regrettable move. Nervously he set his phone down on the desk so he could use his hand, and then grabbed his helmet out from under his arm. "Sorry Randy." The hard, heavy helmet came from seemingly nowhere and hit the unsuspecting lieutenant on the side of the head. Randy fell to the ground quickly and quietly.

"Shit! I'm sorry Randy. You'll be OK, I promise." Scott bent down and rubbed his friend's forehead. Then he picked the thin, young man's body up by the armpits, dragged it into the simulator room and strapped the slumped body into the pilot's seat. Nobody would discover him there. The young man would eventually wake up with a hell of a headache, but that should give Scott enough time to steal the copter and be long gone.

Leaving the sim room and his friend behind, Scott rushed back to Randy's desk and grabbed his cell phone and helmet. Scott slid the phone into his pocket and, without wasting any more time, he rapidly walked toward the main flight line and the waiting helicopters.

Green Bay, Wisconsin:

Charcoal grills were scattered around the parking lot with their owners searing hamburgers and bratwurst over white-hot coals. The huge expanse of asphalt and cars was filled with excitement for the anticipated matchup between the rival teams. Each fan, regardless of the side he or she was rooting for, was sure their team would win. Each tailgater enjoyed his or her beverage of choice, which in this case was mostly Wisconsin beer. Even the Chicago Bears' fans appreciated the fine art of tailgating and partied hardily next to their arch rival's fans. A loud noise was heard above the crowd and all looked up to the spectacular sight of Air Force One as it made a slow pass for landing at the nearby airport. The airport was so close to the stadium that the airplane had to descend to just over the stadium for its approach.

The president looked out his window and saw all the football fans below waving up at the plane. He realized what an opportunity this was for him. The president picked up the phone on his desk and with the push of one button, he was talking to the pilot. "Ricky, can you make another low pass over the crowd? They seem to enjoy it."

"Yes Mr. President. I'm sure the aircraft controllers won't mind."

Captain Rick Wegner made a few radio calls and cancelled his approach. He was right, the control tower didn't mind, but all the aircraft that had to continue holding patterns because the president decided to create a bit more free publicity certainly did. There was little they could do but endure, as Air Force One always got priority.

Air Force One banked, making a slow circle around the stadium to the delight of the crowd below. At the end of the turn, Captain Wegner tipped the wings level and started on the final decent into Austin Straubel International Airport. Tailgating would be out of the question for the president and his family, *or would it?* The president wondered as the aircraft's wheels touched down. A little folksy camaraderie with the fans would certainly play well on the news. *The risk might not be that great*; surprise was on his side, though he knew already that the secret service would object. However, one does not become president of the United States by playing it safely.

Army National Guard base, West Bend, Wisconsin:

Captain Seaver opened the door to the flight line just a crack and waited a few minutes. The sole guard was making his rounds. Scott looked at his watch and thought, *if I timed it just right.* Then a tremendous, thunderous roar and a cloud of dust could be seen on the other side of the building. The RDX had done its job and produced a major hole in the landscaping on the other side of the grounds. He watched the guard run around the building toward the sound. Hopefully he bought enough time to get the aircraft off the ground before security realized it was being stolen. Scott knew the rules and the rules were to shoot to kill. These aircraft could be lethal in the hands of the wrong person. The sentry's orders were to shoot first and ask questions later.

The lone watchman turned the corner and Scott ran out to the flight line. He looked at the two copters already prepped for flight and stopped cold. The helicopters didn't look right; something was wrong. They were longer, sleeker and bigger, much bigger. The tail rotor had four blades as did the main rotor; his copter only had two. Scott spun his body, looking for other aircraft. There were none, at least none ready for flight. The odds of him completing his mission suddenly dropped significantly.

Scott felt confused and realized the potential consequence, but he couldn't forget why he came. In desperation Scott recited over and over again, "You have to save your wife and daughter. They were kidnapped and are somewhere on the lake." Scott repeated it again. "You have to save your wife and daughter. They were kidnapped and are somewhere on the lake." He couldn't let his confused mind lapse into forgetfulness.

Scott always bragged that he could fly a rock if somebody put wings on it. He had no choice; he raced to the first copter in line and repeated out loud again, "You have to save your wife and daughter. They were kidnapped and are somewhere on the lake."

Inside the chopper, Scott strapped himself into the pilot's seat. Suddenly things didn't look quite so foreign to him. It was as if he had sat in this seat before, even though he was certain he hadn't. Captain Seaver grabbed the startup checklist out of the small pocket that held it. For a reason he didn't understand, he knew where all the buttons and switches were as he went down the checklist. His hands and fingers reached out, turned dials and flipped switches without him thinking about it.

He hit the start button on the left engine and watched it spool up and ignite. The sound of a jet engine igniting was unique and rewarding. If he could get it started, he could fly it. Scott's confidence grew. By the time the second engine started, the guard had turned the corner of the big building to where the explosives left a receding dust cloud and a gaping hole in the ground. He held his rifle cocked and ready. Something was positively amiss. Inside the building a group of officers from the flight room were equally curious about what the loud boom was about. They emptied out of the back of the building in time to see the cloud of dust.

Bewildered, they heard another sound, only it was coming from the opposite side of the building. The guard couldn't see what it was, but the sound was the very familiar sound of a Black Hawk spooling up. He had seen no orders for practice flights today. Somebody was taking a helicopter. It was his job to make sure nobody took a copter without his knowledge. He had been purposely misdirected to the farthest point away from the choppers he was supposed to be guarding.

Sergeant Lenny Sidowske started running. He was the closest, but he still had to run completely around the building to see the aircrafts. The rest of the soldiers ran after him, toward the sound of the jet engines. The guard was dressed in full army fatigues with his rifle loaded. Lenny never thought he would have to shoot somebody. His house was only ten minutes away and this wasn't war.

The engines were spooling up; the chopper was preparing to depart, somebody was stealing a Black Hawk, a Black Hawk called 210HK specifically. Lenny dropped down to one knee; he would only have time for a few shots. He had to make them count. The lone sentinel aimed at the pilot through the front windshield. Carefully he pulled the trigger. The gun recoiled and the bullet hit the target.

Scott saw the shot hit right in front of him. He glanced in the direction of the shooter. It was little Lenny Sidowske, Dan's son. Thank god for the bulletproof glass surrounding him. Scott stared at Lenny and pushed the throttle forward. The huge turbines sped even faster. Lenny couldn't believe his eyes. He ran up just a bit closer for confirmation; the pilot was Scott Seaver, his dad's bowling buddy. Lieutenant Sidowske had known Scott since he was a young boy! He and his dad had even gone fishing a couple of times with Mr. Seaver. The soldier couldn't shoot again. What if he got a lucky shot and it killed the captain? He knew he couldn't kill a man he had known his whole life, so he shot over the top of the rotating blades and aimed a few rounds just below the chopper's belly. It was hard to hit the moving target, his superiors would believe him.

By this time, a crowd had gathered in back of the guard and witnessed his apparent, valiant attempts to stop the thief. They all watched in disbelief as 210HK lifted off the ground.

Scott pulled up on the collective lever and the copter moved from the ground. At the same time he pressed the cyclic stick forward. The big

Black Hawk helicopter lurched forward and the rotating blades tipped toward the ground. Lenny ran for cover, as did everybody else. By this time, everybody at the base knew that the thief was Captain Seaver. They also knew that the captain didn't have his wings for the Black Hawk and shouldn't be trying to fly one. There was little doubt the pilot was going to kill himself in a ball of fire. The copter moved across the ground; the giant lifting blades skimmed forward just a foot or two above the landing area. If one blade touched the ground at that speed, the blades would shatter and destroy the transmission, the engines and lastly, the body of the copter itself would disintegrate as the ruptured fuel tanks exploded.

Scott pulled back on the cyclic too fast; he over corrected the sensitive fly by wire controls. This caused the nose of the aircraft to shoot up and the tail of the Black Hawk to hit the ground. It was only beginner's luck that the tail hadn't hit hard. Scott sensed what was happening and was already in the process of correcting; leveling the huge machine. Captain Seaver concentrated on just working the collective smoothly and carefully. Altitude would be his friend; another close encounter with the ground would probably be his last. Slowly the copter climbed straight up. At two thousand feet of altitude, Scott played with the hand controls a bit to get used to their sensitivity. Then he did the same with the foot controls, trying to adjust to the feel of the tail rotor. With a gentle push on the cyclic, 210HK moved forward, not completely under control yet, but enough to get him out of harm's way.

It was right about then that another explosion was heard. The second Black Hawk jerked violently up from the ground and then crashed back down with a severely broken tail. Scott couldn't take the chance of being followed and forced down, so as he ran to 210HK, he had thrown a bundle of RDX under the other helicopter; he prayed nobody was hurt by his criminal stunt.

The rest of the flight lesson would have to be learned en route. It didn't take long before the slick, dark-green Black Hawk was cresting the bluffs overlooking Lake Michigan. Scott didn't have time to double check the yellow dot on his phone, but he remembered his daughter's general location. Spotting his own sailboat shouldn't be much of a problem.

****

Major Hamid Shukah and Sergeant Nassir Azodi wrestled the case containing the nuclear bomb out of its hiding place on the ship and onto the Seaver's small craft. The crew of the Damascus Star was still below deck attending a mandatory crew meeting on safety. The meeting would continue until the sergeant said otherwise.

"What about the women?" Nassir asked.

"I will take a hostage with me in case the husband demands to talk to one of them again. Keep the other one in the container until you are out to sea. After you are on the Atlantic for a couple of days, dump the body into the ocean."

"Which one do you want?"

"Doesn't matter!" Hamid said quickly, and then he thought about it before changing his mind. "I will take the mother to pilot the boat; if her daughter is here, she will not dare disobey."

Sergeant Azodi opened the container door wide. The daylight streamed in, along with some welcomed fresh air. The airtight shipping container was already very hot and stuffy. Two people couldn't last more than a day before suffocating. The bright sunlight temporarily blinded the mother and daughter, who were huddled together.

Major Shukah pointed his weapon at the mother. "You will come with me," he ordered forcefully to the older woman.

"I will go nowhere without my daughter!" she shouted back. Still blinded by the sunlight, Liz held her hand up to partially block the streaming light.

"The young one must stay here," Nassir insisted.

"I said no!" Elizabeth shouted back as firmly as she could.

Hamid shot off a burst from his Israeli made Uzi machinegun into the back of the container, just over the heads of the women.

"Please do not argue. I will kill her now and still take you with me. It is your choice." Kassim spoke loudly with a hint of indifference.

"Mom, it's OK. Go with him. I am not afraid; I will be OK until you come back."

Liz thought about her options while hugging her daughter. She would gladly give her life to save her daughter. But Liz had no doubts that the gunmen would kill Avery in a second if they thought they had to. They were both powerless. At any moment the terrorist could kill them both. It was a sad and humbling experience to be so completely helpless. The fact was, the men could do anything they wanted with either of them. Maybe it would be better for both of them to die right now in each other's arms. Liz slowly let her daughter go. In the human spirit, hope springs eternal; if there was life, there was hope. Maybe somebody on the crew would take pity on the young woman and help her. Liz realized the odds were small, but if she was alive at least there was a chance.

Hamid roughly grabbed the mother's arm and yanked her out of the container. Liz rethought her logic, she wanted her daughter back. But before she could do or say anything, the door to the container slammed shut. Her daughter was gone and Liz was helpless to do anything but scream and pound on the heavy steel door. The mother fell to her knees sobbing, afraid she would never see her daughter again.

Under the threat of gunfire and the death of her daughter, Elizabeth Seaver was roughly forced off the deck and made to climb down the rope ladder and onto My Chopper. Once on the boat, Hamid gave her a grim warning. "If you do exactly as I say, your daughter will be safe, but all it will take is a telephone call from me, and your daughter will never see the light of day again and die in that container."

Liz was ordered to the rear deck steering pedestal. As she walked to her position, she glanced at the spot where her daughter had been sitting. Avery had told her mother about her phone, which was nested in a coil of rope. There was still hope for her and her daughter if she could get to the phone, press 911 and convey a message of some sort. Scott once told her that the police could find the location of every phone on the planet if they wanted to. Elizabeth Seaver hoped that was true.

With a stiff salute, Hamid and Nassir parted ways. The sergeant untied the mooring lines and tossed them down to his superior officer. With the hostage at the helm, My Chopper headed off under diesel power toward Green Bay and its destiny. The bomb was sitting comfortably at the stern of the sleek sailboat, not far from the off-center steering pedestal. The major looked at his watch. In a few more hours he would be the greatest martyr of all time, or possibly the greatest living hero. It would depend on the timing of the bomb and his escape from its effects.

Aboard Black Hawk 210HK:

Captain Seaver scanned the calm lake waters looking for his boat. He passed over many different boats and small ships, but the one that he was looking for was absent. In the distance was an old container-freighter going north. Scott took out his IT-Tech and hoped that it would still work so far out over the lake. If it did, he could track the yellow dot that showed his daughter's phone. Flying the Black Hawk was demanding, but with the proper trim, precious seconds could be devoted to something else. He turned on his phone and the screen lit up.

Something was wrong, terribly wrong; the application for tracking his daughter's phone was missing, as were many of his other personalized features. He didn't have time to study the phone, but the bottom line was that he couldn't use it to find his family. "SHIT!" He swore. Scott glanced at the horizon to make sure the copter was tracking true, and then he looked at the IT-Tech in his hand again. He became so fixated on trying to understand what had happened to his phone that what should have been a few seconds glance, had turned into a minute. Scott looked up just as the copter shot over the container ship, much lower to the lake than he should have been.

Nassir looked up at the military helicopter passing overhead at a high rate of speed. He wouldn't have been concerned except for the extremely low level it was flying. Much lower and it would have risked hitting one of the tall radio antennas on the ship.

Scott tossed the phone onto the copilot seat, realizing his blunder. He regained some of the lost altitude and continued north-west over the lake, away from the old freighter. The controls were so touchy that the pilot nearly lost control of the copter again as he corrected the pitch. The combined distractions had caused him to miss seeing the small boat sailing away from the freighter.

Hamid and Liz were also surprised by the chopper. Liz's heart skipped a few beats. *Could it be a rescue attempt?* She prayed.

The major was also suspicious and watched the craft speed away, more concerned with it than his hostage.

Liz knew the copter was one of the new Black Hawks from her husband's unit. The chopper was low enough that the she could easily see the insignia. She didn't even think that the pilot could be Scott, but she knew most of the pilots from the base. *There's a chance if I act quickly enough.* Liz thought.

Liz opened the water-tight lid on the outside radio stack. The lid was functional as well as decorative. When not in use, it was meant to protect and conceal the radio stack behind mahogany trim that matched the fine woodworking of the outside steering pedestal. Scott always had one of the two radios tuned to the guard frequency. Her husband loved to monitor the frequency to see what his fellow guardsmen were up to. Liz turned the speaker volume off, and then took the microphone in her hand. "Mayday, Mayday, guard copter. My daughter and I are being held against our will on the freighter below you." Liz had enough time to repeat the message one more time. Her hope was that the pilot would hear her message and recognize her voice.

Liz lowered the microphone from her mouth just in time. The terrorist turned back to her, as low flying helicopter disappeared over the

313

freighter. He focused on Liz again, as he walked toward her. With nearly imperceptible movements, she slid the microphone back into its case, but she couldn't close the concealing lid without being suspicious.

The receding noise from the twin jet engines of the copter had drowned out her voice during the radio call. Apparently the kidnapper didn't realize that she made the distress call. But if he saw the radio stack open, a call would be assumed. Liz had to close the case without being noticed. The kidnapper was nearly to the steering pedestal. Liz had to do something quickly. "Hang on!" she yelled and turned the wheel sharply left. Hamid did hang on and looked over the bow of the ship to see why the woman was turning the boat so sharply. All he saw was a small spray of water wash the front of the deck. At that exact movement, Liz quickly lifted the cover and concealed the radio stack again.

"What was that about?" the major asked angrily.

"The wake from the freighter was going to broadside us; I had to turn into it to keep us from swamping or keeling over."

Hamid looked over his shoulder again at the lake. Yes, there was a wake from the freighter, but he didn't think it was a danger. Still, apparently the woman knew her boating and the proper procedure was to turn into a potentially dangerous wave. He gave her the benefit of the doubt.

The terrorist held a hand-held GPS display in his hand and showed it to the woman.

"You will take the boat through the shipping lane of Sturgeon Bay into Green Bay. It cuts the peninsula in half and will save hours. Make your heading 300°; that should take us directly there."

Elizabeth knew what he wanted her to do; Scott and she had been through the channel many times before. Hamid was right, the channel cut through the heart of the city of Sturgeon Bay and would certainly be the shortcut to Green Bay. Maybe he didn't know that the route would put them very close to the operators of the huge drawbridges that spanned the passage. The only way the tall mast of the sailboat could traverse those waters was if the bridges were lifted. It would be another chance for Liz to escape or get assistance. Apparently her call to the copter went unnoticed because the Black Hawk was nowhere to be seen.

****

Scott was fighting with the controls of the Black Hawk. While certain things seemed normal, other things were completely foreign to him. He could fly it if nothing went wrong, but even little distractions seemed to cause him to lose control. It wasn't his helicopter, and he understood little more than the basics. Scott lifted the chopper to a higher altitude. Height above the cold, blue waters below would give him time to react if the chopper became unstable under his control again.

Captain Seaver's heart was pumping hard. Stealing the chopper, being shot at, learning to fly the craft and nearly crashing it several times, was taking its toll. Sweat was soaking his flight suit. He was struggling for control of the helicopter and focused his mind on the problem at hand. Now that he had the copter stable again, he had time to think about the message he heard over the radio a few moments earlier. The voice had been nearly drowned out by the sound of jet engines in the background. There was something about the urgency in the voice that was familiar to him. How long his mind was focused on the mysterious voice he didn't know. But now he became occupied with another riddle: what was he doing out here, over the lake in a Black Hawk? Nothing was making sense. His phone wasn't as he remembered and he was flying a machine that he didn't think he knew how to fly. He was becoming scared. How would he get back to his base? How would he land this thing without crashing it? He swore that if he somehow got to the ground in one piece he would never leave Liz's side again.

Scott thought about his condition and the doctor's advice. "Stay calm. If you are safe, there is nothing to worry about. Just relax and you will eventually remember what you need to."

Scott thought to himself. *How can I stay calm when one little false move of either of my hands could send me crashing into the lake?* "I am anything but safe," he screamed at the doctor who wasn't there.

The fact that the IT-Tech phone on the seat next to him could hold the key to his memory kept gnawing at him. He knew the answers were in it somewhere, if he could only have time to use it. Too bad the chopper didn't have an autopilot. Then, just as if God had heard his request, he suddenly saw a small placard that said "AUTO PILOT" "ON/OFF." Scott remembered something from the far reaches of his mind. *The new Black Hawks have Auto Pilot controls to assist you. Don't be afraid to use them.* It was part of his training, training to fly this helicopter. He pressed the switch to "on" and then slowly let go of the controls. The copter stayed in place in the sky.

After he let go of the controls, Scott realized that his hands were shaking. He was scared to death and with good reason. He reached for the IT-Tech and turned it on. Upon further examination, he realized that it wasn't his phone, it was Lieutenant Schmidt's. How he got the

Lieutenant's phone he didn't remember. Worse, he didn't remember how he got here and into this predicament. Scott did remember his condition and reached for his bottle of pills. If there was ever a time for the magic memory pills, now was it. The bulky flight suit carried many useful things for emergencies, but it didn't contain the bottle of pills he needed.

The jet engines were pounding in his ears, even though his helmet muted and electronically canceled much of the noise. Scott was five-thousand feet above the water and felt totally helpless. He was caught in a death trap with no way out and no one to help him. At least with the autopilot in control, he was safe for now, but it would only be a matter of time before the machine ran out of fuel and crashed into the frigid lake. Scott looked out over the large expanse of blue, trying to calm himself down and slow his heart. It was a beautiful day, and a beautiful site to see the blue waters with boats and ships moving in it. *"Calm yourself, you are safe,"* he reassured his mind. The pilot tried to pretend that he was on a sightseeing tour of the lake. To his left, a freighter piled high with huge cargo containers slowly plodded north. West of that was a sailboat, sails down and headed toward Sturgeon Bay.

Something about the sailboat caught his eye; it looked eerily familiar. Then Scott realized why. It was his boat. The message replayed in his mind over the roar of the engines. He could hear his wife's voice. "Mayday, Mayday, guard copter. My daughter and I are being held against our will, my daughter is a prisoner on the freighter below you." It was the voice he was trying to place. The voice was his wife's. Nothing was making sense. He tried hard to remember. A car crash at a toll both came to mind. There had been a fire, a terrible fire somewhere. He was trapped in it.

Terrible nightmares were coming to life. Why couldn't he remember? Another memory haunted him; it was a pickup crash late at night; there were lights blinding him. The marina in Port Washington, his boat, it was gone! He remembered being shot at by young Lenny Sidowske as he stole a helicopter, this helicopter. *You have to save your wife and daughter, they were kidnapped and are somewhere out on the lake. Mayday, Mayday, guard copter. My daughter and I are being held against our will on the freighter below you,* flashed again in his mind. Scott glanced again at the freighter moving north ever so slowly.

"It's not a nightmare; it's true," Scott said to himself. "My family is on that freighter."

Without another thought, Scott flipped the autopilot off and masterfully flew the helicopter toward the ship. Movements were now automatic. As long as he didn't think too hard about what he was doing, his hands and feet did what was necessary. Somehow he had to get onto that ship and save his family.

Port Washington, Wisconsin:

Bob Allen was rushing to finish cutting the grass around his home in Port Washington. He had lived in the small town all his life and was as proud of that as he was of the Green Bay Packers jersey he was wearing. The game would start in just a few hours. Finished or not, he wasn't about to miss the kick off. The lawn tractor he was using on his spacious lawn howled, but even through the ear protection he had on, he could hear the familiar thump, thump, thump of helicopter blades. The base commander stopped cutting and looked up. There was no doubt that the sound was from a Black Hawk, one of his Black Hawks from the base. An emergency call must have come in because he knew there were no scheduled practice missions today. That meant that even though it was Sunday, and his official day off, he would expect to be notified as soon as the base had time to contact him. And that unfortunately meant he would probably have to go to the base and miss the start of the game, if not the entire thing. *Go figure!* He thought as he shook his head in disappointment.

The deputy post commander issued an immediate base shutdown, then had security do a complete person-by-person check of signed in personnel. It was possible that Captain Scott Seaver had an inside accomplice for his crime. Nobody would enter or leave the base until everyone was accounted for and his or her whereabouts during the theft was verified. Fortunately, most everybody was together in the same room. The security tapes would also tell a tale. Deputy Post Commander Hooper raced for the security room. "Find Lieutenant Schmidt," he yelled to no one in particular. "I want him to get on the radio and tell Seaver to get back here with my helicopter. And tell Schmidt to remind the captain that he doesn't know how to fly a Black Hawk," the deputy commander added angrily and sarcastically.

Although the Mayday call that Liz made was on the guard frequency, nobody at the base heard it. Lieutenant Schmidt had volunteered to monitor the frequency for emergency calls, but unknown to anyone, he was incapacitated. In fact, the lieutenant was still unconscious and strapped to the pilot's chair inside the Black Hawk simulator. It took ten minutes for Hooper to account for everybody except the lieutenant. He knew that Captain Seaver and the lieutenant were buddies but he didn't think that the lieutenant was capable of helping him steal a helicopter.

It was time for a call to Major Allen. This wasn't going to be pleasant Hooper realized. "And find Lieutenant Schmidt!" Those were the last orders hollered at the deputy post commander over the phone. Major Allen raced toward the base. Normally it was a twenty-minute ride; he did it in ten. The camera showed an unconscious Schmidt being dragged to the simulator room. Security entered in time to find a semi-conscious Schmidt holding his head where the helmet had banged him.

Someone had just given the lieutenant a bag of ice for the huge bump alongside his head when Major Allen walked in. "What the 'F' happened Lieutenant?"

"I was talking to Scott when he out and out jacked me with his flight helmet. I don't remember anything else."

"Hooper, call an ambulance and get this man to a hospital!" the major ordered.

The major huffed out of the room and nearly bulldozed a few soldiers down as he rushed down the hallway. He was upset at himself, upset at his good friend Scott and upset that his unit had let a helicopter be stolen. *This couldn't be happening*, he reasoned.

"Where is the security guard?"

"Here, Sir! Sergeant Lenny Sidowske, Sir."

"Can you tell me what the hell is going on? How did Captain Seaver steal a helicopter from a secure base? Can you tell me that, Sergeant?"

"No sir! I mean, Yes sir! He snuck into the helicopter as I did my patrol. It appears that he set off some sort of explosion on the other side of the building. Just as I made it around the building to see the explosion, I heard the sound of engines starting. I ran back toward the choppers sir. I identified Captain Seaver and fired a round at the chopper; it struck the windscreen. I believe it bounced off. I fired more rounds sir, but none of them hit."

"Are you aware that Captain Seaver is not trained to fly a Black Hawk? How did he get away from you so fast?"

"Yes sir, I am aware sir. In fact he almost crashed it sir. I dove for cover; somehow he recovered and flew off under high power. That was when the other Black Hawk blew up sir."

"What do you mean? What other Hawk?"

"The other Hawk on the line sir. It appears as if Captain Seaver blew it up sir."

The major didn't say a thing. He just ran for the flight line. Out on the tarmac and looking at the destroyed chopper he brought his hands up to his face and then brushed his hair back in frustration. "You really did it this time buddy," he said to himself.

The major was glad the sergeant missed. Scott was ill; they all knew it from one source or another. Bob was worried about his friend but didn't think he was trying to hurt anyone. What could be going through his mind to make him take such a drastic measure? And did Scott Seaver even understand what he did? Or what he was doing?

Bob had to call Liz. She should be told what was going on and she should be at the base. Maybe she could help talk him back if they got him on the radio. "Hooper, drive to Scott's house. I'm going to call Liz and tell her what is happening. You bring her back with you; I don't want her driving under these circumstances, and hurry."

"Yes Sir!"

At the other side of the air field, Agent Matthew Mitchell was checking over his helicopter once again. He felt so helpless waiting for the bureaucrats to make a decision that he felt he had to do something productive. Michael Stark and Dieter were just as impatient and paced up and down the sidewalk outside the FBO's office thinking that there must be something they could do.

All three of them heard the explosion outside the building. A huge dust cloud confirmed that something big had happened. Then they heard a helicopter start and a series of gunshots. The departing helicopter nearly crashed. Then there was another explosion and a second copter jumped off the concrete flight ramp, and just as quickly came down again in a noisy collision with the hard surface. They watched as the first helicopter departed quickly to the east while the second became a ball of flames. Something was definitely amiss at the 823rd Army National Guard Base next door. Their suspicions were confirmed moments later when the lockdown siren went off.

Lake Michigan, East of Green Bay:

210HK buzzed the top of the freighter a few times as Scott searched for signs of his family. Nobody was visible on deck, which in itself was strange. Then he settled the aircraft in a hover, low over the top of the rows of cargo containers. The ship was proceeding very slowly, but it was steadily moving north. Why was he here? Was his family on the ship below or was his mind playing a trick on him? Scott had an idea; with the

319

flick of his wrist he pointed the chopper at his sailboat. If he saw his family on their boat, then they were obviously not on the freighter. If he didn't, that would mean they were obviously someplace else, and the freighter would be a good place to start looking. He knew that his wife would never take out My Chopper without him unless she was forced to.

It only took the Black Hawk a few minutes to catch up to the sailboat. Scott was upon it before the occupants realized. Liz and Hamid had their backs to the freighter and were keeping a watch on their heading. Scott buzzed his boat, then came around as low as he dared over the small swells that were forming on the lake. He was lower than mast level and saw his wife at the helm. He breathed a sigh of relief.

Liz couldn't believe her own eyes. It was Scott behind the controls of the Black Hawk. He was so close she could almost touch him.

Scott saw his wife frantically try to wave him off. That was when he saw the sparks of small gunfire bounce off the frame of his aircraft. The windows were bullet resistant, but that didn't mean a lucky shot at some of the critical components of his helicopter couldn't cause serious damage. Scott knew that hovering at this close range made him very vulnerable. But before he peeled away, Scott clearly saw his wife pointing to the freighter. Her mouth was saying Avery over and over again. He was sure of it.

Scott took the chance of circling the small craft one more time. This time he saw the face of the same man from the toll area, and from by the elevator in Chicago. It was a face even he would never forget. The killer had his wife and for some reason, his daughter was nowhere to be seen. Scott made the decision to let the sailboat go. It was not going to get far. He would catch up to it again, that was a promise he made to himself and his wife as he blew her a kiss. Captain Seaver tipped the copter away from the boat and sped back toward the freighter.

Hamid cursed and caught himself as he almost used Allah's name in vain. The pilot was the woman's husband. *Impossible! He was supposed to be on his way to the football stadium. How did the man know where he was? How did he get the military helicopter? And were more military aircraft and police boats coming?*

Hamid angrily pointed his pistol at Liz Seaver's face. "Your husband cannot save you."

"I don't care about me, asshole." Elizabeth was energized and defiant. Seeing her husband coming to their rescue emboldened her. "You can't threaten me with my daughter anymore."

Standing right next to his hostage, Hamid called his compatriot on the ship. "Nassir, use whatever means to bring down the helicopter. There is only the pilot aboard. It is imperative that he is killed. Do not let him get near the young girl."

"I understand major." Sergeant Azodi did understand. Imperative meant just that, at all costs, including his life. The Revolutionary Guard Corps sergeant opened a heavy steel watertight door for the back bulkhead and sped down the stairs to a special, locked hold. The locked area contained just the sort of weapon he needed. The shoulder fired grenade launcher would send the helicopter and its pilot into the cold waters of the lake. He ran back up the stairs, not bothering to re-lock the door; time was precious.

Scott worked the controls gingerly as the craft hovered over the slow moving freighter. Somehow he had to get down to the ship. Then Scott came up with a desperate plan. He saw no other choice. He was alone and had to get to the deck of the ship below. Scott shot the Black Hawk ahead of the advancing freighter.

West Bend Municipal Airport:

After much too long of a wait, Agent Mitchell's cell phone played his alma mater's fight song. He was leaning lazily against his copter when he answered it. "Hello!"

"Matt, we intercepted a Mayday call on a military reserved frequency." Dan Price, Matt's boss, skipped any formalities and got right to the point and it wasn't the conversation Matt was expecting.

"What kind of Mayday?"

"The transmission wasn't very strong and there was loud background noise. But after boosting it and filtering it several times we confirmed that it was a woman's voice saying "Mayday, Mayday, Guard copter. My daughter and I are being held against our will, my daughter is a prisoner on the freighter below you."

"Freighter?" Matt's voice involuntarily shot up a couple of decibels.

"That's right. We narrowed down the general location of the transmission; she was talking about your freighter."

Matthew thought for a moment. "She said Guard copter?" he asked confirming.

"That's right, 'Guard copter.' We also identified the background noise during the transmission. It was from a jet engine."

"Or two," Matthew added as he looked at the guard station across the airfield and stared at the damaged Black Hawk and its dual jet engines.

"Dan?" Matt asked. "Just how much authority do I have?"

"What the hell are you talking about?"

"I think the copter you are talking about came from the Army National Guard base across the airfield from my position."

"And just where the hell is your position?" Senior Agent Price didn't know if he really wanted to find out.

"My team is at an airport in West Bend, Wisconsin. It was the closest we could get to the freighter when we landed hours ago. I was hoping for authorization to fly to the freighter and board it."

The news wasn't quite as bad as Dan was expecting from the sometimes rash field agent. "You won't believe this, but the politicos still haven't gotten back to us."

"Dan, listen!" Matthew paused for effect. "I know this sounds crazy but I think somebody stole a helicopter from the guard base across from us. A little earlier I heard gunfire and then the base alarm went off and things just went nuts over there. Can I crash their little party and find out what is going on?"

"It's not clear who has final authority in a case like this."

"Never mind Dan, forget I ever asked."

"I will. Good luck." Price knew what was going to happen next. The Guard base was going to have an unexpected visit from the NNSA.

"Mike, Dieter, saddle up. We are going for a short flight ASAP," Matthew called to his team.

Chapter 23

Army National Guard base, West Bend, Wisconsin:

It only took a minute for Matthew to pilot the small copter over the security fence and across the field to the reserve base. It took much less time for the tripled security team at the base to surround the copter with rifles pointing directly at its occupants.

Michael and Dieter had no idea what was going on. They had only enough time to buckle in. Before they could ask any questions the copter was already setting down. Matt shut the engine down, carefully placed his hands behind his head and suggested his friends do the same.

Major Allen furiously stormed toward the copter, its lifting blades still rotating, though slowly coming to a halt. "Do you have any idea what kind of trouble you are in son?" he growled.

Matthew didn't move a muscle. "My ID is in my back pocket. We are with the National Nuclear Security Administration."

"I don't give a crap who you are, or what government agency you are with. You have no business landing here. I could have my men shoot you right here and now as spies."

Matthew was afraid that they might be less than welcome. He was right.

"Sergeant, take his ID. If he makes one false move, shoot first and ask questions later."

"I think I know where your Black Hawk is."

Agent Mitchell suddenly had the major's attention.

"What Black Hawk?" Bob pretended he didn't know what the man was talking about as he examined the government issued ID.

"The one that was stolen from this base." Matthew took the gamble, hoping he was right. If he was wrong, it wouldn't matter, but if he guessed right, the major would at least listen to him.

"Security, stand by." The major lowered the threat level a degree. The shoot to kill was now canceled.

"Sir, I would like to talk to you privately. What I have to tell you is sensitive government security information."

By this time, the security team had all three men standing in a line with their hands behind their heads and the major had three security badges in his hand.

"Come with me," the major growled once again. He turned and walked toward the base office.

Slowly Matthew took his hands down from behind his head. He felt silly keeping them there. Nobody objected, so Michael and Dieter became equally as brave, still wondering what their boss had gotten them into.

The four were alone inside Major Allen's office. "You have three minutes, I am very busy."

Finally Michael and Dieter, along with the major, heard the reason they were there.

"My team and I have been tracking a potential nuclear threat against this country. We detected nuclear radiation in and around Chicago, and it all seems to have emanated from a certain freighter traveling on Lake Michigan. By now, that freighter is well north of here."

"How does that give you the right to violate military air space?" The major was a very impatient man today.

"A Mayday radio transmission was picked up by the military and forwarded to our offices. That Mayday was from a woman calling to a Guard helicopter. She said she and her daughter were being held against their will on a freighter. I suspect it's the same freighter that we have been tracking going north."

The major said nothing as he sat down at his desk chair, propped his elbows up on his desk and placed his head in his hands deep in thought. He was thinking about his friend Scott and why the man would steal a helicopter, a helicopter he should not even have been able to fly.

"Liz!" the major said.

"What was that, sir?" Matthew prompted.

"Liz... Elizabeth Seaver. The man who stole the Black Hawk is Captain Seaver. He is a guard captain and chopper pilot. His wife is Elizabeth, Liz for short. He must have known where she was and went out after her. He has a daughter, Avery. As strange as this all is, it's the only thing that makes sense."

"Major, we need to have the police check their house immediately."

"No need." The major hit a radio button.

"Hooper, are you at Captain Seaver's home yet?"

There was an immediate, excited response over the hand-held radio.

"Sir, I was just about to call you. Send the police. I saw blood on the ground and investigated. The door was open. There is a lot of blood all over the place and a very badly cutup dead man is lying on the floor. It isn't Captain Seaver though."

"Did you find the family?"

"No sir!"

"Stay there and wait for the police." Another couple of calls over the phone's intercom and police were dispatched to the Seaver residence.

Major Allen nearly chewed off the end of the telephone receiver when he yelled into it with his next command. "Sergeant, get Hawk 340HK out of the hangar and prep it for flight, full fuel."

210HK somewhere over Lake Michigan:

Captain Seaver pressed his helicopter ahead of the container ship's path. To the best of his ability, he guessed at the ship's current heading and parked the helicopter in the sky directly over its path. Scott moved the autopilot button to hover. The aircraft would now use its internal GPS to stay exactly in that position in the sky.

Sergeant Nassir Azodi cursed as the helicopter flew over his head and out of range of the grenade launcher. It stopped a quarter mile away in front of the ship. The copter hovered in the air and stayed there.

Scott picked up the IT-Tech that was on the co-pilot's seat and used its record function to leave a message to himself. "Your daughter is on the ship somewhere; she needs your help. Liz is on your boat going west; she said that Avery was on the freighter." He also repeated the phrase to himself over and over again. The medicine he took in the hospital was wearing off quickly and he didn't have any of the magic memory pills with him. Scott was frightened that his memory would fail him at a critical time. There wasn't much time left; the ship would be passing under the stationary chopper very shortly. Captain Seaver trusted the controls to the autopilot and went to the back of the craft. Without using the typical safety devices, he slid open the wide side door. He found the rescue ladder that was stowed under the rear seat, and after securing it, he tossed the rope ladder out the open side door. The ship below was gaining on the position of the chopper. Scott climbed down the ladder quickly. His plan was to lower himself onto the top row of containers that would soon be directly under him.

Nassir realized what was happening and called the captain of the ship over the ship-wide intercom. As the ship approached the helicopter, it would be his opportunity to blow it from the sky. If done quickly enough the sole soldier climbing down the ladder dangling from the chopper would crash into the lake along with the aircraft.

Captain Zarin ran up to the terrorist in alarm. Disappointing the sergeant was something he learned could be a very painful experience.

"Make sure the crew is locked below, then turn the ship; don't let that man climbing down reach us. NOW!" Nassir shouted.

The ship's captain ran to the forward superstructure, and with a bar through the watertight lock, the crew was contained. Then he rushed up to the helm. He wondered if the sergeant realized that a ship of this size didn't turn very quickly at all. He would do his best, but it took miles to turn a ship of this mass. Luckily, the ship was going very slowly; that would help.

Army National Guard base, West Bend, Wisconsin:

As Major Allen and the NNSA agents pondered how the events taking place were connected, Lieutenant Schmidt was being loaded onto a gurney for transit to the local hospital. His head was throbbing; ice was packed on the baseball size bump on his head. The lieutenant's vitals were OK but an MRI was already scheduled to check for head trauma and internal bleeding.

"My phone, I need my phone," the lieutenant insisted to the ambulance personnel.

"Where is it sir?" he asked.

"On my desk, just across the hall."

"Is this it?" The nurse held it up.

"Yea, that's it; it's my IT-Tech. I have to call my mom and tell her to come to the hospital."

The lieutenant felt tired and laid the phone at his side as the attendants locked the gurney in place inside the ambulance. Once secured, Randy picked up his phone to call his mother. The ambulance driver turned on the lights and siren and started out the drive.

"Hey, this isn't my phone. You guys took the wrong phone." The ambulance continued down the drive toward the security gate. "I'm telling you this isn't my phone." Randy was becoming upset.

"Please sir, you must relax."

"Stop the ambulance. This isn't my phone. I want my phone." The Lieutenant made an even bigger ruckus."

"Derik, stop the ambulance!"

"Sir you must calm down; you have severe head trauma."

"This is not my phone; it's Captain Seaver's phone." That was when Lieutenant Schmidt realized that he had something special in his hand. "Take me back, NOW! I have to talk to the commander."

****

Bob Allen was pacing back and forth in his small office, trying to put the pieces of the puzzle together. Soon he made a command decision. "I'm going to get a security team together. We'll take one of the Black Hawks out to help Seaver."

Matthew dared to put his hand out to stop the call as the major reached for the phone on his desk.

"We need to precede carefully, sir," Matthew reminded respectfully. "We don't know what or who we are up against yet. We are making an awful lot of assumptions. We don't know why or how Captain Seaver and his family are involved. In fact, we don't even know for sure that they are. If I'm right, these are very dangerous people and they might have a nuclear device. We can't take a risk of scaring them into detonating it. As much as we want to help your captain and his family, we need to have more information and maybe much more help."

The commander sat down again, not quite ready to accept the fact that he was helpless to do anything about the situation. But the security agent did have a point. To rush into an unknown situation was not standard military operations; it was sheer emotion.

Lake Michigan, East of Green Bay:

Scott had positioned the Black Hawk perfectly. The bow of the ship crossed directly under him as he started his descent. The rope ladder would only be close enough when it was directly over the topmost cargo containers. He was dangling on the flimsy apparatus, about half way between the top of the ship's cargo and the Black Hawk, when he noticed that the ship had started to turn away from him. The bottom of the ladder swung in the wind, several feet above the topmost containers. Scott's plan would work if the giant ship didn't turn out from under him before he climbed the rest of the way down the ladder. The chopper pilot was so concerned about not missing his one opportunity to jump onto the boat below that he never saw another more pressing danger. Just as he was moving toward his target, each passing second was also bringing deadly danger from the terrorist onboard closer. The freighter would soon be close enough for the soldier to take a fatal shot.

Alan D Schmitz

Nassir Azodi climbed on top of a stack of the giant steel boxes so he could have a clear shot at the hovering chopper. The grenade launcher didn't have much of a range, so Nassir knew he had to wait for the precise moment when the copter was close enough to destroy, yet off to the side of the ship enough that when it fell, it wouldn't fall onto the moving vessel. He waited for the perfect moment. Even at the slow speed that the old freighter was moving, he would be allowed only one shot. There would be no time to reload and fire again as the ship moved under and away from the hovering helicopter.

Scott struggled against the wind and the twisting motion of the ladder. He was trying to climb down two more rungs when a flash of steel caught his eye. He stopped his decent when he recognized the weapon being aimed at him. The man holding it stepped out into the open for an unobstructed view. Nassir steadied himself on top of the line of containers. Captain Seaver was waiting for the ship to position itself underneath him even as it was beginning to turn away. At the rate of turn, Scott calculated that he would soon be positioned past the edge of the ship and its cargo. His only chance was to drop onto the top level of containers and there wasn't much time left to do it. If he waited too long, he would miss the boat completely and fall one-hundred feet into the freezing waters of Lake Michigan.

He soon understood that he wasn't the direct target; the man with the device was clearly adjusting his aim toward the aircraft above him. The fact that the helicopter was expendable was of small consolation. If it were shot out of the sky right now, he was too far from the ship to jump. Scott reached into his flight suit to pull out his service revolver. It would be an impossible shot; the rope ladder he was on was anything but a stable shooting platform. With each second the captain's target got closer and closer, he needed each gained foot to make the impossible only improbable. It was a game of chicken, which man would fire first?

But instead of lifting his service revolver out of his pocket, he pulled out something else with a bit of suspicion. When he saw it, he immediately knew what it was, it was the very last RDX bundle and it was already prepared for immediate use. Still dangling on the unsteady ladder, he locked his arms around the nylon ropes to secure himself. He turned the timer to the smallest amount of delay available, hoping it wasn't too short of a delay and praying that it wouldn't blow up in his hands before he could toss it. With a press of his hand, the detonator was secured and the timer set. Scott threw the explosive as hard as he could. Which man would hit his target first?

328

Sergeant Azodi steadied himself, making his body as balanced a platform for the weapon as possible. His eyes were on his target; soon the helicopter would be past the edge of the ship and in prime position. Killing the man dangling from the rope ladder would be automatic; he would fall to his death in a fiery crash. With his eyes locked on the body of the chopper, Nassir didn't see Scott throw the red bundle.

The terrorist was as solid as a rock on the huge ship and the calm waters; he had perfect footing for his shot. Scott was anything but. He was dangling on a rope ladder being pushed around by his own weight and the prop wash coming from the powerful copter above him.

The RDX bounced on the top of a container. The terrorist looked at what caused the noise. He saw the bundle settle not twenty feet away from him. It only took him two seconds to understand the significance and another second to quickly re-aim his grenade launcher and then press the trigger. It was too late to run, the sergeant flew through the air from the compressed concussive wave the bomb created.

Captain Seaver watched a projectile zoom past his body and saw it explode just as it passed him and the beating Black Hawk. Then he heard the sound of deadly shrapnel coming toward him and locked his arms around the ladder, preparing for the worst. In an instant the whizzing sound of white hot metal stopped. The Hawk was still dutifully beating the air above him and he felt no strikes. Scott looked down and only had seconds to get to the ship as it passed under him; the ladder was nearing the end of the long line of stacked containers. He climbed down farther on the ladder as quickly as he dared. He needed to get onto the ship immediately or he would be dangling one-hundred feet over the water with no place to go. The end of the stacks of containers was starting to disappear below him. He didn't have time to descend the last few feet of the ladder so he started to swing it back and forth. At the last possible second he let go of the ladder, hoping his momentum would carry him far enough as he dropped the last ten feet.

The huge ship didn't seem like it was moving very fast, but when he landed on the top-most steel cargo container, the forward momentum of the ship made him fall and roll backward. The fall and roll had absorbed some of the impact but as Scott tried to regain his footing, the hard turn of the ship caused him to slide off the smooth, slippery steel roof. The fall from the top container to the icy water below was about eighty feet. It wouldn't matter if he survived the fall. The suction from the ship's giant propellers would drag him under water and churn him into small bits of flesh.

His feet were soon off the side, dangling in the air above the icy waters. The only thing to grab onto was the steel bars that were used to lock the container. Scott's hand missed; there wasn't room to grab around it. His feet went off the edge and fell against the side of the huge box. He dug his flight boots against the side of the container, hoping they would find a foothold. The very tip of his boots caught a thin steel reinforcing ridge. Miraculously it stopped his fall for the moment. In that instant, Scott was able to grab the rim of metal along the top of the container with one hand, then the other. Survival instinct and adrenalin allowed him to push off with his boot tips and at the same time hoist himself by his hands and arms until his torso was on top of the edge of the steel box. Slowly he crawled inch by inch until his entire body was prone on the corrugated steel. There he lay, at first too tired and stunned to even think about his lucky save. Eventually he crawled away from the edge of the box and stood. Scott looked at his helicopter as the ship left it in its wake. His thoughts went over the nearness of his death and how scared he had been. Then he promised to his God, *I will never, ever take my life for granted again. I will live out whatever you have planned for me. Just help me save my family.*

Nassir Azodi was starting to regain consciousness and as he did, tremendous pain in his ankle let him know he wasn't all right. At least he wasn't dead. The blast must have made him crash down on his ankle; it was most likely broken inside his heavy military boot. In the distance, the sergeant could see the soldier who had climbed down from the helicopter. Somehow the man had avoided death. For now, he was in no position or condition to fight further, so he faked unconsciousness and stayed lying on the deck.

Aboard My Chopper:

Elizabeth managed to take a quick look back toward the freighter, which was now off in the distance. But even at that distance, there was no mistaking that the helicopter wasn't following it. Her heart sunk.

Major Shukah had the same observation; apparently the sergeant on the freighter was somehow successful at stopping the copter pilot from following them.

With the freighter far behind them, the outline of the small lakeside city of Sturgeon Bay came into view. Hamid knew of the city of Sturgeon Bay. It had a proud history of building seagoing vessels, including submarines during World War II. Currently it was producing expensive yachts, many that were delivered to his own brethren in Saudi Arabia and Dubai. It disturbed Hamid that so many of his kind had succumbed to the decadence of this country. Yet another reason it should be destroyed.

Elizabeth Seaver was trying to be stoic, though inside her mind she was crying and heartbroken. To casual onlookers, such as passing boat passengers and bridge tenders, she was persuaded to wave and smile. The persuading force was a knife pressed against her side. The ox handle knife poking her was out of sight, though never out of her mind, and neither was the threat that with a simple phone call back to his associate on the ship, her daughter would die. Hamid had further promised that her daughter would not die quickly or painlessly, just the opposite.

Soon they had navigated through the Sturgeon Bay Canal and entered the waters of Green Bay. Hamid asked, "How long until we arrive at the city of Green Bay? Be truthful; your daughter's life depends on it."

Liz looked back in the direction of the old freighter and her daughter. The cliffs of the Door County Peninsula blocked her view east. Not being able to see the ship her daughter was trapped on made her heart collapse. Any connection she had was now gone. Liz felt as though she was suffocating from the loss. The only way she could protect her daughter was to obey the madman. Her own survival now depended on simple faith, faith that God and her husband would save her daughter if she gave them enough time. She studied the charts in front of her and took an educated guess. "Probably an hour, maybe less," she responded without emotion.

Hamid looked at his watch. The football game would soon be underway; that was good. The crowd would be captivated by the sports game for another three to four hours, which was plenty of time. Hamid opened the lid of the bomb while keeping his gun trained on the woman steering the boat. He looked at the timer for the bomb. Major Shukah remembered his instructions: "Once the timer is set, it cannot be stopped or turned off. When the timer hits zero, the initiation sequence begins and nothing can stop it." The terrorist would have to make a careful guess at the time needed. If he didn't give it enough time, the bomb would go off too soon, missing the maximum number of people and the president of the United States. Hamid also hoped to give himself enough time to escape the blast, but that was secondary to the mission. If he died in the blast, he would be the greatest martyr in history. The thought of everlasting glory was something he would gladly die for.

The terrorist looked at the serene waters of the bay; he could see the buildings that outlined the city named after it. The time was now; there

331

Alan D Schmitz

was no turning back. For the occupants of the city just south of their current position, there would be no escaping their fate. He set the timer for exactly one and a half hours from now. With a press of a button the timer started counting down. It was done. The United States was going to experience a nuclear attack in its heartland and there was nothing anybody could do about it.

Army National Guard base, West Bend, Wisconsin:

Lieutenant Schmidt burst into the commander's office. "Sir, I have something you need to see."

"Schmidt, you are supposed to be on your way to the hospital."

"Yes sir, but sir, I somehow have Captain Seaver's phone. His phone and mine must have been switched."

Michael immediately understood the implications and suggested, "If we go over his recently received calls, we might learn who is behind all of this."

Lieutenant Schmidt realized that none of them understood the real significance of his discovery. "Sir, with all respect, this is his IT-Tech phone. It's more like a computer than a phone, and Captain Seaver knows how to use it. He recorded all his phone calls, I listened to some of the recordings on it; we need to study it carefully. It sounds like somebody killed a man and Scott has it on video somewhere. The man is using Scott's wife and daughter as hostages to get the video back. I have a phone just like this and I think Captain Seaver took mine by mistake."

Dr. Michael Stark tried to put two and two together. "There was a fire in Chicago and a young man was found murdered in the old building. I'm guessing that your Captain Seaver saw that murder."

Then he asked the lieutenant an important question. "What would Captain Seaver have used to record a video with?"

"He could have used his phone; it has a video recording feature."

Schmidt began searching the video function of the phone before he was done speaking. "Do you have a date of the killing sir? The videos are sorted by date."

Matt Mitchell shouted out the presumed date excitedly.

"There is a video here on that date."

The lieutenant played it and the team crowded around the small screen.

"It seems like an old building. Scott loved old architecture," Schmidt volunteered.

332

The video was obviously focusing on old molding and intricate woodwork. Soon it ended but there was no fire and no one killed.

"Anything else, anything?" The Commander tried to will more information from the phone.

"Sir, beside date stamping the video, the phone also does a location stamp," Schmidt continued to explain. "With GPS technology, the phone knows exactly where videos and pictures are taken. It automatically stamps the location so that if you are on a vacation or something, you will know where the photo was taken.

"If I press here...." Lieutenant Schmidt talked to himself. "....it should show me a map of where the video was made." It only took a few moments while everyone held their collective breaths. "Chicago!" he said.

Even Michael was amazed. "Zoom it in more. What street?"

The scientist peered over the young man's shoulder.

"My god, that's it. That's the site of the fire. He was there!" Mike shouted.

"There might be more information. I'll keep checking sir. I'll look through the videos, photos and messages."

Mike Stark volunteered his services. "I'll help the lieutenant; I might recognize something he won't."

Matt went over what they knew; he repeated everything out loud so that they could work as a team. "We know the captain was in the old building on the day of the fire and the murder. We also know that the murderer thinks that the captain not only saw the murder, but has a video of it. I'll believe the lieutenant, Seaver was not only capable of recording a video, but actually did."

Matt paced back and forth in front of the commander's desk, then continued. "I think we can now safely assume that Mrs. Seaver and her daughter are being held somewhere as hostages. The Mayday call was not a coincidence, and everything is centering around the freighter, so we have to assume Mrs. Seaver made the radio message and it is accurate."

The commander was becoming impatient. He was a man of action and sitting around, repeating information they all knew, was wasting important time. "What in the hell are we waiting for? Let's get to that freighter and kick some butt."

"Sir," Matt said respectfully. "What we still don't know is why someone from the freighter killed the man in Chicago."

"So what! Let's arrest his ass and find out."

"Who's ass?" Matt questioned. "We can assume it has something to do with some sort of bomb, but we have found nothing but X-ray radiation.

Our equipment isn't finding evidence of a nuclear device, we only have our suspicions."

"Sir, I think there is another video," Schmidt announced. "This one wasn't taken by this phone though. There is a WEB address that is highlighted, that's why I didn't see it before. It was streamed over the Internet from some other device. It is from the same date though."

"Play it!" The commanded ordered.

"I can't, it isn't actually on the phone, and I can't access it."

"Could it have come from a computer with a camera attachment?" the team leader asked.

"Sure! Any source that could access the Internet."

"I think I know whose laptop it was in the fire; it was Captain Seaver's. He must have used it to record the video. But it was destroyed in the fire, so he was bluffing. He didn't have the video anymore; it was destroyed."

Lieutenant Schmidt countered. "I'm not so sure; his laptop might have streamed the video directly to a server somewhere else. Just because it's not on this phone or his computer, doesn't mean he doesn't have it somewhere."

Mike Stark remembered something else they had found. In one of the messages the captain told the kidnapper he had proof that he wasn't bluffing.

On the Damascus Star:

Captain Seaver caught his breath. It was soundly knocked out of him when he plunged onto the containers. With adrenaline flowing through his blood and his heart pumping hard, he quickly remembered why he risked his life to board the ship. His daughter was being held somewhere on this freighter and he needed to find her. Scott could see the man who tried to kill him; he was still down, maybe dead, and at least fifty yards away. Scott didn't see him as an immediate threat and looked for a way off the sets of stacked containers.

Scott saw a way down to the deck. It took some careful climbing but soon he was standing on the deck of the ship in a valley between forty-foot high rows of huge shipping containers. He realized that he would not be able to effectively search the entire ship. His daughter could be anywhere. He needed his own hostage to force a confession.

Sergeant Azodi stood up on his swollen ankle as soon as he saw the soldier disappear. The pain was immediate and searing, causing him to collapse as he tried to stand. He got up again and limped on his ankle as best he could, sure that it must be broken because the pain was nearly unbearable. Blood was dripping from a hole in the side of his boot; something had penetrated though his foot, probably bone.

He was slowly adapting to the pain as he watched the ship steer away from the copter. It didn't take long for the chopper to fall far behind the ship and out of range again. The grenade launcher was useless to him now. The soldier was already on the ship and the copter was being left unmanned in the distance. The Uzi machine gun strapped to his back was another story; it was the perfect tool for hunting the intruder. His current position gave him the high ground to use to his advantage. Nassir tried to be quiet as he limped across the rows of containers. He carefully scanned the deep valleys created by them. Somewhere between them was his prey; it was only a matter of time.

Scott thought about the evasive action the ship had taken as he tried to board it. Somebody was steering the ship. He needed to find that somebody and persuade that person by any means necessary to tell him where his daughter was. He ran through the maze between the stacked giant containers, each the size of a semi-truck, and moved toward the front of the ship and pilot house. Scott had his gun in hand with the safety off; the ship was clearly not friendly territory. Just as he was about to turn past another high alley, a series of bullets pounded the metal around him. A grated walkway that scattered the bullets with a rain of sparks saved him. Captain Seaver dove for cover, then realized that the shooter would soon be directly over him and spraying him with bullets from above. He jumped up to his feet and ran as quickly as he could; trapped between walls of containers he was a sitting duck.

Nassir tried to run over the tops of the steel boxes but the pain in his ankle barely allowed walking. The wind rushing over the top of the ship masked any noise his prey made, so he strained for a visual sign. As he peered over the edge of a series of bins, he saw the direction the runner was taking. It wasn't easy navigating over the slippery steel; several times he had to make a very painful jump from one side of a steel canyon to the other. Each crevice was a two-foot jump, the same maze of two foot wide crevices that the soldier below was using to elude him. The sergeant didn't ask Allah for much, just a clear shot at the man below. Even at half a ship away, his machine gun would easily cut the intruder down.

Captain Seaver ran through the maze, realizing that to travel in a straight line would be suicide. He turned and crisscrossed his path continually while trying to make forward progress toward the front of the ship and hopefully the person steering it. Scott dashed right; it was the widest alley he had found and it looked like a path that would take him to his destination. He guessed wrong, it was a dead end. He was trapped.

Scott was lost in the maze. He couldn't remember which direction he came from, but he knew he couldn't stay where he was. He dashed around a corner and was greeted with another rain of bullets. Scott immediately dropped back and took cover. He was safe for now, but his position was compromised and there was no exit.

Sergeant Azodi didn't have a clear shot yet, but he couldn't let his trapped target escape. Scott ran back to the dead end. It would only be moments before the shooter above would have an open target in the sights of his gun. Nassir ignored the pain in his ankle as much as possible. Soon it would be over and he could get medical attention, but not until the soldier was dead. He had each exit covered as he moved toward a clean shot into the dead-end canyon of containers. He saw his target desperately trying to climb out of the trap he was in. Nassir savored the moment and aimed his gun carefully; the volley of bullets would soon pierce the thin flesh. The rapid fire of bullets would slice him to pieces.

Scott pulled a heavy container door open. Many of the containers were locked. Thankfully, not this one. It was empty. Scott ducked behind the open door just in time. The bullets made a deafening sound as they pounded against the steel door protecting him. Nassir swore profusely. He would have to make one more painful jump over another canyon to get behind his target. It would normally be easily done; today it would be much more difficult and painful. But once on the other side, the soldier would have no place to hide. It would be worth it.

Scott knew what the shooter had to do to finish him off. The man above would have to cross the opening between the stacked containers. The captain took his side arm and aimed it carefully alongside the edge of the giant steel door protecting him. He would have only one chance, one shot. Scott tried to steady his hands and slow his racing heart. A leg was visible. Scott shot just as the man jumped the crevice above him. Then he heard a fall. He hit his target.

Nassir fell, his ankle collapsing on him. The pain was excruciating. The terrorist heard the shot from below. It missed but it had distracted him enough to cause him to land sideways on his already painful ankle. He dared not take off his boot to look at the throbbing joint because he was sure that he would never get it on again. The sergeant used his machine gun as a crutch to push himself up. He peaked over the side of the top container to confirm that his target was still trapped, and he was.

Nassir figured he could crawl to the next container and take out the man trapped below, and that was just what he was going to do.

Scott heard movement above him that sounded like metal on metal. He was still trapped and the door wouldn't shield him any longer. A dash to the next opening would expose him for a deadly period of time. The captain felt he had one chance; he reached into the leg pocket of his flight suit and pulled out one of two signal flares he was required to carry. It was waterproof and self-igniting. He twisted it open and it ignited. Red rescue smoke filled the valley between the containers, masking his position. Scott held his breath and tossed the flare down the row; it filled the entire area with red smoke.

Sergeant Azodi peered over the edge of the crevice, ready to shoot, but all he saw was dense, red smoke pouring out in all directions, filling the valleys below. In desperation, he shot into the thick red haze. He poured bullets in all directions, not sure where in the maze the trapped man was. Bullets bounced and ricocheted everywhere as he emptied his clip into the smoke.

The Iranian Revolutionary Guard member's gun was empty; he didn't have another clip of ammunition with him. That meant he would have to make a painful climb down the sides of the containers and get another full round. Then he would go back to the dead end that was now filled with smoke and see if he had killed the intruder.

Army National Guard base, West Bend, Wisconsin:

The team spent a fair amount of time researching the information on the phone. Lieutenant Schmidt navigated its features for them and played back the recorded phone calls and memory aids that Captain Seaver left to himself. There was no doubt that the captain's family was in danger and that he somehow discovered where they were and had gone after them.

The commander heard enough and ordered a rescue team to board the copter. Black Hawk 340HK was standing by. The commander would ride co-pilot with Captain Dan Fredric as pilot in command. Matthew Mitchell, Michael Stark and Detrick Michael Krier understood the commander's anxiety to get started on a rescue. They knew that there were pieces of the puzzle missing, important pieces. So far there was no mention of a bomb, or of threat of a bombing, or of using any kind of nuclear device as a dirty weapon in the messages. It appeared that all the kidnappers wanted, was the video that the captain had somewhere.

Alan D Schmitz

What they did know, was apparently Mr. Seaver had somehow videoed the kidnappers as they killed the young Behrouz Golzar. It would be understandable why the kidnappers would want that video. According to the recorded phone call, the kidnappers would give Captain Seaver his family back at the crowded stadium in Green Bay in exchange for the captain's promise to never release the video. Everybody's safety and identity would be guaranteed by the threat of death to the Seavers if it was ever released. The killers on the other hand, couldn't harm the Seavers or the video would be automatically released somehow, possibly through a lawyer. *The plan could have worked, should have.* Matthew reasoned, *unless the kidnappers found out that the captain was bluffing and that he didn't really have a video.* But from the recorded phone calls they had studied, it certainly appeared that he did and had proved it.

The commander kicked everyone out of his office as he prepared for the rescue flight to save his friend Scott and his family. As Lieutenant Schmidt, the commander and the NNSA team walked down the hallway toward the flight line, Matt continued to ponder the questions. *Why did they kill Behrouz in the first place? Why did they kidnap the Sever family before they even knew Scott had a video identifying them? And then why would they decide to risk double-crossing the one man who could identify them? Why did they take the hostages to a radiation contaminated ship? How did Seaver learn of the deceit?*

"THAT'S IT!" Matthew shouted and turned to the lieutenant. "We need to find the video immediately." He looked at his partners and explained. "At first the killers didn't know there was a video of them, they thought that if they killed Captain Seaver, their identities would be safe. Their plan was to hold his family hostage so that he would stay quiet until they could lure him to his death. When they found out he had a video that would be automatically released upon his death, killing him was no longer an option, at least, not until the video wouldn't matter.

"So they changed their plan slightly. All they had to do was to stall him long enough. They did that by dangling the safety of his family in front of him and promising him that if he didn't show the video to anyone, his family would be OK."

"I still don't get it. Stall for what?" Dieter asked.

"They weren't worried about double crossing Captain Seaver, or being exposed in the video. The Captain and his family were going die anyway, and by then, a video of the killing wouldn't matter because their main objective would be accomplished. But first they had to get something from the ship."

338

"A bomb!" Dieter and Michael uttered immediately.

"A big bomb! Big enough to kill everyone at the game, including Scott Seaver. And once Scott was dead, his wife and daughter would no longer be of any value, so they would be killed also."

Michael stared at the map of the Great Lakes that was hanging on the wall of the hallway. "Dieter, your friend has the freighter located east of the city of Green Bay, off the west shore of the lake. Is that right?"

"That was what she said; as of a half-hour ago, just south of this area," Dieter confirmed, circling an area of the big lake with his finger.

Michael pointed to the city of Green Bay Wisconsin. "The president of the United States just happens to be at the same game the killer wanted Captain Seaver at, the Packer/Bear game going on right now. It can't be a coincidence that the freighter is so near this area at just the right time."

"The video. We have to find the video that Captain Seaver has."

"Are you telling me that this isn't about a kidnapping, it's about a plan to kill the president?" Bob Allen asked, not believing his ears.

"Commander, I have no proof, but I'd stake my career on it. Your Captain Seaver and his family somehow became pawns in the plot when he saw and recorded a murder in Chicago three days ago."

"You said you have no proof. Are you prepared to evacuate the entire city of Green Bay, along with the president of the United States, on a hunch? You realize what will happen once you yell bomb in a crowded stadium. People will be hurt. And why is the video so important? You might stake your career on it, but are you willing to gamble other people's lives on a hunch?"

"I believe that the reason the kidnappers wanted Captain Seaver and the video so badly was because it would identify them and give away their plan. My suspicion is that the perpetrators are known to us. With a positive ID of a known terrorist, my superiors can and will issue a red alert and evacuate the president and the city."

"Lieutenant Schmidt, we really need that video," the commander pressed.

Chapter 24

Deck of the Damascus Star:

Captain Seaver ran through the dense red smoke. For the first thirty feet he ran in a straight line with bullets nipping at his heels. With his right hand he felt for an opening in the steel walls. Finally he found one and dove into the smoke filled alleyway as the bullets pounded the area behind him. The sound of dozens of bullets hitting the steel sidewalls and steel deck of the ship was deafening. Then suddenly there was silence. Scott couldn't hold his breath any longer even though he wasn't clear of the choking haze. The smoke hit his lungs causing him to cough. He took small, short breaths and walked toward clear air, hoping that the gunman didn't hear him.

The lack of air winded him and made him light headed. Scott kept walking slowly between the mazes the stacks created. He wasn't headed in any particular direction, just away from where he had been. Scott managed to stumble his way across the ship. On the opposite side was a walkway wide enough to take a forklift truck from one end of the ship to the other. Leaving the relative safety of the shadows created by the high containers would be dangerous. For now he needed a place to rest, to collect his thoughts. He was out of breath and his heart was pumping hard. He went back into the maze and found a hidden corner. There he slumped down to rest for just a minute. He closed his eyes.

****

With the Uzi slung over his shoulder, Nassir very tentatively climbed down from the top row of containers, frequently cursing. His ankle was in pain even when it was dangling in midair. And when he needed it to steady his body, it became so unbearable that it made him feel nauseous. Eventually he was back on the deck; cautiously he walked toward the aft structure. He could still see the helicopter; it was small in the distance. If his commander was right, and this man was alone, then he was also the pilot. That had to mean that the helicopter was flying on automatic control and would eventually crash into the lake when it ran out of fuel.

Extra ammunition was below deck. The blood oozing out of his boot left a trail on the metal flooring. The sergeant realized that he was hurt much worse than he originally thought. Taking the stairs down would be painful; coming up again would be worse. His field commander said he needed to kill the intruder and he would do his duty no matter the pain.

****

Scott woke still feeling lightheaded and dazed. The thick smoke had nearly suffocated him. He noticed that he was surrounded by high steel containers, not unlike the one he and his crew had been locked in for three days in Iraq. He hated the steel box in the desert. It lacked sufficient oxygen and was stifling hot during the day, and at night it was unbearably cold. Then Scott remembered the torture, how they hit him over and over again. He remembered the Iraqis bringing his crewmembers back after an interrogation session and throwing the near lifeless bodies into the damned steel cage. Scott began to weep as he relived the ordeal in his mind. He made a mistake and now his men were paying the price. He didn't care what they did to him; he just wanted them to leave his men alone. The Captain pulled himself together. He had to save them. He couldn't let them be tortured any longer. Somehow he escaped, and now it was up to him to find his men and free them.

Captain Seaver looked around. There were many steel boxes. Where was he and where were his companions? He cautiously explored his surroundings with his pistol at the ready. Eventually he walked to the wide alley where he had been before, only he didn't remember it. There was a cable rail and a wide expanse of water on the other side, the top of the deep blue swells sparkled like diamonds. He was on a ship; he looked out as far as he could and didn't see land, so he assumed he was on an ocean somewhere. His men might be locked in one of the containers. He had to free them and capture the ship.

Carefully he scouted for enemy eyes. He scanned the doors of the steel boxes; most weren't locked on the outside. But to someone trapped inside of one, it would be impossible to open just the same. He assumed his team members would be held in a cage that was easily accessible for interrogation reasons. Captain Seaver cautiously opened the container nearest him. It was empty. Leaving the door open, he went to the next container. The door squeaked loudly as he opened it; it too was empty. Nobody heard him. The captain continued down the long row, opening each and every container, hoping he would soon find his crew. He noticed the trail of blood going toward the aft superstructure. Somebody was injured; he hoped it wasn't one of his. The more steel boxes he opened, the more he was certain his crew was being held in one of them

341

and probably being tortured for information. It was his duty to rescue them. Scott went down the row of steel boxes, opening each one and peering in. Some had equipment in them, but so far there were no weapons to steal. If a container was locked, Scott took careful aim with his pistol and shot the lock apart. He looked down the row of boxes behind him; the doors were all open. As soon as the deck was patrolled, they would know an intruder was aboard. He had to hurry.

Scott shot at another locked door; he opened the steel door enough so he could see into the dark container. "DADDY!!" the sole occupant cried.

"Are you OK?" Scott asked hesitantly, scanning the area outside the container nervously.

"I'm hurt a little. Daddy, I'm so scared," she answered.

"Are there more hostages?" Scott asked as he concentrated his surveillance in the direction of the bloody trail.

Avery Seaver wasn't sure why her father asked, but she answered, "Mom was taken by the terrorist."

"Mom?" Scott questioned, glancing at the girl. He then insisted, "Let's go!" Scott motioned for the young girl to move out in front of him. He would cover her escape. His mind had transported him to Iraq; the steel cage put shivers up and down his spine. He could feel the danger and pain here. Escaping with his crew was his only objective, there were bound to be more prisoners and he had to find them.

Avery couldn't help but give her dad a big hug. She didn't want to let go. Scott tried to pry the scared young girl away from him, time was of the essence. Her powerful hug and the smell of her hair brought back thoughts of his family. He pried the girl away from his neck and stared at her face.

Avery could see the confused, blank look on her father's face and guessed the worse. "Daddy, it's me. Avery!" she cried. "You said you would never forget me. Daddy, I'm so afraid."

The father held his daughter at arm's length desperately trying to remember. Then it came to him in a solid wave of memories. "Princess, Princess, are you okay?" He wasn't sure how he found her. Scott pulled her close, nearly hugging the breath out of her. His baby was in his arms now and nobody was going to harm her.

"I'm OK Daddy but we have to save Mom. The terrorists are going to use a nuclear bomb to kill everybody at the Packer game, including Mom. He took Mom with him to steer our boat."

"Where's your brother? We can't leave without him."

"Brad?" Avery asked, shocked at the question, but now knowing her worst fears were true. Her father's mind was failing, she had to make him remember so they didn't waste precious time looking for her dead brother.

Just then Nassir walked through the hatchway; he stepped onto the deck and saw the soldier with the young girl. Scott noticed the terrorist at the same time and watched him start to bring his machine gun up to his shoulder. Sergeant Azodi knew that if they ran, he would never catch them. The shot had to be taken now.

Scott pushed his daughter back toward the open container and the bullets pounded on the open door shielding them. Nassir kept them pinned down with gunfire as he cautiously moved toward the open door. The shot of morphine he had given himself took away the sharpest of the pain. The terrorist conserved his bullets but kept sporadic gunfire on the door so the soldier and the young girl would stay under its cover. Soon it wouldn't matter; if they tried to run he would easily cut them both down. What the sergeant didn't understand was how the soldier knew the girl was being held hostage onboard the ship, nor how he found her among the numerous identical boxes. The only thought he had was that Captain FarzAm Zarin betrayed them; he was the only other person on the ship who knew of the girl's location.

Sergeant Azodi approached the door; he wanted to avoid a bloody mess on the deck. If possible, he would trap the soldier and the girl back inside a container and then kill them. He glanced back at the helicopter; it was a mile behind the ship though still visible. For whatever reason, this soldier was alone on this mission. There was no support coming from the chopper. In fact, the helicopter would itself become a victim as soon as it ran out of fuel.

Nassir aimed his machine gun, flipped the door to the side and started shooting. They were gone. The terrorist looked down the row of open doors. The two had used the first door as a shield to hide their escape past the rows of partially open steel doors.

Scott checked his gun; he had used all the rounds to open the containers. This fact he didn't let on to his daughter.

"Let's find Brad," Scott said, he pulled his daughter after him as they ran through the maze. Scott remembered the alleyways and he proceeded carefully, trying not to go down the same blind alley as earlier.

"Daddy?"

"Yes Princess."

"Brad is with Mom."

"Are you sure?"

"The men took them on our boat." Then she asked a question she wasn't sure she wanted to hear the answer to. "Are we going to die?"

"No, of course not." Scott rejected the idea.

"I was so scared Daddy. I thought they were going to kill me."

"You're OK now sweetheart. You're with me and I won't let anybody hurt you."

For the first time Scott noticed how badly his daughter's hands and wrists had been cut by the tight bindings. He also noticed the big bruise on her cheekbone.

"Who did this to you?"

"The man who has Mom. He is a very bad man."

"Did he hurt your mother or Brad?"

"Brad is fine, but the bad man kicked Mom real hard and tied her hands and made them bleed like mine. We almost escaped. I shot the man who has Mom, which was why he hit me. I thought he was going to kill me. Why'd they do this to us?"

"I don't know Princess, I don't know," Scott answered honestly. "Where did you get a gun?" he asked his daughter incredulously.

"It was from the first man who captured us. Mom hurt him real bad before he tied her up, that's when he dropped his gun. She cut him real bad with your saw. I got untied and then found his gun. I tried to hide. Mom said to shoot if the other man came near me and so I did."

"Where did you shoot him?'

"In the shoulder."

"How badly did you hurt him?"

"I don't think it was very bad because he is still using that arm a bit."

"I'm so proud of you sweetheart. I'm sorry you have to go through this."

"Dad," Avery said slowly. "I don't think the man shooting at us will stop until he kills us."

Scott looked at his daughter and nodded his head. She was right; she was growing up very quickly. If they wanted to live, he had to kill this man before he killed them, and Scott had to do it fast.

"Listen honey, I've been forgetting things a lot lately. I don't have my medicine, so you might have to remind me of what we are doing and where we are going from time to time. OK Princess?"

"Okay. How are we going to save Mom?"

"I don't know honey; we'll think of something. Right now we have to stay clear of the guy with the gun until we have a plan to escape."

"Dad, I have a plan."

Army National Guard base, West Bend, Wisconsin:

"I think I can hook up Captain Seaver's phone to my computer. Then I can use the computer's software to synchronize with his phone. With my computer searching his phone's memory I might find more information."

"Just do it Lieutenant," Major Allen ordered. "We don't need a play by play."

Just about then, Dan Price called Matt with an update. "The police have identified the dead body at the Seaver residence. He was an ex-convict, no link to any terrorist group. The NSA and FBI were both trying to make a connection. It seems that your hunch has finally gotten the attention of the higher-ups. Reports of exceptional radio chatter were detected. What that means isn't exactly clear, but your team's scenario is starting to be taken very seriously in Washington."

"Thanks Dan, gotta go, I will call with any new developments."

Lieutenant Schmidt then announced success at the first step of his plan and explained what he was trying to do. "Captain Seaver had to send an Internet link to the kidnappers so they could watch the video, I'm sure that is what this WEB address is about.

"I have the link. All I have to do is click on it and we should be able to see what the captain recorded."

The team watched impatiently as a computer video player appeared like magic. Nothing happened, then a warning. "Please enter the password."

"What's wrong, Lieutenant?"

"It's password protected. This is his company's site; he has it security locked so not just anybody can access it. Maybe somebody at his office knows the password?"

Matthew pounded on the desk in frustration. "Lieutenant, we don't have time to try to find somebody who might know the password. The president and a hundred thousand lives are at stake here."

"I know, sir. I'll try to crack it, maybe we'll get lucky. I know the Captain pretty well, I'll try to think like he would."

Michael picked up Scott's IT-Tech and started to look at some of its functions. The rest of the team started to shoot off words or phrases that might have been used as passwords for the video. Lieutenant Schmidt entered the names as the team went through pet's names, children's names, birthdates, mother's name and father's name; nothing worked.

345

Alan D Schmitz

Michael shuffled through the pictures on the phone looking for clues. One particular picture stood out. It was just another long shot but he said, "Try 'My Chopper.'" The lieutenant's eyes brightened. It was a good guess. He typed it in. It didn't work. Schmidt tried a few more variations of the two words, his gut told him it had to be right. Then he tried it in all upper case and as one complete word. It worked! Soon, the old office building was on the screen in front of them.

The team watched the video until the end. There was no doubt; somehow Scott had captured a murder on camera. A terrible fire raged and eventually burned the camera.

Matthew wasted no time. "I want you to freeze on the face of the killer. We already know who the murdered young man is. Send a photo of the face to this e-mail address. Can you send the entire video through that thing?"

"I can try sir, it will take more time."

Michael explained why. "There is a possibility that they can also get a voice print match."

Then he said to the major, "The department will run the picture through very sophisticated face recognition software for a positive ID. It's time for us to get into position. My team needs to ride along. Our copter doesn't have the range or the speed. We have some equipment that might be needed to locate and disarm the bomb, assuming there is one and we find it in time."

The major did some quick math in his head to calculate whether the extra weight would be acceptable. "We'll be cramped and on the edge weight-wise, but it can be done. Board up!"

Approaching the Fox River:

Hamid and Liz had the sailboat throttled very slowly; they were entering the mouth of the Fox River, the largest tributary to the waters of Green Bay. Even more important was the fact that the huge football stadium was built not far from a marina within the river. Soon he would be able to dock the boat and leave it floating casually with the bomb sitting unsuspiciously on deck. No one would suspect that in a little more than an hour, the idyllic setting would turn the city of Green Bay into a burning, radiation-polluted hell.

Liz wanted to yell for help to other boaters, yet her motherly instincts prevented it. Her mind told her that the lives of one hundred thousand people outweighed her's and her daughter's, but her heart told her to not give up hope. Scott would save them somehow.

Damascus Star:

Nassir limped along, searching the openings between the high containers as he walked. He contemplated climbing the containers and taking the high ground once again. It would be a good plan, but in this case he didn't feel that his ankle could take the abuse of the climb and descent again. Then he heard a sound. Somebody had slipped and fallen. To go after the soldier would be dangerous because he had a gun and obviously knew how to use it. But the sergeant also knew that he couldn't play this game of cat and mouse much longer. The crew was still below deck, so the noise was positively his prey. Nassir reasoned that even if the soldier got off a shot, it would have to be instantly deadly or he'd be able to use his machine gun to finish the man.

Sergeant Azodi entered the cavern carefully with the Uzi held before him and his finger on the sensitive trigger. Inside the maze of alleys between the containers, nobody would see the bloody corpses. He would have time to clean up the bloody mess before any crewmembers saw it. The sergeant heard a faint sound. As he turned, he saw a foot running from him; on it was a young girl's tennis shoe. The soldier wouldn't be far away. There was another noise. In their haste they were running toward the same dead end the soldier was trapped in before. *He should have remembered this mistake from the first time,* the sergeant thought. Nassir could still smell some of the remnants of the red smoke but the smoke itself had cleared away. He had them. The running footsteps went down the fateful corridor.

Nassir turned a corner. In the middle of an intersection of alleys there was another noise. It was the sound of something dropping, like.... Nassir tried to think of what it reminded him of. Like..., *a hand grenade!* He looked at the floor and saw it. Without hesitation the sergeant ran a few steps and then tossed his body to the ground, forgetting about the girl just a few yards away. He smelled the smoke. It wasn't a hand grenade. It was another harmless smoke flare. The distractions had worked, but not for long enough. Nassir stood up; he was in the middle of an intersection with four possible exits. He fired blindly down one direction then another. Turning around, he fired into the two remaining alleys. Anyone in those alleys would be dead. The flare continued to burn and produce thick red smoke. With nowhere else to go, the terrorist decided that he had no choice but to climb up to get out of the choking smoke.

He slung his gun over his shoulder and started the painful climb. After he climbed the first eight-foot high box, his head poked through the top of the red haze. In an instant he was painfully smashed back into the smoke and his ankle hit the deck hard. Nassir had never in his life screamed in pain before. Today was a first time.

The soldier had jumped onto his back, forcing him back into the dense red smoke. Captain Seaver fell to the deck with the terrorist. Scott ignored the painful scream and blindly punched at the terrorist over and over again. When his lungs couldn't take another breath of the smoke, Scott grabbed the machine gun and went as far down the alley as he could before collapsing breathless and out of oxygen.

Avery Seaver tried to pull her father to clear air but she couldn't move him. It was her idea to use herself as bait to lure the terrorist into a trap. It was her father's idea to further confuse and hamper the terrorist with the smoke flare. Avery never imagined her father would leap off the top container and drop twenty feet onto the terrorist's back. It was nothing short of amazing to see her father act so heroically. Avery held onto the Uzi. If she had to, there was no doubt in her mind that she would use it to protect her father and herself. The smoke was clearing away ever so slowly. Scott coughed now and again, though he was still unconscious.

"What happened?" Scott eventually recovered to see his daughter guarding over him.

"You beat the shit out of the terrorist and stole his gun. I haven't seen him again; I think you might have killed him." Avery was relieved to have her father back.

Scott stared at the young woman for a few minutes and then tried to sit up but failed. He recognized the teenager after a while. "What are you doing here? Where am I? Where are we?"

His daughter explained the entire situation to him. She realized that he had just been through a traumatic event, but it was scary to see her father in such a confused state of mind.

"You just need a few more minutes, Dad. You were fighting in the smoke and it filled your lungs. Try to take some deep breaths."

Scott was dazed and confused. Though the large ship was steady in the water, he felt as if it was twisting and turning, making him feel sick to his stomach. Scott took the teen's advice and breathed deeply. That caused him to cough up red dust, which made him heave onto the deck. But slowly he was taking deeper breaths and starting to feel better. He lifted his body half up and rested on his side, slowly getting his orientation back. The red smoke was diffusing into intermittent wisps of red fog.

"Don't move or I will throw this knife into the young lady's heart. Be assured that I am very good with a knife. My friend Hamid saw to that." Sergeant Azodi walked out of the fog and back into their lives. Nassir had been too incapacitated by Captain Seaver to inhale as much smoke as Scott did. That worked to his advantage.

Scott lay motionless on his side facing the terrorist. Avery tried to slowly reach for the big machine gun.

"Pick up the gun by the barrel and hand it to me very slowly," the terrorist commanded.

"Don't do it honey! As soon as you give it to him he is going to kill us with it," Scott warned.

"Honey!" Nassir sounded surprised. "So this is your daughter. You are a brave man to risk your life for her. Too bad you will not be successful. Young lady, you should be very proud of your father."

"I am, and he kicked your ass before, and he can do it again," she threatened.

"Honey, hush..., now is not the time to antagonize the man; he has a knife." Scott tried to settle down his daughter's bravado, though he had to admit her spunk in the face of death made him proud. And whether she knew it or not, she was providing a needed distraction.

"This is correct and if you don't give me the gun very carefully, I will kill you with the knife very slowly and make your father watch. I am a trained fighter; your father is no match against me."

"Fuck you!" Avery shouted.

The strong language from the young mouth took both men by surprise.

"Avery!" Scott scolded. "That is no way for a young lady to talk."

Nassir chuckled at the bizarre scolding, as if the young girl's manners would ever matter again in her short life.

While the terrorist was distracted by the banter, Scott took his left leg and swung his metal-tipped army boot as hard and fast as he could at the gunman's blood stained ankle. The bone in it had been so tortured and weakened that it cracked in half. Nassir dropped like a rock. Scott easily twisted the knife out of his hand and proceeded to pummel the Iranian with years of pent up anger.

"Where is my crew?" Scott angrily cried, never waiting for an answer. "What did you do to them?" Scott straddled the man's chest. He didn't have a chance against the furry being unleashed against him. "They were just doing their job," he cried as he continued the pounding with his right fist, then his left, over and over again. "They were just boys doing their job," Scott sobbed, slowly becoming tired.

The Iranian's nose was broken and his face was severely swollen.

Avery watched her father batter the man. That didn't bother her, but her father's blind rage over past memories scared her.

"My son, what did you do to my son? Where is my son Brad? Why is he gone?" Scott started pounding on the man in slow motion, with almost no strength left in his arms.

"Dad," Avery spoke softly. "Brad is with Mom. We have to find Mom. Your soldiers are OK. They are all OK Dad."

Scott looked at his daughter and nodded his head in tired agreement. The Iranian's eyes were swollen shut. He was unconscious and near death from the beating. Scott sat off to the side, resting.

"Brad is dead," Scott said factually and calmly. "He died in an accident, didn't he? I killed him."

Avery didn't know what to do; she didn't understand her father's condition enough to deal with the contradictions, so she told the truth. "Dad, it wasn't your fault. There was big deer that bolted onto the road. You tried to miss it. You lost control trying to miss another car. There was nothing you could have done."

"But I killed Brad in the process."

"Brad would have died in a head on crash too," Avery comforted. "You couldn't have known."

Scott was crying, slumped against a steel container. "I know, I know that now. I tried to save him. I really did. I begged him not to die, but I couldn't save him. I can see it all like it just happened. Avery, honey, it was terrible. But I did everything I could. You have to believe me."

"Dad," Avery said as she hugged and held her father. She felt it appropriate to confirm his actions. "We all know you did."

"I miss Brad so much; I couldn't bear to lose you too. That asshole had it coming." Scott looked at the bloody mass that was Nassir's head.

"Dad, he would have killed me if you hadn't saved me."

Scott felt better; his crying was starting to stop. "I was just doing my job in Iraq, as was my crew. We were captured and the Iraqis did what they thought they had to do. I remember coming back into the equipment container after a particularly brutal beating and started singing "My Country, 'Tis of Thee". Then the whole group inside the hot bin started singing. The Iraqis got so pissed they started banging on the outside of the container box, but we just sang louder. We talked about that for days, even though they really got me the next time I was interrogated. They had purposely beaten me so that I couldn't talk, or sing. But that didn't stop the men from singing when I came back and I conducted with the only thing that wasn't bruised and that was my finger. I think that was what helped to get us through the ordeal, all of us, including me. We were sure glad when the Special Forces guys showed up."

Scott smiled a bit at his daughter. His rage was completely gone.

"We really need to find Mom," Avery reminded her hero.

"Yea, let's go. I'm feeling better now."

Scott and Avery walked toward the helm, but not before Scott picked up the Uzi. Right now, Scott felt invincible.

Avery looked up at her father and asked, "I thought you couldn't remember any of those things?"

Scott put his arm around his daughter's shoulder as they walked. "I guess I couldn't, or didn't want to. But something happened when I thought about you being harmed by that man, I just got so angry. I knew then that forgetting just wasn't an option for me anymore; I couldn't hide from my memories any longer because it put you in danger. Suddenly all those past memories filled my mind; they were all I could think about. And as painful as they are, seeing you hurt or killed because I didn't want to face them was even worse."

"So how are we going to find Mom? All I know is that the terrorist was taking her to Lambeau Field in Green Bay and the bomb is going to go off sometime during the game."

Scott glanced at his watch. "I have a risky idea, but we can do it, I know we can."

Father and daughter found their way unhampered to the front of the ship and the control room. Scott entered the room quietly. Captain Zarin didn't see them coming, not hearing Scott until he clicked the lever of the Uzi, setting its firing pin.

"What do you want? I have nothing." The captain of the ship acted very nervous.

"I want you to turn the ship around."

"I can't. I have a schedule to keep."

"I have a schedule to keep also, and I have a gun pointed at you, so I win. Turn the ship around. NOW!" he shouted.

FarzAm Zarin realized that the Revolutionary Guard Corps sergeant must have been disabled or this man would not be here. He turned the wheel, which started the huge ship turning toward the eastern shores of Wisconsin.

Alan D Schmitz

"Honey, get ready and do exactly as I told you."

"OK Dad, don't worry, we'll make it."

"What is it you want from me?" FarzAm asked.

"I want you to turn this ship around and steer this boat straight toward the helicopter. If you don't, I will shoot you and steer it myself."

The ship captain didn't know what the man had in mind. It would take a while for the big ship to turn and what possible good would it do to steer the ship toward the unpiloted helicopter?

Chapter 25

Fox River, Green Bay, Wisconsin:

The Iranian Revolutionary Guard Corps major and Elizabeth Seaver were nearing their destination. Hamid looked at the huge stadium just a few blocks away. Soon they would dock the boat and pretend that they were going to the game. Mrs. Seaver was dutifully guiding the boat down the wide river, every so often increasing the speed of the engine. Almost imperceptibly she increased the speed enough to create a wake. Her hope was that if she did it slowly enough, the terrorist wouldn't notice the increase in speed. If the craft was going too fast for the river conditions a DNR patrol might stop them.

Hamid noticed the growing wake and rushed to the helm. He moved the power lever back, and then he grabbed Liz's right hand and made a long bleeding cut down the palm of her hand as a warning. "The next time I will remove a finger."

Hamid tried to call his companion on the freighter once again; there was no answer. The terrorist was becoming concerned that something on the ship was amiss. He talked loudly into the phone, pretending that everything was fine on the big ship and that the young teen was still captive.

Checking the timer on the bomb, only ten minutes had passed since they entered the river, but as the clock ticked down, he became more nervous. He had no desire to be a martyr if he had the option of being a living hero. It wouldn't take him long to get into a safe zone once he stole a car. The scientist who loaded the bomb with the fissionable material estimated that he needed to be at least five miles away from the blast to be safe, as long as he was upwind of the bomb. Hamid wanted ten miles for added security; the bomb could be more powerful than the scientist estimated.

On the Damascus Star:

Scott kept the gun pointed at the captain of the ship as it turned toward the south. "You are a crazy man. My company will make you pay for the cost of delaying this ship."

353

Alan D Schmitz

"Well, you are going to have a bit of a problem explaining to the police and your company why you had my daughter held as a hostage on your ship."

"I know nothing about that," the ship captain insisted.

"You don't seem too surprised to hear it."

Scott glanced out the window overlooking the cargo and saw that his daughter was in place just as he had instructed. Avery was very athletic; if anyone could do what she needed to, it was Avery.

"Keep this course and slow the ship down."

"If I slow the ship down anymore than it already is, I will lose steering."

"Slow it down, NOW!" Scott insisted and emphasized his point with the machine gun pointing very close to Captain Zarin's head. The ship's captain pulled back the throttle and the ship began to slow to a stop.

They were approaching the hovering helicopter; Scott took the butt of the gun and hit the captain against the back of the head. FarzAm Zarin went down. Scott guided the ship with the helm wheel as long as he could. The ship was moving directly under 210HK. He could see the flimsy rope ladder dangling down from the Black Hawk. There wouldn't be much time left. He had to outrun the speed of the ship and stay in front of the ladder. Scott crashed through the door and down the stairs as fast as he could. He slung the Uzi around his back as he bolted down the wide side alley toward the aft superstructure. He had no time to look at how his daughter was doing; it was up to the athletic teen now, he couldn't help her.

The ship was moving faster than he anticipated. Scott climbed up the last row of stacked containers. "Shit!" he cursed. The helicopter was almost overhead and the ship was veering off course. The bottom of the rope ladder was only a few feet above the steel boxes. Unfortunately it was moving over the containers on the opposite side of the ship from Scott.

"Dad hurry!" He heard over the roar of the beating blades. The chopper was only twenty feet above him. His daughter had made it; she grabbed onto the ladder and climbed into the helicopter. Now her life depended on him doing exactly the same thing.

Captain FarzAm Zarin crawled back to the wheel of the ship. If the man and his daughter died, they would not be able to tell the American police about anything. The ship's captain immediately increased the speed of his ship and turned the rudder as hard as he could. A ship of this size didn't speed up very fast, or turn quickly, but anything he could do to

354

keep the man from reaching the dangling ladder was worth a try. He watched the unfolding scenario. The young girl had nearly slipped off the rope but she managed to hang on, and then, rather expertly, climbed the wobbly thing. But now the speed of the ship had picked up and a turn was initiated. The crazy man with the gun was on the wrong side of the ship to catch the ladder, which was moving farther and farther away from him all the time.

The rope he needed to grab dangled above the top containers by no more than three or four feet. It was plenty low enough. The problem was that it was moving very quickly toward the aft of the ship. Soon it would be off the side of the ship completely.

"Daddy, please hurry." Avery Seaver knew their only chance to save themselves and her mother depended on the pilot of the chopper. Without her dad at the controls of the aircraft their lives would all be lost.

Scott ran across the tops of the stacked containers. He jumped an open valley, continuing to run. He tried to straddle another wide gap,,but fell. The ladder was across from him and going off the edge of the ship. Scott got up and bolted toward the ladder. Avery saw the ladder leave the edge of the last container; her father didn't have a chance.

Scott didn't wait. He didn't think and he didn't anticipate. He jumped off the edge of the last container as if his family's life depended on it. Scott grabbed for the ladder. He missed his target. Avery saw her father's hand grasping at thin air. In an instant he would start to fall toward the white foaming water churned up by the ship's propellers.

The pilot clenched his fingers together, but they had nothing to hold onto. He fell toward the frothy cold depths. Scott was certain of his impending death. Nobody could survive the gnarled cold waters below him. Memories of his wife and children flooded his mind. That instant lasted forever. Memories of all the people in his life passed before his eyes. In desperation, he slammed his left hand against his right. His right arm had shot completely through the last rung of the ladder. He laced his fingers together just in time to stop his fall, only just hanging on.

"Daddy, hang on," Avery shouted.

It was a strange time for the thought, but Scott reflected about how his daughter always called him "Daddy" when she wanted something. Usually it was a new I-pod, DVD or his charge-card to buy something new. In this case, she wanted him to live. That was a nice change.

"Daddy!" she hollered again. "Don't fall. Don't let go."

It wasn't that he didn't appreciate the encouragement, but a few of those same thoughts had already crossed his mind. Scott dangled for a bit. The aft section of the ship was passing by, only yards away from him. Scott looked down at the giant white churning wake it left behind; it wasn't someplace he would want to be.

Very carefully, Scott pulled himself up by his arms, one rung at a time until his feet rested on the bottom rung of the ladder. He rested for a second. Climbing the wiggly ladder could be difficult and one careless mistake could plunge him into the lake. Step by step he lifted himself up, wishing he was a teenager again. His muscles ached all over. Eventually, with his daughter's help, encouragement and added strength, he was inside the Black Hawk.

Avery hugged her father intending on never letting him go. She hadn't realized how much she loved him and needed him. Some daughters might say their parents or a particular parent was their hero, but in her case, her father had gone above and beyond the definition. Avery Seaver became a changed young lady; her teen years would never be the same from this point of her life on.

Black Hawk 340HK:

The Black Hawk NNSA team was heading north out of West Bend as fast as the Hawk would take them. They would stay over land as long as possible. Dieter had the freighter's latest position; it was somewhere east of the city of Sturgeon Bay with the Door County Penninsula to the north.. To save time, the chopper would start to look for the ship by going out over the lake on a northeast heading near the city of Manitowoc. The one thing going for them was the weather. It was one of those fall days in Wisconsin that creates perfect post card pictures. Leaves were changing into their bright colored hues of red, orange and yellow. Mixed with the vivid colors was a smattering of green leaves that were trying to hang onto life for as long as possible. 340HK left the Wisconsin woodlands behind, flying low at one thousand feet above the lake. The multicolored scenery gave way to miles upon miles of solid dark blue water. The freighter wasn't yet in sight.

Matthew got a call from the department chief, Dan Price. They had a positive ID on the killer. The man's name was Hamid Shukah, who sometimes used the alias of Kassim. He was a known assassin for Iran, and a high-ranking officer of the elite Revolutionary Guard. By any measure he was a very dangerous man.

"Matt!" the chief said in a somber tone. "We believe your scenario is credible. The president's team has been alerted; as soon as Air Force One is airborne, an evacuation of the stadium and the entire city of Green Bay will be authorized unless you tell us differently. You are authorized to detain and arrest Hamid Shukah. Use any and all force necessary to apprehend him. Be aware he will be armed and very dangerous, even with his bare hands." Then he added, "We would really like this guy alive, but that might not be possible. Do not underestimate this guy, Matt. If you have to kill him, then do it. Protect yourself and your team. I am uploading several more photos of him. Pass them around. Make sure everyone understands just how dangerous he is.

"If Iran wanted to take a bomb into this country, Hamid would be their man. I am issuing a code red to Homeland. If this guy is on our soil, he is up to no good in a major way. We are dispatching all available assets to help you, but be advised, for now you are on your own."

Agent Mitchell hung up. He gravely looked at his team and the armed security force on board. "Gentlemen, we have a new mission."

Aboard the Damascus Star:

Scott took off the Uzi slung over his shoulder and slid it under the pilot's seat as he got behind the controls of the copter. Captain Seaver stared at all the dials and controls in front of him. They all seemed so foreign to him. Father and daughter buckled themselves into their seats. Dad helped his daughter with the complicated straps that went over both shoulders and snapped into place around the hips. Scott slid on his helmet. His daughter was a fast learner. She found the co-pilot's helmet and strapped it on as tightly as she could, though it was too big for her small head.

"I can't fly this thing," Scott said nervously into the microphone built into his helmet.

"Yes you can Dad, you just don't remember," Avery encouraged.

"That's the problem. I do remember. I have never flown this aircraft for real. I only flew it in simulation, basically a big computer game. And I remember crashing it a few times too many."

"You must have flown it here." Avery could hear the panic in her hero's voice.

"I must have, but I don't remember. I can't take the chance with your life, honey. If I make one mistake, I could start a spiral into the lake that I can't stop." Captain Seaver was feeling the stress of the situation. Experimenting with only him in the aircraft was one thing, but taking his daughter's life in his hands trying to learn to fly this beast was not something he was prepared to do.

"You have to Dad, we have to find Mom. She is with a very bad man." Avery tried to make her father remember. "If we don't find her in time, he will kill her. I don't care about my life if Mom dies."

Scott hadn't forgotten about his wife. In fact, he knew that Avery's mother's wishes would be exactly the same as his. She wouldn't care what happened to her if her daughter's life was safe. He thought about his options. He could call for a rescue boat and wait until it arrived, then he could very slowly lower the helicopter to a point where his daughter and he could jump into the lake and swim to it. At the very least, he could get his daughter safely into the lake, even if he didn't survive, but that would mean Liz would most certainly be doomed. Scott remembered what his daughter had told him about the terrorist with a bomb. His mind was as clear as it ever had been. He believed his daughter because it was the only thing that made sense of all the crazy things that had happened to him and his family over the last few days. But if there was a nuclear bomb on its way to Green Bay, Liz certainly wouldn't want Avery to be flown right into harm's way. If Liz was here she would undoubtedly want Scott to not take any chances with their daughter's life.

Avery saw her father's hesitation. "Dad, you always told me you could fly anything. I know you can do it. You have to try. You flew it here Dad. You can fly it. I know you can."

Staying alive in the cold waters without survival gear would be measured in minutes. Scott didn't know why but his pilot's instincts, or possibly just old habits, told him to glance at the fuel gauges.

"Strap yourself in tightly, honey; this might be a wild ride." Both fuel gauges were near empty. Waiting for a rescue boat to reach them was not an option. One way or the other, Scott had to get the aircraft to shore before the fuel ran out. Either way, the copter would soon be going down.

Captain Seaver prepared himself as much as possible. Then he clicked off the autopilot and hoped for the best. The helicopter had trimmed itself for the hover mode, but as soon as Scott changed anything, there was no guaranty it would remain stable. The Black Hawk tipped forward and suddenly pressed for the surface of the lake, flying directly toward the cold waters. Scott was caught completely off guard. The Huey was much more forgiving. Scott instinctively pulled the cyclic back. Without adding power, the abrupt change in pitch brought the tail down and the front of the helicopter up but it still was losing altitude.

The young teen pressed her small fingers into a tight ball around the edge of the flight seat. *Maybe this wasn't such a good idea,* she thought as she screamed, "Daaad!"

Scott added power with the collective. The helicopter shot up and spun to the right. "Wow, this thing has got power," Scott said out loud.

Scott tipped the cyclic and used the rotor pedals to straighten the craft. "I think I'm getting the hang of it," he said just before the chopper took another quick descent.

"Oops!" Scott apologized just after he righted it.

"Dad, please don't crash us." Avery was terrified.

"Don't worry, piece of cake," Scott said as he took time to smirk at his daughter to calm her nerves a bit.

The helicopter rode like a roller coaster for a while. It didn't take too long for Captain Seaver to become more effective on the controls, though it was much too long for his daughter's liking. Some of his simulator training was coming back. The simulator was even more sensitive; he just needed a bit of time to settle in to flying the actual aircraft.

After Avery caught her breath and a bit of composure, she asked her father, "How are we going to find Mom? I know they were going to Green Bay, but I don't know where."

"I have an idea; we can find them the same way I found you. Where's your phone honey?"

"I hid it on the deck of our boat. If the jerk who took Mom didn't find it, it should still be there. Why do you need my phone?"

Scott pulled out Lieutenant Schmidt's IT-Tech phone, which had the same features as his. "Type in your phone number, and then we can tell the GPS mapping function to locate your phone."

Avery Seaver suspiciously did as she was told. "Now honey, I want you to touch the picture of the GPS symbol."

She did. It didn't take long for a map to be displayed along with a flashing yellow dot. "I see a flashing dot."

"That's it!" Scott confirmed. "We just fly to the dot!"

Avery was trying to process the information her father just told her. Somehow, her father's phone was able to locate her phone. If her phone was with her mother, then it would lead them right there. Avery thought about the flashing yellow dot a bit more. Despite their perilous situation her blood began to boil in an angry teenage fit. Avery started to shout at her father once she realized the implications. "You were spying on me?" she demanded to know.

"I wasn't spying on you." Scott defended himself.

"What do you call this?" She held up the map with the dot flashing.

"It's not spying honey; I just wanted to know that you were OK and where you were."

"You were tracking my every move. You LoJacked my phone and you don't call that spying! I hate you Dad!" she said to her former hero. "You gave me your old phone just so that you could spy on me, and I thought it was because you loved me," she pouted.

"Listen, your majesty..." That was what Scott called his little princess when she was being a demanding teen. "I'm not debating this right now; in case you haven't noticed, I'm a little busy saving your princess butt. Besides, it was for your own good. How do you think I found you on the freighter?"

"You are so lucky," The angry teenager insisted. "If I had known you were SPYING on me, I never would have let you give it to me."

"I was lucky? How about you? Or did you like it in that cozy little box? I did give it to you because I love you. Why do you think I risked my neck to save you in the first place?"

"Maybe you wanted your precious phone back, and you wanted to see how good your little spy machine worked."

"That's silly; you're just being unreasonable now. You know I love you. "Besides, I'm your father and I will SPY on you anytime I want to. How do you like those apples?" Scott said smugly.

Avery folded her arms together in a huff. She hated it when her father used the old... "Because I'm your father" argument. There was no defending against it. She looked outside and saw the Door County Peninsula as they crossed over Sturgeon Bay. "The SPY phone says Mom isn't far," she added as sarcastically as she could.

Scott took a quick look and adjusted his heading. It made sense; there was a small marina in that area. "You're sure there is a bomb?"

"Yes, they were all happy about killing the president. They thought we were going to be dead so I guess they didn't care that we heard them."

"We have to get Mom away from there."

"What about the president and all the other people?" Avery asked.

"I don't know. I'll try the radio, but I don't know if they are going to believe somebody who just stole a helicopter!"

"You stole this?" Avery asked in disbelief.

"How do you think I got it? They don't just rent these things out like a car."

"You stole a helicopter to save us. Cool!" The teen was impressed with her father.

Scott smugly grinned back at her; under the circumstances, it was pretty cool. He was in deep trouble, but in the situation, he would do it again if he had to.

The helicopter shook and gyrated a bit. One of the engines started to flame out.

"What was that?" Avery was back to gripping her seat.

"We're running out of fuel. It's not far; I think we can make it."

The copter was entering the mouth of the Fox River; the marina was only a mile away.

Black Hawk 340HK over Lake Michigan:

The Army Guard team was within site of the freighter. Captain Dan Fredric thought he spotted another chopper heading west as they flew northeast toward the freighter, but he couldn't be sure. The major saw it too, but it would do no good to chase the unidentified craft. The freighter was their first priority.

Green Bay Marina, Fox River:

Just before arriving at the small marina, Hamid had ushered Elizabeth Seaver below deck. The marina could possibly be populated and he didn't want to take a chance that the woman would become overly brave and risk her life to warn others of his plan. Before locking her there, he made sure she was bound and gagged tightly. Hamid guided the craft into the dock at the end of a line of piers as far away from any other boat as he could. Because of the late season, the docks were sparsely occupied by other boats. It seemed as if all the owners of those boats were either at the game or watching the game at home, because he didn't see any pedestrians around the marina.

The terrorist tied the boat to the slip, and when he was confident it was secure, he checked the bomb one last time. His timing had been planned well. There was half an hour left and it was counting down as planned. Hamid glanced at the cabin door and contemplated the fate of the woman in the cabin below. He would kill her now. He didn't need her alive any longer. Even though the bomb would certainly disintegrate her and any evidence, he had to be certain that on the chance it didn't go off, she wouldn't be alive to describe him to the police.

Major Shukah pulled his long knife from its case in the small of his back. A bloody mess below deck would not be a bother to him at this point. Soon he would be in a stolen car heading north, away from the stadium and toward the rendezvous with the freighter. Hamid heard a sound in the sky. It was a strange sound, quiet, yet powerful.

Black Hawk 210HK:

"Honey, I want you to strap yourself into your seat as tightly as possible. I am going to have to auto-rotate the copter down." There was only one engine still running and it was starting to flame out. The Black Hawk was going to lose powered flight. "How far away is Mom?"

Avery stared at the miniature computer screen on the IT-Tech. "It looks like she is right below us."

The second engine stopped. All their fuel was completely exhausted. Scott's hands automatically flew to switches he didn't even know existed, he secured the engines and set up the copter for gliding down. The rotor blades spun freely from the gearing of the transmission. This kept the helicopter from crashing straight down. Helicopters made for terrible gliders, but the good news was, they did glide. A crash was survivable. Scott had done it before.

"I see our boat; the kidnapper is on deck," Scott told his daughter, though he was talking more to himself at the time.

"Daddy, are we going to crash?" Avery asked, not sounding very frightened.

"We are not going to crash, but we are going to land very hard, so hang on."

By now, Scott had become proficient enough with the controls of the Black Hawk to maintain a good auto-rotation forward and vertical speed. The electronic assist from the fly-by-wire controls made the job easier, as long as he didn't get too aggressive with the controls. If the pitch wasn't maintained perfectly, the copter would crash. It would fall from the sky like a rock if the rotors stopped spinning at the proper speed and the aircraft stalled out.

****

Hamid stared at the huge chopper coming toward him. He suspected that the craft was in some sort of stealth mode because it was so eerily quiet. Hamid swore in Farsi. Apparently his Revolutionary Guard Corps teammate on the Damascus Star didn't have any more luck in killing the aviator than he did. The man was extremely resourceful. Then Hamid realized the copter was coming to earth much too fast. The terrorist had seen auto-rotation before and knew the copter coming toward them was going to crash; its engines were not running at all. Captain Seaver would not leave the copter alive, Hamid promised himself.

The Black Hawk shot over his head, the pilot wouldn't have much choice where it landed, but it would be very soon. Hamid dashed off the dock and ran after the descending chopper. The pilot would undoubtedly be severely shaken up, if not unconscious, after the crash landing. Major Shukah was intending to take full advantage of that moment to kill the captain and finally be done with him.

The treetops were buzzing past the windows. The ground was approaching fast. Scott had just an instant to glance at his boat as the copter raced over it; his heart sank when he didn't see his wife. "I love you princess!" Scott cried out to his daughter in the last seconds. "Hang on, here we go."

"I love you too Dad!" Avery managed to reply just as the copter hit ground.

****

Hamid heard the loud crash. He waited for a few moments, expecting to see a fireball in front of him. He did not intend on running into it. A fiery crash could happen instantly on impact, but often it happened after the fuel had time to leak from a ruptured tank and sparks from destroyed electronics ignited it. He couldn't take the chance of waiting; he had to see Seaver dead now, before he left the doomed city.

Lucky for the two occupants of the chopper, they landed in a marshy area of the river, just up from the marina. The marsh had cushioned the fall, though they both were battered by the impact. Scott caught his breath first. "You OK princess?"

"Yea Dad, I'm OK. That was a shitty landing."

Scott laughed a bit. "I always told you I could fly a rock if there were wings on it, but I never said I could fly it well. Come on, we have to get out of here, a fire could start any second." Scott kicked at the door on the pilot's side to try to open it. The door was wedged between the frame on impact. It wouldn't budge and Scott started to panic a little. He had to get his daughter out of the helicopter before it was too late. Somebody was helping him from the outside. A Good Samaritan had undoubtedly seen them come down and was trying to help. Scott and Avery were still strapped into their seats. Scott gave one mighty push with his shoulder into the side door.

Alan D Schmitz

Finally the door creaked open a small bit, then wider as the man outside pulled on it and Scott pushed. He recognized the killer immediately and the knife in his hand. It was the same ox handle knife that was used to kill the young man in Chicago. Hamid intended to slash the pilot's throat as soon as the door opened far enough but was stunned when he saw the man's daughter in the co-pilot's seat. Now there were questions to be answered.

"How did you get the girl?" Hamid snarled.

"I made a little deal with your friend on the freighter."

"What are you talking about?"

"I told your friend that he could live if he gave up the girl."

"You are lying; my friend would never do such a thing."

"You are right; he didn't. So he's dead now," Scott said, without emotion. "Look, asshole," Scott said with disdain, refusing to play the game any longer, "it's over. The ship is captured. The captain surrendered and told us everything," Scott bluffed. "We know about the bomb; it's going to be defused."

"I assure you, it is far from over. And if you had thoughts of saving your wife, you are too late. She is dead. I slit her throat myself. But do not fret; you will soon join her in hell."

Avery screamed from across the chopper. "If you hurt my mother, Dad will beat the crap out of you like he did to your friend."

Hamid believed the young girl. She was too angry to make such a thing up. Somehow this pilot had overtaken Nassir. The captain of the ship probably did talk. He was such a coward. If the sergeant wasn't there to protect him, he would have been an easy source of answers.

"It is time for you and your daughter to die. But before you die, I want you to know that soon your president, and all the people within miles of him, will be incinerated."

Suddenly there was a huge roar in the sky. Air Force One had just taken off and was departing the area almost directly overhead. Hamid couldn't help being distracted by the huge white and blue jet.

"That plane doesn't go anywhere without the president. Looks like Allah didn't want the president dead after all," Scott retorted.

Hamid's anger couldn't be contained. The man in front of him was responsible for saving the president. He wasn't sure how, but he would die for it immediately, and then his daughter and then his wife. The terrorist lifted his knife; it would be easy to kill the man and young girl who were both still helplessly strapped tightly into their seats.

364

Scott had tried to distract the terrorist with his conversation. It wasn't until Air Force One flew overhead that the murderer looked away long enough for Scott to reach his right hand down to the Uzi under his seat. Scott pressed the trigger and tried to aim the gun under him. Bullets exploded out of the barrel, he only needed one to hit the target.

Hamid knew the sound instantly; he looked down at the white light of the rapid explosions exiting the gun. The end of the barrel was only inches away from him. He tried to move his body out of the direct line of the weapon. Steel ricocheted off the open door, sparks flew and the noise was deafening. The terrorist tried to avoid the un-aimed bullets, but they seemed to come from everywhere. He felt the deadly searing of hot metal penetrating his body. The morphine he had been injecting himself with enabled him to endure the pain for a few moments before he fell back into the weedy depths of the river bank. His last thoughts contained more anger than anything he had ever experienced before.

Scott quickly unbuckled himself and his daughter. He shielded her eyes from the broken flesh of the man in the blood stained water as he grabbed her from the helicopter and lifted her down to the ground. A moment later they were both running toward the sailboat.

Black Hawk 340HK:

The team aboard the Black Hawk saw the freighter turning from a southbound heading. Why the ocean bound freighter had been heading back south was impossible to guess.

"Captain, can you set this thing down on the top layer of containers?"

"Can do major. I'll keep it at a hover so the full weight of the chopper isn't on them. I don't know if they could support the full weight."

Don turned to the back of the chopper and gave the instructions. "When we land, the security team will secure the ship. Agent Mitchell, your team must not leave the chopper until I say so. If there is a bomb, we can't risk your team. You might be the only chance we have of stopping a nuclear disaster."

"Understood, major," Matthew acknowledged.

Dr. Michael Stark didn't need to be off the chopper to start taking readings. If he got lucky, he would pick up strong matching radiation signatures. That would be a sign that they were on the right track.

Captain Fredric gently set the Black Hawk down on a set of steel boxes near the center of the freighter. The armed security team jumped out of the copter and proceeded toward the bow of the ship. Major Allen wasn't as armed or protected as the security team, but he went with them, bringing up the rear and protecting the team from an ambush. Over the man-to-man radio all heard: "We have a severely injured man down here. He needs medical attention ASAP."

"Roger that," the major acknowledged. "It'll have to wait. Get to the bridge. Find the captain of the ship. I need this freighter secured now."

"Yes sir."

Five minutes passed. "We have the captain of the ship; he is injured also, although not very badly."

Ten minutes later, aboard the ship, Dr. Stark found the same strong X-ray signatures as days before, only these were very strong, indicating the bomb may still be on the ship. It didn't take long for Major Bob Allen to convince the ship's captain to tell the truth about the ship's mission and soon he admitted that there had been a bomb on board the ship but it was now on its way to Green Bay.

"The two of you stay aboard; this ship is impounded." He pointed to two of the security detail men. "Keep the crew confined below deck. The only thing the captain is to do, is to keep this ship from going anywhere. Circle in the middle of the damn lake if you have to," Major Allen ordered. "The rest back onto the chopper. We have to find that bomb and disarm it. Make no mistake; we are going into harm's way."

Green Bay Marina:

Scott cautioned his daughter as they approached My Chopper. "Honey, we don't know what he might have done to your mother. You wait here. I'll check below." Avery wanted to follow, but for a change, she listened to her father's advice and prayed for the best.

Slowly he opened the cabin door, afraid of what he might find. When the daylight streamed through the door and Liz saw her husband, her eyes opened wide and she cried with relief. Scott yelled loudly. "Your mother is fine." Avery rushed down the few wood stairs into the galley area where her mother lay on the floor, still bound. Scott was untying the gag so Liz could breathe easier and talk.

"I can't believe it. Thank god you two are all right. How did you find me?" Avery looked at her father and they both laughed. Scott said, "It's a long story, but we have to get you out of here. The kidnapper is dead, but there is a bomb on the boat and you two have to get out of here."

Liz was soon untied and the three headed out to the deck. "What do you mean the two of us? Where do you think you are going?"

"I have to get this bomb out of here or it will kill tens of thousands."

"No you can't. I thought you were both gone forever. I can't lose you again Scott," Liz pleaded.

"Elizabeth, trust me, I have a plan. I'll be all right. Besides, if I don't get this thing out of here, it will kill us all anyway." Scott lifted the lid of the container carrying the bomb. The timer said fifteen minutes and it was counting down.

Avery was starting to understand what her father was suggesting. "Dad, you can't die, I need you. You promised to teach me to drive, and sail the boat, and scare away my boyfriends."

"I am just going to take the boat out far enough so that it will explode in the middle of the bay. I'll jump off into the water before it goes off. Hopefully the bomb is a dud, nuclear bombs are very difficult to make."

Liz had enough time to think about her husband's unselfish act to realize he was right. If the bomb was a dud, he would be OK; if it wasn't then they would die in the blast along with the others. To do nothing would be cowardice and that was something her husband could never live with, regardless.

"Dad's right, honey. You have to stay here and tell the police what happened and where the body of the terrorist is. People have to know what happened here."

Now Scott was upset. "What do you mean SHE has to stay here?"

"You can't get any distance without the sails, and you can't rig the sails and sail at the same time. Together, we have a chance."

Scott realized he didn't have time to argue about it, his wife was right. They had one chance of saving their daughter's life; both parents knew it without saying it. Scott saw his daughter's phone on deck. He tossed it to her. "Call 911 and try to explain. They might not believe you until you show them the body. Sorry to leave you like this princess, but we don't have time. Just remember we love you so much."

Liz and Scott worked together to untie the boat moorings. Then Scott started the engine. There was no time for goodbyes. "Run as fast as you can away from the dock. We'll call you when we're OK," Liz said as the boat was already backing away from the slip.

Except Avery didn't run; she cried. She was afraid that she would never see her parents again. Scott yelled as loudly as he could toward the dock. "Run, run as fast as you can. Then in ten minutes hide in a road culvert. Go, go now." Avery needed to have faith, so she ran. She ran back toward where the helicopter crashed, away from the boat that might be

Alan D Schmitz

taking her parents away from her forever. She ran toward the first road she could find.

Scott knew that every yard farther away gave his daughter a chance at survival; he pushed the big diesel engine to the maximum setting, not paying attention to the "NO WAKE" signs. If he didn't get the bomb away from the river and out into open water, the DNR would have a lot more to worry about than the eroding shoreline. Scott reminded his wife, "Liz, put your survival suit on. We will have to jump into the water when we are clear of the river and the sails are up," Scott reminded.

Liz nodded in agreement; there wasn't much for her to do until it was time to set the sails. Liz located both of their cold-water suits. She slipped hers on and set her husband's out so he could easily put it on the second he was ready. The mouth of the river was approaching and at the first hint of open water she would be very busy.

Chapter 26

Black Hawk 340HK:

Captain Fredric expertly piloted the Black Hawk toward Green Bay; somehow he got a few more forward knots out of it than the book said was possible. The stadium full of people was being evacuated. Under normal conditions, it took hours to empty a stadium and the parking lots surrounding them. That was if it was an orderly departure. Today was not orderly; panic was ensuing. People ignored police and the orderly evacuation routes; this caused mass traffic jams in all directions. Most would be stranded just blocks from the stadium for many more hours.

The team aboard the copter didn't know exactly when the bomb was set to explode. But from the information given to them by the captain of the Damascus Star, they had to assume the bomb would be detonated to kill the most people possible. That time was now. The people in and around the stadium didn't know it, but their lives depended on the team finding and disarming a nuclear bomb planted somewhere along the river. Michael researched a map of the area around the stadium. If he were a terrorist with a floating bomb, he would certainly try to get as close as possible; that would be at or near the Fox River Marina.

"Head for this spot here," he suggested to the major riding in the co-pilot seat.

Aboard My Chopper:

As My Chopper approached the open water of the bay, Scott yelled, "Liz, raise the sails, all of them." Liz ran from station to station, pressing the electric winches that hoisted the sails. Then she tied them off in the correct position. "Give me ten feet of deflection of the main sail," Scott ordered as he lowered the keel with another electric motor.

Immediately, Scott started jibing the boat. Because a sailboat cannot go directly with the wind, Scott alternated his angle across the tack of the wind. Each time he did, he warned his wife with a loud yell, "Boom on the move."

Liz had time to take another look at the timer counting down on the bomb. Scott saw her. She looked at him and shook her head back and forth. "We won't make it honey; only five minutes left." She started to walk the deck toward her husband at the helm; she would stand by her man till the end.

Scott jibed the boat quickly, only this time he didn't warn his wife. The big steel boom caught her across the chest and threw her overboard. Scott watched closely to make sure she was OK. The automatic flotation device worked and filled with air. Soon his wife was floating upright. The cold-water survival suit would protect her until she could be rescued or swim her way back to shore. Scott ran to the rail of the boat and yelled, "Sorry honey, you have to take care of princess. If you see a bright flash, don't look directly at it. Take a deep breath and go under water for as long as you possibly can. The water should protect you. Remember, I love you, and tell Avery that I will never forget her and that I love her dearly."

"Scott, Scott Seaver, don't do this to me, don't leave me. Jump, you can jump too; the boat is far enough away," Elizabeth cried and screamed. In her heart she knew that the boat was still too close to shore for her husband to risk abandoning it, but she wanted him to anyways.

Scott cried out to his wife, "I love you so much, you will never know." Liz watched the boat and her husband sail softly away. It looked so peaceful moving away from her as it created a serene wake in its path. The fact that it carried a deadly of cargo seemed dreamlike. Captain Seaver prayed for a miracle. He was afraid the boat wouldn't be far enough away in five minutes to save his wife. Then he had a thought. He opened up the radio stack and turned on the emergency Guard radio, the same one Liz had cried out for help on.

"Mayday, Mayday, this is marine vessel 'My Chopper.' I need assistance. There is a passenger in the water at 44 degrees, 32 minutes and 38.38 seconds by 88 degrees, 0 minutes, and 11.65 seconds." Scott read off the exact coordinates his GPS navigation display showed.

Scott hoped that the President's security helicopters were still in the air. It was a long shot but if they were and monitoring the emergency frequency, maybe they could help.

There was no answer. Scott franticly repeated the call. There was a crackle over the airwaves, then Scott heard a familiar voice.

"Scott? Scott Seaver? Is that you?" Bob asked over the radio.

"Bob, your voice is a blessing. Bob, please listen; Liz is in the water at the coordinates I just gave. Are you in the air?"

"Yes, we know everything; the captain of the freighter told us everything. Do you know where the bomb is? That is our first priority. I have people on board who may be able to diffuse it."

"Sorry major, your first priority is my family. You save my family and I will tell you where the bomb is. How far out are you?"

"Scott, they will kill everyone in the city of Green Bay if you don't help us," Bob argued.

Scott knew that the major and his crew wouldn't deviate from their mission profile no matter how helpless the situation. With only minutes left, unarming the bomb was not an option, but only he and Liz knew it.

"Scott!" Bob repeated into the headset microphone. "You have to help us; it's the only chance your family has."

"No dice Bob. You have to do it my way. Promise me you will pick up my wife at the coordinates I said and then get my daughter. Once they are safe, I will tell you exactly where the bomb is." Scott knew it was a long shot, but it was the only play he had. If the bomb went off per the timer, soon they would all be dead anyway. Scott looked to the sky and saw the chopper behind him coming from the east.

"Scott, I see your boat. Come about, let's talk," the major urged. "Help us save Liz. I can't believe you would turn tail and run, and abandon your wife in the middle of the bay."

"She's back a ways in my wake; you should see her any moment now."

Bob nodded to Captain Fredric as soon as he saw the orange vest in the blue waters. Saving lives was what they did. He couldn't let Liz flounder in the cold water and fly right over her. It might be a mistake but they had to save her. If Scott wouldn't tell them where the bomb was, maybe Elizabeth would. It would save valuable time. Bob felt ashamed for his friend. He never thought he would see the day when Captain Scott Seaver of the Army National Guard turned yellow and abandoned his family to save his own skin.

Fox River Marina:

Avery ran on a well-worn path toward the fallen chopper, taking her away from the receding sailboat. She ran past the broken tail rotor and just as she past the open cockpit door, she fell. Major Hamid Shukah tripped her with his blood-drenched leg. When he heard footsteps coming his way he found a hiding spot behind one of the many trees along the path. When he saw the Seaver teen and she was alone, he thanked Allah. The determined terrorist had dragged his shot-up body out of the marshy waters and back to the chopper for his knife. As long as he was still breathing, he was willing to fight for his life. How fortunate for him that the young girl had come back to help him escape.

371

Despite having been directly hit by only one bullet, which went right though him, many others had ricochet off the door and injured him quite badly. He needed a doctor's help, but if he didn't get out of the blast zone first, it wouldn't matter. Hamid fell on the small girl and pressed his knife to her throat. "You will help me escape, and if we don't escape the bomb you will be the first virgin Allah blesses me with."

They both got back onto their feet. The bloody mess of a man leaned on the young girl for support, his knife never far away from the teen's throat. "We must find a car to steal."

Avery Seaver knew the cruelty of the man. As much as she wanted to run, to tell the man she didn't care what he did anymore, she couldn't. The truth was, she wanted to live too. They needed to find a car very quickly; she realized that she needed the terrorist's help to escape just as much as he needed hers.

Aboard My Chopper:

Scott glanced backward several times. The helicopter was hovering with its belly just inches over the water. He saw Liz being lifted into the copter. There was a call over the radio. "We have Liz, Scott. She's OK, a little cold, but OK." Scott couldn't see the timer on the bomb but he knew it was set to expire any minute. The Black Hawk with his wife on board was still too close to save it from an atomic bomb blast.

Liz could hear her husband's voice over the helicopter's intercom, a voice she never thought she would hear again. "Fly toward the marina right now. Liz can show you where," Scott yelled into the microphone. "Find my daughter and I will tell you where the bomb is."

Liz heard her husband's demands over the Black Hawk's rear speakers and realized what Scott was up to. She had lost track of time, but she knew that her husband was as good as dead. Nobody could save him now if the bomb did go off on schedule. And if the helicopter didn't immediately put some serious distance between them and the bomb all of its occupants would also perish.

"Elizabeth!" Bob pleaded. "We need to find the bomb. These men might be able to diffuse it."

"We need to find my daughter first." Liz supported her husband. "She is by the Fox River Marina, just east of the stadium. Then we will tell you where the bomb is."

Liz looked at her watch; the second hand had stopped moving. *Was time really standing still?* She wondered as the copter peeled away from the rescue scene and toward the mouth of the river.

Scott locked the tiller in place, giving him a moment to check on the timer. By his calculations the bomb should be close to detonation. He had to know. Maybe the bomb was a dud and he was safe. The helicopter was quickly moving away. Scott guessed it wouldn't take the pilot long to be traveling at one hundred and sixty knots or about three miles a minute. If they had one minute more they might make it. With another minute for the decreasing blast wave to catch up to them, it was possible.

The timer was reading ten seconds, nine, eight, seven, six, five, four, three, two, one....

Black Hawk 340HK:

Elizabeth dared to look back toward the speck of a boat. She prayed to God that he would keep her man safe. *The bomb had to be a dud or it would have gone off by now*, she willed.

Road Side, Green Bay:

Horns were honking furiously; people were panicking, many in fistfights, trying to get other people to give them the right of way. Some cars took dangerous paths to a gridlocked freeway system. Others used their own cars as battering rams to open what they hoped would be paths to safety. Police were trying to unlock the congestion of cars. But even as they did their jobs, each officer considered the possibility that he or she had already been exposed to the radiation of a so-called dirty bomb. The officers couldn't help but wonder, just like everyone else around them, would they all be vaporized in the next instant.

The second the President's plane had lifted off, an emergency announcement was made over the Lambeau Field speaker system. Moments after that, emergency sirens started blaring all over the city of Green Bay. Then pandemonium broke out in the stadium and throughout the city. The only thing people knew was that there had been a call for immediate evacuation. It didn't take much imagination to conjure up the worst scenario, as all had seen the President leave unexpectedly and then watched as Air Force One departed the area.

Hamid found a vehicle and pushed his captive into the front seat of an already running SUV as the owner fought with another motorist. "Strap

Alan D Schmitz

yourself in tightly if you want to live," Hamid warned. The call of self-preservation is strong. Avery Rose Seaver wanted to survive the holocaust even if it meant trusting her life to the man who had created it.

Hamid didn't make a run for the freeway. It was uselessly clogged. He put the black SUV in reverse and pushed the car in back of him out of the way, nearly killing both of the men fighting and severely injuring one of them. The terrorist turned the SUV onto the manicured lawn of an adjacent property, then used it and the properties adjoining it as his personal roadway. The truck traversed over small trees and bushes at will. Picnic tables and lawn ornaments were no obstacles. Each city block they passed was an appreciated gift.

Avery had never been so scared in her life. At least with her father behind the controls of the helicopter, she knew he was trying to be safe. This man was a maniac. People, small buildings and gardens were ignored as if they didn't exist.

Aboard My Chopper:

The timer went to zero. Scott closed his eyes. He didn't want to see the end coming even if it lasted only a microsecond. Nothing happened. The bomb didn't go off. Scott opened his eyes daring to take a look. The clock clearly spelled 00:00. The bomb was a dud, a dead bomb. If it didn't go off by now, the bet was that it wouldn't.

Scott thought about his family again. He would see them again; soon he would be able to hold his wife and daughter in his arms. Then Scott had a worried thought. *My daughter? How were they going to find Avery?* He told her to run and hide.

Captain Seaver pulled the IT-Tech out of his pocket. With a couple of button clicks he located his daughter. She seemed to be moving at a high rate of speed away from the marina. "Major, do you have your ears on?"

"Yes Scott, I do. Are you ready to tell us where the bomb is?"

"Not quite yet. You promised to save my daughter first. I will give you the coordinates of her location." Scott read off their immediate location, it would be a starting place. By the time the chopper got there, she would be gone, but they should be able to follow from there. "Tell Liz that it looks like we will be cooking at home tonight. The take out was a dud."

Liz heard the message and laughed with relief. "Elizabeth!" Bob warned. "This is no laughing matter. Scott is in serious trouble. The bomb is a real threat; we don't know when it is set to go off. It could be timing down at this very instant."

374

"Trust me Bob, Scott knows what he is doing. Let's find my daughter."
Scott was so relieved he felt giddy and started to do an Irish Jig on deck. The bomb still had to be disassembled in a safe area, and he had a plan. Just past Washington Island, off the tip of the Door County Peninsula, was another small island that was uninhabited. It had an unmanned lighthouse on it and a sufficient dock. He would take the bomb to that island, where it would be safe until the proper authorities could decide what to do with it.

The Black Hawk turned toward the giant stadium, now empty of fans. The coordinates were along a side street. Elizabeth and Bob scanned the street below; they were the only ones onboard the chopper who knew what Avery looked like. "Scott, do you copy?"

"Copy Bob, are you at the position?"

"Affirmative, any help?"

"Proceed west."

"Scott, if she is in a car, I can tell you she isn't going anywhere; it's gridlock down there."

"Look for a fast moving vehicle; somehow, she is moving west fairly rapidly from your location."

The copter moved west and then they spotted a single car ignoring the roadway completely, tearing through backyards at an alarming rate. "We have the vehicle." Bob let Scott know. "Scott, your daughter must be with somebody because she certainly is not driving that vehicle."

That was when Elizabeth saw a face she never wanted to see again. "Scott," she screamed into a headset. "It's the terrorist. He has Avery."

Scott's heart sank. Here he was, in the middle of the waters of Green Bay. He was miles away from his daughter, unable to help her.

Agent Mitchell looked out the open side door at the driver of the car. Captain Fredric was doing an excellent job of pacing the vehicle with the helicopter. Matt spoke into the microphone, "It's him alright. Dieter, tell Price that we have Hamid Shukah on the ground, fleeing in a vehicle. We can assume the bomb is armed, that is why he is taking so many risks."

"You know him?" Elizabeth was shocked.

"Only by his picture, Mrs. Seaver. He is a known terrorist. He came into the country illegally on the freighter your daughter was held on. We believe he brought a nuclear bomb into the country and is trying to use it to blow up the President and the people in this area. He is undoubtedly trying to escape the blast. We must be close to the blast zone. The bomb must be set to explode soon or he wouldn't be so desperate to leave the area."

"Bob, I know where the bomb is. Scott has it. It didn't go off. There was a timer, it was a dud. That was what Scott's message to me was about. He's taking it away from the city."

Bob thought about the verbiage of the strange message and knew Liz was telling the truth.

Matthew's voice came over the headsets. "We have to try to capture the man below alive. Do not shoot to kill unless there is imminent danger to the hostage."

"What do you mean, don't shoot to kill?" Liz was outraged. "He's kidnapped my daughter. He has to be stopped. Bob, you promised Scott you'd save her."

"We will Liz, she is our top priority. But there could be more bombs. We have to know. And that nut down there is the only one who has that information."

"What about some ground support?"

"No good. The police are spread too thinly already and as you can see, they couldn't help us even if they wanted to. The roads are just too gridlocked."

"Can we shoot out his tires?" Michael, the scientist, suggested.

Bob looked at the security team's officer. "Can you?"

"We can try!"

****

What Scott, Hamid, Elizabeth or the team in the helicopter didn't know was that the bomb wasn't a dud, at least not yet. In his written instructions, the professor had been very specific when he told the Iranians that the timer started the detonation sequence. The professor managed to omit exactly what that meant.

The timer itself took very little power to operate; in fact the timer could be powered for over a full year with a small battery. However, the twin computers that the bomb needed to run the detonation sequence took much more power to operate, so much power that to have them running continuously would have limited the bomb's useful life to days, maybe a week at most. The professor had solved this dilemma by simply having the dual computers wait to turn on until the timer went to zero.

As soon as the timer counted down to zero, the initiation sequence began. A relay opened a switch and batteries packed tightly inside of the foam container started two computers. The twin computers were merely protection in case one or the other became unstable. It was good planning on the part of the mouse. In this case, the intense, repeated X-rays delivered by the Iranian scientist had destroyed some of the all-important 1's and 0's on the magnetic drives.

The first thing the computers did was to boot up. The second was to examine each other's hard drive to see if the proper coding was available. At this particular time the computers detected some abnormalities that would have to be corrected. Because each machine was identical to the other, the fix was simple. The machines would copy the code, line by line, from one computer to the other and check it again and again until they matched.

When the codes matched, the computers would initiate the ignition program. Only then would a perfectly timed sequence of events start. It would only take seconds for the bomb to mature into a beautiful and immensely deadly mushroom shaped cloud of dust, vapor and debris.

****

"Scott, Liz told us you have the bomb," Bob radioed.

"That's affirmative Bob, I have a pretty good wind behind me and I'm making good time. The city of Green Bay should be out of the blast zone by now. The bomb was a dud; the timer went to zero five minutes ago. I'm taking the bomb to Lighthouse Island, just north of Washington Island. I would suggest that you order an immediate evacuation of Washington Island and the Door Peninsula just as a precaution."

"Scott, that was a very brave thing you did," Bob conceded.

"No problem," Scott humbly accepted the flattering remark.

"We are going to try to shoot the tires on the car. We'll get your daughter."

"I know you will Bob, keep me posted."

"Roger that!"

Two members of the security team strapped themselves into safety harnesses and stood firm by the chopper's open door. It was up to Captain Dan Fredric, the Black Hawk's pilot, to keep the copter completely still in the air so the shooter could aim at the moving vehicle.

"Take your shot as soon as you can." The major gave the order.

The first two shots bounced off the dirt in back of the car. The driver was unaware he was being shot at. Hamid looked at his watch. Per his calculations the timer should have reached zero by now, but he knew that a nuclear detonation wasn't as simple as igniting plastic explosives. A delay could be expected. The SUV raced and bounced around heavily. It skidded through a playground, then the terrorist aimed the car toward an empty church parking lot. Avery was as frightened as she had ever been.

Alan D Schmitz

A few more bullets struck the pavement alongside the vehicle. The occupants were still unaware. The man sped through the parking lot and onto a street. He managed to move them far from the panicked crowds leaving the stadium. From here out, the roads would be clear of the traffic from the departing fans. Hamid was prepared to see the reflection of an immensely bright flash of light at any time, but until that instant he would put every block he could between them and the explosion.

"The SUV is bouncing around too much," Lieutenant Michaels told his boss as the truck bounded through the playground and out through the church lot.

"He's back on the street now; if you can get me in front of him I think I could disable the vehicle."

"You'd better," Bob reminded. "Once he knows we're here, he isn't going to make it any easier."

Elizabeth wanted to jump out of the copter to help her daughter. It was an irrational thought, but doing nothing other than watch her daughter nearly get killed a dozen times by the madman was making her desperate.

"I want to talk to Scott," Liz said.

Bob hit a few switches and told her he was standing by.

"Honey, the kidnapper still has Avery. They are going to try to stop him by flying in front and taking some shots, but the kidnapper will know we are after them. If they miss, there is no telling what he will do to Avery. What should we do?"

Captain Seaver thought for a few seconds. "Who's the Black Hawk pilot?"

"It's Dan Fredric," Liz answered, not knowing what that had to do with it.

"Who's on the rifle?"

Elizabeth didn't know the man but she read his nametag. "It's Lieutenant Michaels."

"Dan, can you hear me?" Captain Seaver asked.

"Got you Scott. What's up?"

"If anyone can hold the bird still enough it's you. Tell Lieutenant Michaels that it's his call." Scott turned the wheel of the tiller and the rudder swung the boat sixty degrees opposite. He was making good time; the farther away the small sailing ship was from heavy population centers, the better.

"Scott, they're going for it; he'll see us at any time."

"Bob, don't underestimate the man; he's a ruthless killer."

378

"Copy that Scott."

****

Hamid heard the sound of the chopper before he saw it. Then he caught a glimpse of it and wondered how in the hell the husband of the woman had found another helicopter so fast. As the copter pushed past him he quickly realized that it was a troop of armed men. "Golole," he cursed, wondering what they were up to.

The copter came to an abrupt midair stop, the side of the chopper facing Hamid as he stuck his hand out the open window and started to shoot his high-powered pistol at the open door and the two rifles pointing at him. Lieutenant Michaels decided to go for the kill; in his mind the hostage was in imminent danger. A careful shot through the windshield would finish it; he hoped the young girl had fastened her seatbelt.

Avery saw her mother peering out the side door. She couldn't let her mother get shot, so she flung herself at the injured shoulder of the terrorist. It was the same instant that the lieutenant took his shot. The SUV turned abruptly sideways and flipped; it made one full roll, and slid on its side down the city street.

Captain Fredric started to land the Black Hawk on the roadway; the security team rushed out of the copter, jumped down to the hard pavement and ran toward the vehicle before the Hawk's wheels touched the ground.

Hamid crawled out of the shattered windshield. Lieutenant Michaels had his rifle trained at the terrorist's head. Agent Mitchell hoped they could still bring the man in alive. The terrorist bent down, as if he was stuck in the opening. Then with a mighty tug, he had the body of the young girl between him and the rifles aimed at him. The girl seemed bloody and banged up, but she stood under her own power in front of the terrorist. Hamid aimed his gun directly at her head.

"Everybody out of the helicopter except the pilot, or the girl dies," Hamid ordered. "How nice of you to provide me with a ride," he smirked. "So we meet again, Mrs. Seaver. It seems our lives are intertwined."

Elizabeth pretended to be too confused to leave the chopper. She hid her mouth from the terrorist and spoke into the mouthpiece she was wearing, calling her husband again. "The terrorist is still alive. He wants to steal the Black Hawk, and he's pointing a gun at Avery's head."

Scott, in a near panic, thought for a moment then said, "Tell Avery that Dad says, now is the time."

"What?" Elizabeth didn't understand.

"Just tell her!" Scott demanded. "Bob, have your pistol ready."

Bob was the second to last to depart; Elizabeth was the last to step out of the copter. "Wait," she demanded.

Everyone stopped including the terrorist.

"Wait?" The terrorist questioned the order from the woman. "I have waited my entire life. Get away from the helicopter, all of you, or the girl dies. I will not be taken alive and I will not die alone, that I promise."

"Avery, your father says, 'Now is the time!'" Elizabeth shouted.

Avery immediately understood what her father wanted her to do. She took a step forward, flung herself around and gave the terrorist a well-placed roundhouse kick into his knee. Then Avery dropped down. In that instant, Bob fired three rounds into the terrorist's chest.

Liz ran up to her daughter and hustled her away from the dying man. The team was already trying to stop the bleeding and stabilize the terrorist. Perhaps his life could be saved so that he could be interrogated.

Liz and Avery hugged and cried. Finally it was over. "Is Dad OK?"

"Dad's fine, want to talk to him?"

"You bet. Mom, you should have seen what dad did to the terrorist on the ship." Avery Seaver couldn't be any prouder of her father than she was. Liz and Avery ran back to the waiting chopper.

"Dad? Dad? Can you hear me?" she asked with giddiness in her voice.

"That you princess?" Scott acknowledged his daughter's voice with tears in his eyes. His plan must have worked.

"That move you showed me, it worked. It worked just like in practice."

"Atta girl. I knew you could do it, just like in practice."

The move that Scott's daughter had done was just one of the many Tae-Kwon-Do moves she learned on her way to earning a black belt in the sport. Scott was a black belt in the martial art and often helped teach the class at the local YMCA. It was common in practice for Scott to announce to the students, "Now is the time." This was when they were to imagine their lives were in danger and they had to take matters into their own hands. That was when "Now is the time" became a sort of class mantra. It was his signal to his students that it was time to fight for their lives and escape whatever hold was being practiced.

"Are you going to be home soon?" she asked.

"As soon as I can, princess."

Liz interrupted on another headset. "I'll never trust you again when we go sailing, you know."

"Sorry about that. I hope it didn't hurt too much."

Liz rubbed her shoulder a bit. "Not too much. See you soon; let somebody else be the hero from now on."

"You don't have to say that twice. Over and out."

Scott looked out over the expanse of blue water. It was a peaceful calming scene. His family was safe. He was safe. In that knowledge came a feeling of peacefulness he hadn't felt in a long, long time. In the distance Scott saw the beautiful expanse of the Mackinac Bridge. He got lost in thought, enjoying what had turned out to be a beautiful day for a sail. Time passed unnoticed by the small vessel's captain. He took a look around him. There was mostly open water in all directions, though he did recognize the entrance to the waters of Green Bay behind him. What he didn't remember was the large wood crate perched on the back of his boat. He didn't recall putting it there, or what it was for. Undoubtedly his destination was Mackinac Island; it was probably some special delivery for the Grand Hotel, one of his favorites. It bothered him that he couldn't remember exactly why he was sailing on such a beautiful day, but he knew where he was and remembered the wise words of Dr. Maslow. "As long as you're safe, don't panic and you will be OK. NO BIG DEAL!" So Scott enjoyed the wind at his back and the gentle sway of the craft. One thing he did know was that on such a beautiful calm day he was as safe as he could possibly be.

The sailor's thoughts went to his family. Scott remembered the video feature of his IT-Tech and decided to take a little movie of himself and the fun he was having on the open waters. He would e-mail it to his wife, daughter and son. They would get a kick out of seeing old Dad sailing solo on the great lake.

A few miles later the computers inside the large crate had finally agreed that their programs were now compatible. The timing sequence was started; a few solenoids were switched on, which in turn released small high-powered sparks. All the detonations were successful; the professor had delivered on his promise.

The chopper crew and everybody on the east coast of Wisconsin and the west coast of Michigan saw an immense flash. It was followed by a thunderous blasting sound wave. After that, anyone who didn't know what happened could quickly see the telltale sign of a huge mushroom shaped cloud of vapor forming over Lake Michigan.

Alan D Schmitz

Epilogue:

Yuri Kromonov was enjoying a cigar. He looked out over the small Swiss lake that Anzhela and he had moved to. The professor looked at the paint that was chipping off the modest pier upon which he was sitting. *It would be fun to paint the boards,* he thought. For the first time in his life, he owned a piece of land and the home on it. Yuri touched the worn, chipped wood bench he was sitting on. With great pride he considered his change in fortune. The wood belonged to him. They were his boards to paint, not some uncaring government worker's, and he would take good care of his boards.

His pleasure was a guilty one, but it was a guilt he could live with. The official death count from the bomb had been only one hundred. The scientist was happy about that. The news story that came out of the United States said that the bomb was moved to a safe place just in time by a hero. The hero died in the blast, as did some inhabitants of a nearby island; but most of the deaths were from the evacuation of a very large and crowded stadium. Still, Yuri was proud of his bomb. By the reports he was able to piece together, the bomb was even more powerful than he had anticipated.

Anzhela came outside to enjoy the sun for one last time before it set. "Ahh..., my angel, sit down next to me and let's enjoy the sunset together."

"My Yuri, you sit here, a king on his throne. Would a mere commoner like me be allowed to sit next to his majesty?"

"You are my queen and always shall be. This beautiful sunset was made for both of us."

The professor's angel sat next to him and he held her hand. His angel was happy at last.

Yuri heard a hunter's gun in the distance. Then his wife's hand became limp and he caught her slumping body just as it rolled forward. Yuri saw his angel's face blown wide open; his face didn't have time to register the horror. In another instant he had taken a bullet to his own head. Husband and wife fell off the wood bench and into the water. Their bodies made a small splash when they fell, but nobody heard, not even the shooter who was a half mile away.

382

The Russian officer leisurely knocked down her gun and carefully placed it back in the carrying case. It was convenient that the professor and his wife had chosen such a remote location to retire, not that the end result would have been any different. When the FSB wants somebody silenced forever, a way is always found.

The Russian government decided that the professor had turned from an asset to a liability. The very few at the highest level of government who knew of the plan to destabilize the current fragile world peace decided that it would be too risky to ever use the professor's services again. And if he could not be used by them, the asset should not be available to anyone.

The shooter thought about her previous target. The mafia boss thought he was protected because of his powerful position within the mob. But his girlfriend Natasha, the shooter, found it very easy to slowly poison the man. He died a slow, yet tragic death with her by his side the entire time. She had been loyal and comforted him to the end.

Port Washington, Wisconsin:

Elizabeth Seaver walked along the tall bluff overlooking the great lake. It was spring in Wisconsin. The red-breasted robins had returned. The trees and bushes were showing signs of life. Tiny buds with just the slightest hint of green were proof that life went on. Liz took a small twig with its new life, snapped it off in her hand and stared at it. It made her angry. She broke it in half and threw it to the ground.

How dare God to ignore her pain. How dare he have life go on as if nothing happened to her, to Scott and to their daughter. How often during the last few months had she come up to this bluff, dreaming of seeing her Scott miraculously sailing back on their boat? How often had she wanted to tell Avery that her father would be returning soon? Reality meant that Scott wasn't ever coming home again. Miracles didn't happen in real life. Tonight she would cry herself to sleep, alone again.

When Scott received the highest commendation from his country, The Congressional Medal of Honor, Liz and Avery stood proud during the ceremony in Washington D.C. It was what her husband would have wanted. And when the military asked if Scott's official resting place could be in Arlington Cemetery, buried there as a war hero, she also agreed. It was an empty casket that was lowered that day. Scott and My Chopper had been instantly disintegrated in a moment of total nuclear annihilation. The thought that even the smallest atom of Scott's existence was gone, affected her deeply. How could she ever have closure? At least when her son Bradley died, she could look at his face one last time. An empty casket in the ground, no matter where it was, was still empty, as empty as her heart that ached from the sheer volume of its emptiness.

Avery and she would go on; Elizabeth looked at the fresh buds again. Life went on whether you wanted it to or not. Dr. Maslow assured her during their weekly talks that, in time, her heart would heal, perhaps never completely, but time always healed. Her daughter seemed to be doing better now; the nightmares of being chased by a man with no face and a bloody knife had stopped. With the doctor's help, she was back in school. Liz knew that in time, some young man's love would fill her heart and all would be as it should.

Mrs. Scott Seaver looked out over the deep-blue, shimmering lake, searching for a sailboat and praying for a miracle. She cried out loudly and begged, "Please come home Scott. I love you so much. I miss you so!"

Across the Lake in a Black Hawk:

Dr. Michael Stark listened to his headset as the Black Hawk flown by Captain Dan Fredric crossed over the lake along the main western shore of the state of Michigan. In the aftermath of the explosion, he had been given a new assignment by the government. He was no longer working with Dieter or Matt Mitchell, they still stayed in touch though through e-mails.

The explosion had contaminated one of the world's largest fresh water supplies. It was an ecological disaster of unprecedented scale. In their failure, the terrorists had triumphed. In direct lives lost, the bomb was unsuccessful, but the environmental and economic damage was unimaginable.

All the cities around the lake, from Green Bay to Milwaukee to Chicago, used the fresh water system. The thriving cities around the lake had ground to a halt. Dr. Stark and his new team were charged with monitoring the spread of the contamination. The hope was that somehow it wouldn't spread into the remaining fresh water systems.

Canada had already initiated an international lawsuit against the United States for environmental contamination, because the nuclear contaminated moisture from evaporated lake water was carried by upper winds over Toronto. There it came down as poison rain. Canada was holding the United States responsible for not doing enough to protect its borders from terrorists. The long-term effects that the contaminated rain would have on people and property were still unknown.

The Damascus Star was held in quarantine and likely would stay that way for the next hundred years or so. That would probably be as long as its captain would be incarcerated too. As of this date, Captain FarzAm Zarin had not divulged any additional information. The trial would be complicated, possibly not even held in the United States, but in some international court. There was a great deal of politics going on behind the scenes and the defendant and his attorneys were taking advantage of it all. It would take years before an agreement on the proper course of action for a fair trial was reached. Many things could happen during those years. Possibly the captain could become the victim of some mysterious disease and die before a trial could even begin.

Sergeant Nassir Azodi, however, was another case all together. When the bomb went off, Nassir gloated to the rescue crew. He proclaimed that he and his partner had created great jihad. It hadn't taken long to discover his true identity and country of loyalty. His partner, Major Hamid Shukah, alias Kassim, was enjoying the fruits of martyrdom.

The president of the United States forestalled a retaliatory attack against Iran, afraid that the international community would rebuke his actions. Ongoing talks were a near daily occurrence for the United Nations Security Council, and the President was frustrated that the overwhelming evidence wasn't enough for the Security Council to come up with the required unanimous vote to sanction Iran. It seemed that Russia and some of its allies felt that despite the apparent evidence against Iran, it could not be held accountable until all the facts and the trials were completed. Russia and its allies were also fairly certain that because of bureaucratic maneuvering, such trials would not end in their lifetime.

****

Elizabeth Seaver came back from one of her walks and entered her lonely home. As difficult as it was, she knew that she had to move on with her life. Somehow she had to come to terms with her husband's death. Liz held the Medal of Honor her husband had earned with his life. Yes, the country won a victory over the terrorists. Most of the news articles remarked at how fortunate the country had been this time. Liz Seaver didn't feel so lucky.

She turned on her computer and started to check her e-mails. It was a daily chore. There were so many well-wishers that finding the more important documents was very time consuming. Elizabeth deleted about twenty unrecognized and unsolicited e-mails. Then she came upon one from Lieutenant Randy Schmidt.

Randy had been particularly distraught over Scott's death. Everybody at the base was of course affected, but Bob Allen and Randy Schmidt were close friends of her husband and that made it much more difficult for them.

Over the last few months, both men had provided her with emotional support and helped with all the many details of her life. There were so many things involving her husband that needed to be brought to a close. They had formed their own support group and just being together helped them all cope better.

Mrs. Seaver clicked on the title line and opened it. *Strange*, she thought, *there was a video attached.* It was a video sent from the lieutenant's IT-Tech. An instant later, the hair on her back stood straight up and a cold shiver ran down her spine. The date on the e-mail was indelibly etched into her mind. The video was made on the day Scott died. Her fingers started trembling. *Why would Randy send this without warning her first? What could it possibly be?*

If there was new information about that fateful day she needed to know. Without Scott's body to lay to rest, closure had been difficult. Mrs. Seaver was still searching for that one thing that might give her the comfort she craved. With trepidation she opened the video. It automatically started to play.

"Hi honey!" Scott's voice and a close up of his face came into view. "This is such a beautiful day to be sailing. I thought I would send you this video to rub it in a bit."

The shock was too much. Liz clicked on pause; the video stopped on Scott's smiling face. How could this be? It was months since the disaster, months since the video had been taken. And how did Randy get it? And why didn't he tell her, instead of just e-mailing it to her like some flyboy humor he might send? Was this a hoax, a terribly cruel hoax by someone, certainly not the lieutenant?

Liz thought back to that day, a day she had been trying to put out of her mind. Then she remembered. Scott had Lieutenant Schmidt's IT-Tech on the boat. Scott had accidentally taken Randy's by mistake.

She re-examined the time stamp on the e-mail. Randy didn't send this to her, Scott did, using Randy's phone. But why did it first come now? Mrs. Seaver ran to the kitchen and the newspaper. She remembered reading something about the nuclear explosion and the widespread panic causing an Internet shutdown.

There it was, the article said, "Because of the huge volume of text messages, e-mails and attempted voice calls, the Internet system stored as many messages as it could to be sent out immediately after the volume of calls permitted. However, because of the electromagnetic pulse, or EMP, given off by the bomb, the system crashed and lost the time stamps and order of the incoming messages. Technicians have since been able to rebuild the database, and those messages and e-mails are being sent out today even though they are months old."

Liz ran back into the den and her computer. It was Scott, it wasn't a hoax; she had her Scott back. Mrs. Seaver pressed the play button. Soon Scott was moving on the screen waving at the expanse of blue water and shouting over the wind.

"Isn't this beautiful? I wish you, Brad, and Avery were here with me. I'm headed over to the big island to deliver a big box on the back of the boat. Don't have a clue what's in it and don't remember how it got there, but somebody always cons me into hauling something for them when they know I'm heading this way."

Scott ran up to the tiller and tacked the sailboat as he hammed it up for his audience. A small spray of lake water glistened over his head. Listen love, I have to go now. Just remember, I love you more than you could know. Goodbye and be brave, I will always be with you."

The video stopped. Liz cried out. "No Scott, No." It was like losing her husband all over again. As much as it hurt, she had to play the video again, and then she played it again. She thought about his last words to her. *At least Scott didn't know he was about to die, or did he?* He wished Brad was there with him, but so did she, every day. His message at the end was unlike her Scott. "Goodbye and be brave, I will always be with you." *Did Scott somehow know his end was near?*

In the weeks that followed, she shared the video with no one, not even her daughter. She found herself going to it less and less often. Scott was helping her to put it behind her and find closure. "Be brave!" he said and for Scott, she would be. And he was right about something else. He would always be with her in her heart. Eventually Elizabeth would share the video with her daughter and she would make sure that those memories never die.

Alan D Schmitz

"Even [with] all these steps, we know that [in] a free society there's no such thing as perfect security. That's the challenge. To attack us, the terrorists only have to be right once; to stop them, we need to be right one hundred percent of the time. And so we're working to ensure that if an attack does occur, this country is ready. We'll do everything we can to stop attacks -- and we are. I can confidently tell the American people, a lot of folks are working hard to protect them."

President Bush Commemorates Fifth Anniversary of U.S. Department of Homeland Security

(03/28/2008)